For my parents

"To eat well is to live well."

—CHINESE PROVERB

PART I

The North

"Ann Mah's *Kitchen Chinese* is a delicious debut novel, seasoned with just the right balance of humor and heart, and sprinkled with fascinating cultural tidbits. Read thoroughly. Share with friends."   —Claire Cook, bestselling author of *The Wildwater Walking Club* and *Must Love Dogs*

"Suffused with humor, genuine warmth, and mouth-watering culinary descriptions, *Kitchen Chinese* is, first and foremost, about the adventure of self-discovery."
—Irina Reyn, author of *What Happened to Anna K.*

"Ann Mah's sizzling portrait of life in Beijing serves up more than just scrumptious banquets, identity crises, and fraught, intercultural romances. It's a story of how we find and nourish ourselves in unexpected ways and places, so delicious that I took breaks from reading only to dash to the phone and order Chinese."
—Rachel DeWoskin, author of *Foreign Babes in Beijing* and *Repeat After Me*

"With a light, self-deprecating touch, Ann Mah portrays the quirks, pleasures, and surprises of life as a young Chinese-American woman finding her way in an alien motherland."
—Jen Lin-Liu, author of *Serve the People: A Stir-Fried Journey Through China*

"Ann Mah's richly detailed *Kitchen Chinese* is humorous enough to make you laugh out loud, and so delicious you are sure to begin craving Peking duck and dim sum. A true tale of reinventing oneself in a new and foreign world."
—Patricia Wells, author of *Vegetable Harvest* and *We'll Always Have Paris . . . and Provence*

KITCHEN CHINESE

WITHDRAWN

A

A V O N

An Imprint of
HarperCollins*Publishers*

Excerpts from *Classic Food of China* copyright © 1992 by Yan Kit So. Reproduced by permission of the Estate of Yan Kit So.

Excerpt from *Swallowing Clouds* by A. Zee (Simon & Schuster, 1990) is reprinted by permission of the author.

Excerpts from *The Food of China* by E. N. Anderson copyright © 1988 by E. N. Anderson. Reproduced by permission of Yale University Press.

Excerpts from *Oxford Companion to Food* by Alan Davidson reprinted by permission of Oxford University Press.

FIRST AVON PAPERBACK EDITION PUBLISHED 2010.

Designed by Betty Lew

Library of Congress Cataloging-in-Publication Data
Mah, Ann.
  Kitchen Chinese / Ann Mah. — 1st ed.
    p. cm.
    ISBN 978-0-06-177127-9
    1. Chinese Americans—China—Beijing—Fiction.   2. Sisters—Fiction.   3. Beijing (China)—Fiction.   I. Title.
PS3613.A34923K57 2010
813'.6—dc22

                                            2009012087

10 11 12 13 14   OV/RRD   10 9 8 7 6 5 4 3 2 1

Peking Duck

" . . . It was only in China, and indeed for a long time only in Beijing, that the special dish known as Beijing *kaoya* (in China), Peking duck (in English), and *canard lacqué* (in French) was prepared. [The] cooked bird has a shining golden exterior, attractively crisp, and a moist, succulent inside, the whole having a fine aroma and being free of excess fat."

—*THE OXFORD COMPANION TO FOOD*

My first meal in Beijing is roasted duck, or *kaoya* as it's called in Chinese. Glossy and brown, with crisp skin and meltingly moist flesh, the bird is cut into over one hundred pieces, in the traditional way. We silently fill our pancakes, dipping meat and skin into the dark, salty-sweet sauce, adding slivers of scallion and cucumber, and rolling the packages up like cigars. I arrived in Beijing only two hours ago, and my head feels pinched with tiredness and jet lag, but I eat until my fingers are greasy and my jeans feel snug. When the pancakes run out, I eat the duck alone, dipping morsels of skin into the brown sauce, relishing the crisp richness.

My sister, Claire, watches me from across the table. We haven't seen each other in almost two years, yet the sly arch of her eyebrows is still familiar.

"It's delicious," I say, smiling to hide my nervousness. "Almost as good as Mom's."

"Mom's is better," she replies. But I see her hands falter as she lights a cigarette. I try not to stare at the unfamiliar purse of her mouth as she exhales a plume of smoke. The cigarettes are a new accessory, but then again, everything seems a little different about my sister.

I devour almost the whole duck, savoring its familiar, gamey flavor, so evocative of the scraps I used to scrounge from my mother's cutting board. The other dishes are stranger, and after one taste I ignore the cubes of tofu that drift within a deep puddle of bright red oil, and the plate of stir-fried mutton that releases an unwashed whiff. Around me, voices warble incomprehensibly in Chinese, faces grow rosy from beer, my sister, ever vigilant of her waistline, coolly smokes a string of cigarettes and watches me eat.

"Aren't you hungry?" I ask.

"I had a huge lunch." She slides her plate away. "How's your jet lag? You should take a melatonin before you go to bed tonight. Or I have some Ambien if you're really desperate. They say that's what all the flight attendants take between shifts." She flits from topic to topic, like she's trying to avoid something.

"I'm pretty sleepy." I swallow a yawn. "But thanks again for letting me stay with you," I say, feeling shy under her gaze.

"It's great to have you here, *mei*." She uses the Chinese word for younger sister, something we never did as children.

After dinner we stroll among the narrow tangle of *hutong* alleys that make up old Beijing. The warm summer evening feels festive; families sit outside, trying to escape the close heat of their tiny, traditional courtyard homes. Men, their pants rolled to the knees, T-shirts pushed high to expose solid bellies, smoke cigarettes and turn to stare balefully at Claire's tall and sleek figure.

Bicycles whiz perilously close to pedestrians, and everywhere the air is heavy with odors—garlic, grease, and other, grubbier, smells.

We wind our way through the slender alleyways, and suddenly the quaint, village atmosphere disappears, choked off by a vast avenue that teems with bicyclists and honking cars. Claire stops abruptly. "I'm supposed to meet some friends," she says. "But if you're too tired . . . " Her voice trails off.

"I'm exhausted. But don't worry about me. I can find my way back to your apartment."

"It's your first night," she says distantly, before hailing me a cab. As I climb in, she leans over me to give the driver directions, I hand my check, and closes the door. "See you tomorrow, Iz. Sleep well."

As the cab speeds away, I see her chatting and laughing on her cell phone, her whole face alight with animation. I remember those abrupt mood swings from my childhood, along with something else: Claire has always hated Peking duck.

Why did I move to China? I still don't know. But if I think back, I guess it all started one Friday night, the kind of New York winter evening that features seeping cold and flesh-freezing winds. As I sat at the kitchen table of my friends Julia and Andrew, sipping Prosecco and watching the sky turn to a deep, hopeful blue, I couldn't help but wonder if I could blame the biting winds for freezing my life.

"I think I'm having a quarter-life crisis," I announced, and pushed a bowl of pistachio nuts across the kitchen table.

"I think you're a little old for a quarter-life crisis, Iz, unless you're planning on living to a hundred and twenty," said Julia gently. As my best friend, only she was allowed to comment on my approaching advancement into my thirties.

"It's my job," I said glumly. "If I'm not photocopying, I'm babysitting. Today, I'd finally finished making copies of Nina's articles from the past six months—"

"Your boss's clips?" Julia interjected. "Why didn't you send them to the copy shop?"

"Nina said no one could match my photocopying talent. Apparently I make the cleanest copies in the entire company."

"You should mention that at your next review," Julia said with a smile.

"Anyway," I continued, "I'd just lugged everything back to my desk, when Nina shows up with Nicky. Her son. She didn't have time to take him home between his Jungian and Freudian therapy appointments and so she asked me to keep an eye on him."

"*How* old is he?" asked Andrew incredulously.

"Six." I sipped my wine. "He ran straight into the men's room and I had to coax him out. I went in there and saw Rich taking a leak. I'm not sure who was more surprised."

"Isabelle, Rich is a bastard." Julia calmly refilled my glass.

"I know he's a little . . . unreliable." My voice sounded uncertain, even to me. "But he's . . . interesting. He knows a lot about art and books and wine, he speaks fluent French . . . "

"And you work together. He dumped you in the conference room, for God's sake."

"Come on," I objected, "we're still . . . seeing each other."

"You mean, sleeping together. Iz, you deserve more. You're not going to get over him until you cut him out of your life."

"We both work in journalism, we have the same friends. He's everywhere!"

"What you need," Julia twirled the stem of her wineglass, "is an adventure. Someplace different, where you can totally get away."

"Yes!" said Andrew, wrestling the cork out of a fresh bottle. "Like Paris! Everyone speaks French there."

For a moment I imagined myself living in Paris, strolling down a bustling avenue, thin and chic, with a slender scarf wrapped around my neck . . .

"Nooooo, not Paris," said Julia, interrupting my reverie. Seeing the look of protest on my face, she continued, "I'm sorry, Iz. But what would you do? You don't speak French, and you'd never get working papers. The French are notorious sticklers about that sort of thing."

The three of us sat contemplating this unhappy fact, and I started to realize the preposterousness of Julia's idea. I couldn't just go off on some overseas adventure. What about my friends? My family? My career? After five years of slaving over a hot photocopier at the glossy women's magazine, *Belle*, I was finally on the verge of making the leap from fact-checker to staff writer. In just a few days I was meeting with our editor-in-chief to discuss a job in the features department. After so many years of embarrassing fact-checking calls, paper-pushing, and midnight pizza runs for the deadline-dazed production crew, I felt sure the time had come for our editor-in-chief to finally take notice of me, finally start calling me Isabelle, not Irene. I started to speak, but Julia got there first.

"I've got it!" she said, her face alight with enthusiasm. "Beijing!"

"What?" I managed to screech before choking on a sip of wine. My thoughts spun, but I had to finish coughing before I could continue. "How did we go from the City of Light to the City of Smog?"

Julia ignored me. "China is totally hot right now. You could finally start writing articles under your own byline, instead of just fact-checking someone else's work . . . Just like you've always dreamed of."

"I hardly think that'll pay the bills—"

"You speak Mandarin . . . "

"Only kitchen Chinese," I protested.

"What's that?" interjected Andrew.

"Just basic conversation," I explained. "Simple words I picked up in the kitchen, spending time with my mom. I hardly have the Chinese vocabulary to work as a journalist."

"You'd have no trouble getting a visa," Julia continued, undeterred. "And you wouldn't be totally alone. You could live with your sister."

"My *sister*?" I couldn't keep the incredulity out of my voice.

"Yes, your sister. Claire. Doesn't she work for some high-powered law firm in Beijing?"

"I haven't seen Claire in almost two years. I really don't think I can just show up on her doorstep."

"I didn't even know you had a sister," said Andrew.

"We're very different," I said flatly. "She has a dynamic career as an attorney and my parents think she's perfect."

"Claire cares about you, Iz," Julia said. "She just has a funny way of showing it. I bet she's lonely."

Suddenly, the baby monitor crackled to life and the kitchen filled with the demanding cries of a hungry infant.

"Feeding time," said Julia as she scraped back her chair.

"I'll go," said Andrew, kissing the top of her head as he brushed behind her.

"So . . . China." Julia turned to me with a smile.

"You're not trying to get rid of me, are you?" I joked, but sadness seeped into my voice.

"Oh, Iz. No. We'd miss you so much. It's just—" She sighed a weary, sleep-deprived sigh. "I love Andrew and Emily. I love our life together. But everything happened so fast—you know, shotgun wedding, and then the baby six months later." She hesitated. "This is my life now," she said, gesturing around the cluttered kitchen. "But sometimes I wish I could have one last adventure.

Not everyone gets to live overseas . . . and I think I've missed my chance."

"You mean, you want to live vicariously through me."

"Exactly." She giggled. "I'm practicing for when Emily gets older."

"But *China*?" I crossed my arms and looked at my friend, her topknot of golden curls, the clear blue eyes that matched her cashmere sweater. "I'm not some banana who needs to search for her roots," I said slowly, not sure she'd understand.

"Banana?"

"You know—yellow on the outside, white on the inside."

"Oh, Izzy Iz." She sighed impatiently. "Just because you visit China doesn't mean your life is turning into some Amy Tan novel. Besides," she added, a familiar sparkle in her eyes. "Just think about the food!"

I laughed. Julia was one of the few people who shared my near obsessive interest in food. We pored over cookbooks the way some women scrutinize fashion magazines, and spent hours talking about leaving our jobs and opening a combination cookbook shop, test kitchen, and café, an idea that made Andrew break into a sweat with its impracticality.

Julia and I met on my first day at *Belle*, when she helped me free a mass of wrinkled paper from the overheated photocopier and gave me a Band-Aid for the seeping paper cut on my index finger. We became friends the way colleagues usually become friends—through gossiping about our coworkers—but cemented it with a shared interest in food, books, and the Barney's shoe department.

Now, Julia is a literary agent, with nerves that live up to her last name, Steele. She needs them to negotiate multifigure advances for her stable of best-selling authors. Sometimes, when I watch her cuddle her chubby daughter, I'm amazed by her ability to juggle work, marriage, and motherhood. In less than two years Julia has morphed from a single saketini swilling girl-about-town, to someone who quotes Sponge Bob Square Pants. But Julia and Andrew give me hope that true love exists. That there's someone out there for everyone. Plus, they've promised me the attic in their dream home, just in case I don't find him.

"Maybe we could teach a Chinese cooking class in our bookshop's test kitchen!" said Julia excitedly as Andrew returned, bearing a smiling, rosy-cheeked Emily in his arms.

He groaned. "Not the cookbook shop idea again! I swear our bank account diminishes five percent every time you even utter those three words together."

Julia held her arms out for the baby. "You're just jealous you didn't have the idea first," she said, firmly swatting Emily's small bottom.

"Huh!" Andrew snorted, but his gaze lingered upon her affectionately before he turned to wrench open a kitchen drawer. "I don't know about you guys," he said, rooting through the mass of overflowing paper. "But all this talk about China has given me a craving for takeout!" He unearthed a folded paper menu and held it up triumphantly.

"Ooh! General Tso's chicken!" I exclaimed.

And so, Julia called Mee's Noodle House with our usual order and we opened another bottle of wine while waiting for the delivery. Later we scarfed peanut noodles and sweet and sour pork and the topic of China didn't come up again. After all, life in New York had its challenges, but with such good friends, good food, and a job that might finally become rewarding, why would I ever want to leave?

On Monday morning, stacks of paper threatened to overtake my cubicle. Yellow Post-it notes flapped from the pages, each scrawled with my boss's untidy handwriting. *Invoice immediately!* . . . *Xerox—3 copies,* . . . *To art dept., ASAP!* Suppressing a sigh, I gathered up everything, dreaming of the day when piles of paper wouldn't mushroom overnight on my desk. A day when I'd have my own office, complete with a door, so my colleagues wouldn't know when I was making a gynecologist's appointment.

Heaving the reams of paper off my desk, I spotted a red folder at the bottom of the pile. The mere sight of it made my neck muscles clench. A red folder could mean only one thing: urgent fact checking. Urgent, like the article was supposed to be fact-checked last week, but my boss, Nina, neglected to give it to me until today. Urgent, like I would need to have every quote confirmed and every detail quadruple-referenced by early afternoon. Urgent, like Nina would be stopping by my desk every fifteen minutes to check on my progress.

Sure enough, she had slapped a note on the front of the folder: *RUSH! Fact-check and to production by 2:30 P.M. Thx!* Repressing the urge to scream, I started scanning the article, a juicy, tell-all profile of Jolly Jones, Hollywood's newest rags-to-riches-to-rehab starlet. I began making notes, so absorbed in my work that I didn't notice Richard strolling down the hall until he'd stopped in front of my cubicle.

"Hi, you." He cocked his head and regarded me with a tender look that he probably thought I'd find irresistible.

"Hi," I said shortly, ducking under my desk to turn on my computer.

"You seem chipper this morning. Does that mean I'm forgiven?"

I shrugged. "There's nothing to forgive. I haven't heard from you since Friday. Obviously you've been busy." I brushed by him and headed toward my boss Nina's office to unlock her door and boot up her computer.

I lingered in the office, turning on the lights and straightening Nina's stacks of back-issue magazines. But Richard was still there when I returned, a look of indulgent fondness on his face. "I love this cranky, pouty Isabelle," he said. And then, when I remained silent, he cajoled, "Come on, Iz. I'm sorry I didn't call. Let me make it up to you over lunch."

I felt myself weaken as I looked at him, the lock of dark blond hair that flopped over his forehead, the way his gray eyes crinkled. But then I remembered the red folder. "Sorry, I can't," I said. "I'm on deadline."

"Deadlines, shmed-lines." He threw me a careless smile. "Let's go to Pearl Seafood and get oysters and a bottle of wine."

"I can't . . . I don't want to piss Nina off. They're making a decision about the job in Features next week, you know."

Richard gazed at me admiringly. "You know, Iz, this might finally be your big break. You could finally make the leap to staff writer."

Behind my back I crossed my fingers and squeezed them together with an intensity that surprised me. "Here's hoping," I murmured.

I spent the rest of the morning with the telephone receiver wedged under my ear as I struggled to reach all the sources named in the article, while my fingers typed agitated bursts into the LexisNexis search engine. The journalist, a freelancer named Zara Green, was considered one of *Belle*'s rising stars, known for her assertive reporting. I'd met her once at a brownbag lunch for assistants, and found her unreserved enthusiasm and determination compelling. Unfortunately, she'd left so many holes in this story about Jolly Jones, I was starting to feel more like her ghostwriter rather than a fact-checker.

At lunchtime my boss appeared at my cubicle.

"Almost done?" She shot an agonized look at my computer screen. As *Belle*'s managing editor, Nina was arguably one of the most powerful women in New York media, yet she lived in constant fear of getting fired for missing a deadline.

"Not quite."

"When?" Nina spoke in one-word sentences when she was stressed.

"I don't know. I need another couple of hours. Actually, I had some questions . . ."

She heaved a sigh so forceful it ruffled the papers on my desk. "What is this, like the eight hundredth story you've fact-checked for the magazine? You should be able to do this in your sleep by now."

"It's just that there's so much information missing from the article . . . and I can't reach half her sources. And Zara's not picking up the phone or answering any of my e-mails. Are you sure this piece is ready . . . ?" My question hung in the air.

"Why don't you just do your job, Isabelle, and I'll do mine," she said crisply. "Zara Green is a highly respected journalist and I highly doubt she's making up sources."

"But—"

"If you can't finish in time, I'm sure I can find someone else to take over."

"The deadline is not a problem. But—"

"Good. I'll expect it on my desk in an hour."

Swallowing my frustration, I turned back to the phone, picking it up to call Zara one more time. To my surprise, she answered on the third ring.

"Hi, Zara? This is Isabelle Lee from *Belle* magazine. I'm fact-checking your piece and I had some questions about reaching some of your sources . . . " As we started to go over my notes, I noticed that Zara had a habit of calling me "kid," as if she couldn't be bothered to remember my name.

"Kid, don't worry about reaching Henry Collins . . . he's on some sort of meditation retreat in darkest Tibet. He's totally out of contact," Zara reassured me.

"Henry Collins . . . " I scanned my notes. "You mean the extra on the set of Jolly's latest movie who claims he had a one-night stand with her?"

"Yes, and she made him dress up in a bear costume while they had sex."

"His quotes are pretty, er, revelatory." Bizarre was more like it. "All that stuff about her ursine fetish—her fixation with bee-hives, smearing honey all over him, using a stuffed salmon as a sex toy, and then retreating into a darkened room for days and calling it hibernation . . . it all just seems a little . . . unusual. I would really like to talk to him. Are you sure he's out of contact? He's not checking e-mail or anything?"

"I doubt the monks will let him, kid." She laughed. "Apparently they're very strict. Must be all that yak butter tea."

"But . . . I really need to verify everything."

"You can try to reach him, kid, but believe me, it would be a waste of your time. I used to be a fact-checker. I know you probably have a million other things to finish today."

"Are you sure you don't have a telephone number or anything for him?"

"No." Her voice sharpened. "I told you, he's in Tibet. He doesn't want to be contacted. Trust me."

I felt uneasy, but Nina's words came echoing back to me: Zara Green was a highly respected journalist. Why would she invent her sources? And so, I finished up my conversation with Zara and put the article through to production. The rest of the afternoon passed in a blur as I made Nina's photocopies, answered her phone, and ordered her son's organic, gluten-free, vegan Wiggles birthday cake. Three days later, when the issue hit the newsstands, even I had to admit that the article looked stunning, illustrated with Annie Liebowitz's photos. Yet despite my best intentions, I still couldn't shake the feeling that something was wrong.

The morning of my review, I searched the skies for an omen and decided that the bright sun and puffy clouds could only signal a positive outcome. Three people smiled at me on my walk to work, I found a penny on the sidewalk, and the Starbucks barista started making my nonfat cappuccino the minute I walked through the door.

My good luck continued at the office, where someone had left a glazed doughnut on my desk. I took a sticky bite and turned toward my phone, whose message light was flashing more frantically than an ambulance siren. "You have . . . eight . . . new messages," announced my voice mail. That's odd, I thought, as I punched my code into the phone. But maybe Nina was having a crisis. She once left me fourteen voice mails while I was in the bathroom just because she couldn't find her metro card.

In fact, the first message was from Nina. "Iz, could you come down to my office, please!" she said cheerfully.

My heartbeat slowed. Nina sounded perfectly normal in her message. She probably wanted to discuss next week's production schedule, or something.

Except, messages two, three, four, five, six, and seven were also from Nina, her tone growing increasingly sharp. "Where are you?" she said finally. "I need see you *now*."

Before I could cross the hall to her office, she was there at my desk.

"Do you know anything about this?" she demanded. "Did you have any idea?"

"What?" I asked. "What is it?" Searching for clues, my eyes slid from her ashen face to her hands, which held a copy of the latest issue of *Belle*.

"I just got a call from the legal department," she said, her hands trembling slightly. "Jolly Jones is threatening to sue us. She's furious about Zara Green's article."

I swallowed hard. "Oh, no . . . "

"She's claiming that," Nina leaned in and enunciated slowly, "some of the quotes were fabricated."

"Are you sure?" I said, and managed to keep my voice from cracking.

Nina started pacing the corridor in front of my desk. "How could she have done this to us? How could we have let this happen?" She leaned in close. "You spoke to every single source, right?"

"I— I . . . " My pulse skyrocketed. "Have you spoken to Zara?"

"Not yet." Nina's lips thinned. "Get her on the phone for me, okay?" She bolted back to her office and closed the door.

Zara was not at home and her cell went straight to voice mail. I pressed redial again and again, willing her to answer, and when she didn't, slumped back in my swivel chair. This could not be happening to me. Zara Green could not be a pathological liar.

My heart leapt at the ringing phone and I pounced on it, but it was only Julia. "Iz, I just heard what's going on."

How? I thought wildly. Does everyone know?

"Are you okay?" she asked.

"I'm still trying to reach Zara," I admitted.

"Well, don't freak out before you know all the facts."

"Jules?" I said in a small voice. "If something did . . . happen . . . you don't think I'd get . . . fired . . . do you?"

She sighed. "I don't know." Her voice was grim. "But I promise that no matter what happens, everything will be okay. *You* will be okay."

My other line beeped, signaling another call. "Look, that might be Zara on the other line. I'll call you back, okay?"

I switched lines and heard Nina on speaker phone, her voice distant and echoey. "Can you come into my office?" she said.

I tried to respond, but could only squeeze a croak beyond the lump in my throat.

If, as they say in journalism, getting fired is a badge of honor, then I was surely on my way to a long and illustrious career.

Nina regarded me from behind her desk, her shoulders slumped. "I just got off the phone with Elaine," she said quietly.

I swallowed. Elaine was our editor-in-chief.

"I'm . . . She wants . . . " Nina shifted in her seat. "Look, the magazine can't let this slip through the cracks. *Belle* is not the kind of publication that allows shoddy journalism."

No, just articles on how to fake an orgasm, I thought bitterly.

"We'll give you six month's severance. If you agree to the terms, I need your signature." She gestured at a sheaf of documents before offering me a pen.

"You're firing me?" My voice cracked. "But how— Why—"

"Elaine feels that we need to send a message. Make a clean start. Clear the slate."

"But—" I couldn't untangle my thoughts to form a sentence. "It wasn't me. Zara—" The words caught in my throat.

Nina sighed. "You didn't hear this from me, but Jolly's lawyers have agreed to drop the lawsuit against us if we identify the
responsible parties and terminate their employment," she said
quietly. "We'll never use Zara again, but she's just a freelancer.
She's not under contract at *Belle*. And it was your responsibility
to fact-check the article . . . "

I opened my mouth to protest but nothing came out. It wasn't
fair, but Nina was right. I had fact-checked the article—and I
hadn't verified every source. I didn't think it was possible that
Zara would fabricate quotes. I trusted her. I stared at Nina's wide
hands for a moment before reaching for the pen and signing the
papers. I pushed them back toward her and searched her face,
hoping for a glimmer of compassion, but the expression in her
eyes seemed closer to relief.

I managed not to cry until we had politely shaken hands, until I had cleaned out my desk and hugged the other fact-checkers
good-bye, until I had walked out the double glass doors of *Belle*
magazine, my dreams of journalistic success tarnished black by
my tears.

By the next day (and three boxes of Kleenex later) I had started
wandering the streets, officially unemployed. Well, maybe not
actually wandering. But I was tucked up in my apartment, Aunt
Marcie's hand-knit afghan pulled up to my shoulders, TV turned
to *The View*, when Rich called and asked me to dinner. "I'd love
to!" I said, trying to keep the surprise out of my voice. As much
as I adored him, Richard wasn't exactly known for his caring,
nurturing side. Nevertheless, he'd booked a table at my favorite
French bistro for eight o'clock.

I arrived first and ordered a glass of champagne. One sparkling sip and my mood lifted. After all, I was young, I lived in the
media capital of the world, I had tons of contacts, and a sophisti-
cated, thoughtful boyfriend . . . I had nothing to worry about.

"Darling!" Richard advanced from the door and swooped down to kiss me on both cheeks.

"Hi, sweethcart," I said, and felt a smile spread across my face. He looked so handsome in his black turtleneck and tweed trousers. Of course we'd had our ups and downs, but it meant so much that he was there. That he cared.

We ordered steak frites right away, and after our waiter disappeared, Rich reached across the table to wrap his hands around mine. "My poor, sweet Isabelle," he said. "This must be so awful for you."

"It's worse than awful," I groaned.

"Any job prospects lined up?"

"No," I admitted. "Julia wants me to go to some book party tomorrow but I don't know if I can face the humiliation." I gazed at him hopefully. "You wouldn't want to go with me, would you?"

"Oh, Iz, I don't know." He removed his hands from mine. "Look, I know you've got a lot going on right now . . . but I think we should take a break."

A leaden feeling tightened my chest.

"I've always loved how undefined our relationship has been," he continued. "There's never been any pressure to make it last two weeks or two years—"

"A year and a half," I said faintly, squeezing the words past the lump in my throat before the anger, shock, and pain combined to turn me silent.

"We didn't force ourselves to label it, put limits on it, you know?"

The waiter delivered our food, and I cut into my steak and watched the red juices seep out. It's the last thing I saw clearly before the tears started falling down my cheeks, before I pushed my chair away and left.

Thank God for Julia. I lay on her green velvet sofa and wept, my head and heart aching. She bit down on her lip, but made nary an I-told-you-so peep. The next morning she forced me out to the farmer's market, where we dug through a bin of winter apples. The sharp wind dried my cheeks and numbed my hands, and when Emily, tucked up in her stroller, received her first sip of warm cider with a clap of her chubby hands, I even tried to smile. Later that afternoon we baked a pie, and I took comfort in the precision of the measurements, fiercely chopping apples, lightly rubbing butter and flour together with my fingers.

"Will you think about Beijing?" asked Julia.

But I'd already decided.

I couldn't disappear, of course. But two months later I'd sublet my apartment, sold most of my furniture, and become skillful at decoding the tide of opinion about my decision.

"What an adventure!" exclaimed my neighbor, Liz. "But what will you *do*?" Translation: You're crazy!

"You're moving back to China?" said my hairdresser as she clipped layers into my long, dark hair. "How exciting that you're going back to your homeland!" Translation: Your life is an Amy Tan novel.

On a weekend visit to my parents' house in the suburbs, I casually mentioned my plan over lunch. My mother beamed. It was the first smile I'd seen from her since I told them I'd been fired (actually, I used the handy term "laid off"). "Your father will be so happy," said my mother. Translation: I'm ecstatic.

I glanced at my dad, but if he was happy, it proved hard to decipher. A second generation Chinese American born in Queens, his ties to China faded before he was born, when his parents left Guangdong over eighty years ago for the United States. Later, as I climbed sleepily into my childhood bed, he tiptoed into my room and tucked a hundred dollar bill into my hand. "For emergencics," he said. "Don't tell your mother." Translation: I'm worried about you.

His concern didn't surprise me. My parents had been worried about me for years. For starters, there was my choice of college: "You want to go *where?*" my mother had said, when I told her I wanted to apply to NYU. "Is that a four year university?" And then, once I'd graduated, there was my career: "Journalism?" she'd said, when I got my job at *Belle*. "Oh, you don't want to do that. You'll never support yourself!" Getting fired amidst a blaze of scandal only seemed to confirm their fears: straying from the white collar, model minority path led to disaster, and, worse, loss of face.

Being at home with my parents was like reverting back to my childhood. I visited them once a month—not as often as they would have liked—and every time I entered via the garage door, I knew exactly what to expect. The modest colonial still smelled the same, a not unpleasant mix of steamed rice and tiger lilies with a faint trace of mothballs. My father still sat in his overstuffed lounge chair watching golf and working the crossword puzzle. My mother, home from her trio of hair salons (the largest Asian hair empire on the East Coast) whizzed around the kitchen stirring bubbling pots of pork stock, or chopping spring onions with an oversized cleaver, all while chattering on the phone in Chinese with my aunt Marcie. Claire's diplomas still hung in the hallway, a pair of gilt-framed curlicued documents that haughtily announced her Ivy League education. And I still felt the same feelings of adolescent insecurity.

Upstairs, our bedrooms also remained the same, even Claire's, though she hadn't been home in two years. The closet held her collection of plain trouser suits, arranged by color; in the desk drawer I found a stack of gift cards to Barney's, which I'd given her in the hopes that she'd abandon Ann Taylor forever. They looked untouched. I peered at a row of her college textbooks, arranged neatly by height.

Claire had said that opening her law firm's Beijing office was a huge promotion, the opportunity of a lifetime, but the thrill hadn't reached her pale face when she announced the news to us all those months ago. She'd always been ambitious—valedictorian of her senior class, editor of the law review—but it still seemed strange that work could have kept her away for all this time.

My mother caught me leafing through Claire's old Mandarin textbooks, examining the characters with familiar fascination and frustration.

"Have you heard from her?" she asked, her voice wistful, though her expression remained impassive.

"I haven't e-mailed her yet," I admitted.

"It would mean so much to me for you two to be together in China," she said, heaving a theatrical sigh.

I resisted the impulse to roll my eyes. My mother's feelings for China were filled with the wistfulness of an exile, expressed with all the melodrama of a soap star. Even after thirty years in America, she still regarded herself as Chinese; her deepest regret—expressed many times over family dinner—was that I didn't speak fluent Mandarin.

"Mom, just because I go to China doesn't mean I'm going to have some enormous ethnic epiphany," I said impatiently. "Or that Claire and I will become best friends."

She pursed her lips together and looked at me with an air of disappointment that I recognized all too well.

I feared Claire's reaction the most, but finally typed her an e-mail and waited nervously for her reply.

To: Claire Lee
From: Isabelle Lee
Subject: Beijing

Dear Claire,
    I know it's been a while since my last e-mail, but I think of
you often and wonder about your adventures in China. Things
here are fine but work has been a little rocky and I've been
thinking about making a change . . . maybe coming to Beijing,
which seems so exciting right now. There's no easy way to ask
this, so here goes: Am wondering if you'd have room for me in
your guest room, just for a little bit while I get on my feet? If this
is too inconvenient, just let me know. I won't be mad, promise.
Hope you're well. Mom and dad say hi.
    Love, Isabelle

Her response, when it finally arrived two weeks later, revealed
nothing.

To: Isabelle Lee
From: Claire Lee
Subject: Moving to Beijing?

    Darling Iz, of course you can come and stay for as long as
you like. My apartment is gigantic and Beijing will give your New
York literati lifestyle a run for its money . . . Am swamped with
work so will wait until I see you to catch up on everything.
    xxxx C

And so, one brilliant June morning, I found myself crammed
into a coach seat, on a sixteen hour flight for Beijing via San

Francisco. The sun shimmered off the East River as our plane took off, and I said a silent good-bye to New York with dry eyes and a pounding heart. I'd gotten what I wanted: a chance to start over. Except it felt an awful lot like running away.

Now, back in Claire's cavernous apartment, I sit in the living room wrapped in a sweater yet still shivering from the aggressive air-conditioning that chills the air to a frigid sixty-four degrees. The vast space spreads around me, ostentatious in its enormity, with eerie hums and electronic squeals of feedback occasionally breaking the silence. "Don't worry about those sounds," Claire assured me earlier. "They like to keep an eye on us. It's annoying, but our local legal counsel says there's nothing we can do about it." I'm still not sure who "they" are: Chinese spies? That seems absurd.

Claire's apartment, part of her white-shoe law firm's expat package, drips with flamboyant grandeur. Marble columns rise throughout the three-thousand-square-foot space, and giant gilt-framed mirrors cover several walls. In contrast, Claire's own refined furniture, shipped directly from the States, cowers within the rooms, its normal size shrunk to miniature next to the floor-to-ceiling windows, her prized collection of Central Asian rugs like scraps of patchwork on the pink marble floors.

I try to read my book, skipping whole paragraphs as the words blur, but eventually, as my head jerks up for the tenth time, I creep to bed. Falling asleep is easy, but 2:00 A.M. sees me wide-awake, my mind as alert as if it were two in the afternoon, which, considering the twelve hour time difference between Beijing and New York, it is. As I slip out to use the bathroom, I pause in the hall to see if Claire has returned, but find only silence, her bedroom door wide-open, her bed still smooth.

My sister and I are six years apart, but there is a greater gap between us. As children, we were allies against a steady stream of dried black mushrooms and crunchy wood ear fungi, thousand-year-old-eggs that wobbled like jelly and endless, countless bowls of white rice. To my mother, whose family fled Shanghai in 1949, these familiar tastes and textures were a safe and steady bridge; they linked her to a world to which she could never return.

For my sister and me, both born with a second-generation horror of being different, nightly Chinese feasts assured a craving for Taco Bell and tuna noodle casserole, or anything that our friends wouldn't think of as weird. It was one of the few things we ever agreed upon. Once we grew up to have kitchens of our own, we banished bok choy and chicken feet from our diet. Eating at home with Mom and Dad, though, remained the same.

My mind races over the meal we ate tonight, the soft cubes of tofu that drowned within a deep pool of fiery oil, the fat-streaked slices of mutton so redolent of stale sweat. After a childhood spent eating Chinese food, I didn't expect culture shock to strike at the dinner table.

I've only been in China for a day but I think I've discovered that what expats say about the country is true of its cuisine: the more you know, the less you understand.

Home Style Cooking

"In China, dietary practice involves two extremes; 'eating to live' and 'eating for pleasure'. The make-up of the Chinese menu reflects this opposition/correlation between what is necessary and what is superfluous."

—*THE OXFORD COMPANION TO FOOD*

3:00 A.M. Wide-awake.

5:00 A.M. Still wide awake.

7:30 A.M. Getting sleepy . . .

The telephone wakes me, ringing and ringing until even the two pillows shoved over my head won't block the noise. I stagger out of bed and into the living room, blindly lurching from corner to corner in the cavernous space, pausing occasionally to allow the phone's shrill bleat to guide me. Just as I'm about to retreat to my room and jam three pillows over my head, I spot the phone lying underneath a marble-topped gilt side table and pounce on it.

"Hello?"

But it's only the dial tone, and even it sounds different here, hollow in its high-pitched drone.

I hang up and totter back to my cozy, soft bed. The light streaming through the windows suggests that the day is not young, but I don't stop to look at the clock. Right now I feel the same passion for sleep that I once felt for the Barney's end-of-the-year shoe clearance: I need as much as possible, damn the consequences.

I collapse into bed, fluff my pillows and pull the down-filled duvet up to my chin. Claire's sheets are so soft, I think as I drift away. They must be 800-count Egyptian cotton. I am just about to sink into blissful unconsciousness when the phone starts ringing again.

This time I get it after only five rings. "Hello?" I say, and then because, after all, I am in China, I attempt a greeting in Mandarin. "Wai?"

"Hold the line for Claire Lee, please," says a cool voice. I wait. And wait. And wait.

Perhaps my jet-lagged brain misunderstood. "Hello?" I say experimentally, but only a series of clicks answers me.

I'm about to hang up and crawl back to bed when Claire's honeyed tones come floating over the line. "Isabelle? I'm so sorry to keep you waiting, darling."

"Hi." My voice emerges in a croak.

"Oh, did I wake you? You weren't still sleeping, were you? It's two o'clock!"

"Sleeping? At this hour? Oh no, no, no. I've been up for ages." My laugh sounds like a gurgle.

"Oh good. Because I meant to phone earlier, but today has been insane. Listen, I ran into a friend at that party last night . . . "

I try to focus but my brain refuses to absorb any information. If I closed my eyes, would I be able to sleep standing up like a horse?

" . . . and he really wants to meet you," Claire concludes. "Isn't that great?"

"What?"

"Ed Watson. At the expat magazine. Is expecting your phone call. Honestly, Iz, haven't you been listening?"

Expat magazine? A dart of alarm shoots through the fog of jet lag. Is that all she thinks I can do? I try to keep the irritation from my voice. "Claire, I'm not sure if an expat magazine is really the right fit for me. I mean, I worked at one of New York's *biggest* women's magazines . . . " Why does she always underestimate me?

"Oooh," she squeals. "Sophia! I didn't know you were in town! Hold on a sec, okay? I'm just getting off the phone."

"Hello?"

"Iz? I have to run. Ed's card is on the kitchen counter. Just tell him you're my sister."

"Will you be home later tonight?" I ask, my voice more hopeful than I intend.

"Ohhhh, I'm sorry, darling . . . I have to work late and then I'm supposed to go to this dinner party. I'd bring you but it's going to be horribly boring. All legal mumbo jumbo . . . " Her voice trails off. "But maybe I could get out of it."

"No, no. I'm fine." I struggle to sound confident. "Don't worry about me."

"Well, if you're sure . . . "

"Definitely. I should try to get over my jet lag anyway."

"Well that probably makes sense." Is that relief I hear in her voice? "I'll talk to you soon then, yes? Big kiss. Mwah. Byeeeee!"

She hangs up leaving me staring blankly at the phone. I didn't expect Claire to spend all her spare time with me but I'm a little surprised that she's so, well, social. Back in New York, the only dinner parties she attended were at the office—late night deli sandwiches while preparing for a trial. And what's up with her accent? It seems to have evolved from mid-Atlantic to British. Darling? Big kiss?

Something else is different too . . . something more intangible than the red highlights in her dark hair and new wardrobe of sleek outfits. It's almost as if she's . . . hip. Yet how could that be possible? The Claire I remember wore thick glasses and graduated valedictorian of her class. She was the first person from our high school to go to Harvard, but I don't think anything ever erased the sting of staying home from the prom. Once she graduated from law school (Yale), her life in New York revolved around making partner at her firm and visiting our parents on the weekend. My parents constantly urged me to emulate Claire's grades and discipline, her obedience. "Why can't you be more like your sister?" cried my mother, casting aside my report card of straight B's and C's. She didn't understand that I worked as hard at appearing effortlessly cool as Claire did at school. We both viewed the other with a mixture of envy and disdain.

Shrugging my shoulders, I wander into the kitchen where a business card lies stark white against the black granite counter. BEIJING NOW MAGAZINE proclaims the logo, and below it, *Ed Watson, Publisher.* Chinese characters on one side, English on the other.

I push the hair out of my eyes and sigh. Claire may have moved halfway across the world, but nothing could alter her brisk sense of order, her need to tidy everything into its proper spot. A place for everyone and everyone in her place. Her spic-and-span methods now extend to me. Apparently, I'm the mess that needs to be cleaned, the stain to scrub.

I bury my face in my hands. I need to find a job soon—my plane ticket to Beijing used up most of my severance pay. But I didn't come to China to work for some no-name expat rag. A bubble of resentment rises in my throat. Why does Claire constantly have to remind me that I'll never live up to her Ivy League education?

I leave Ed Watson's card on the counter and stalk back into my bedroom, where I open the curtains to a smoggy gray day, turn on my laptop, and connect to Claire's wireless. Thirty minutes of Googling turns out a bevy of e-mail addresses for Beijing's newspaper bureau chiefs. I quickly start typing:

> Dear Simon Bank (or Mary Ellen Bates, or Kathy Woo, or Dennis Frank),
>   I recently relocated to Beijing from New York, where I was an editorial assistant at *Belle* magazine. I'm interested in covering news and am wondering if you'd have time to meet to discuss opportunities at your Beijing bureau. I am a great admirer of your work at the *New York Times* (or *Newsweek, Chicago Tribune, LA Times, Washington Post,* etc.) and look forward to speaking with you soon.
>   Sincerely,
>   Isabelle Lee

I fill in their e-mail addresses, attach my résumé and send off a dozen messages, crossing my fingers as they flit away.

In the next few days I check my e-mail three, four, five, six times a day, but after a week my hope starts to fade. I wander through Beijing's great sites, pushing my way through the crowds. Claire offered to accompany me, but her enthusiasm for the capital's tourist spots seemed weak, and so I explore alone. At the Forbidden City, I inch into the maze of courtyards and ceremonial halls, the surrounding high walls making me feel insignificant. The sun breaks free of the pollution for the first time in nine days at the Temple of Heaven, shining with dazzling

strength against the white marble walkways and elaborate pago-
das. I tramp a steep section of the Great Wall, my legs straining
with every step, until I finally survey the sweeping landscape
from a stone watchtower. I stroll Tian'anmen Square's wide concrete swaths at sunset, pausing with the crowd to watch a quartet of round-cheeked guards lower the flag. Around me people
shuffle and sigh, snapping quick photographs. From the back,
everyone looks the same, distilled into an indistinct black-haired
head. A sudden realization shocks me: I look just like everyone
else.

After two weeks I've realized that silence is the new rejection
letter. The fear of pennilessness is hovering around me like a cloud of
gnats. After three weeks Claire's nagging about Ed has become
certifiably maddening. I try to think up a Plan B that doesn't
involve expat magazines or teaching English.

And then, on another humid, gray morning I wake to a phone
call.

"Isabelle Lee?" says a man's voice, clipped and efficient.
"Dennis Frank from the *Washington Post*. Got your e-mail . . .
as it turns out we're looking for a news assistant. Why don't you
come in this afternoon?"

Trying to keep my hands from shaking, I scribble down the
address and hang up the phone. Thank God something finally
came through. I was beginning to think I might actually have to
take my sister's advice.

A few minutes later I am tearing at my suitcase, which has
stood untouched in the corner of my room since I arrived three
weeks ago. I poke around, hoping to avoid unpacking for at least
a few more days, and pull out . . . a flower-splashed bikini, a
sequined top, a tweed skirt—good grief, what was I thinking
when I packed? Finally, I unearth a pale linen suit and blue silk
blouse. Perfect, crisp and professional. Since it's too hot to wear

the jacket, I throw it over my arm in the manner of a jaunty cub reporter.

Outside, I step out onto the street, dodge a herd of bicyclists wearing scary Darth Vader–style shaded visors over their faces, and hail a cab from the tangle of cars inching their way along Guanghua Lu. The car is cool, but smells strongly of stale cigarette smoke, and the cotton-covered seat feels slightly damp beneath my back, from someone else's sweat, I realize with a grimace. As we edge along, I try to prepare for the interview. Topics to highlight: my experience at *Belle*, interest in journalism. Topics to avoid: getting fired.

"Ni shi na guo ren?" says the taxi driver, breaking into my thoughts. Where are you from?

I answer haltingly in Chinese. *"Wo shi meiguoren."* I'm American.

He removes his eyes from the road to stare at me. "No! You're not American!" he continues in Mandarin.

"Yes, I am!" I bare my teeth at him in a big American-style grin.

"Americans have yellow hair and big noses. And they're fat," he retorts.

"Well, I was born in America. I grew up there." I want to continue, but my Chinese falters. I don't know the words for pop culture or second generation, and even if I did, I don't know how to tell him that right now China seems as foreign and indecipherable as Mars.

"You look Chinese."

"I am Chinese. But I'm also American."

"No wonder your Chinese is so bad," he says acidly. "You should study harder." He snaps on the radio with an air of displeasure.

We creep along the Second Ring Road, one of the major highways that encircle the city. I know from my guidebook that the road is built around the old city walls, and I peer out, hoping to catch a glimpse of an ancient stone barricade or crumbling watchtower, but instead see only sleek, bland high rises, dazzling and empty, and shabby cereal box apartment buildings that seem late for an appointment with the wrecking ball. Construction sites blossom on almost every block, the bright yellow cranes a splash of color against the gray sky. The air crackles with energy, excitement, opportunity, and for the first time in months I feel hope flutter in my chest. Perhaps there's a place for me too in this brave new Beijing.

Before I know it we've clattered to a stop. "Dao le," announces the driver. We're here.

"Where is . . . the . . . uh . . . place?" I ask in my broken Chinese.

He gestures vaguely into the distance.

On the sidewalk, I gaze up at the blocky buildings and down at the address in my hand: 2 Dongzhimen Nei Dajie. Hmmm . . . the nearest building reads 43. Are we even on Dongzhimen Nei Dajie? I pull out my cell phone. Should I call Dennis Frank's office for directions, or will that make me look like I don't have a clue about this city? Which I don't. I scroll through my phone, looking for Dennis's number. Wait a second. Why isn't his number in my phone? I could have sworn I'd programmed it into my contacts list. My phone only operates in Chinese and I must have confused the characters for "save" and "delete," I realize with horror.

Okay, no problem. Deep breaths, deep breaths. Squaring my shoulders, I begin to walk the long block to the next office building, ignoring the beads of sweat that start streaming down my forehead. Phew! These wide blocks seem designed for the girth of a tank, not pedestrians. And who knew Beijing was this hot? And humid? Ten minutes later . . . None of the buildings have numbers. Okay . . . I'll just ask someone for help. I approach a young woman, about my age, elbow-length gloves covering arms that wield an Olympics 2008 umbrella. Is it supposed to rain? I glance at the sky, which is oddly bright with sun straining through the layers of ozone.

"Er, excuse me?" Damn. How do you say "excuse me" in Chinese?

At the sound of my voice the girl's eyes grow huge and she moves her hand rapidly from side to side—the international sign for "go away!"—before scurrying down the street, her umbrella bobbing with every step.

Five long blocks later my face drips with sweat, but by some miracle I've finally found the right address. In the cool, dark elevator, I gaze at myself in the reflective doors with horror. My silk shirt is drenched with sweat, my linen trousers look limp and wrinkled. My face is flushed and sweaty like I've just run a marathon; or worse, like I'm going through heroin withdrawal. I try to cover my soaked shirt with the suit jacket, pulling it on only to discover a rust-colored stain on the lapel. Ketchup. I remember the night Richard dropped a splodge while trying to feed me a french fry at the Corner Bistro. Now it looks like I've had a messy accident with a handgun. Great. I can look either sweaty and disheveled, or bloody, sweaty, and disheveled. I pull off the jacket as the elevator doors open.

Dennis Frank ushers me into his office right away, tactfully ignoring my sodden appearance. We sit down and he tactfully directs his gaze to my face.

"Would you like a cup of tea?" he finally asks.

I've just walked five miles in ninety degree heat, I think. The *last* thing I want is a hot beverage! I shake my head.

"So . . . " Dennis pauses and looks down at my résumé. " . . . Isabelle. Tell me about your experience in journalism."

Despite the air-conditioning—which is like an arctic blast, given my damp clothes—I feel my palms grow damp. "Well . . . I worked at *Belle* magazine for five years . . . as a fact-checker. " I tack on the last word like it's an afterthought.

"What about reporting? Ever written for any dailies? Maybe in college?" He bobs his head encouragingly.

I take a deep breath. "Well, I did work for my college newspaper—"

"Yes?" He leans forward eagerly.

"Selling classified ads."

"Oh."

The uncomfortable silence settles on us again. I stare outside, where the sun struggles to break free of the pollution.

"How's your Chinese?" Dennis asks abruptly. He looks down at his thin, dry hands.

"It's uh . . . okay. Pretty good. Conversational," I hedge.

"Are you familiar with news terms? Like . . . say . . . nuclear nonproliferation?" He raises his eyebrows.

Should I lie? Is he going to test me? The silence grows as I furrow my brow, pretending to search my brain for the word. "No," I finally admit. "I don't know." I consider snapping my fingers in a "darn it, the word escapes me" gesture, but when I see Dennis narrow his eyes, I reconsider.

"Your résumé says you speak Mandarin," he says, and I catch a glimpse of impatience in his face.

"It's a little rusty right now," I admit.

He stands up. "We're really looking for someone who speaks Chinese."

"I understand," I say, and try to avoid offering him my hand, which is still hot and sticky, but I can't, and we awkwardly shake.

"We'll be in touch," he says as he ushers me out the door.

I nod even though I know I'll never hear from him again.

Downstairs, I am relieved to find one of the many Starbucks outposts that dot the city. I treat myself to a latte, in the hope that the smell of ground coffee and their familiar little wooden tables will somehow comfort me. My iced coffee tastes reassuringly familiar but does little to solve my problems. I've gone from being unemployed in New York to being unemployed in a country where I can't even speak the language.

Well, at least I can make more of an effort to study Chinese, maybe try to learn a new word every day. I dig around in my bag for my pocket dictionary. Let's see . . . here are the N's . . . nuclear nonproliferation . . . *bukuofan hewuqi.*

Oh, for heaven's sake. What the hell am I doing? I barely know what nuclear nonproliferation means in English, let alone Mandarin Chinese. I swallow the last of my cold coffee along with my pride and dial *Beijing NOW*'s number on my cell phone.

Barely two days later I once again regard myself in the reflective doors of an elevator. At least today I'm clean and cool in dark jeans and a crisp white blouse. After my disastrous interview with the *Washington Post,* I crumpled my soiled linen suit into a ball, shoved it to the back of my closet, and rejoiced when Ed said the *Beijing NOW* office was casual. The elevator lifts me with slow majesty to the tenth floor, where I find a portly, curly-haired man smoking next to a grimy window. He shoots me a curious glance, and I venture, "Ed Watson?"

"Yeah, that's me." A sunny Australian accent warms his vowels.

"I'm Isabelle." A blank look crosses his face, and I quickly add, "Claire Lee's sister?"

"Isabelle! Of course!"

"I'm sorry I'm late . . ."

"No worries," he says with a bemused smile. He blows a stream of smoke toward the ceiling and stubs out his cigarette in one swift motion. "Come on, let me show you around."

From the dim hall, he ushers me into a large room that's bright with fluorescent lights and the stir of people. "The newsroom," says Ed. "I think the mismatched furniture and scuffed walls add to the charm." The eyes of the room glue to me, and I manage a soft "Hi."

"Hey mates, this is Isabelle. She's an ABC from New York." American Born Chinese. Ed is obviously well-versed in his expat lingo. "That's Lily," he says, pointing a thick finger at a slender girl in the corner, who smiles shyly before tucking a silky black strand of hair behind her ear. "She covers fashion. Gab is from New York too," he says, nodding at an Asian guy on the phone, short sleeves hacked from his T-shirt to reveal wiry arms cuffed with tattoos. "He writes about the local music scene. His Chinese is amazing." Gab nods briskly and smiles a hello. "Over there, that's Tang Laoshi." Ed gestures at a balding Chinese man with thick glasses and a stare that oozes suspicion. Teacher Tang. "He's our censor," Ed hisses out of the corner of his mouth.

"And I'm Geraldine," says a voice behind me. "Welcome," she says with a warm smile.

"Geraldine is our food editor and resident fashion model," says Ed as we shake hands and I note her intriguing East-meets-West style, the Japanese-print miniskirt she's thrown over dark jeans, the thick twist of golden hair held in place by a carved red lacquer comb.

"I've got a brain too, Ed," she says with a laugh, though there's a smooth touch of sarcasm in her voice.

"She's moving to the culture page," says Ed as we move away from the center of the room to his office.

Inside, the door closes with a flimsy snap. I perch on a one-armed chair while Ed settles his stocky bulk behind a tiny desk and eyes me speculatively. "I'm not sure how much Claire has told you about our magazine . . . "

"Not a lot," I hedge politely.

"Basically, we're a weekly English-language magazine for expats. We cover the local art scene, live music, new bars and clubs, restaurants. Our readers are mostly young, mostly men—so is our staff, for that matter, though we're trying to soften our tone, add a more feminine touch. Anyway, one of our editors just moved back to the UK, and Geraldine, who you just met . . . " He pauses and I nod. " . . . is going to take over his beat. Says she's tired of eating out all the time." He straightens a stack of papers on his desk. Despite his rumpled clothes and hair, his office is pristine. "So, Ger's going to do the arts section, and we're looking for a food critic, someone to write features about wine and regional cuisines, review restaurants, that sort of thing."

It sounds like a great job. Despite my initial prejudice against expat magazines, I find myself leaning forward and nodding with interest. Claire was right about *Beijing NOW,* I realize with faint chagrin. Buzzing with energy and ideas, covering food, fashion, and the arts, it's a perfect fit for me. Is it possible that my sister knows me better than I thought?

"Ideally, we need someone who speaks great Chinese," Ed continues. "But Claire really gave you the hard sell."

"She did?"

"Oh yeah, yeah. Beautiful girl, Claire . . . hilarious too." He stares into the distance for a minute with a small smile on his lips before recovering himself. "Anyway, she told me all about your work at *Belle,* and how you're a great writer—"

I am? I think wildly.

"And how you've loved Chinese food ever since you were a kid—"

"But my Chinese really isn't very . . . fluent."

"I'm sure you know enough for the job. Like, do you know how to say . . . "

Oh dear. Here we go again.

"Steamed rice?"

"Bai mi fan!" I exclaim.

"Braised beef?"

"Hongshao niurou."

"Broccoli, carrots, potatoes?"

"Xi lan hua, hong lun lui rudun."

"See?" says Ed. "I knew you'd be fine. Claire told me about how your parents forced you guys to go to Chinese school on Saturdays and how you both hated it. Her Chinese is really spot on, though, isn't it?"

Claire hated Chinese school? I remember the stiff set of her shoulders as she copied characters into a gridded notebook, her long, schoolgirl hair lying in a thick tail upon her neck. She was always the first one in the car on Saturday mornings, the one who sang folk songs in the bath and recited four character sayings in front of guests. "You should study like Claire," my mother always said. "Like a good Chinese daughter."

"So, what do you think, Isabelle?" Ed leans forward, interrupting my reverie. "Are you interested in the job?"

"I wasn't really a journalist in New York. Only a fact-checker," I blurt out.

Ed ignores me. "Bluster, Isabelle, bluster," he declares. "Journo, fact-checker; tomayto, tomahto." He shrugs. "Everyone reinvents themselves in China. Except for me, of course," he adds hastily. "I actually *was* a features editor at the *Sydney Morning Herald.*

Anyway, I know your sister." Seeing the surprised expression on my face, he adds, "In China, you have to rely on your *guanxi*."

Guanxi. Connections. In the States, connections are like a strand of fishing wire—strong enough to reel in a heavy fish, yet so cunningly transparent they're almost invisible. I had forgotten that in China, *guanxi* is like flashy jewelry—flaunted, fawned over, and, at times, used to bribe. *Guanxi* forms the base of every relationship; from work to friends, it's the only way most business gets done.

I take a deep breath, but before I can say a word, he plunges into a discussion about salary—naming a figure so tiny it makes my former slave wages at *Belle* look grand—benefits, and my visa situation. "We'll help you get you a Z visa. You'll need it to work legally in China."

"But—But—" I stammer.

"What's wrong, mate?"

"I haven't said yes!"

"Don't be coy, Isabelle. No other prospects on the horizon, are there? Listen, if you don't like the job, you can quit. No hard feelings. And if you're not up to snuff, don't worry. I'll fire you." Ed roars with laughter.

I chuckle a tiny bit to prove I'm a good sport, but inside, my heart beats fast in a mixture of terror and excitement.

My new desk is part of a square in the center of the room, facing Gab and Lily, with Geraldine sitting to my right. Only Tang Laoshi has a private corner, with his desk angled so he can watch us. The room buzzes with activity—the phones ring constantly, bilingual conversations flow over one another, ideas and suggestions are tossed around.

Lily finds me a stack of back issues and I start leafing through a copy. Typos and awkward layouts litter the pages, but the articles strike just the right note of informative and sassy. Scattered as Ed seems, he seems to keep a sharp eye on the writing. I've just started reading his weekly "Editor's note" when my cell phone rings.

"Did you get the job?" Claire's voice is high with excitement.

"Er, can you hold on a sec?" I feel self-conscious talking in front of everyone, and leave the newsroom to slip into the corridor.

"Don't you love Ed? Isn't he totally hilarious? And come on, you have to admit that *Beijing NOW* is the perfect place for you to work."

"Everyone does seem really energetic and full of great ideas," I admit.

"So, was I right, or was I right?"

"You were right." I resist rolling my eyes, even though she can't see me.

"See? You should listen to me more often." She laughs. "When do you start?"

"Soon. Right away. Actually, tomorrow."

"Wow, Ed really doesn't mess around. That's wonderful! I'm really happy for you." She does sound happy, but I'm not sure if it's because I finally took her advice. "Anyway, darling," she continues, "I should probably get back to work. I just called to say congratulations! Oh, and I'll probably be home super late tonight, so don't wait up, 'kay sweetie?" Before I can respond, she's ended the call.

I return to the newsroom, where I start to peruse the current issue, laughing out loud at a witty article by Geraldine about the wild side of Cantonese cuisine. She glances away from her computer and over my shoulder. "Yuck," she says with a shudder. "I actually had to eat dog meat for that piece. It was horrible."

I look at her with new respect. "What was it like?"

"Tasted like chicken, of course. Very stringy, gamey chicken."

As if on cue, my stomach resonates with a loud growl. "I'm sorry," I say, embarrassed. "I'm not a fan of dog meat, I'm just hungry."

"Do you want to grab a bite to eat? It's just about dinnertime."

"It's only six-thirty!" My voice rises with surprise.

"Yeah, but this is China. Lunch is at eleven-thirty, dinner at six. Stray from those hours and you're in trouble. Come on." She closes down her computer with a few efficient clicks of the mouse. "I've got a hankering for *jiachangcai.*"

I'm not sure what *jiachangcai* is, but am too famished to protest. Geraldine waves a cheerful good-bye to the newsroom and we find our way outside. We pass a narrow alley that's lined with tiny food stalls, and I pause to admire the griddle-fried pancakes that gleam with hot cooking oil, and breathe in the fragrant steam that rises from the vats of spicy soup.

We arrive at a small, bright restaurant that's crowded with dark heads, the walls scuffed and stained, the floor littered with chopsticks and chicken bones. As we enter, I realize we are the only two foreigners, and that the entire restaurant, both customers and staff, have turned to stare. "Look!" A pimpled girl points a bony finger at Geraldine's bright hair. *"Laowai!"* Foreigner. Their eyes swivel between us, but linger on me, curious to see what kind of Chinese person would befriend an outsider.

I stand by an empty table, awkward and unsure. For the first time, I realize how difficult it will be to live in China, a foreigner by nature, with the appearance of a local. For a moment I feel overwhelmed by the prospect, but then Geraldine sits, and I sit across from her.

A waitress appears and hovers impatiently over our table, her

pen poised. "Are you ready to order?" she asks me, her eyes resolutely avoiding Geraldine. I flip through the menu searching for
familiar characters, but can't decipher much more than "meat,"
"vegetable," and "rice."

"Do you eat everything?" says Geraldine.

"Yes," I say with relief.

"Okay," she says, without even a glance at the menu. *"Women
lai yi fen'r mayi shang shu, yi fen'r mapo doufu, yi fen'r di san
xian* . . . that's probably enough," she muses. *"Liang wan mi fan.
Gen can jing zhi'r, cha shui."* She bestows a sweet smile upon the
waitress. *"Xie xie."* Thank you.

The waitress writes it all down, her expression impassive, and
shuffles away "What did you order?" I ask with admiration. "You
didn't even look at the menu!"

"Oh, it's easy!" Geraldine laughs. "The food is the same at
every home-style joint."

Ah! *Jiachangcai.* Home-style food. The simple, comforting
dishes that people eat every day.

"Chinese cuisine is like poetry—everything has a beautiful
name," she continues. "Ants on a tree. That's just ground pork
and cellophane noodles. *Mapo doufu*—you probably know—
it means pockmarked tofu, but it's actually just tofu in a spicy
sauce. And *di san xian* is my favorite. Earth's three fairies—eggplant, potato, and bell pepper combined in a brown sauce form
a magical flavor."

My mother never translated the names of dishes; she simply
cooked and we ate. I feel suddenly excited by the idea that such
unadorned fare could be entwined with poetic charm. "Your
Chinese is so fluent!" I marvel at her ease.

"Well, after six years in China, I should at least know how
to order my dinner." The waitress slaps down a pot of tea and a
stack of dishes still wet from the sink.

"You should dry everything." Geraldine hands me a paper napkin. "Germs," she explains.

"So, what brought you to China?" I ask as we busy ourselves with dripping, doll-sized plates and teacups that are chipped and stained with age.

"I came on a Fulbright scholarship with the firm intention of only staying a year," she says, and laughs. "But then I fell in love and we got married . . . six years later, I'm divorced and still here."

"What happened?"

"Culture clash. He was too Chinese, I was too American." Her smile is wry. "How about you?"

"Me? Oh, I just wanted to discover my roots," I say lightly, hoping she'll drop the subject.

"Really? A returnee? You don't seem the type." She eyes me shrewdly, but the waitress returns with our food, plunking everything down in the middle of the table, and the moment passes. *"Dong kuaizi,"* says Geraldine, unwrapping her chopsticks and placing a tiny paper napkin in her lap. "Move your chopsticks—it really just means, dig in!"

The food, fresh from the wok, glistens with oil. But the cellophane noodles are spicy, savory with ground pork and laced with chili flakes, and the tender vegetables in earth's three fairies are salty and sweet with a rich, brown sauce. I alternate bites before piling cubes of tofu into my rice bowl, allowing the fiery chili oil to seep into the fluffy grains and then scooping everything into my mouth in a hot, delicious bite.

If I've had food like this before, I can't remember. It's peasant fare, simple and cheap, spicy and salty, filling and delicious, and we eat it as such, with no pretensions of daintiness. Geraldine tells me about her courtyard home, which sounds like a dreamy relic of old Beijing, and I confide that Claire's vast apartment seems icily cold.

"I think I've met your sister," says Geraldine, selecting a slice of eggplant. "Tall, thin, great clothes . . . sort of looks like an Asian Nicole Kidman?"

The thought has never occurred to me, but now that she's mentioned it, I realize that Claire and Nicole Kidman are a cross-racial ringer for each other.

"Yep, that's her." I help myself to another scoop of tofu and try to think of how I can change the subject. It's not that I want to avoid talking about my sister, I'm just not sure I have much to say. In the weeks that we've lived together, I've watched Claire whirl from work, to cocktail parties, to art openings, to charity benefits, to dinners with clients and colleagues. Her phone rings constantly, heralding laughing conversations that are peppered with "darling," and her bedroom sees more clothing changes than the fashion tents at Bryant Park.

She's always inviting me to go with her, and I did once, tagging along to a cocktail party hosted by one of her friends. From the moment the elevator doors opened directly into the duplex penthouse apartment, I felt uncomfortable. When I went to lay my handbag in the guest room, my knockoff Miu Miu looked decidedly forlorn next to its couture counterparts. In the living room, the conversation revolved around charity balls and overnight jaunts to Hong Kong.

"But you have no reason to go!" exclaimed Vanessa, a tall Chinese woman with jutting cheekbones. She entwined her arm around her Italian boyfriend, Marco.

"Oh, but I'd love to see Hong Kong!" I exclaimed.

"We don't go to sightsee," she reassured me. "We go for Botox!" She laughed and her face remained immobile.

I glanced at my sister, but she seemed more amused than surprised—or maybe she'd had one too many treatments herself. Ten minutes later I told Claire I wasn't feeling well and left. I couldn't explain that the party made me feel even more isolated than staying at home. Lately, I've been dodging her invitations and hiding out in my room.

Across the table, Geraldine regards me with a hint of sympathy in her clear eyes. "Hm. Living with Claire must be—" She hesitates, then seems to change her mind. "I know moving to Beijing can be really scary, Isabelle," she says. "So if you need anything, please don't feel shy about asking me."

"Thanks." And suddenly, sitting in the litter-strewn restaurant, with Chinese voices rumbling around me and my belly filled with warm food, I begin to relax, despite the heads that still turn around to stare.

Street Food

"Peking street food stalls and hawkers supply substantial snacks, such as steamed buns, plain or stuffed with meat, baked sesame cakes, oily spring onion cakes, deep-fried bean curd triangles or squares, and roasted sweet potatoes, which are more popular in the winter . . . Unless you are an early riser, you run the risk of them having been sold out before you get to the street corners where they are sold."

—YAN-KIT SO, *CLASSIC FOOD OF CHINA*

Watch out," whispers Lily as I slip behind my desk at the office. "Da Wang is in a bad mood this morning." After a month at the magazine, I'm already familiar with Ed's volatile moods, which can slip from jovial to irate at the sight of a typo. The staff calls him Da Wang, or Big King, behind his back, and, indeed, visiting his office is a little like being a royal consort: you're either fondled and adored—or your head is chopped off.

I lean under the desk to turn on my computer, and as I struggle to my feet, Ed looms over my desk looking pointedly at his watch. "How nice of you to turn up this morning." I try not to cringe at the ooze of sarcasm. "All right, mates," he roars, "Meeting now!"

After we've settled ourselves in the conference room, he snaps,

"Let's hear some ideas!" I glance discreetly around the table. Lily seems absorbed in examining her new manicure, magenta with pale pink heart decals. Gab is nursing a hangover, his skin sallow, eyes bloodshot, probably the product of another eardrum rattling night hanging out post-set with his favorite rock band, SUBS. *Long night?* I mouth at him.

Very, he silently replies, running hands through his tangled mat of hair. Geraldine sips a hot glass of green tea with a pensive look on her face. Winston, Ed's assistant, who always seems to pop up whenever we start complaining, scribbles streams of Chinese characters—minutes, I suppose, though no one is talking.

"Come on, mates! What am I paying you for?" Ed glares at us.

Silence.

"Okaaayy. Let's try something new. Obviously, none of you bothered to prepare for this meeting, and obviously I have to hold your hands like lit-tle ba-bies." When Ed gets angry he over-enunciates. "So, we're going to sit here for ten minutes, and at the end of the ten minutes you will each have five ideas. Or you're fired."

Out of the corner of my eye I see Geraldine roll her eyes.

Ed glances at his watch and the six of us sit in the silent room. Despite my best efforts to concentrate, I find myself gazing sleepily out the window. The sky looks bright, free of its usual coat of pollution, and above the whir of the air conditioner, I can hear the shrill thrum of cicadas. My eyes grow heavy, only to pop open at the snap of Ed's fingers.

"Time's up," he barks, appraising us with a challenging gaze. We hunker down in our seats, each doing our best to appear invisible. "Let's see . . . I think we'll start with . . . " I keep my eyes fixed on my notebook. "Gab."

The rest of us exhale silently, shooting sympathetic glances toward Gab.

"Let's hear it, punk man," barks Ed. "What's new on the local music scene?"

"I've been working on a preview of this year's Midi Festival—" Gab begins.

"Bo-ring!" snaps Ed.

Gab's skin seems to grow three shades paler as three days of work get dismissed. "How about a profile on Cui Jian?" he suggests weakly.

"Are you living in 2005? We want new *new* new. Cui Jian is so over he's considered Chinese rock history. Do you have any brain cells left in your head or have you killed them all smoking hash?" A long silence descends while Ed glares at Gab's bowed head. "Actually, what *is* going on with your head? Your hair looks like a wombat's nest."

"I'm . . . trying to grow dreds," Gab mutters.

"Dreds? *Dreds?* Can Asian hair even *do* dreds?"

"I saw them on this guy at the Chaoyang Rock Festival last year. You can't wash your hair for months . . . I have to wear a cap in the shower, this big flowery plastic thing like a fucking grandma."

Silence hangs over the room. Ed's face turns bright red before he bursts into laughter. "And there, ladies and gents, is a feature story," he gasps. A few of us chuckle tentatively. "A-thousand-words-on-how-Chinese-people-grow-dreds—I-expect-it-on-my-desk-Monday," he says in a single breath. "Next! Geraldine."

She launches into a string of ideas, each featuring a chain of incongruous words I didn't even know could be linked together. "There's an exhibit of post-eighties generation neobaroque social realism . . . "

My mind starts to wander. Outside, I watch a crowd as they gather around a storefront window, eager to buy myriad breads and pancakes, all called *bing,* that make up Beijing street food. Geraldine claims there are more types of *bing* in a Beijing street food stall than there are bagels in a New York deli. She's probably right; the assortment, which ranges from giant *laobing* that resemble tortillas, to savory, meat-filled pockets called *xian'r bing*, to flat, fried egg-filled pancakes called *jidan guanbing*, could rival the poppy seed, plain, sesame, and everything at H&H's counter any day. So far I've only sampled a few of these street treats, though they beckon from every corner with greasy allure.

"And then, I thought we could do a Venn diagram showing the proportion of neoclassic brush calligraphers versus the cynical realists and Eastern mystics," Geraldine says smoothly.

"Uh, sure. That sounds great, Ger." Ed's eyes look slightly boggled. "Er, who's next? Isabelle."

Shit. I consult my notebook and find an empty page. "Uh . . ." I shift in my chair and will an idea to pop into my brain.

"Yes? Let's hear it Ms. I-lived-in-New-York-and-I'm-full-of-good-ideas."

My eyes wander back outside to the street food vendor. A young man walks away from the window, swinging a heavy sack of food with one hand, while hungrily biting into a pancake with the other. "How about something on . . . " *Think, Iz, think . . .* "Street food!" *Yes!* "A piece on Beijing's famous street food—what is it, where do you find it . . . We could interview local movers and shakers about their favorite snacks . . . " I babble away, the ideas coming thick and fast.

"Hmmm . . ." Ed frowns. "Not bad. You'll need a better angle, of course, but it'll do." He makes a note. "You're off the hook for now, Isabelle," he adds. "But don't think you can fly by the seat of your pants in this office. Next. Lily." He turns away and I sigh with relief.

The meeting continues but my mind wanders. Six months ago, if someone had told me that I'd be sitting in a bilingual meeting in Beijing contemplating street food, I would have laughed.

Back in New York, I dreamed of Sancerre-soaked dinners in the south of France, not discovering northern China's wheat-based cuisine. My lack of curiosity about China dated back to—well, as far as I could remember, really.

"You're a banana," my college roommate, Karen, herself Korean American, once said. "Yellow on the outside, white on the inside." It was our freshman year at NYU and I just confessed that I'd never seen a Bruce Lee movie. Maybe she was right, but her accusation stung.

Karen fit almost every Asian stereotype—she majored in engineering, wore glasses, grew red when she drank alcohol, was obedient and filial toward her parents—and I both envied and scorned her. Part of me wished I could be so comfortable in my own skin, so willfully oblivious to Barbie dolls and blondes, and all the other icons of beauty that little American girls measure themselves against. But the other half of me wanted to rebel against the model minority stereotype, to be adept with words, not numbers, to be creative and carefree, not parceled into a bland, white-collar career.

On weekends, Karen would hang out with friends from the Korean Culture Club. They'd pile in a car and head to K-town, where they'd buy Seoul's latest top-of-the-charts CDs and feast on barbecue. She invited me to come along once, and I spent the evening hanging on the edge of every conversation, not understanding their mix of Korean and English, not comprehending any of their inside jokes.

Later that night, Karen encouraged me to join the Chinese Students Association. "I can see how much you want to be in touch with your cultural roots," she said, her eyes wide and solemn.

When sorority row threw open their gracious, white-columned houses to potential rushees, I'm not sure who was more surprised that I joined—Karen, who couldn't understand why I'd want to call seventy frivolous young women who shared little more than a penchant for bulimia and booze "sisters," or me—I couldn't believe they wanted me. The next year I moved into the confines of the sorority house, and though I soon discovered that wearing Greek letters across my chest didn't guarantee glamour, popularity, or even happiness, I was still thrilled that I had infiltrated their world. Karen and I still met for lunch sometimes, but after I moved out of the dorm, we no longer had much to talk about. She treated me with a grave formality, as if I had become a stranger. I could feel disapproval in her quiet gaze, but I'm not sure if she sensed the guilt in mine.

Street food day, 5:15 A.M. The alarm shrieks but I'm already awake, my mind racing while my body struggles to catch up. As I scramble out of bed to splash cold water on my face and slip contact lenses into my bloodshot eyes, I try to work up my courage. Breakfast on the streets awaits me and though I'm excited to sample the fare, I'm nervous about asking too many questions. Chinese people can be decidedly unfriendly to outsiders. I've practiced the Mandarin vocabulary over and over but I'm still afraid the words will stick in my throat.

I pull on my clothes and tiptoe from my bedroom toward the kitchen, which is already flooded with light. The rubber soles of my running shoes pad silently over the marble floor, and so there's a moment when my sister doesn't know that I'm watching her gulp sweetened green tea with greedy thirst. When she sees me, Claire jumps, almost dropping the bottle on the floor.

"Jesus, Iz! You scared me!" she says, replacing the bottle's cap with a sharp twist.

"I'm sorry." I gesture to the bottle of tea. "You must really like that stuff."

"Not really. I just . . . drink it for the antioxidants. It's really good for you. Prevents cancer." She examines me, taking in my crumpled clothes and unwashed hair that's scraped back into a ponytail.

In contrast, Claire looks crisp and powerful in her dark suit, her hair shining, her makeup smooth. But as I peer at her face, I see the red and puffy eyes that her carefully applied foundation can't hide.

"Is everything okay?" I try to keep my tone light to hide my surprise.

"Of course! Just a touch of allergies." She swiftly changes the subject. "Why are you up so early?"

I'm working on an article on street food . . . and you know what they say about the early bird . . . it, um, catches the fresh street food!" I feel clumsy and tongue-tied, but she seems too distracted to notice.

For a moment we stand together in an awkward silence. Claire's eyes are focused on the floor and her posture is painfully tense, as if she's holding back a flood of tears.

"Claire—" I reach out, but at my touch she pulls away, glancing at her watch.

"Oh my goodness! I'm late for work!" She snatches a heavy stack of manila folders from the counter and hefts a soft suede bag across her shoulder. "I have to go."

I glance at the kitchen clock as its hands creep to five-thirty.

"I have a conference call to New York," she says swiftly.

"Let me get my bag and I'll walk down with you."

"No, it's okay. I'm already late." The sharpness in her voice fades as she moves toward me. "I'm sorry, honey. There's just so much going on right now . . . " She puts her arm around my shoulders and squeezes, enveloping me in a cloud of scent. "I'll give you a call later, okay?" She throws me a smile, which reveals a mouthful of dazzling teeth before hurrying out of the room.

I lean against the counter and listen as the front door slams behind her. Claire and I have never been close, but when she moved to Beijing she snipped the familial ties with a swiftness that surprised me. I missed her during the holidays and on my weekend visits home, missed the spark in her eye when Aunt Marcie would tipple too much mulled wine at Christmas, the calculated way she would whip us all at Scrabble.

Now, I turn on the stove to heat the kettle and heave a sigh. It took me a while to figure it out, but this morning has confirmed my suspicions: Claire is unhappy. She puts up a good show, but despite the constant swirl of parties and drinks dates, gallery openings and late night karaoke, she seems to be struggling to keep a smile on her face. Every time her cell phone rings, her eyes light up with hope, followed more often than not by a cloud of disappointment when she checks the caller ID.

She hasn't volunteered any information and her face closes like a slammed door every time I ask her about her love life. Nevertheless, the whispered wee-hour conversations, frequent weekend absences, and manic mood swings seem to point one direction: an unhappy relationship. I wish I could help her, but I know better than to offer her advice. I learned that lesson the hard way, years ago.

When I was eleven, my best friend was a girl named Shannon Lee. My mother actually picked her out, one late summer afternoon, the day before I started sixth grade. "Oh, look," she said, her finger running down the list of names that composed the class roster. "Shannon Lee! Another Chinese girl for you to be friends with."

I rolled my eyes—even then I was conscious of not selecting my friends by race—and ignored her. But thanks to alphabetical seating, Shannon Lee and I were placed next to each other the next day in homeroom. Imagine my surprise when a red-haired girl showed up, her nose dusted with copper freckles. Shannon didn't have a drop of Asian blood in her. Sure, her name was Lee—as in Robert E. She was a direct descendent of the Confederate general.

Shannon and I soon became BFFs. She lent me Sweet Valley High books—banned by my parents—and taught me all the words to "Like a Prayer." I introduced her to the Hello Kitty aisle at our local Japanese grocery store. We pretended we were sisters.

Shannon had an older brother, David, the tall, blue-eyed captain of the high school volleyball team. He wore checkered Vans and a letterman's jacket, but his distinguishing feature was his niceness. There's no other word for it. He always smiled, said hello, opened doors, and was pleasant and helpful—not only to grown-ups but to us, two preteen girls. Needless to say, I wished he was my brother.

David and my sister were in the same class in high school, both graduating that year. I didn't expect him to know Claire, but when I mentioned her one early evening at White Castle, he seemed impressed. Shannon was in the bathroom and I was alone at the table with David, searching for something to say.

"Claire Lee is your sister?" he said. "She's in my AP Chem class." He raised his eyebrows. "She's crazy smart. She has the whole periodic table, like, *memorized*." This did not surprise me. "Hey!" His face brightened. "You don't think she'd be willing to help me sometime, do you?" He unwrapped a slider and took a bite. "I didn't do so hot on the midterm . . . Coach says if I don't raise my grade I'll be suspended from the team." He grimaced. "Can you ask her?"

"Sure." I was delighted to help him.

I waited until that night, when Claire was alone in her room making Latin flash cards.

"David Lee wants *me* to help him? He doesn't even know who I am," she said, her eyes narrowing. "I don't think so." She snappily turned the tissue thin page of her Latin dictionary.

I should have left well enough alone, but I couldn't disappoint David. "He totally knows who you are." I cajoled. "Plus, he's super nice and . . . and I think he likes you."

She looked up. "Really." It was a challenge, not a question.

"He said you were really smart . . . " Claire picked up her scissors and started snipping index cards in half. "And that you seemed . . . funny."

"He said that?" I could feel her weakening.

I nodded vigorously. At least the smart part was true.

She took a deep breath. "Okaaayyy . . . tell David . . . I'll meet him after school on Tuesday. In the library." She pushed her glasses up her nose and smiled.

And so I became Claire and David's intermediary. They had a standing study date twice a week, but if anything changed—if David had extra volleyball practice and had to cancel, or Claire knew she'd be late because of her cello lesson—they would rely on me to relay the information. For a while everything went swimmingly. David raised his AP Chem grade from a C– to a B+ and Claire started singing in the shower and wearing lip gloss. And then May rolled around. Prom season.

I knew something was up when Claire baked a batch of chocolate chip cookies and brought a plate of them to my room. "So . . . I'll be graduating from high school this month." Her eyes darted everywhere but toward me.

"Yeah." With my foot, I surreptitiously nudged a candy pink stack of Sweet Valley High books farther under the bed. Claire thought I should spend my spare time reading the classics.

"And in a few months, I'll be living in Boston." She had received her acceptance letter to Harvard a few weeks ago.

"Uh-huh." I bit into a cookie and braced myself for the usual lecture on how I should listen to Mom and Dad and start early prep for the SAT.

"Do you know what David's doing for the prom?" she blurted, her face turning bright pink.

Wow, I hadn't seen that coming. "No." I paused. I had just finished reading *Harriet the Spy* and was eager to try my own hand at a little snooping. "Do you want me to ask him?" I asked casually.

"If you want." She shrugged, but her face stayed red.

I saw David the next day at Shannon's house, eating pizza with some guys from the volleyball team. "My sister wants to know what you're doing for the prom," I said, feeling very important.

His friends erupted immediately. "Oooohhh! Does four-eyes Claire have a crush on Davey boy?"

"Guess you two really have been studying *chemistry*!"

"Yeah, like how to turn a frog into a princess!"

"Cut it out, guys! Sorry, Lee." David sometimes called me by my last name, which I loved. "I dunno. A bunch of us are going in a group. She's welcome to come with us, I guess." He shrugged.

His friends burst into groans. "Dave, she's a total nerd. If she's going, then I refuse to get a limo with you guys." David's friend Brian, dark-haired with a high, imperious nose, crossed his arms.

"Dude, I know Claire's kind of a drag, but I owe her. She's saving my ass in chemistry." David looked at me. "Tell her she can ride over with us, if she wants."

Shannon and I quickly ran to her room to record the conversation in my Harriet-the-Spy notebook. "He said you could go with him and his friends," I told my sister that night, when she cornered me in the bathroom.

"Really? In a group?" She seemed uncertain. "What does that mean?"

I wasn't sure if she was asking my advice, but I decided to give it to her anyway. "You should go! He likes you!"

"Really?" Her eyes turned shiny.

Claire kept her emotions concealed as tightly as a sphinx, so it was no surprise that she didn't mention prom again until a week before the dance. "Can you ask David what time he's picking me up next Saturday?" She ducked her head while her cheeks burned bright.

I squirmed behind my desk, where I was copying Chinese characters—thirty times for each one—under Claire's watchful eye. The whole prom thing was starting to make me feel a little uncomfortable. The AP Chemistry test was over and David had started hanging out after school with Candy Andrews, a long-limbed brunette who was cocaptain of the tennis team. She came with us on our White Castle runs, where they held hands under the table and fed each other french fries. "Ummm, I haven't really seen David in a while—"

"If you ask him, I'll tell Mom you finished your Chinese school homework," she said quickly.

I looked at the vocabulary list. Twenty characters still remained and *Who's the Boss?* was on in ten minutes. "Okay," I said.

True to my word, I found David the next day in the kitchen. "Um, so my sister was wondering what time you were coming by before prom . . . " My voice trailed off. Shannon climbed up onto a chair and got down a box of Nilla Wafers from the top of the fridge.

"Oh, man, Lee, I totally forgot about that." His brow furrowed. "Uh, the thing is, we're not—um, she's totally welcome to come but I'm—"

"Aren't you going with Ca-andy?" Shannon broke in, punching her brother's arm.

I grabbed the box of cookies from Shannon and started eating.

"I just don't know if it's going to work out this time . . . " David's mouth turned down at the corners and he shifted uncomfortably in his chair. "Do you think you could let her know?"

"Oh," I said, through a mouth full of Nilla Wafers. "I . . . " I had no desire to be the bearer of this news.

"You wouldn't mind helping me out, would ya, Lee?" He reached out and patted my shoulder.

"I really don't want—" I made another desperate attempt.

"Or I could call her. I should totally call her."

"Ye—"

"But you know what? I bet she doesn't even care about the prom. Claire Lee seems like the last person who would want to go to some lame high school dance." He laughed weakly.

"Um, maybe, but—"

"Really? You think so?" He turned his clear blue eyes upon me. "Thanks, Lee. I totally owe you. Next White Castle run is on me." He reached for the cookies and grabbed a handful before leaving the room. I watched him retreat from the kitchen, my heart sinking with disappointment. I'd thought David was perfect, but it turned out he was selfish and flawed just like everyone else.

What is it they say about shooting the messenger? I stared at the ground when I told Claire, unwilling to meet her eyes, my shoulders heavy with guilt.

"He said *what*?" Her face drained of color.

"I told you. All he said was that he didn't think it would work out this time. Anyway, Shannon said he's taking Candy."

"*Candy Andrews*? Do you know where she's going next year? White Plains Junior College. She couldn't even get into a four-year school." She barked a bitter laugh. "I just—" Her eyes flashed wet with tears, but she bit her lip to stop them.

"Claire . . . please don't . . . " I reached out to touch her arm, but she snatched it away.

"I don't need your help," she hissed, before turning into the bathroom and closing the door with a quiet click.

And so, prom night came, and Claire stayed home. In the years since, she's joked about missing the prom, laughing it off with an airy shrug that can't quite conceal the lingering sting. I'd like to think that by now she's forgiven me for misreading David, for convincing her to tutor him, for leading her on, for being a busybody. But I know that's not true. Because Claire has never again asked me for help.

The kettle whistles, and I hurry to turn off the stove, pouring scalding water over my tea bag. As Ed has said, China is the land of reinvention, and so it doesn't surprise me that my shy, dowdy sister could transform herself from a duckling into prom queen. But that doesn't mean I'm not concerned. The stainless steel kettle reminds me of Claire: polished to a gleam on the outside, boiling within.

By the time I get outside it's almost 6:00 A.M. and Ed's voice is echoing in my ear. "You better make like a granny and get out there early, Isabelle, or your story is fucked."

I have no idea what he means by the granny reference, but I know he's right about the early start. Most street vendors cater to hungry construction workers, and by 8:00 A.M. they've sold out of food and are pedaling back home, already finished with a day's work.

The early morning air feels cool and silky as I turn down one of the narrow streets that wind through our neighborhood. Back here in the alleys, people cling to the old way of life. Wiry hawkers squeeze three-wheeled carts through the slender lanes and announce their wares in a singsong chant. Stooped old men swing round wooden bird cages from their hands, giving their pets a breath of morning air. I once watched a white-haired woman hobble down the street and gasped as I looked down at her feet, which were bound into minute stumps.

Above, our apartment complex looms sleek and tall, a harbinger of doom for this lively, grubby area. Soon it will be destroyed, its crowded alleys turned first into a pile of rubble and then into a series of bleak and bland office buildings, all created in the name of modern China. But for now, life continues as it has for centuries, closely packed and bustling with the smells and sounds of old Beijing.

Chubby toddlers run in circles, their split potty-training trousers winking open to reveal bare bottoms. A small Pekinese prances along the gutter, enjoying his last gulps of freedom before being shut up, as Beijing law dictates, until evening. In a shady corner of the neighborhood's playground a group of tiny wrinkled women stroke the air in the graceful motion of the Chinese martial art, tai chi. Their tranquil movements remind me of my mother's mother, an elegant stiff-backed woman we called Laolao, who proclaimed the benefits of tai chi and a smoke-free lifestyle until her death at ninety.

The exercise concludes and the group erupts into a cacophony of chatter. These gray-haired grannies certainly look vigorous as they mill about, swinging their arms and gulping deep breaths.

I vow to reform my own high-fat, low-exercise existence, when I see them dive into their pockets and light up a tobacco field's worth of cigarettes.

I continue down the street until I reach a small stretch that's lined with ramshackle storefronts. Here each step brings a different smell, first an acrid wave of cigarette smoke, then the reek of garbage, then the cozy, wafting scent of fried dough. It's a reminder of how closely packed life is here, where generations share bedrooms, neighborhoods share bathrooms, and stacks of napa cabbage are stored next to trash heaps.

I pause in front of a young woman who is deep-frying *youtiao*, long strips of dough, in an enormous, portable vat of boiling oil. As a kid, I used to eat these greasy, heavy wands of dough on Saturdays after Chinese school, accompanied by a salty bowl of soy milk and a stern lecture from my mother on my lack of discipline.

The wet dough puffs and sizzles as it hits the oil's scalding surface. The vendor, an unsmiling woman with a toddler clinging to her legs, stacks a pile of fried dough sticks and makes an impatient gesture with her tongs. *"Ni yao bu yao?"* she asks. Do you want one? Shaking my head, I continue down the street.

I spot a crepe vendor and join the long line, admiring his compact, portable kitchen. He's packed a coal-fired stove, grimy buckets of batter, and bowls of chopped cilantro and hot sauce onto the back of a three-wheeled cart, ready to be pedaled away at a moment's notice. I watch as he swirls batter onto a flat griddle and delicately distributes a raw egg across the surface. After a jaunty flip, he sprinkles the other side with sesame seeds, cilantro, scallions, brushes it with a dark sauce, and adds a thin sheet of fried dough before folding the pancake into a square and tucking it into a wisp of plastic bag.

The line in front of me shuffles with hungry impatience, but the vendor's movements remain unhurried. I admire the artful twist of his wrist as he spreads the batter into a large, paper-thin crepe, the flick of his spatula as he turns it over, the meditative sprinkle of sesame seeds. By the time it's my turn, the long line has shrunk. As he pours a scoop of batter onto the griddle, I gesture at the griddle and ask, *"Zhongwen zenme shuo?"* How do you say it in Chinese?

"Jianbing!" he replies with a glance that's at once hostile and curious. I brace myself for the inevitable question. *"Na guo ren?"* Where are you from?

"I'm Chinese but I have an American passport." I rattle off the words in Mandarin. Geraldine taught me the phrase last week and already it's proved to be indispensable, short and tidy, though not strictly accurate.

"Mm." He concentrates on turning the crepe.

"Are *jianbing* from Beijing?"

He snorts a scornful laugh, and for a moment I consider snatching the pancake from the griddle and running for the hills. But then I picture Ed's impatient face as he shouts, "What do you mean you were afraid of the street food vendor? Are you a bloody pansy?"

Switching tactics, I smile broadly and try again. "Are *jianbing* from Beijing?"

"They're from Tianjin. Do you want hot sauce?"

I nod, and as he brushes chili sauce on the crepe's delicate surface his mood seems to soften. "Have you eaten *jianbing* before?" he asks, placing a thin, crisp piece of deep-fried dough in the center, and folding the crepe into a thick, piping hot square.

"No, this is my first."

He scoops the heavy package into a gauzy plastic sack and

hands it to me. It swings between my fingers with a pleasing weight, like a pendulum.

"Taste it!" he urges, but without napkins the crepe burns my fingertips.

"Did your mother teach you to make *jianbing*?" I ask instead.

His face brightens. "Yes! This is her recipe! The secret is when you mix this . . . " He points to the batter, making a stirring motion and continuing in a happy flood, much of which I don't understand, though I continue nodding, smiling, and mimicking his hand motions. I think he says that the trick to delicate crepes is letting the batter rest overnight, but I make a mental note to ask Lily to find out for sure.

"How long have you been making street food?" I hand over two *kuai*, the equivalent of about twenty-five cents.

"I've owned this cart for almost ten years. I was one of the first snack sellers back when there was only cabbage stacked in the streets." He straightens a plastic bowl with fingers that are stained with tobacco.

"Are you from Beijing?"

"No, I'm from the country near Tianjin. My parents are farmers . . . they don't understand why I moved to the city. I don't get to see them that often, but sometimes I can send them some money." He sighs and I notice the tired lines that surround his eyes, his frayed trouser cuffs.

I pat the heavy mass of crepe; it's cooled slightly, and so I take a bite, relishing its eggy warmth and salty, spicy sauces, the contrast of soft and crisp textures.

"Do you like it?"

It reminds me of the crepes I used to eat from the French café in my old New York neighborhood, fresh off the griddle, gooey with melted Gruyère, or sweet with Nutella. Except, this crepe, which I would have never recognized as Chinese, combines salty and spicy, the sharp bite of scallion and lingering fragrance of cilantro giving it an enticing, exotic flair.

"It's delicious," I mumble through a full mouth, and he smiles.

"Chinese people love *jianbing*. But our family recipe is special." He puffs with pride, and I feel a pang of sympathy for him and his old parents. I imagine them scrambling to put food on the table, tilling the countryside's harsh, arid fields with gnarled hands and hunched backs.

Suddenly, the vendor's cell phone trills a familiar mournful tune that I can't quite place. What is it? I rack my brain as it repeats again and again, calling to mind images of pine trees, swaths of red and green, turkey (turkey?) . . . finally I pin it down: "God Rest Ye Merry Gentlemen."

The vendor extracts his phone from his pocket. *"Wei . . . ? Ni hao, mm. Mm, mm, mm."* I recognize "mm" as Beijing's all-purpose sound of affirmation, and lean in to eavesdrop on the rest of his conversation.

"Waaa? Zenme hui shi . . . ? Shi huaile ma? Shi bu shi che zhuang huaile?" Uh-oh, sounds like something is broken. I examine the vendor's battered cart, which hardly seems able to withstand Beijing's potholed streets.

"Mm, mm, mm." More of the universal sound. Maybe I should try using that more.

He continues rapidly. *"Ni zai na'r?"* Where are you? *"Mm, mm . . . Hao, wo mashang jiu lai. Hao, hao, hao."* I shift my bag to another shoulder and start to wonder if I should move on.

"Eh . . . zaijian." Oh, he seems to be wrapping it up. *"Eh, eh . . . zaijian."* He lingers over the good-bye. *"Eh, eh, eh, zaijian!"* Finally, he punches a button to end the call and emits a heavy sigh.

"Who was that?"

"That was my younger brother . . . he's had an accident . . . a donkey cart ran into his *jianbing* cart. Eggs and batter are running all over the street! I have to go help him."

"Your brother also sells *jianbing*?"

"Yeah . . . he rents a cart from me, so do a couple of people from my hometown."

"How many carts do you own?"

"Oh, only about thirty right now. When I save up some money, I buy another one and rent it out to someone from my village. I'd like to have one on every street in Beijing!"

"Like McDonald's!" I joke.

"Exactly," he says seriously. "*Jianbing* are part of China's culture and cuisine. And this is the right time to expand. Right now, in Beijing, anything is possible." He clips a plastic lid on his bucket of batter, secures a few cartons of eggs with rubber bands, and walks to the front of the cart where he swings a leg over the bicycle-style seat.

"*Zaijian!*" he calls out. Good-bye. "I'm here every morning. I hope you'll bring your foreign friends to eat *jianbing*."

I take another enormous bite as he pedals away. The growl in my stomach subsides, satisfied by delicious crepe, and I walk slowly to the office through narrow streets, pausing occasionally to examine the other *bing* on offer.

Sunday morning. Outside, the sky is dark with rain and the heavy, hanging pollution I'm beginning to associate with Beijing. But inside it's bright and dry, a cozy nest far from the deluge that streaks the streets. Claire has disappeared for the weekend. "We're riding Harleys out to Weiwei's house in Huairou, darling. You'll be all right, won't you?" she'd called out while cramming Seven jeans and silk pajamas into her LV overnight bag. Too embarrassed to remind her that she said we'd hang this weekend, I waved her off with an assured smile.

Now, as rain streams across the windows, I decide to recreate a bit of my former New York life, reading the weekend paper while eating a tender cheese omelet. Claire may be enjoying a weekend of pampering at her friend Weiwei's cold, concrete-and-glass country house—more postmodern showcase than home, from what I can tell by the spread in *Elle Décor China*—but I can indulge in my own lazy morning. After the stress of last week, I feel like I deserve it.

Ed liked my article on Beijing's bounty of *bing*, but was nonplussed that Lily would have to double check the Chinese. "Speaking Chinese is part of your job, Isabelle," he bellowed, sweat breaking out on his forehead. "I don't give a shit about your identity crisis! *Improve it*."

"I know I should make more of an effort." I glanced guiltily at Geraldine. "I mean, I *am* Chinese."

She shrugged. "You don't see me learning Polish. Anyway, don't worry. Your Chinese will get better. Just give it time. I can help you find a tutor."

"What she needs is a Chinese boyfriend!" barked Ed.

But as I hover over the newsstand counter in our apartment lobby, I find myself hampered by the language once again.

"Do you have the *International Herald Tribune*?" I ask.

The blank look on the shop girl's face indicates she doesn't understand me, so I make a weak effort to ask in Chinese. "*Guoji . . . shenme shenme baozhi*." International . . . something something newspaper.

Nothing.

The image of myself spending a happy morning lounging at the kitchen table, mulling over the crossword puzzle, is slipping away.

Determined, I make a final attempt. *"Guoji . . . shenme shenme baozhi?"* Inside, I'm cringing.

"Guoji Xianqu Daobao," I hear a voice say. "Is this what you're looking for?" A paper is placed upon the counter, fresh and new with the seductive scent of newsprint.

"Yes!" I exclaim. Turning around, I find a grave young man, politely attentive with tousled light brown hair and tortoiseshell glasses.

"Thank you so much." I gush to cover up my scrutiny. "But, I'm afraid this might be the last paper . . . "

"That's okay. I'm getting too addicted to the crossword anyway. I'm Charlie, by the way." His voice is quietly courteous, with a light American accent.

"Isabelle, from the twentieth floor."

"Hello Isabelle-from-the-twentieth-floor. It's nice to meet someone else young around this mausoleum."

"Oh, are you new here?"

"No, I've been in Beijing for almost two years. But I have to admit I don't know too many of my neighbors. Too much time at work." He laughs ruefully.

"What do you do?" Oh God, I sound just like my mother.

"I work at the American embassy." He shoots me a piercing look. "And you? How long have you been in Beijing?"

"Me? Oh, almost a month. I live with my sister, Claire."

"Are you Claire Lee's little sister?" He raises his eyebrows. "She mentioned you, but I didn't realize . . . hm. So, how do you like writing for *Beijing NOW*?"

"How do you know Claire?" I don't know why I'm asking. Claire is the queen bee of Beijing's expat society, her oval face always in *Beijing NOW*'s society page, her name on every guest list.

"Claire? Doesn't she know everyone?" says Charlie, and I think I detect a slight, ironic note in his voice. "She's Wang Wei's girlfriend, which automatically makes her one of Beijing's beautiful people."

I manage to arrange my face into a knowing smile and nod. Who is Wang Wei? Is that who's been making her cry?

"Um . . . ." I try to cover up my confusion. "How do you like working at the embassy?"

"Oh, it's busy." He sighs, and I notice the graying temples that belie his youthful face. "I think morale's a little low, but it's fine."

"I've heard that."

"Really?"

"Yeah. One of Claire's friends works in the visa section. He was complaining about the ambassador . . . said he was a tyrant, stuck-up and arrogant." The words tumble out.

"Hm. And I was ready to chalk the poor morale up to America's bad global position." For a second Charlie's shoulders seem to slump, but then he glances at his watch and says with a smile, "Well, speaking of work, I better be off." He shakes my hand. "It was very nice to meet you, Isabelle. If you ever need to borrow a cup of sugar or want help with the crossword puzzle, just let me know. I'm in 3002."

"Thanks."

"And tell your sister hello, if you see her." His glance is thoughtful as he steps into the revolving door with a small wave.

Back in Claire's kitchen, I pile eggs, milk, cheese, and butter on the shining granite counter and begin grating and whisking. I turn to the stove, which our housekeeper, Wang Ayi, scrubbed clean yesterday. Her biweekly visits mean Claire and I don't argue over laundry or cleaning the bathroom, and we split her pay, the equivalent of fifty dollars a month, between us. Claire has met Wang Ayi only once, but I often come home to find her ironing Claire's beautifully tailored suits and my ragged jeans.

Sometimes she helps me with my Chinese, revealing the names of fresh herbs and vegetables, and pointing out the best foreign grocery stores. We call her *ayi*, or aunt, though she's unlike my mother's big-haired, sharp-tongued sister, but more like a kind and cozy grandma.

I heat a nonstick pan over a low flame and melt a lump of butter, breathing in its milky scent, careful not to let it brown and burn, and slide in the eggs, stirring constantly. My first omelet was a disastrous combination of rubbery and runny, caused by an overzealous blast of heat. I'd made it for Rich after our first night together. He'd taken one look and dumped it in the trash with one hand, while reaching for the eggs and milk with the other. "*Ma petite* Isabelle," he said with a smile that surely wasn't patronizing. "Let me show you how it's done."

Now as I break the curds that form on the bottom of the pan, I sigh. I'm certainly better off without Rich, with his arrogance and affectations, but cooking reminds me of our weekends together, our companionship. I slide the omelet onto a plate and admire it: light and pale yellow, tender to the touch and filled with melted cheese. Perfection.

I take my plate and newspaper to the kitchen table and close my eyes for a minute. Outside, the summer storm rumbles, the dark skies reflecting my heavy mood. Right now Rich is twelve time zones away, probably on a date, sipping vodka martinis and regaling her with tales of his crazy ex-girlfriend who got fired and moved to China. And I am alone. In a strange city. I open the paper and fold it to the crossword puzzle.

A six-letter word for one forced into the aesthetic life? H-E-R-M-I-T.

Hot Pot

"The Mongolian chafing dish or steamboat, known as 'fire-pot' or 'hit-the-side stove' in Chinese . . . is a ring-shaped vessel that fits over a chimney that holds burning charcoal. The charcoal heats water in the pot. Diners boil thinly sliced foods in the water and then dip them into sauces and eat . . . This do-it-yourself dinner is regarded by many as the high point of Chinese cuisine."

—E. N. ANDERSON, *THE FOOD OF CHINA*

I find the postcard after work, wedged beneath our doormat with only a bright corner peeping out. It's a picture of Tintin crouched in a boat, his quiff of hair blowing in the sea breeze. I flip it over and am surprised to find that it's not from one of Claire's admirers, but is addressed to me.

Dear Isabelle,

It was nice meeting you the other day. Did you finish the crossword puzzle? I was wondering if you're free for dinner this Thursday? There's a Japanese-Italian restaurant next to Guomao (my colleague says it's eclectic) that sounds interesting. Sorry not to call, but I don't have your number.

See you soon, I hope—Charlie

At the bottom is his cell phone number, neatly printed. I examine the front of the postcard, remembering Charlie's warm smile and intelligent blue eyes. A flurry of nerves flutters into the pit of my stomach.

"Don't be silly," I mutter to myself. "He's not interested in you. He's just being friendly."

"Who's just being friendly?" says Claire, strolling into the room.

I hide my surprise at seeing her, along with the mess of bag and shoes I've just dumped in the hall. Claire's exacting neatness has prodded me into tidiness, but it's an unnatural state. I force myself to conduct a sweep every night, gathering up the flotsam of clothes, books, and mugs that magically accumulates in my wake.

"Hi! You're home early!"

"I took the afternoon off." She swigs from the bottle of green tea in her manicured hand. "Anyway, who's just being friendly?"

"What? Oh, just someone at work," I say, feeling the heat creep into my cheeks.

"Is Ed hitting on you?" says Claire with a tinkling laugh. "He's such a cad. Ignore him, darling. He's totally harmless."

"Um, yeah." I slip the postcard into my pocket and try to change the subject. For some reason, I feel shy talking to her about Charlie. "So, you took the afternoon off? I didn't know you were planning that."

"I was supposed to pick a friend up at the airport but he decided to stay in Shanghai an extra night." She picks up the current issue of *Beijing NOW* and starts to flip through it.

I peer over her shoulder. The magazine is open to the society page, with a snap of Claire at the Latin Ball in the center. In the photo, she's in profile, her fine features edged by a long swish of silky hair, her laughing face turned toward someone outside of the frame.

"Did you guys crop this photo? Wang Wei's not going to like that," she mutters.

Ah, the elusive Wang Wei. After Charlie mentioned him last week, I did a little nosing around. As it turns out, Wang Wei has quite a reputation. When I asked Geraldine about him, she visibly recoiled.

"You don't know Wang Wei?" Her eyes widened. "He's the head of Capital Property. You know, Beijing's biggest real estate developer?" She dropped her voice. "According to the rumors, he's emptied two-thirds of Beijing's *hutongs*. He forces residents to leave by harassing them or paying them a pittance, promises to preserve the historic area, then turns around, rips down their houses and develops multibillion dollar blocks of condos."

"Diabolical," I breathed.

She shrugged. "Or brilliant, depending on who you're talking to."

Now, I glance at my sister, her smooth, pale skin, the nervous crease in her forehead. "Who's Wang Wei?" I ask, as casually as I can.

To my surprise, color floods into her face, her ears and neck turning scarlet. "He's a friend of mine." She flips hurriedly through the rest of the magazine before snapping it shut. "He and I—we see each other. Out. At parties, sometimes. He's in real estate. He developed Midtown East. You know, that huge apartment complex near the East Third Ring Road." The words tumble out in fits and starts, as if she wants to stop herself but can't.

In the past, I might have dispelled the awkward silence that follows by blurting out the first inane thought to pop into my head. But Ed has been trying to teach me the art of nonresponse as an interview technique. "Make the silence work for you," were his exact words.

"Mm." I try to make my voice sound encouraging.

To my surprise, she continues, jolting along in the same broken rhythm. "In fact, he's—the friend. The one I was going to pick up. At the airport. Today. But he had to stay in Shanghai an extra night." She crosses her arms and sighs.

Another stretch of silence descends, during which I immobilize my lips through sheer willpower.

"It's still pretty new," she adds finally. "We're not serious. Or anything. That's why I haven't introduced you yet . . . " She fiddles with the buttons on her shirt. "You're not going to tell Mom, are you?" she asks suddenly. A look of panic—or is it guilt?—flashes across her face.

Telling our mother is the furthest thing from my mind, but I'm surprised Claire wouldn't want me to mention Wang Wei. We both receive regular e-mails from our mom in which she expounds upon her concern that we're still single and in our thirties. "You're not going to be young forever," she wrote to me just last week. "Your father and I would feel so much better if you settled down." I'd have thought Claire would be excited to tell Mom she has a new boyfriend—anything to stop the endless suggestions that she set us up with her mahjong partner's sister's son, or sign us up with some ridiculous dating service in Taiwan called the Love Boat.

"Of course I won't tell her, if you don't want me to," I promise. "But I would love to meet him," I can't resist adding.

"Yeah . . . " Claire looks doubtful. "Maybe. Sometime. Coordinating our schedules is crazy—he's super busy and you know how things are at my office!" She flaps a hand to indicate a flurry of activity. "I hardly get to even see *you,* and we live together!" She laughs and her cheeks return to their normal color. "What are you up to tonight? I was supposed to go to Samantha Hong's party at Centro with Wang Wei, but since he's still in Shanghai . . . Do you want to go as my plus one?"

"Oh! I would love to, but—"

"You have plans," she says crisply, and my heart sinks.

"I'm really sorry. Look, why don't I call Geraldine and cancel. We can go out to dinner, catch up . . . "

"It's okay, sweetie." She lightly touches my shoulder. "Let's just do it another time. I should probably put in an appearance at Sammy's soiree, anyway." And before I can say another word, she's gone into her room and shut the door.

I feel so guilty!" I groan and lift my heavy goblet of too-sweet sangria for another sip.

"Isabelle. You're being ridiculous." Geraldine crosses her arms. "Just because Claire is suddenly at a loose end doesn't mean you have to drop everything to hang out with her. She never makes time for you."

"That's not fair," I say. "She's always inviting me to do things. I just . . . don't always enjoy seeing her friends." Can't stand them, is more like it. Especially her expat friends, a wealthy crowd who seem determined to forget they live in China. The last time I met her best friend, Mimi, a twiglike blonde from Brussels, she told me the best thing about living in Beijing was the cheap domestic help.

Geraldine and I are sitting outside at Kasbah, a Middle Eastern restaurant opened by Joey Han, a budding entrepreneur from Sha'anxi who has never set foot in a souk. Rough kilim cushions support our backs and a bouquet of lit incense sticks wards off the summer's final mosquitoes. I squint my eyes against the table's candlelight and watch a belly dancer shake her way around a table crowded with expat men—Americans, I'd bet from their whoops and whistles.

"And she'd just opened up to me about Wang Wei . . . " I sigh.

"What? What about Wang Wei?" Geraldine's voice sharpens.

"They're dating. She claims it's not serious, but I think she really likes him. Why?"

Geraldine's mouth is twisted into a grimace. "Let's just say Wang Wei has quite a reputation."

"You mean, a girl in every port? That type of reputation?"

She hesitates. "More like a girl on every block." She slides the pitcher of sangria toward her and starts refilling our glasses. "Ugh, what a mess! Poor Claire. I feel sorry for her."

"Don't." I think of my sister's pale face, secret and closed. "She would be mortified by our pity." I offer her a rueful smile.

"So I shouldn't invite her to the karaoke and hot pot night I'm organizing for Thursday?" Geraldine teases.

"Not unless the hot pot is Kobe beef and the karaoke features gold-plated microphones." I crunch down on an ice cube.

"But you're coming, right?" Geraldine fishes an apple wedge out of her glass and gives me an expectant look.

"Oh, I don't think you want to hear me sing." I laugh. "Anyway, I think I have plans with my neighbor."

"Realllllllly?" Geraldine raises her eyebrows. "The mysterious crossword-loving diplomat asked you out on a date? Have you found out any more details about him?"

"No. Just that his name is Charlie and he lives in our building." I shrug. "Anyway, I don't think it's a date. He's just being nice. He left me a postcard because he didn't have my number."

"Very clever." She nods approvingly. "Where are you going?"

"I'm not sure . . . " I fumble in my bag and pull out the postcard. "Some Japanese-Italian restaurant . . . near Guomao?"

"Le Café Igosso. Wow."

"Have you heard of it?"

"Heard of it? It's only Beijing's most romantic restaurant. Cozy, intimate. Interesting food. Great wine list. As the city's foremost restaurant critic, you're supposed to know these things," she teases.

"You don't think it's a date, do you?" The waitress deposits a giant platter of lamb kebobs on the table, but I suddenly feel too jittery to eat.

"A date? No," says Geraldine, tearing meat off a skewer with a pair of chopsticks and stuffing it into a piece of bread.

Despite myself, disappointment nips a tiny, stinging bite.

"I think it's a hot date." She grins before sinking her teeth into her sandwich.

By Thursday, I am plucked, polished, and pulled into a frenzy. Charlie and I are meeting in the apartment lobby at eight, and I leave work early, with the hopes of calming myself with a hot shower and chilled glass of wine.

"You're leaving?" booms Ed as I try to slip out the office back door.

"I, uh, have to interview someone for that story I told you about," I say, as my palms grow damp. I glance at my watch. "Oops, I'm running late. I'll catch up with you tomorrow." I stride to the elevators without glancing back.

I return home to a silent apartment, kick off my shoes, and pad through the cavernous hall to my bathroom, where I turn on the shower and allow the water to heat. In my bedroom I throw open my closet doors and examine my clothes, wishing I could phone Julia. Every girl needs a fashion advisor and she's always been mine. Our daily contact at work meant she knew my clothes better than I did, and her sage advice even led to my first successful story pitch (pleated skirt, ballet flats, string of pearls).

I glance at the clock, but it is still too early to call New York. I squeeze into my favorite jeans, wincing at the snug waistband— must cut back on the greasy *jiachangcai*—rifle through the closet and find Julia's going away present, a dainty chiffon top with ruffled sleeves that flutter when I move. Wearing it seems like receiving her seal of approval, and I smile as I dry my hair into a lustrous mass, slick on a bit of lip gloss, and pull on a pair of gold sandals before clicking my way out the door.

Dawdling over my clothes has made me late. Charlie waits by the mailboxes, and as I cross over to him I feel the eyes of every person in the lobby watching us. I give them all a small wave, the sullen-faced doorman, the skinny, acne-pocked girl behind the front desk, the matronly woman who runs the dry-cleaning service, but their curiosity remains unabashed. I feel their eyes bore into my back as Charlie leans down and politely kisses me on both cheeks.

"It's great to see you," he says, and his smile is so warm that I almost forget my nerves.

"Thanks." I smile back and note with some dismay Charlie's dark suit, the crisp white shirt, and elegant slash of red tie. "Sorry, I think I'm a little underdressed," I say. Suddenly, my jeans and skimpy top seem juvenile and sloppy.

"Actually, I'm the one who should be apologizing. I meant to change, but ran out of time."

"Do you want to run upstairs? I'll wait for you."

"Nah, it's okay. A few more hours in this monkey suit won't matter."

We walk into the dry summer evening and Charlie hails a cab from the cars inching along Guanghua Lu.

"Do you spend most of your life in a suit?" I ask after we've clambered into the backseat and Charlie has given the driver the address.

"Yes. I feel like I should just wear them to bed. Someone should design a sleep-and-go men's wear line."

"It would have to be made out of wrinkle-free material," I say with a nervous laugh. A faint smile makes his eyes crinkle.

For a moment silence descends, and I worry that the evening will be awkward, but then Charlie starts asking me questions about the magazine and I tell him about Ed's temper and our family-style staff lunches, and the sound our censor, Tang Laoshi, makes when he reads something deemed inappropriate.

"His face turns beet red and he'll start shaking his finger and going *Juh juh juh juh!*' It's really awful, because on one hand it's so irritating that he's spiking a story, but on the other hand you're afraid he's going to have a stroke."

"I'm going to have to try that when the Ministry of Foreign Affairs tells me something I don't what to hear. *Juh juh juh!*"

"No, it's more from the back of the throat—like '*juh juh juh juh juh!*'"

The cab driver turns around to give us a disapproving stare that lasts the length of a red light. "*Laowai,*" I hear him mutter as he turns around and snaps on the radio at top volume. Foreigners.

Charlie shoots me a glance and we both stifle a laugh. He grins and it occurs to me that, despite his polished calm, perhaps he was also a bit nervous.

The restaurant's plain wooden door offers no hint of its romantic reputation, but it swings smoothly open, revealing a lush den dark with mystery. We climb a short flight of stairs, and I run my hand along padded walls that are covered in velvet. Upstairs, a jazz trio plays softly in the corner, tiny tables for two are scattered at discreet distances, and the whole room has the promise and glow that only candlelight can create.

I glance at Charlie in time to see a wrinkle of concern crease his forehead. "Wow," he says. "I didn't realize this place would be so, uh—"

"Romantic?" I wiggle my eyebrows in what I hope is an ironically amused gesture.

"Dark," he says firmly.

A hostess clad in a black chiffon dress floats up to us. "Hello," she says to Charlie with a gracious smile. She turns to me: *"Ni hao."* Her up-and-down glance rips my outfit to shreds.

"We have a reservation, Ai Xiansheng, two people."

"You used your Chinese name?" I ask as the hostess checks the computer. Virtually all students of Chinese have a name in the language. If you're ethnically Chinese, it's given at birth, a reminder of your parents' mother tongue that you'll probably bury in the middle of your name, the short sounds too difficult for most Americans to pronounce. For everyone else it is bestowed by their Chinese teacher, the singsong of words a faint echo of their English name. But I don't know many people who use their Chinese name in their English-speaking life.

Charlie shrugs. "Sometimes it's easier to make reservations in Chinese, don't you think?"

I nod, but am not sure if I agree. Too often my Chinese name feels like an unwanted alter ego. As Isabelle, I am articulate, confident, even, sometimes, witty; as Li Jia, I feel tongue-tied and slow, able only to understand the edges of a conversation. Despite his light brown hair and blue eyes—or perhaps because of them—Charlie is clearly more comfortable than I am in China. His foreignness, his otherness, is obvious from a glance. Unlike me. I can slip into a crowd unnoticed, but in a country that highly values foreigners—particularly white men—I am often dismissed with disdain simply for being young, Chinese, and female.

As we walk through the dining room, I peek discreetly at the other customers. Couples bend their heads together, sipping wine from oversized balloon glasses or feeding each other forkfuls of food. But there is a uniformity here that I can't quite put my finger on until we sit and I am able to glance again around the restaurant: at more than half the tables, the men are white and the women Chinese.

My cheeks begin to burn as I remember how indignantly my colleague Lily dismissed the idea of dating a foreigner. "I come from a good family," she said. "I went to college. I have a good job. I don't need to date some white buffoon who can't even get a date in his own country." Her meaning was clear. Lucky enough to make her own choices, Lily doesn't need a *waiguo* boyfriend to provide her with a better life. As I peer around the room one more time, I note the stares directed at our table. Some are knowing, some are curious. None are sympathetic.

"Should we order a bottle of wine?" Charlie's voice breaks my reverie and I smile and nod.

"That sounds lovely."

But before we can decide on red or white, a figure materializes at our table. I open my mouth to ask for a glass of water, and quickly realize it's not our waitress, but a woman, tall and blond, with glittering blue eyes spread wide with astonishment.

"Well, hello there! I haven't seen you around the embassy lately!" She shakes a playful finger at Charlie and smiles broadly to reveal large and even teeth.

"Uh, hi! Kristin!" Charlie shifts in his seat.

"You know Scott, of course." She pulls forward her companion, a stocky man with closely cut hair and muscular arms. "He works in DAO?"

"Scott, it's good to see you."

"Hello, sir." They shake hands.

"I ran into Scott on the way out of the embassy and convinced him we should grab dinner. I just hate eating alone, don't you?" Her voice is soft and Southern, with an adorable drawl.

"Kristin Morgan, Scott Cooper, this is Isabelle Lee." Charlie stands to introduce me, and I awkwardly rise. Beside their three all-American faces, I feel short, dumpy, and extremely ethnic.

"Scott, the White Sox played a great game last night," says Charlie. "I caught the box score online this morning."

"Aren't they cute talking about sports?" Kristin crosses her arms and gazes down at me. "I just love your top. It's so hard to find clothes that fit me in this town. Everyone's mini, like you!"

"Um, thanks."

"So, what do you do in Beijing?"

"I'm the dining editor at *Beijing NOW*." Her brow wrinkles in puzzlement and I add, "It's an English-language magazine for expats."

"Oh, there are so many of those rags I can't keep them straight—but I'm sure it's very good," she adds hastily, glancing over at Charlie. "Do you write restaurant reviews?"

"Yes, and features about food, fashion, art . . . "

"What a *great* job! I'm green with envy. You make me want to quit the Foreign Service and jump right into writing."

An awkward silence descends. Kristin bobs her head up and down with a friendly smile, but I can feel her pale blue eyes probing me.

"What do you do at the embassy?" I ask. Across the table, Charlie and Scott turn their attention to us.

"Oh, I work in the Econ section," she says vaguely. "Anyway, we're keeping you from your dinner. We should really get going. Charlie, we're having a countdown meeting for Senator Allan's visit tomorrow. I hope you can come. And Isabelle, it was nice meeting you. You know," she leans in confidentially, but doesn't quite drop her voice, "you should be proud of yourself. Your English is really impressive, honey."

I look down at the floor. "Um, thanks." I struggle to keep my voice even. "But—"

"Kristin," Charlie breaks in. "Isabelle is American. She grew up in New York."

"Oh!" She covers her mouth in surprise. "I just thought . . . because of your outfit . . . " She stops and shrugs. "I'm sorry. My mistake."

"No problem," I manage.

"Well, now that I've put my foot in my mouth, I really think it's time to go." She smiles sweetly, revealing again those large white teeth. "Good-bye." As they turn to leave, Kristin catches my eye one more time before she walks away. The look she gives me is hard and steely, like a challenge.

Charlie and I sit down again and place crisp napkins across our laps and dutifully study the menu, but though I pretend to mull over sea bass poached in a lemongrass broth and sautéed filet mignon with black truffle jus, my mind skitters. Though I've only been in China for a few months, has my Americanness already been erased? Or is there another reality: that no one has ever considered me American in the first place?

"How about a drink?" asks Charlie gently. He signals to the waiter and orders a bottle of Bordeaux, and I try to compose myself in the ritual of its opening, forcing myself to concentrate as Charlie swirls, tastes, and approves.

"Cheers," he says with a smile. "Here's to being neighbors."

We clink glasses and I take a sip that tastes of berries and summer skies and the slow pace of the French countryside.

"This is delicious," I say, and gulp another large sip. "Do you know a lot about wine?"

"Just a little. I spent a year after college working in a vineyard in Burgundy."

"Wow. That sounds amazing."

"It was wonderful . . . I love that region of France. I still dream about it sometimes."

"How could you tear yourself away?"

He grins. "I'm still asking myself. After that summer, I lived in Paris for a couple of years, working at an English-language magazine for expats, sort of like *Beijing NOW*. But I never had proper working papers and eventually the long arm of the law caught up with me."

"What happened?"

"I moved back to my parents' house in Connecticut. I heard about the Foreign Service exam from a friend and took it on a whim."

"Have you been back to France?"

"To visit, yes, but not to live. When I was in Eastern Europe covering the Violet Revolution—which was challenging, but very rewarding," he inserts hastily, seeing a look of dismay cross my face, "it was a little easier to go back to see my friends, but since moving to Beijing, it's been more difficult."

"Do you think you'll ever live in France again?"

"I hope so. But how can I complain? Beijing is one of the most exciting places in the world right now—at least according to the front page of the *New York Times*." His mouth twists into an ironic grin. "The truth is, aside from all the superpower hype, I've always been interested in China. I studied in Shanghai one summer in college and I always wanted to come back. But what about you?" He leans forward slightly and I brace myself for the same old question, the one that everyone asks: How does it feel to be back in your homeland? I take a sip of wine and stifle my annoyance, but he surprises me. "Have you ever been to France?" he asks.

"Oh! France! No . . . but I would love to travel there. I really feel like I have an inner French girl—" I'm interrupted by an insistent ring that grows louder as Charlie reaches into his suit jacket and extracts a cell phone.

"Excuse me," he says, glancing at the number. "I think it's the embassy. Do you mind if I take this?" He offers an apologetic smile and leaves the table.

I sip my glass of wine and feel its warmth spread through me. Charlie's wineglass stands too close to the edge of the table and I move it, imagining his long fingers along the stem, or brushing across my hand, or neck. A smile creeps across my lips and the knot in my neck starts to loosen as he returns to the table.

One glance at his face and I know something is wrong.

"Isabelle," he says, "I feel awful about this, but I have to cut our evening short."

"Oh!" I search his face for clues, but his expression is guarded, as if he's afraid to reveal too much. "Is everything all right?"

"Something has come up and I have to be at a meeting in half an hour." He signals for the check and fails to meet my eyes. I feel terrible. A car is coming to get take me to the embassy, but it can take you home after."

"That's okay. I can just take a taxi."

"No. I insist." Too hurried to wait for the bill, he lays down a few hundred *kuai* notes. I stare at their garish pink color against the white tablecloth. "We have to go."

"The car is here already?" I stand up shakily, a bit light-headed from the wine.

"They sent it before they called." He smiles ruefully. "That's what I get for asking my secretary to make my dinner reservations."

We head into the warm night, and sure enough, at the restaurant's door stands a dark sedan with black license plates that are stamped red with the character *shi* for embassy. A driver climbs out of the car and rushes to open the back doors. I climb in on the right side and reach to pull the door shut. To my surprise, the driver holds the door and motions for me to slide to the left.

"You can't sit there," he says.

"*Moiyou wenti,*" Charlie inserts quickly. "It's no problem. I'll just sit on the other side." He walks around the back of the car.

"That's so odd," I remark once he's settled himself. "Why didn't the driver want me to sit on this side?"

"Oh, there's some silly protocol rule," he says vaguely. His phone rings again. "Yes," he barks. And then, "I'm in the car. I should be there in fifteen minutes . . . Yes. I reviewed the talking points this afternoon . . . It's probably going to be a long night . . . Okay, see you in a few minutes." He ends the call. The car glides through streets filled with chattering, laughing people, but inside we are silent. Charlie crosses his arms and presses his lips together; he seems intensely focused, as if he's trying to speed through traffic using sheer force of will.

But the brake lights flash like neon as we creep down Guanghua Lu in fits and starts, the driver alternately accelerating and braking until I am woozy from the motion mixed with the wine. Finally, the car passes through a gate and stops outside the darkened embassy. Charlie reaches over to grab his briefcase and then wrenches open his door.

"Isabelle." His smile is like an afterthought. "I'm really sorry about this."

"It's okay. I understand."

He hesitates for a second and then says: "I'm going to be away for a few weeks in Washington. But I'll give you a call when I get back and maybe we can get together then."

"Great!" I reply cheerily as my heart sinks. Maybe I'm jumping to conclusions, but everyone knows that going away for a few weeks is code for "I'm not interested."

He waves good-bye and slams the door shut. I watch the briefcase swing from his hand as he swiftly walks into the embassy.

"Xiaojie. Ni xiang qu na'r?" The driver turns and stares at me. Where do you want to go?

I glance at my watch: 9:00 P.M. I could go home, but the

thought of our cold, empty apartment tightens my chest. "Wait a sec," I say to the driver.

Geraldine answers on the first ring, but I can barely hear her over the din of music. "Hold on! I'm going outside," she shouts.

"How's the karaoke?" I ask when she returns.

"Fun." She giggles "More importantly, how's the date going? Are you calling me from the bathroom to tell me you're in lurrrve?"

"Actually, the date's over. Charlie had some sort of work emergency and—"

"Where are you?" ·

"You're not going to believe this, but I'm sitting outside the American embassy in a car, and the driver's staring at me like I have two heads."

"Come meet us," she says immediately. "A bunch of us are heading over to Gui Jie for hot pot."

"Hot pot? It's like eighty degrees outside."

"That's why they invented industrial air conditioners, my friend. Come on, give the phone to the driver and I'll tell him where to go."

Geraldine gives swift instructions and soon we are gliding toward Gui Jie, or Ghost Street, a bright and blinking stretch packed with twenty-four-hour eateries, popular for late night, postdrinking binges, the Chinese equivalent of an all-night diner. Touts surround me as I exit the car, clapping their hands and crying out, *"Xiaojie! Xiaojie!"* But I ignore them and make my way toward Xiao Shan Cheng, which beckons with all the electric glitz of a Las Vegas casino.

"Huanying guanglin!" exclaims the staff as I enter the restaurant. Welcome honored guest. Their voices are faint against the roar of diners, who are packed elbow-to-elbow at round tables of ten. A bubbling cauldron of broth fills the center of each table, and patrons jostle each other to dunk paper-thin slices of meat, or

plop fat mushrooms and triangles of tofu, within its oily depths. Already my skin feels sweaty from the humid room, despite the promised air conditioners that ineffectively blow out lukewarm gasps. The place veritably embodies the term *renao*: it's hot, noisy, and chaotic, a dining atmosphere beloved to most Chinese.

I wander through the crush of people wondering how I will locate Geraldine and her friends, when I hear a shout. "Isabelle! Over here!" She's ensconced at a table of ten, the only blonde in the room. I'm not sure how I missed her. "I saved you a seat." She pats the chair next to her and calls out: *"Dajia! Zhe shi wo de tongshi,* Li Jia."

"Why did you use my Chinese name?" I ask as I wave and smile at everyone.

"It's just easier." She shrugs. "So, tell me what happened."

The story tumbles out, aided by a few healthy swigs of Yanjing beer.

"It doesn't sound that bad," says Geraldine. "I mean, he's probably really busy."

"I thought it was going really well. But when he had to go, he became a different person, all serious and stern."

"Sounds kind of sexy." Geraldine raises her eyebrows.

"What's sexy?" The guy on my left leans over and flashes a grin that dimples his round face. Even in my distressed state I note his smooth, muscled arms and spiky, tousled hair, the dark flash of his eyes.

"Meet Jeff Zhu," says Geraldine. "Friend to all single women," she says loud enough for him to hear. "And some who aren't single." She turns to Jeff. "Be nice to Li Jia. She's new in town and she doesn't need any of your shenanigans."

"What's a shenanigan?" He stumbles over the word, his accent slurrily Chinese.

"You know what I mean." Geraldine rolls her eyes as a waitress sets down small dishes of sauce at each place. "*Majiang.* Some of the yummiest sesame sauce in the world. I'm addicted to the stuff."

We stir dense scoops of sesame paste into a rich, thick liquid. I can't help but lick the ends of my chopsticks and exult at the salty, nutty intensity. Jeff sees my expression and laughs. "Have you ever had hot pot before?"

"No."

"There are rules, you know."

"What kind of rules?"

"You have to put the potatoes in first—they take the longest to cook. Meat cooks fast, but people like it the most. The *baicai* and *bocai* come last. You know, cabbage and spinach," he adds.

"I speak Chinese."

His laugh rises above the rumble of voices.

Platters of ruby red meat arrive, thinly sliced to cook in an instant. "Let's put everything in so it's like a big stew," says someone. Thick potato slices, black mushrooms, gauzy mung bean noodles, pale sheaves of cabbage and curled leaves of spinach, and sliver after sliver of meat get thrown in, until the cauldron threatens to overflow, bubbling volcanically while a brave few reach in with their chopsticks to snatch up scraps. Jeff dives into the food, slurping up noodles and wildly swirling bits of meat into his sauce. Our faces grow red from the heat of the boil and the fiery chili-laden broth.

"*Hao chi!*" remarks someone, and the rest of the table agrees. "*Hao chi! Hao chi!*" Good eating.

The food is honest and hearty, perfect for unthawing frozen limbs—or making the sweat run on a sultry summer evening. I slip paper-thin slices of meat into the sauce, rich and nutty with sesame, and allow the evening's disappointment to fade into the haze of noise and heat and beer. As the bubbling broth relaxes to a simmer, our table grows rowdy. Jeff lobs a *shaobing* bun across the table and everyone erupts in laughter. I can't quite pick up the joke but I forge a hearty chuckle.

"What are you laughing at?" Jeff turns to me, his wide brown eyes running down the low V in my shirt.

"Nothing," I chirp, enjoying his attention.

Soon the check arrives and we divide it equally, each offering up twenty *kuai* notes, the equivalent of two dollars.

Jeff finds me as I'm straggling out the door. "Hey, Li Jia! Give me your cell phone number," he says. "You can practice your Chinese on me."

I dig in my purse and extract a card. "What makes you think I want to practice my Chinese?" I ask, and, really, I'm not trying to be flirtatious.

He takes the card and examines it. "Isabelle Lee. Your Chinese name suits you better."

"Isabelle!" Geraldine waves at me from the curb. "Do you want to share a cab home?"

"I have to go," I say to him. "It was nice meeting you."

"I'll be in touch!" he calls after me.

I crawl into the cab and crank open the window to release the clouds of cigarette smoke issuing from the driver. "I think Jeff likes you," Geraldine says. "You should go for it."

"Oh, I don't know . . . Chinese guys aren't really my thing. Besides, he's way too good-looking for me."

"Don't underestimate yourself, Iz," said Geraldine. "It could be fun . . . a Beijing fling . . . "

"Do I *need* a fling?" I ask, and cross my arms.

"Yes." She turns to look me in the eye. "You do."

Lao Beijing

"For home cooking, the most celebrated northern food has to be *jiaozi,* or dumplings. Made of wheat flour dough skin or wrappers, they are stuffed most commonly with vegetables and minced pork, then boiled or steamed ... The whole family gather together both to make them and eat them, while at the same time reinforcing family reunion and social contact."

—YAN-KIT SO, *CLASSIC FOOD OF CHINA*

I should be finishing an article on Beijing's best dumpling restaurants, but who could concentrate on such a beautiful morning? The skies hold only a smidgen of haze, the taxi driver who drove me to work was blissfully incurious, and I didn't run into anything freaky while crossing through the construction site in front of our office. (Last week Ed saw a human skull lying in the dirt. He took photos of it with his iPhone, of course.)

Oh, and there's Jeff. I thought I wasn't interested. And I'm not. Really. But after meeting him for coffee this weekend, I have to admit it's kind of nice being wooed. He's the type of guy I've always been wary of, a little too handsome, a tad too coolly confident, but being with him makes me feel dangerous and sexy. And he's Chinese. My mother would be so happy.

He called Saturday morning to ask if I wanted to meet to practice my Chinese. I agreed, mostly because I'd promised Geraldine to give him a chance. He showed up at the café fifteen minutes late, his tousled head cocked in apology. "Forgive me," he said, shaking my proffered hand and then pulling me in for a hug. I was surprised. Chinese people don't usually hug.

We stood together at the café's counter and I felt a small jolt of electricity as our hips touched. *"Ni yao shenme?"* asked the cashier. What do you want? She stacked a tower of paper cups and looked at me expectantly.

"Wo lai yi ge chuan zhen," I said, forgoing coffee for an orange juice.

"Shenme?" What? The cashier wiped her hands on her green apron and glared at me.

"Yi ge chuan zhen," I said firmly. Then, to Jeff: "I guess I'm having one of those days where nobody understands me." I rolled my eyes.

"You just asked for a fax," he gasped between bursts of laughter. "What were you trying to order?"

"Orange juice."

"Cheng zhi," he said, patting me on the shoulder. "Orange juice is *cheng zhi.*"

We ferried our drinks to a table and Jeff pulled his chair close to mine. "So," he said, resting his elbows on the table. "I've been dying to ask you something."

"What?"

"Was your life in New York just like Carrie's in *Sex and the City*?"

I laughed and caught myself tossing my hair around. "What makes you think that?"

"Well, Geraldine told me you worked at a magazine just like Carrie. And you're beautiful and stylish like her . . . "

"Flattery will get you everywhere."

"So?" He smiled, flashing his dimple. "Was it?"

"Well, I went to parties, and wore high heels, and lived in Manhattan. But I didn't have Carrie's clothing budget. Or as many boyfriends. I definitely experienced the city. But maybe not the . . . sex." Oh my God. Did I just say that? He raised his eyebrows and I felt my face warm.

"I don't perceive you," he whispered huskily. It took me a minute to figure out he meant "believe" me.

We spent the rest of the hour talking about New York. At first I was afraid of boring him, but he pressed me for details and I soon found myself describing the things I missed the most: the dark coziness of my favorite East Village bar, my solitary Sunday morning walks across the Brooklyn Bridge, making snow angels in Washington Square Park with Julia. It was the first time I'd talked about home since moving to Beijing three months ago, and I was surprised to find that thinking about New York no longer carried a sharp sting. When Jeff ran a hand down my shoulder and said he had to go, I couldn't believe how quickly the time had passed.

Later, I realized that we hadn't spoken a word of Chinese.

I turn back to the mocking glow of my computer screen with a sigh. Since our Starbucks encounter, I haven't had so much as a text message from Jeff. I gaze at my cell phone hoping it will beep, but there is nothing. Nothing.

Why haven't I heard from him? Wait. I don't even like him. But why hasn't he called? Out of the corner of my eye I see Ed skulk into the newsroom. I reluctantly tear my eyes from my cell phone and turn back to the computer.

"Working hard, or hardly working, Isabelle?" Ed's sarcastic tones float over my shoulder. He looks pointedly at the empty document on my computer screen.

I jump. How did he sneak behind me? "Just . . . trying to come up with something snappy."

"Yes, well I'd hate for you to feel underused— Ooh! Are those moon cakes?" His eyes light on a gilt box of the indestructible pastries, leaden with preservatives, a gift from the publicity manager at the Shangri-la Hotel. Ed's moods are as unpredictable as the lottery, but I've learned that nothing changes them faster than free food.

"Help yourself!" I push the box toward him cheerfully.

"Mmmmmmmm! Salty duck egg . . . I love these!" He takes an enthusiastic bite. "Ishabel," he mumbles, spraying me lightly with crumbs. "Geraldine called in sick. I need you to fill in for her this morning." He pauses to examine the chalky interior of his moon cake. "I wonder what they do to keep the egg yolk from spoiling . . . "

"What—"

"Tina Chang," he says. "Eleven o'clock. That coffee place at Pacific Century Place. That's Yin Ke Zhongxin in Chinese."

"But—"

"I'll text you Tina's number so you can confirm. Ring Geraldine if you need more info!" he mumbles through another mouthful of moon cake, his long legs already striding back toward his office.

I call Geraldine from the cab and she gives me the scoop between coughing fits. Tina Chang was born in Beijing, immigrated to Great Neck as a kid and moved back to Beijing after graduating from Stanford. "She started out doing subtitles for Hollywood blockbusters," says Geraldine. "And sort of wormed her way up from there. Five years later she's the rep for Topanga Films in China. She's tough, a real *haigui*. Very aggressive. A lot of people can't stand her."

"What's *haigui*?"

"You know, a returning Chinese. Someone who's immigrated overseas but come back to the mainland. It literally means sea turtle."

"Huh." I scribble the word in my notebook.

The cab screeches to a halt at a red light and I look up to check our location. Only at Chaoyangmen, I realize with a frustrated sigh, before a billboard catches my eye. Spread high in the sky, across half a city block, is a photo of a long-limbed blonde frolicking with two children in a grassy field, their golden heads glinting in the sun. BE A FOREIGNER'S LANDLORD AT MILANO CHAMPAGNE APARTMENTS! proclaims the sign in English. Something about the model's posture seems familiar . . .

"Oh my God!" I shriek, interrupting Geraldine's etymological explanation of the term sea turtle. "Is that *you*? On the billboard?"

"Are you on Chaoyangmen Nei? Um. Yeah," she says reluctantly. "My friend Xiao Pan needed a foreign face for his ad campaign." She groans. "It looks like an ad for the Aryan nation. Every time I ride by it on my bicycle I cringe."

"You're a supermodel!" I tease.

"Only in China . . . " Her laugh turns into a sigh.

"And Tina Chang? Is she another made-in-China success story?"

"She certainly thinks so. We're trying to get on the set of Max Zhang's next film, and she's the dragon at the gate."

"Who?"

"He's famous, Iz," she says patiently. "You know, the Taiwanese director. He made *The East is Red* with Zhang Ziyi."

"Mmm." I have no idea what she's talking about.

"And that movie about the eccentric British family? Mitford?"

"*The Pursuit of Love*? I loved that movie!"

"You're such an Anglophile." She blows her nose. "Sorry, that was disgusting. Anyway, this is his first time directing on the mainland, so there's bound to be some controversy."

"It sounds like a great story."

"It is." She hesitates. "There's one other thing you should know—Tina and Jeff Zhu used to be engaged. He broke it off last year and I've heard she's still pretty bitter. So don't mention him. You don't want to cross paths with a jealous Chinese ex-girlfriend."

At Jeff's name, I feel a shiver run down my spine. "Have you talked to him?" I ask casually.

"No . . . why? I thought you weren't interested." Her voice takes on a teasing lilt.

"I'm not," I insist. "I was just you know . . . curious."

"Well, don't mention him to Tina, for God's sake. Even that could send her into a rage."

"I'm nervous."

"Call me when it's over."

After lurching through five more blocks of traffic, my cab finally pulls up in front of a sprawling glass and concrete mall. I find my way to a familiar green awning and plunge through the revolving door to the scent of coffee and . . . cigarettes? Wait a second, I thought Starbucks was a smoke-free zone. I glance at the tables and chairs in blond wood, the long counter with its glass case of pastries and gleaming espresso machine, the baristas swathed in kelly green aprons, before my eye is caught by a logo on the menu board: SPR COFFEE. It seems Starbucks has its very own Chinese coffee emporium knockoff.

Geraldine offered vague details about Tina—"medium height, thin but not skinny, long black hair"—which could easily have described half the customers in the café. For a moment I have the mad, mental image of me approaching each young woman one by one, asking, "Tina Chang? Tina Chang?"

I study the desiccated pastries in the glass case and covertly assess my options. Out of the gaggle of slender young women with long black hair, only five are alone. Girl #1, by the window, snaps impatiently through the pages of Chinese *Vogue*. Girl #2, at the counter, pauses from examining her cell phone to take a sip of foamy cappuccino. Girl #3 studies an English textbook, glancing up occasionally to throw a flirtatious look at the white guy sitting at the table next to her. Girl #4 has been joined by a friend, I note with relief, while Girl #5 shouts into her cell phone, her brow furrowed in anger. Bingo. I can't hear what she's saying, but she looks aggressive.

I approach and hover over her table, shy about interrupting her phone conversation. "Excuse me?" It comes out like a squeak. I clear my throat. "Excuse me? Are you Tina Chang?"

She looks up, eyes narrow with suspicion, pulls her purse close and continues her phone conversation. I try to laugh but it comes out more like a pant. Girl #1 looks up from her magazine and sees me wheezing and breathless by the milk dispensers. She waves.

"Oh, are you Tina?" I call out, feeling heat creep across my cheeks. The edge of a chair catches my knee and I nearly skid into her lap.

"Isabelle?" she says with surprise, her accent tripping charmingly over every syllable. She has the refined features of a doll, a delicate nose, rosebud mouth, and enormous, double-lidded eyes, which I'm experienced enough to know are the result of a surgeon's quick snip and sew. They regard me with an unblinking gaze. I'm wearing my usual *Beijing NOW* uniform of jeans and a scoop-necked T-shirt, an outfit that would look fine with the right shoes, thin-strapped sandals perhaps, or a pair of ballet flats. However, unwilling to expose my bare feet to the grime of Beijing's streets, I have pulled on my usual footwear: sturdy running shoes that scream suburban mom.

"Hi!" I say, and try to hide my discomfort with an oversized smile. "It's so nice to meet you! Tina!"

"*Zhende shi qiguai! Women da dian hua de shi hou wo yiwei ni shi lao wai!*"

It takes me a minute to puzzle out the translation. Ah, yes: that's strange, on the phone, I thought you were a foreigner.

I hesitate. "Ummm . . . *wo shi meiji hua ren*. Uh, *wo de fuqin zai meiguo sheng de, suo yi* . . . Uh, *shi yin wei*. . . " Oh dear, I've painted myself into a Chinese corner. Am I making any sense at all? Didn't Ed tell her I'm American? Tina watches me struggle, a small smile on her lips.

"It's okay," she says finally. "Let's speak English." She crosses her legs, dangling a high-heeled mule from one foot so that I can see the label: Prada.

I smile politely.

"So, Isabelle . . . " Tina raises her manicured eyebrows. "Tell me about yourself. How long have you been in Beijing?"

"Me? Just a couple of months."

"Where do you live?"

"Oh. Uh, Roman Villas," I say, inwardly wincing at the ridiculous name.

"Which phase—Caligula Court or Pompey Towers?"

"Caligula," I admit.

"Wow. I had you pegged as a Haidian kind of girl. Something a little more low-end." She picks up my hand. "No ring. So how docs a girl like you afford digs like Roman Villas?"

Her directness leaves me speechless, but Tina seems unfazed. "Don't mind me, sweetie," she coos. "The Chinese side of me is so frank. I can't help it." Her syrupy tones are reminiscent of Claire and her friends.

"I live with my sister." She stares at me expectantly and so I add, "Claire Lee."

"Ohmigod! Are you Claire Lee's *meimei*? Why didn't you tell me?!" Her face, wreathed in smiles, is almost scarier than before. "Claire is one of my *best friends!*"

"Everyone . . . seems to know Claire," I manage weakly. Privately, I wonder why, if they're such good friends, Claire has never even uttered her name.

"So, tell me . . . " She leans in close and her perfume almost chokes me. "How are things going between Claire and Wang Wei?"

"Um . . . fine?"

"I told Claire, who cares if he's one of the richest men in China? If that two-timing bastard won't commit to you, dump him! He's not worth it! And then Sam saw him at Q Bar with Sophie Wang—you know, the Hong Kong movie star?" She pauses and gives me an expectant look. I nod. "I told Claire she should go after him with a butcher knife. But he just claimed they were discussing business. Huh!"

I keep a pleasant smile on my face, but inside my heart is sinking. I had hoped Wang Wei was some kindhearted but misguided guy who was simply sowing a few wild oats. But the reality sounds much worse than I feared.

"She sometimes seems a little blue . . . " I say, thinking back to that morning in the kitchen, when Claire seemed ready to burst into sobs.

"I knew it!" Tina scoots her chair even closer, and I immediately wish I'd kept my mouth shut. "Do you think they're going to break up?"

"Well, you know Claire," I hedge, wanting to bite my tongue off. "She's very proud."

"That's so true." Tina nods. "She keeps everything inside. I'm always telling her to loosen up, open up, maybe see a shrink. But she always has to be in control."

"That's probably what makes her such a successful litigator," I say snappily, feeling suddenly protective. Only I'm allowed to criticize my sister.

"Oh, she's smart about a lot of things. Just not men." Tina digs through her bag and pulls out a pack of Marlboro Lights. "Do you mind if I smoke?" She taps out a cigarette and lights it before I can respond, blowing a stream of smoke past my shoulder. "How about you? Single?"

"Me? Oh, yeah. Well, you know how it is . . . I just moved here . . . " Nosy old cow, I think.

"A pretty girl like you? Well, I'm sure it won't take you long to find a man." She takes a long drag and regards me with a steady gaze.

How did this meeting turn into a summit on my love life? I attempt to refocus. "About the article—"

"Ah yes. Enough gossip." Tina straightens in her seat and taps cigarette ash onto the floor. "Frankly, we still don't know if we can offer you access," she says. "Shooting starts in a couple of weeks and we'll need to see the interview questions beforehand. We'll need to approve the article before it runs. And," she continues in a crisp tone, "we've moved the set to Shanxi province, so you'll have to make your own arrangements to get out there."

"Shanxi?"

"We have accommodations for the cast and crew, of course, but we're filming during the Pingyao International Photography Festival so most hotels are already full. You better make reservations now."

As I'm scribbling everything down, my cell phone rings and Jeff's name flashes across the screen. My heart floods with joy, followed immediately by panic. He had to call *now*?

"Don't you want to answer that?" Tina peers at the phone as it beeps and hums.

What to do, what to do? I'm dying to talk to Jeff. But if I answer she might cancel everything. Geraldine and Ed would kill me.

Reluctantly, I press End on the phone, sending Jeff into cellular oblivion.

"Nobody important," I assure Tina with a smile.

Do you think she knew it was him?" Geraldine's screech raises a squeal of feedback on my cell phone. "I'm telling you, she has eyes like a hawk."

"I promise you, she didn't have a clue. She was too busy digging for information on Claire's love life. Anyway," I switch topics, "how are you feeling? Did you go to the doctor?"

"I saw my herbalist yesterday." Cough, cough. "He has me on these little bottles of Chinese medicine. They're dark and sweet."

"Hm. Don't you think you should see a real—er, I mean, a Western doctor?"

"Why? It's a total waste of time and money. Anyway, I'm getting moxibustion this afternoon and that should clear everything up."

"Is that where they stick needles in your spine?

"No," she says patiently. "It's when they suck the toxins out of you with hot glass cups. I'll have hickeys all over my back. And hopefully I'll be cured by Sunday." For weeks, Geraldine has been planning a mid-autumn festival party, to be held at her home, a restored courtyard house that Gab says is like an untouched corner of old Beijing. It's hidden in a tangle of narrow *hutongs* in the Back Lakes district, and, unlike many old-style homes, which were divided during the Cultural Revolution, is complete with four buildings and a spacious central courtyard. "I told you I invited Jeff, right?" she adds.

"Yeah." I shift the phone against my ear.

"I got an e-mail from him this morning. He asked about you."

"Really?" A smile creeps across my face.

"He likes it when women play hard to get."

"I'm not sure that's what I'm doing."

"He said you're intriguing."

Hmmmm. Intriguing. Not that I care what he thinks, of course.

On Sunday, a brisk wind scrubs away the pollution, leaving behind a deep, pure blue sky. I linger in the kitchen over a cup of Earl Grey tea, allow the sun to warm my back and absorb myself in the crossword puzzle. As I fill in the clue for 17-across "Parisian river" (S-E-I-N-E), my thoughts wander to Charlie. I haven't heard from him since our aborted date, and I have no idea if he's still traveling or simply avoiding me. I've looked for him at the lobby newsstand, but found only a tall stack of *International Herald Tribunes*.

Claire wanders into the kitchen, dressed in a baby blue trailer-chic velour sweatsuit that reveals a strip of taut stomach. "Hi, sweetie," she croons, opening the fridge and peering inside. "Shoot! We're out of milk."

"I'm going to Jenny Lou's in a minute. I can pick some up."

"I'll come with you," she says. "Just hang on two secs while I get ready, okay?"

An hour later we are strapped into the backseat of Claire's silver Audi while her driver, Mr. Wang, weaves his way in and out of traffic. Claire pulls out a compact and smooths on another glistening coat of lip gloss. "Want some?" she asks, her eyes fixed on the tiny mirror.

"No, thanks." Before leaving, I'd brushed on some mascara and changed out of my hooded sweatshirt into a pale pink cashmere sweater and dark jeans. It seemed silly to dress up for the grocery store, but one look at Claire's sexy suburbanite outfit— Juicy sweats, kitten-heeled sandals, tousled mane of hair, and full foundation-wearing makeup—and I know I've made the right decision.

Claire closes her compact with a snap and pushes her dark hair behind her ears so her diamond solitaire glitter in the morning light, I know those earrings. They were a gift from our parents, Claire's reward for getting into Yale Law School: a pair of diamonds so large and perfect and sparkly that I called them the Elizabeth Taylors. I still remember the day she got them. They appeared on her dinner plate, nestled into a red leather box that had been tied with a white satin bow.

Claire stared at the box and we stared at her. "Aren't you going to open it?" our mother finally asked.

Her face solemn, Claire slowly picked up the box and loosened the ribbon. Prying open the hinged cover, she gently touched one of the diamonds with her fingertip.

"Do you like them?" Mom plucked one of the earrings out of the box and held it up so it caught the light. "Aren't they beautiful?"

We watched the sparks of light bounce off the wall. "Thank you," Claire finally said. She fastened first one diamond and then the other into her ears.

"They look nice on you, honey," said Dad.

"Remember, I promised to get them for you if you got into law school? We're so proud of you." Our mother beamed.

"Thank you," Claire repeated, and helped herself to a spoonful of bitter melon in black bean sauce.

"Aren't you proud of your sister?" Mom nudged me. "Maybe you'll follow in her footsteps. Claire could tutor you on the LSAT."

I busied myself with balancing my chopsticks on the edge of my plate. I was sixteen and I hadn't even taken the SAT yet, let alone the LSAT.

"Have you thought about what you want to do after you finish college?" my mother pressed me.

I took a bite of pork, chewed, and swallowed. "I don't know . . . Maybe work in magazine publishing?" I wasn't even sure what that meant, but I knew I liked to read.

"Magazine publishing!" My mother widened her eyes. "You'll never make a living doing that!" she said. "Tell her, Claire."

"You'll never make a living doing that," my sister repeated, except her voice seemed flat.

Now, I touch the skin of my narrow earlobes, which are empty and bare. Unlike Claire, the model nerd teen, I ditched SAT class and didn't get into the Ivy League. Instead of jewelry, I received my mother's enduring disappointment, which extended to my choice of college, career, and companions. Now, in the car, I gaze at my sister's diamonds. If diligence could sparkle, it is in the shimmer of those earrings.

At Jenny Lou's, Claire and I each grab a basket and split ways to wander through the narrow aisles. Jenny Lou's, J-Lou's, J-Ho's, call it what you will, the shop is the Beijing expat community's lifeboat of sanity. Geraldine brought me to the store my first week at *Beijing NOW,* and I gasped with relief at the sight of boneless, skinless chicken breasts, the boxes of cereal and Twinings tea bags. Here, one hundred *kuai* notes fly freely out of our hands, spent on the things we miss the most: the tastes and textures of home. Now, I wind my way through the pasta aisle, lingering at the cheese counter to eye the hunks of Gorgonzola and wedges of Brie. I examine the rows of old and new world wine, the jars of Nutella, the produce aisle with its avocados and fresh basil.

Rumor has it that Jenny, an enterprising young woman from Anhui, once eked out a living selling fragrant bunches of dill, basil, and mint at the local wet market. Ten years later she presides over an empire, with five stores that bear her name.

I finish gathering the rest of my list, and find Claire at the cashier. She must have spent her time investigating the beverage aisle. Her basket contains:

SWEETENED GREEN TEA, 12 BOTTLES

SKIM MILK, 1 CARTON (SMALL)

SPECIAL K "LOW-CARB LIFESTYLE" CEREAL, 1 BOX

I see her glancing at my basket, her brow furrowed as if she's having trouble adding up the calories. In my basket is:

HUNK OF PARMAGIANO-REGGIANO, CAVEMAN-SIZED

PASTA, 2 PACKETS

FULL-FAT RICOTTA CHEESE, 2 TUBS

FROZEN SPINACH, 1 BAG

EGGS, 1 DOZEN

SALTED BUTTER, 1 KILO

EXTRA VIRGIN OLIVE OIL, LARGE BOTTLE

"My, what a lot of dairy!" she exclaims, her eyes traveling down to my waistline. "Are you sure you want to . . ." She pauses. I can feel her weighing her words in her bossy big sister way, and resentment flares within me, hot and familiar. Why does she have to be so smug? Why do I always feel like she's making the right choices while I'm killing myself with saturated fat?

"You're so critical, Claire," I snap. "Why are you always so critical?"

She shrugs and we move to separate cashiers to pay, before gathering up our groceries and riding home in silence.

It's 2:00 P.M. I'm standing over the kitchen sink, squeezing liquid out of defrosted spinach. Geraldine asked me to bring dumplings to her moon festival party, and of course I said yes. There's only one problem: I don't know how to make Chinese dumplings and I don't have an Asian cookbook. Solution? Spinach and cheese ravioli. After all, everyone knows Marco Polo stole ravioli from China.

When people find out that I like to cook, they always ask if I make Chinese food, and they're always surprised when I say no. "Why not?" they say, raising their eyebrows, as if Chinese recipes are something passed along in the DNA, along with black hair and single-lidded eyes. It's a question I've been dodging with a smile and a shrug, ever since I was eight years old and we lived next door to Melanie Stansfield.

She and I weren't best friends or anything—she always wanted to dress up Barbies and parade them around in the dream house caravan, while I wanted to redesign their ball gowns into mini-skirts with the help of pinking shears—but we lived so close, of course we played together. I ate at Melanie's house all the time; her mother served things like pot roast and mashed potatoes, or meat loaf. Melanie would nibble at her meal, but I always cleaned my plate, delighting in its ordinariness—it was just like the food I saw on TV. One night, in the spirit of reciprocation, my mother invited Melanie to stay for dinner. I still remember that feeling of panic, thinking: Oh please God, just let her go home.

But Melanie didn't go home. She stayed and sat at our round kitchen table, spun the lazy Susan too fast, and watched us manipulate chopsticks while she pushed her food around with a fork and knife. Her eyes grew wide when she saw the thick-stalked, stir-fried *jielan*—"It's like Chinese broccoli," my mother said—and I thought she would scream when the steamed fish appeared, with its gaping mouth and unblinking eye. She tried a spoonful of *mapo* tofu, her eyes streaming as the chili caught her tender tongue, and hid a black bean sparerib in her napkin. I watched her pick at her food and felt embarrassed by the meal, which, to Melanie, was not exotic, but simply weird.

A few days later, at Melanie's house for an after-school snack of graham crackers and milk, her mother turned to me. "What exactly do you eat for dinner at your house, Isabelle?" She eyed me appraisingly, as if noticing for the first time that I was Chinese.

"Oh, just Chinese food." I tried to avoid specifics.

"Was that *tofu* that Melanie ate the other night?"

"Um, yeah. I think so."

"Huh." She moved away to empty the dishwasher and the topic was dropped.

After that meal, though, Melanie became distant and cool, in the cruel manner that little girls know best. She started hanging out with another neighbor, Anna Carpenter, and sometimes I would see them staring at me across the playground, whispering and giggling. At home I still ate Chinese food—I had no choice—and I enjoyed it. But each bowl of rice, each pink shrimp, with their spiny antennae and crunchy shell, each cool, creamy slab of tofu, had become a symbol of my Chineseness—the thing that made me weirdly, unquestionably, different from my peers.

By the time I had a kitchen of my own, ethnic food had become chic. As college students at NYU, my friends and I rode the 7 train to Jackson Heights and feasted on masala dosas, we saved our pennies for jars of duck confit and scoured Chinatown for delicate sprigs of lemongrass. I sampled everything—from French to Filipino—each bite a discovery. Of course, I ate Chinese food, but constant exposure as a child made it ordinary. I never craved it. And I never cooked it.

Now, I open the stained pages of my favorite cookbook, *Donatella's Italian Kitchen*, which I brought from New York. I've experimented with almost all the recipes—except for fresh pasta, which I've always been eager to attempt.

I open the book. *Fresh pasta sounds hard, but it's really not that difficult,* I read. Great! *Once you develop a feel for the correct consistency of the dough, you will be able to make such delicious pasta that even Marco Polo would be impressed.* Marco Polo again! It must be a sign.

Okay, the recipe . . . Three cups flour. I start hunting for a measuring cup. Hm. Not with the baking sheets, nor with the mugs. I search through all the cupboards, unearthing a stash of contact lens fluid, teeth whitening strips, and a mass of tangled yarn and sticks that's either an abandoned knitting project or an avant-garde sculpture, I'm not sure. But no measuring cup.

Well, I'll just have to eyeball it. It's all about proportions anyway, right?

Grabbing a mug, I pile flour onto the counter, wincing as a large flurry dusts the floor white. Claire would have a heart attack over the mess, but luckily she's not home, having sped off for a coffee with her friend Samantha immediately after we got home from the store.

I dig down into my mound of flour, scattering another shower over the tops of my sock-clad feet. *Beat together the eggs, olive oil, and salt and slowly pour them over the flour.* So far, so good. I start mixing everything together, trying to control the flour, which seems to have a mind of its own. *Beat until the dough becomes too stiff to mix with a fork.* Fork? What fork? Was I supposed to be using a fork? And why is there flour *everywhere*?

It's coating the counters in powdery white. It's cascading down to the floor, filling the air in thick clouds that are eerily reminiscent of Beijing smog. If I didn't know better, I'd bet our kitchen had been the center of a cocaine bust.

Meanwhile, I gaze with dismay at the ball of dough that I've managed to pull together. Which is the size of a tomato. A grape tomato.

What am I going to do? I promised Geraldine I'd bring dumplings. The creamy, cheesy ricotta-and-spinach filling (delicious, added a dash of nutmeg) mocks me in its bowl, all mixed up with nothing to stuff. Suddenly, I have a brain wave. I grab my wallet and run downstairs to our building's little grocery store, praying that Claire doesn't return before I've had a chance to clean up the mess.

Freaking Jiminy Cricket. I'm back from the store only to find Claire standing in the middle of the kitchen, a look of sheer bewilderment wrinkling her face.

"Isabelle. What. Is. Going. On." She grips the counter for support.

"I'm so sorry, so sorry, sorry, sorry, sorry," I babble. "I was trying to make ravioli and the flour just got everywhere, multiplied like rabbits . . . " I scan her face. Is she mad?

"What are you going to do?" she whispers.

"I'm going to clean it up. I promise. I'm so sorry, Claire. Honestly, it was an accident—"

"What about the ravioli?" she says weakly.

"No problem. All under control." I reach into the grocery sack and pull out a package of premade dumpling wrappers. "It's one of the few useful things they sell at the store downstairs."

Claire stares at them. "You're going to use *jiaozi* skins?"

"Why not? It's like a Marco Polo-Genghis Khan-creamy-cheesy-Chinese-Italian-*jiaozi* thing. You know, fusion."

Silence. And then, to my surprise, she bursts into laughter. "Do you know what this reminds me of?" she says.

I know exactly what she means and the memory makes me giggle. "That time we begged Mom to make us meat loaf?"

"And she thought the recipe was so boring, she kept adding in her own ingredients . . ."

"Minced ginger and garlic, black mushrooms, water chestnuts, *curry powder* . . ."

"And that Lee Kum Kee chili paste!"

"And then she threw some bacon on top, and basted it with Hoisin sauce! It was like . . . Asian fusion meat loaf."

"Yeah, she was definitely ahead of her time." Claire laughs and wipes away a mascara smudge from under her eye. "You know, I thought that was what meat loaf was supposed to taste like until I got to college and tried it in the cafeteria. And then it was so bland, I was disappointed."

"Hey!" In my excitement, I brush another flurry of flour off the counter. "We should invite a bunch of people over and have a meat loaf throwdown! Mom's fusion meat loaf versus the one on the back of the Lipton onion soup box. Geraldine and Gab would love it. We could get the recipe from Mom."

"Recipe? Oh, I don't think there's a recipe." Claire fiddles with her cell phone.

"Well, we should ask her about it. The next time we call home."

"Yeah, I suppose." But the amusement has left her face, replaced by something that looks like annoyance. Did I say something wrong? Was it because I mentioned calling our mother?

"Claire—" A million questions hang on my lips. What's going on between her and Mom? Why did Claire move to China and disappear from our family? But I am suddenly tongue-tied.

"Hmmm?" she says, distracted by her buzzing phone. "Hello? *Wei?*" Her face lights up. *Wang Wei*, she mouths at me, before leaving the room.

I've promised Geraldine that I'll arrive early to help her set up for the party, but of course the cab driver gets lost in the snarl of *hutongs* behind Gulou Dajie, stopping the car again and again to ask for directions with good-humored determination. We creep through the narrow lanes until we rattle to a stop at a dingy *hutong* intersection. A printing press fills the tight space, with reams of newsprint stacked as high as the tiny *hutong* dwellings, and the steady hum of industrial machinery abuzz in the air.

"Na'r!" he points. There!

"Are you sure?" I ask doubtfully.

"It says!" He shakes the sheet of directions, which are a spidery mass of characters. I glance at the English: *Left at the Heping Fandian, right at the dumpling restaurant, and then walk through the* Beijing Daily *printing press to a gate at the back.*

"Okaaay . . . " I pay him, gather my bags, and haul myself out of the cab.

"Man zou," he says. Take it easy.

Hidden behind the printing press compound stands a high brick wall with a rusting metal door. Red lanterns bob on either side, adding a dash of color against cracked black paint. I juggle my bags so that one hand is free and ring the bell. After a lengthy pause it creaks open, revealing Geraldine in a pale blue linen sundress.

"Welcome!" she says, simultaneously hugging me and relieving me of a bag. "Oof! What do you have in here?" she asks, drawing out a bottle. "Australian Shiraz! Iz, you shouldn't have."

She steps aside to let me pass through the gate, and I nearly drop my other bags in astonishment. For behind the high brick wall and dingy gate is a secret garden, a quiet courtyard planted with patches of grass and cooled by the rustling leaves of an ancient gingko tree. A building stands at each of the courtyard's four sides to form the traditional *siheyuan'r,* or four-sided house; each structure is graced with fat scarlet pillars that lead the eye upward to the fading grandeur of elaborately painted eaves. A string of colorful lanterns hangs from the trees, and a domed Mongolian yurt stands at one end of the courtyard, its flaps pinned open to reveal a swath of brightly patterned carpets and a pile of kilim cushions. Across from the yurt rests a long table already laden with food: platters of papaya and mangosteens, large bowls of potato chips, small ones of pale green wasabi peas, and tall glass pitchers of pastel-colored fruit juices.

"Geraldine!" I gasp. "This is like . . . " I search for the right words. "It's like a Chinese fairy tale."

"It's charming, but the plumbing is terrible," she says. "Come on, leave the bags. I'll show you the rest."

She leads me into the nearest building and swings open a set of double doors set with diamond-shaped panes of glass. "The living room," she says as we kick off our shoes. Rice paper screens soften the windows and a curved white sofa snakes across the room. Scarlet pillars soar through the space, while thick Xinjiang carpets, delicate with muted color and intricate patterns, cover the polished concrete floor. Geraldine's Dirt Market treasures intimately fill the corners: a battered gramophone with a trumpet-shaped speaker sits on a nest of carved tables, a flock of jade elephants lumbers across a bookcase, silver frames display photographs of her family. Beyond, a long maple dining table is piled with mail and newspapers, stacks of magazines, and a vase crammed with fragrant white lilies.

And everywhere there is art. Oversized paintings, abstract with bold strokes of color, hang from the white walls. A row of headless Mao busts stolidly stand guard on a bookshelf, while an enormous bright and brazen photograph of Beijing's city sprawl leans casually against a side table. Even my untrained eye recognizes the work of Beijing's biggest art stars, an Ai Weiwei here, a Wang Guangyi there, each selected by Geraldine's impeccable eye.

"It's beautiful," I whisper into the quiet space.

"The rooms aren't connected," she says. "So we have to go outside to enter the next building."

"What's that like in the winter?" I ask as we step out into the courtyard.

"Horribly cold," she says, throwing open the doors to her bedroom. A carved wooden headboard shines with dark varnish, and ornate red lacquer cupboards flank either side. The bed gleams with raw silk pillows in subtle shades of pale blue and celadon green, while above a swirl of mosquito netting tumbles down into a frothy mass.

It's like stepping back in time—or into a Shanghai Tang catalog. I wonder how she can afford such opulence on our meager *Beijing NOW* salary.

"All courtesy of my ex-husband," she says, answering my unspoken question. "This is what you get as the son of a Standing Politburo member. Don't worry, it's not their family home," she assures me, seeing the surprised look on my face. "I found the house and Andy gave it to me as a wedding present. When we split up, he lost no time buying himself a penthouse condo in

one of those flashy developments near Chaoyang Park. He left
this death trap to me."

"He didn't mind?"

She barks a short laugh. "Hardly. He hated living here. Hot
in the summer, freezing in the winter; no doorman, no wireless,
no satellite TV . . . " She ticks off the reasons on her fingers.
"Believe me, he was ecstatic to escape the clutches of his crazy
American wife . . . and run straight into the arms of his little mis-
tress." She rubs her hands over her face. "Anyway, this house . . .
my alimony . . . it's all peanuts to the Zhao family. They just don't
want any *mafan*—any trouble from me."

Before I can respond, she walks out into the courtyard. "The
kitchen and dining room are over here," she calls. "They're still
pretty bare bones. I haven't had a chance to renovate yet."

We squeeze into the kitchen, maneuvering between Geraldine's *ayi* and an army of caterers. The room is spacious but
worn, with stained linoleum floors and an industrial-sized ce-
ramic sink that dwarfs the gas stove. A washing machine stands
between the sink and the door, but there is no dryer, and no
oven. A circular dining table fills the other half of the room, its
polished wooden surface shiny under the fluorescent lights.

I offer my *jiaozi*-ravioli to the *ayi*. "*Shi ni zuo de ma?*" she asks,
lifting out a dumpling to examine it. Did you make these?

"*Dang rang le!*" calls out Geraldine.

Of course! She whisks me out of the kitchen before I have
a chance to explain that I'd like to make a special butter-sage
sauce to accompany them.

"I want to change the floors in the kitchen," Geraldine muses
as we sway gently on the wooden swing that dangles from the
gingko tree. "Put in an oven, add some counter space . . . "

"What's in the fourth building?" I ask.

"Storage," she grimaces. "My ex-husband had aspirations of

becoming a patron of the arts. We collected so much stuff I don't have room to display all of it."

"What kind of stuff?"

"Paintings, photographs, sculptures . . . mostly from the early 798 gallery days. I should catalog everything but it was just a hobby. I don't really have time for it now that I'm at the magazine."

My eyes widen: 798 may have lost its edge, but when the former factory-complex-turned-gallery-district first opened, it was the center of the Chinese avant-garde art world. "They could be worth a fortune by now!"

"Ha. I doubt it." She gets up and the swing jerks. "I should see what's going on the kitchen. Help yourself to a drink. I'll be back in a minute."

I steady the swing until it rocks more gently, and watch the sun creep behind the gingko tree. As the sky deepens to indigo, I help light candles in the paper lanterns. They glow like jewels within the darkening garden, and I step back for a moment to admire them. A rattle at the gate makes me jump, and then voices call from outside. "Geraldine! Are you there? Geraldeeeeen!"

She laughs as she throws open the door, and suddenly the courtyard floods with people who are kissing cheeks and exclaiming, "We got lost!" No kidding, I think. Corks are popped, there's a luscious glug-glug sound as wine is poured into glasses, and the party begins. I hang back for a second to examine a sputtering lantern, but another bright object catches my eye: the full moon, which has started to rise in the sky. Gazing at its pale surface, I try to remember the myth behind the moon festival—something about a woman who flees earthly pleasures to dance on the moon. I'm trying to recall the details when I feel hands lightly touch my waist.

I turn around. "Jeff!"

"Hey babe," he says, kissing both my cheeks. He smells fresh, like green grass, mixed with cigarettes. "Great party. Isn't this a cool pat?"

It takes me a second to figure out what he means. "Pad," I say automatically. "Cool pad."

A look of annoyance flickers across his face. "Whatever." He shrugs.

"Would you like a drink?" I lead him to a corner of the courtyard, where Geraldine has set up the bar. "What's your poison—er, what would you like? There's red wine, white wine, vodka, gin . . ."

The bottles clank as he searches through them, finally pulling out a heavy flask of Chivas. He pours himself a neat measure, adds ice and a generous splash of sweetened green tea.

"Oh, you're part of the Chivas and green tea crowd?" I tease. It's a popular drink among Beijing hipsters, who mix high-priced bottles of Chivas with bottled green tea, swilling the mix down while belting karaoke or dancing at nightclubs.

"Why not?" He takes a sip and grimaces.

I pour myself a glass of red wine and take a ladylike swallow. It slides down my throat in a silky trickle and I quickly take another gulp. Jeff regards me, a tiny smile touching his full lips.

"I don't make you nervous, do I?" he murmurs.

I glance up from the edge of my glass, but before I can think of a flirtatious response I am interrupted by a familiar squeal.

"Isabelle? Hi!" Tina Chang emerges from behind the yurt and walks toward us, her sharp heels puncturing the grass with every step. What is she doing here? "And Jeff! What a surprise! *Zenme yang?* Do you guys know each other?" she asks. Her overly round eyes dart between us, and I wonder if she's been watching us from across the courtyard.

"Not really," says Jeff.

"Isabelle is Claire Lee's little sister," says Tina.

"So I hear," he says.

Tina shoots me a glance and fires off a rapid sentence in Chinese. Jeff responds with a guffaw. My eyes dart between them, but the conversation quickly moves beyond my grasp. There are names: Wang Wei and Li Xiaoping (Claire's Chinese name), the words "yesterday," "dinner," and "wife," but otherwise I have no idea what they're discussing. I feel as if I am drowning in an ocean of Mandarin, clutching at familiar words like they're pieces of driftwood. Tina runs her fingers through her silky hair and Jeff's gaze lingers on her chest, which is prominently displayed in a lingerie-style bustier.

"Guys, I'm going to see if Geraldine needs any help," I interrupt.

They turn to me. "Oh don't go," says Tina. "We'll switch to English."

"It's okay," I say. "Enjoy yourselves."

I find Geraldine in the steamy kitchen, throwing dumplings into an enormous pot of boiling water as fast as her *ayi* can fold them.

"Oh, thank God, it's you," she says. "Can you put those salads into serving platters? And dish up some bowls of noodles?" She flaps a hand at the containers of food that crowd the kitchen counter.

"Why is Tina Chang here?" I hiss at her.

"What? Jesus Christ!" She swipes a hand against her sweaty brow. "She told me she couldn't come!"

"But why did you invite her?"

"Are you kidding? Do you know what would happen if I had a party and didn't invite Tina Chang? Instant shit list. She'd cut us off from Topanga Films. Or worse." She turns panicked eyes upon me. "Did she see you and Jeff together?"

"Um. Sort of. Well, just talking."

"Oh, dear God." Geraldine puts down her long-handled kitchen strainer and reaches for her glass of wine, draining it in a gulp. "Can't. Think. About. This. Now." She holds her glass out to me. "Would you mind topping this up at the bar?"

By the time I return with a full bottle (Geraldine seemed pretty stressed), the buffet line snakes around the room. In deference to her lovely, traditional home, Geraldine serves a buffet of old Beijing comfort food. We crowd into the kitchen/dining room and circle the big table, filling small bowls with *zhajiangmian*: doughy, hand-pulled noodles topped with a salty preserved bean sauce, studded with chunks of pork, and showered with an assortment of vegetables, from boiled soybeans to strips of cucumber. Platters of *laohu cai*, or tiger salad, a refreshing mix of slivered cucumber, bell pepper, and cilantro, add crunch to the meal, while thick-skinned boiled dumplings give it heft.

I wander into the kitchen, in search of my ravioli-*jiaozi*. I'll just make a quick sauce, melt some butter, sauté some sage, and serve them in a nice platter. "Have you seen my *jiaozi*?" I ask the *ayi*.

"*Nide jiaozi?*" she says, puzzled. "We put them together with the others." She gestures to the dumplings that bob within a boiling pot of water on the stove.

Oh dear. In her haste, Geraldine has combined everything together, and the round premade wrappers mean my ravioli blend in with all the other crescent-shaped dumplings. Now they're really fusion, cooked together with their Chinese cousins: savory pork and chive, soothing pork and cabbage, bright shredded carrot and egg. Well, *meibanfa*. There's nothing to be done. Shrugging my shoulders, I slip out of the steamy room, find a plate and heap it with food, dumplings and noodles and salad, drizzle vinegar on everything and head outside. Ed and Gab beckon to me from the yurt and I join them, settling against the rough cushions to enjoy the mysterious flicker of candlelight against cloth.

"We thought we'd rescue you from Jeff Zhu and his boy-band fabulousness," says Gab with a curl of his lip.

"Er, thanks," I say, though I have no idea what he's talking about. "Hey, your hair looks good tonight. A little more . . . clumpy."

"It's been forty-two days since my last hair wash," Gab says proudly.

"If only people knew how you suffer for your rocker chic." I bite into a dumpling, verdant within and spicy, like anise. "Mm! Is this . . . fennel?"

"Cheers, Iz," says Ed, raising a paper cup to me. His baggy cargo shorts reveal legs surprisingly muscular and long. I'd never noticed them before, since he's always sitting behind a desk.

"Those fennel and egg dumplings are really good." Gab waves his chopsticks at my plate. "But there are some really weird ones in there. Call me crazy, but I swear there's cheese in one of them."

"Huh," I say casually.

"And it's kind of gross with the soy sauce and vinegar."

"So, how's your gorgeous sister?" asks Ed, ignoring the foodie talk. "Is she here tonight?"

"No, she went to Shanghai with Wang Wei."

"Oh." His face falls.

"I'm going to get some more food," announces Gab. He picks up his plate, which is empty except for five dumplings filled with white and green that look very familiar.

"I'll come with you," I say quickly, before Ed can start expounding on Claire's beauty, wit, and unavailability, which he tends to do when he's had a few.

"Bring me a vodka on the rocks, okay?" Ed calls after us.

We slither out of the tent, giggling like schoolchildren. Gab moves toward the drinks table and I go inside to look for the bathroom, passing through the empty, air-conditioned living room and down a long hallway lined with boxes and Geraldine's Flying Pigeon bicycle. I find the bathroom, dim with candlelight and heady with the scent of lilies mixing with another, pungent, odor. A handwritten sign above the toilet proclaims: *We have ancient plumbing. Please place used toilet paper in the bin. DO NOT FLUSH IT! Thank you!* A trash can heaped with toilet paper stands in the corner, its quiet reek bearing testimony to the obedience of Geraldine's guests.

My ingrained American squeamishness means I hurriedly wash my hands with Geraldine's posh ginger lily soap and leave the bathroom. The living room appears quiet and cool, and I pause for a minute to perch on the sleek white leather couch. Outside, voices rise to a shriek, but inside they're a soothing rumble. The double doors open and shut.

"Are you hiding in here?" Jeff approaches the sofa.

"I'm taking a break." His presence fills the room and I'm suddenly aware that we've never been completely alone together. I cross my arms and swallow. Something about Jeff's lazy smile and lingering gaze makes me very nervous.

He sits down close to me and lays an arm across the back of the sofa, which almost, but not quite, touches my shoulders. "Li Jia," he says, using my Chinese name. "Those were some weird ass *jiaozi.*"

A laugh escapes me. "They were my Marco Polo–Genghis Khan fusion ravioli," I protest. "And I didn't exactly envision them being eaten with soy sauce and chili oil."

"What was in them exactly?"

"Cheese," I admit. "And spinach."

"Chinese people don't really . . . like cheese, you know."

"Are you saying you didn't like them?"

"Welllll . . ." He hedges and I giggle. "But . . ." He leans in and I catch his green grassy scent. "I really like you, Li Jia. *Wo juede ni hen xing gan.* I think you're really sexy."

"Really?" My voice rises with surprise. "We barely know each other. I mean, I don't even know what you do."

"Do?"

"For a job. What do you do?"

He seems startled. "I thought Geraldine told you. I'm like a . . . *zenme shuo? Liuxingge.* Pop star."

I giggle again. "You're joking, right?"

"Noooo . . . not joking. I'm a singer-songwriter. I perform in Chinese."

"Are you famous?"

"Among a certain set of thirteen-year-old girls."

"Well I guess it explains your hair," I say, trying to hide my astonishment.

"You don't like my hair?" He runs a hand through the bleached mop, causing strands to stand on end. "I really like your hair," he whispers, leaning in to tuck a wisp behind my ear.

"Really? I think—"

He stops me with a kiss, his full lips soft and urgent. My stomach flutters with nerves, but he tastes sweet and fresh, like mint mixed with vanilla. After a while he pulls away and strokes my back.

"I thought you were here with Tina," I say.

"We're just friends." He moves his hand to caress my cheek.

"But—"

"Shhhhh." He leans in to kiss me once more, and I feel myself relax into his muscled chest. I'm not sure how long we sit there before I hear the living room doors open and close with a soft thump.

Jeff and I jump apart with guilty haste, but we're too late. Tina Chang stands in front of us, her face frozen in shock.

"I thought you didn't know each other!" she shrieks.

"I thought we had broken up," says Jeff coolly.

Her face flushes as she runs out of the room and slams the door behind her.

"Where were we?" Jeff murmurs, running a hand up my thigh.

But Tina's brief appearance has squelched the romantic atmosphere like baking soda on a grease fire. My heart is pounding so hard I'm afraid it's going to tear my chest open and leap halfway across the room. If anything happens to the Max Zhang story, Ed will fire me. And kill me. In that order. I shake Jeff's hand away and push myself off the couch. "It's late. I better get home."

"Oh, don't go, baby." He purses his lips together in a pout. "You're so groovy."

Despite my panic, I laugh. "I have to work tomorrow. And maybe you should find Tina. She looked pretty upset."

He grabs my hand and plays with my fingers. "Let me help you find a cab."

"I'm okay." The wine and warm summer evening have combined to give me a throbbing headache, and I can't wait to escape to the cool, dark silence of my bedroom. "Thanks, though, for a, um, memorable evening."

"Let's go out again this week. I'll call you." He pulls me down to kiss my cheek but doesn't get up from the couch as I leave the room.

Shanxi

"Shansi and Shensi in the central west are a sort of Chinese England, characterized by thrift, hard work, industrial development, and solid but stolid fare that merits little comment here."

—E. N. ANDERSON, *THE FOOD OF CHINA*

It's past midnight by the time I get home, but despite my headache, I'm too jittery to sleep. My encounter with Jeff has left me feeling unsettled, like the most popular boy at school finally asked me to dance, only to abandon me midway through the song. And then there's Tina. Recalling the deep flush of her face when she saw Jeff and me together makes my mind race with worry. What if Tina kills the story on Max Zhang? Geraldine would be so disappointed, and as for Ed . . . yikes. Ed might actually implode.

I perch at the desk in my room, turn on my laptop computer and bask in its electronic glow. My hands hesitate over the keyboard before I log in and compose an e-mail to the other side of the world.

To: Julia Steele
From: Isabelle Lee
Subject: Beijing Blues

Dear Jules—

Hello from your errant Beijing pen pal . . . Sorry it's been
so long since my last message. Work has been insane—lots of
extreme eating. It hasn't gotten as bad as bull's penis kebabs,
but last week's sheep's brain soup made me think of you,
especially when I tried to hide a chunk in a bowl of rice (didn't
work—my Mongolian host saw me and launched into a soliloquy
about how Westerners need to have their palates "educated").
Claire is still maintaining her Lady Di impersonation—darling
this, sweetie that, air kiss–air kiss. I can't figure out if it's an act,
or if some English-accented alien has taken over her body.

As for my love life . . . I haven't heard a peep from the
Diplomat since he fled our date a few weeks ago. Instead,
I've been hanging with a friend of Geraldine's, a (don't laugh)
Chinese B-list pop star with a minor teenybopper fan base. I
think he likes me, but then again he might just have some sort
of American fetish—he keeps asking me about *Sex and the
City*. I don't know . . . might be fun for a fling, but he's not really
my type . . . Dating in Beijing seems as complicated as it is in
New York with the added disadvantage of a language barrier. It
wasn't a mistake for me to move here, was it?

xxx Iz

I pause for a second and hit Send. Julia is no more than a
mouse click away, but the twelve-hour time difference makes
phone calls impractical and I miss hearing her voice. Instead, we
write messages while the other sleeps. She sends me pictures of
the baby and gossipy news about publishing, but it doesn't compare to living only eight blocks away from her.

I push my chair away from the desk and head into the
kitchen, where I pour myself a glass of water and stare out the
window. The Third Ring Road streaks by our apartment, lined

with colored lights and, even at this hour, whizzing with traffic, like a highway to the future. From twenty floors above, I watch a stream of cars zoom by a giant billboard that's emblazoned with enormous Chinese characters. I've stared at the ad for weeks now but still don't know what it says. Now, I try to puzzle out the words again, one by one, each inscrutable character a reminder that the ad is targeting someone else, that I am an outsider.

I thought moving to Beijing would make my troubles disappear, but in the harsh, neon light of the capital, that hope seems childish. Instead, I seem to have traded one set of problems for another. My career is still at a standstill. My mother still disapproves of my job, my hair, my lack of a boyfriend. I'm still single—in fact, men now actually flee from their dates with me. Instead of making new friends, I think I've made an enemy. And, despite our physical proximity, my sister still feels like a stranger. I lean against the windowpane, allowing the iciness of its smooth surface to cool my throbbing forehead. Below me the unending traffic flows, each burst of light a mocking twinkle.

When I check my e-mail the next morning, Julia's reply is at the top of my in-box.

To: Isabelle Lee
From: Julia Steele
Subject: Don't be ridiculous

Izzie, Iz—

Guess who I ran into yesterday at Michael's? None other than that slimy bastard ex of yours, Richard White. He was out with his new girlfriend, some 22-year-old with mousy hair and a "passion for books." You know the type. It turns out they met when she interviewed to be his assistant! Please don't be upset.

You are not allowed to be in love with someone who uses
Human Resources as a dating service.

Beijing sounds brilliant! It was definitely NOT a mistake
and you know it. Take a cue from your sister and STOP
overanalyzing as usual and START having fun. Kick up your
heels! Put ON some heels! And be sure to fill me in on all the
juicy details.

Love,

Jules

My heart sinks. Richard already has a new girlfriend? I didn't
expect him to stay single for long, but a part of me was hoping
he'd pine after me. That he'd miss me so much he'd follow me to
Beijing. Which is ridiculous, because the most interest Richard
ever showed in China was his weekly take-out order for sweet
and sour pork, which he ate with a knife and fork. The thought
of him perched at his kitchen table, daintily cutting bites of pork
and scooping up the cloying sauce with pork fried rice, makes
me laugh. I've been too busy to think about him for weeks, I realize, with a deep breath that clears my lungs and brushes away a
margin of doubt.

Julia is absolutely right. I can't sit around waiting for Prince
Charming to come along. I should get out there, put on some
heels, put on some makeup, for God's sake. I peer at my face in
the mirror. Living in Beijing has made me lazy—after all, scruffy
jeans and a pilled sweater look like couture when your neighbors are strolling the block in their pajamas. But today I'll make
an effort, I vow, pulling out a black skirt and unearthing a pair
of knee-high suede boots. Today I'll wear mascara and lipstick,
squeeze into tights, and pretend I care about the way I look. Like
in New York. Before Richard dumped me.

And behind the plan for self-improvement is the unspoken

hope that if I try a little harder, perhaps Jeff will call. And, I know, I know, I'm not really interested, but I have to admit it boosted my ego to have the attention of one of China's smoothest pop sensations. (I admit it—I Googled him.)

I perch on the edge of my bed and start rolling up my last pair of unladdered black tights. Beijing is halfway around the world from New York. Maybe my Beijing dating style should be 180 degrees from my New York approach. More honest, less inscrutable. More carefree, less crafty. More casual fling, and less man-of-my-dreams. Maybe I should call him.

Except, what would I say?

I stand in front of the mirror and practice holding my cell phone to my ear. "Hi, Jeff." Good tone. Friendly, casual, not desperate. "Hi, Jeff," I repeat. Er. What next?

"Iz?" Claire pops her head into my room. "Do you want a lift to work?" She sees me with the phone clutched to my ear and stops. "Oh, sorry, I didn't know you were on the phone," she whispers, backing out of the door.

"Wait!" I exclaim, my cheeks tingling. I can't believe she caught me rehearsing a phone call in front of the mirror. It's so geeky, I'm tempted to pretend I'm actually in the middle of a phone call. On the other hand, I can't resist a ride to work in Claire's clean car, versus screeching around corners in another smoke-filled taxi death trap. I reluctantly lower the mobile from my ear. "I'm not on the phone," I confess.

"Darling, what on earth are you doing?"

"Practicing," I mumble.

"Practicing? Practicing what?"

I wildly try to think up an excuse but come up with . . . nothing. "Practicing calling someone."

"Who?" A teasing grin spreads across her face. "A *boy*?"

"Yeah."

"Well, get your stuff together. I'll help you figure out what to say in the car."

Wait a second. Claire is going to help me? *Claire?* The girl who didn't go out on her first date until after law school, and even that was set up by my mother?

"But—you don't—" I bite back the words.

She pauses with one arm in her suit jacket. "What." She fixes me with a challenging stare.

"You don't know how much I appreciate this," I say in a rush.

In the car, Claire issues advice while simultaneously checking her BlackBerry, scanning the newspaper, and smoothing on another coat of lipstick. "Just be casual," she says, her voice as instructive as Dear Abby. "Men don't like it when women are too aggressive. Especially Chinese guys."

"Should I ask him out for a drink?"

"Depends. Is he Chinese or foreign? Chinese guys think good girls don't drink. They like women to be ladylike."

"But I do. Like to drink, that is. I don't want to pretend to be someone I'm not." Like you, I think.

"I'm just trying to help you." She shrugs. "Cross-cultural dating is hard. When Wang Wei first asked me out, I turned him down flat just because he's married. But he kept calling and texting until I finally agreed to have coffee. And what can I say? He swept me off my feet!" She giggles a little self-consciously.

My eyes widen. "Wang Wei is *married*?" I gasp. But as soon as the words leave my mouth, they start to make sense. So that explains Claire's secrecy, why she hasn't yet introduced me to him.

"Oh, don't be such a prissy American, Iz." She rolls her eyes. "He's been trapped in a loveless marriage for years. His wife lives in Shanghai with some Italian guy and everyone knows it." She crosses her arms and lifts her chin, as if daring me to disapprove.

I hesitate. I want to grab her slim shoulders and pelt her with questions, but I know she'd only interpret them as criticism. I ask her instead, "Claire, are you sure you're okay . . . ?" The words hang in the air.

For a second her mouth tenses into a thin line. But then that smooth mask descends again and she brushes away an invisible speck of lint from her lapel. "I'm fine," she says a little too brightly. "Anyway, who's the lucky guy? Do I know him? Is it Charlie?"

Is she changing the subject? And how did she know about Charlie? "Um . . . " I'm not sure what to say.

"What?" She laughs at my confusion. "You think I didn't know you and Charlie went on a date together? I ran into him in the lobby a few days ago and he told me how sorry he was to cut it short." She nudges me with her elbow. "I think he really likes you. He couldn't stop asking about you."

"Really?" I can't stop the corners of my mouth from creeping up. "What did he say?"

She ignores me. "Did he call and ask you out again?"

"Uh . . . no . . . "

"Well, then you definitely shouldn't call him!" She looks shocked. "Never, ever pursue a man. Ever. That's one of the first rules of dating."

"Is Charlie dating anyone right now?" I ask as casually as I can.

"Hmmm? I don't think so. Not for lack of opportunity, of course. But the guy's practically married to his job." She twists her mouth to one side. "Now, let's see . . . how could we get you two together again . . . Ooh, I know! Kristin is having a party on Saturday. Charlie will probably be there."

Kristin was the supercilious blonde who worked with Charlie. I'm pretty sure I have no desire to ever see her again. "I think I'm busy next weekend," I hedge.

"Honestly, Iz. I don't know how you're ever going to meet

someone if you just hide in your room all the time," Claire exclaims crossly. "You really need to—"

"Anyway, I was talking about Jeff. Jeff Zhu," I break in before she dispenses more Claire Lee Dating Advice 101 (which, come to think of it, sounds suspiciously like *The Rules*).

"Jeff!" She looks surprised. "Oh! He's a cutie. But be careful. He has this crazy, completely bonkers—"

"I've heard all about Tina," I insert. "Don't worry."

"When it comes to Jeff, Tina is nuts," Claire admits, as her driver slides to a stop in front of her office building. "But I was going to say, he has a crazy problem with commitment." She climbs gracefully out of the car. "Well, I must fly. Big kiss, darling. Mwah. And good luck. Byeee!" With a trill of her signature farewell, she is gone. I stare at her slim back as she walks briskly into her building and can't help but worry.

Now, I sneak into the hallway at work to see if it's empty. Our open-plan office makes private phone calls impossible, which means there's usually someone in the hall whispering furiously into their cell. A swath of open space means the coast is clear. Well, here goes. Taking a deep breath, I whip out my phone and quickly punch in Jeff's number, shifting my weight from one foot to the other as it rings and rings. Finally, he answers, *"Wei?"*

"Hi, Jeff? It's Isabelle, uh, I mean, Li Jia. Listen, I hadn't heard from you . . . er, I mean, I was just wondering if you might be free sometime this week for a drink." I consider Claire's advice and add: "Or coffee. Or, er, ice cream. You know, to get together. Sometime this week," I finish lamely. So much for my casual, friendly, confident tone.

"Iz—Li Jia! Can you hold on a second?" There's a rustling sound, as if he's covered the receiver with his hand, and I hear muffled voices in the background. He returns a moment later. "Sorry about that." His voice is crisp. "So, you'd like to meet this week? I'm fairly booked, but I could manage say . . . Thursday at four P.M.?"

"Okaaayyy . . . " I shuffle the floor in confusion. "Well, that's not so good for me, because I have to, you know, work."

"Let me call you back," he says. Then, to someone else: "Okay, okay. I *said* okay!" Back to me: "I'll have my assistant call you back."

"Your assistant?" Are we setting up a business meeting? I feel embarrassment creep through me. Perhaps I've misread the entire situation.

Suddenly, there's a loud crackling sound, sounds of a struggle, as if the phone is being wrestled away from him. "Hello?" I say.

"Hello?" says a shrill female voice. "Who is this?" it demands.

"Isabelle Lee," I say faintly. I'm not sure why I give my name, but something tells me the voice on the other side won't rest without it.

"I knew it!" says the voice. "You bastard!"

"Tina," I hear Jeff's voice pleading. *"Mei shi."* It's nothing.

She screeches into the phone: "I'm going to teach you a lesson, Isabelle Lee. You think you can move here and swoop in, and steal all our Beijing men? I don't give a fuck about you. Welcome to my bad side, Isabelle."

I remove the phone from my ear and stare at it in disbelief as she continues screaming. Who talks likes this? Tina has obviously been watching too much daytime TV. I can't help it. A giggle escapes from my lips.

"Are you *laughing* at me?" she shrieks.

"Tina, Tee-nah." Jeff's voice carries a placating tone. "That's enough. Please, honey, stop."

Beep-beep-beep. The call is ended.

I stare into space, my brow wrinkled with confusion. That

certainly didn't go according to plan. Are they together, or not? I'm not sure what's going on, but I do know this: I've finally met a real, live Wicked Witch of the East.

I don't tell Geraldine about my conversation with Tina—why worry her?—though I can see her pupils dilate with fear when I inform her that Jeff and I are going out on Thursday.

Oh, yes. He called back an hour later, with total silence in the background, apologized profusely, and asked if I wanted to grab a bite to eat on Thursday night. Actually, the phrase he used was "grab a mouth to eat," but I didn't have the heart to correct him.

The stodgy New York me would have said no, but the new, insouciant Beijing me said *yes*. I still don't have any real answers about the Tina situation ("I swear to you, we're not together anymore," he'd said) but who cares? We're having dinner, not eloping.

At my desk, I gaze dreamily at the computer, remembering Jeff's dark eyes and soft lips, the intensity of our kiss. Mmmm . . . I picture us sipping cosmopolitans at Suzie Wong's . . . Maybe he'll introduce me to some of his celebrity friends—Faye Wong and Jet Li and, er . . . I'm drawing a blank on other Chinese celebrities . . . Well, whoever is famous in Beijing, anyway.

"Isabelle, Geraldine. I want to see you in my office. *Now*." Ed's florid face looms suddenly over my desk, chasing away my daydreams. He jabs a finger at me before turning and stomping away. Uh-oh. Is something wrong? I tally the possible offenses but the list adds up to zero. I shoot Geraldine a puzzled glance and together we creep toward Ed's office.

Inside, Ed kicks the door shut. "Look," he says. "I don't know who pissed off Tina Chang, but we have a big problem."

"What? Why?" Geraldine's voice rises in alarm.

I shift uncomfortably in my chair.

"She just called to say Topanga Films will not allow Geraldine on the set of *Iron into Gold*," says Ed. "Apparently Max Zhang didn't like your snide comments about *The East Is Red*." He peers at her. "When did you write about *The East Is Red*?"

"I have no idea," Geraldine says slowly. "Unless it was a short description for a listing. That movie came out five years ago. And who cares what I think? It won an Oscar!"

"Tina also said that they'd be happy to accommodate someone else on the set. We all know she loathes Gab, so that leaves . . . Isabelle." They both turn to look at me. "What the fuck is going on here?" says Ed.

"I—I—" I can only stutter in confusion.

"Does this have something to do with Jeff?" asks Geraldine, her eyes narrowed. "Is she *that* crazy?"

"Who is Jeff? Does he work at Topanga?" demands Ed.

"Jeff is . . . this guy . . . " I feel my face growing warm.

"Tina's ex who now fancies Isabelle." Geraldine crosses her arms and turns to me. "I *told* you to be careful."

"I'm hardly interested in Isabelle's love life," snaps Ed. "So what if you're on her shit list? Why would she suddenly want you to have a shot at a *Beijing NOW* cover story?"

"Who knows?" Geraldine shakes her head. "But knowing Tina . . . I'm sure she has some kind of Machiavellian plan up her sleeve."

"It's no use speculating." Ed sighs. "Isabelle, pack your bags—looks like you're going to Pingyao."

"But this is Geraldine's story," I protest.

"I don't think you understand, Isabelle." Ed leans over his desk and I can see a vein throb in his forehead. "We need this story. So get to work. And don't fuck this up. Your ass is on the line. This time I mean it." He turns to his computer screen.

"I'll forward you information on the guest house and how to get to the set," says Geraldine as we leave his office. "The bus leaves at eight A.M. tomorrow."

"I'm really sorry about this."

"It's not your fault, Iz." She squeezes my shoulder. "To be honest, I don't envy your time with Tina."

My laugh sounds hollow, even to my ears.

I've backpacked in the Adirondacks, driven across the U.S., flown across the Pacific, but I've never traveled like this before, with a chicken squashed at my feet. I'm on my way to Pingyao in a bus that's packed to the aisles, and though I'm lucky enough to have snagged a seat, it's impossible to relax amid the roar of voices and acrid smell of fresh cigarette smoke.

Beside me sits the chicken's owner, a stocky woman with round cheeks and a wide, gap-toothed smile. We've exchanged a few polite words about the chicken—its fate is sealed upon arrival—but her thick Shanxi accent means I have to strain to understand her. Miraculously, she thinks I am some sort of slick Beijing city girl and has not questioned my accent or broken grammar. I'm not sure how I could explain to her that I am American.

I sigh and think back to this morning. After waiting all night for the alarm to ring, I overslept by almost an hour and awakened with a racing heart and no time to shower. I snatched at my clothes—yesterday's jeans, lying crumpled on the floor, a clean T-shirt—zipped up a hooded sweatshirt, and ran out of the apartment. When the elevator finally arrived, it was packed. I squeezed myself inside, pulling my overstuffed backpack to one side and hitting someone in the chest.

"Oh, sorry," I apologized, glancing behind me and finding Charlie's calm, blue eyes.

"Isabelle! How are you?" His smile changed his whole face, erasing the worried crease in his brow.

"Hi!" I tried to inject some enthusiasm into my voice. Why did I have to run into him this morning? Why? After all those times I put on lipstick just to take out the trash, I had to run into him now? "When did you get back from the States?" I bit back the question hovering on my lips: Why didn't you call me?

"A couple of days ago," he said. "Listen, work has been crazy but—" He hesitated, looking into the elevator's mirrored doors, at the reflected faces of the other passengers, all listening intently to our conversation, and pressed his lips together. We descended the remaining eighteen floors in silence.

At the lobby, everyone streamed out of the elevator and Charlie paused by the revolving doors. "Isabelle, I want to apologize for not calling," he said slowly. "But things have been really busy at the embassy . . . The situation with North Korea is crazy and . . . " He continued, but it all just sounded like a bunch of weak excuses. How could anyone be so busy they couldn't spare five minutes for a phone call? "Nuclear crisis . . . Six Party Talks . . . uranium enrichment . . . " continued Charlie, worry clouding his eyes. "But I don't want to bore you with the details—"

"It's okay," I broke in, before he could create any more excuses. He obviously found lying disconcerting; his entire forehead was crumpled into a deep furrow. "I understand, you're busy." I shrugged. "And if the choice was between calling me and saving the world from nuclear destruction, you definitely made the right decision!" I barked a short laugh and patted him on the shoulder in what I hoped was a friendly gesture devoid of romance.

"I, it's not like that—" He stopped when I glanced at my watch. "Do you have to be somewhere?" he asked.

"Oh my God, the bus! Taiyuan!" I gasped, my heart suddenly

dropping to my knees. Running into Charlie had momentarily made me forget about my tardiness. But if I missed the bus, I was toast; Ed would fire me, for sure. Through the lobby's plate-glass window, I scanned the street for a taxi, while trying to push Ed's wrath from my mind. "Oh my God, no cabs, no cabs. If I miss the bus, Ed will kill me . . . "

He lay a calm hand on my shoulder. "My car is outside. I could take you to the station."

"You?" My voice rose in disbelief. "Aren't you busy? Don't you have to be at work?"

"I think I can show up late for once."

I followed him outside, and climbed into the backseat of his black sedan, relief causing my annoyance to evaporate. "But won't your boss get mad at you?" I ask. "Isn't the ambassador incredibly demanding?"

"That's what people say," he said wearily.

The driver raced in a special, speedy (e.g., terrifying) manner to the station, but Charlie and I were so busy discussing Max Zhang's filmography, I scarcely noticed the close brushes with oncoming traffic.

"He's such a legend of Chinese film. I can't believe you get to meet him," he kept saying. "Your job is so cool. The only other person I know who gets to meet celebrities is my little sister. She's a makeup artist."

"Your sister?"

"She lives in L.A., works in the film industry. You remind me of her, actually. She's really funny and loves crossword puzzles too."

Hmph. His sister. As the car hurtled along the break-down lane, everything became clear. Obviously, I misread the situation; Charlie's not interested in me romantically. No wonder he never called—he sees me as some sort of surrogate little sister.

I tried to hide my mortification by rifling through my backpack. Happily, the bus station came into view.

"Looks like we're here!" I zipped up my bag. "Thanks again for the ride."

"You're welcome." He leaned forward to help me lift my bag. "When are you getting back from Pingyao? I'm going to Pyongyang next week, but maybe we could get together after that? I think they're still renting boats on Houhai before the lake freezes."

And will the boat ride include a lollipop and a pat on the head? With effort, I swallowed my sarcasm. "That's okay," I said instead. "I'll probably be pretty busy when I get back, closing the magazine."

"Oh! Okay." Again Charlie's brow furrowed.

"But thanks for the ride! I really appreciate it!" I forced a cheerful note into my voice, grabbed my bags and leapt out of the car, running toward the entrance. By the time I reached the ticket counter, I had banished Charlie to the back of my mind.

I hurled myself onto the bus to Taiyuan, a large German wide-load with air-conditioning and doily-covered seats, which lumbered off with a huff of exhaust as soon as I had settled myself. At Taiyuan, I switched buses, going from grand to grungy. The bus to Pingyao has forgone luxuries like shocks and power steering. We jolt along the rough road, the horn blaring continuously, careening left to pass slow trucks carrying loads of mud-smeared pigs or heaps of coal lumps, careening right to avoid the trucks that threaten head-on collision. I watch the girl in front of me, a tiny creature with sallow skin, open the window and quietly retch down the side of the bus. I rake my greasy hair into a ponytail, gaze at the chicken as it presses its long plume of tail feathers against the wicker cage, and promise myself a long hot shower upon arrival.

Tina meets me at the station, and my heart thumps at the

thought of confrontation, but she seems cheerful and chatty. Her sharp-toed boots clatter on the pavement as we walk to the car, and she helpfully hefts my bag into the trunk. We sit side by side in the backseat and wait for the driver to finish his cigarette.

"Thanks for coming to get me, Tina."

"*Mei shi*. It's no problem." Her eyes avoid mine, but her voice is solicitous and I begin to relax. Maybe she's not angry. Maybe it was all a big misunderstanding.

Encouraged, I take a deep breath and attempt to clear the air. "Listen, Tina . . . I just wanted to tell you that I'm sorry—" I break off as she turns her head toward me and blinks.

"Are you tired?" she asks.

"Er, I am a little tired," I admit, confused. Clearly she doesn't want to discuss Jeff, and so I follow her cue. "Are we going straight to the guest house? I'd love a hot shower."

"Actually," she flicks a sidelong glance at me from beneath her lashes, "there's been a change in plans. We had some last minute housing changes and had to move you. But don't worry." She pats my arm. "We found you another spot."

"Where?" Something in her tone seems odd. I cross my arms, suddenly wary.

"Well, I thought you might want to experience the real Pingyao. One of the sound guys knows a local family and they've invited you to stay with them. Won't that be fun?" Her laugh is brittle, like glass shattering against granite.

I stare at her with alarm. The idea of staying with strangers, of imposing myself in their modest home, is unthinkable. "If it's possible, Tina," I keep my voice smooth, "I'd prefer to find another guest house."

"Unfortunately . . . " She shrugs, and I get the feeling she's enjoying herself. "Did I mention the International Photography Festival is going on right now? Everything else is booked."

Pingyao is quaint and shabby, like a miniature village that's been forgotten for a hundred years. Ancient walls surround the center, and low buildings poke their dainty eaves and peaked tile roofs up from narrow streets. The Shi family lives on a dusty lane not far from the main drag. Cars are banned inside the town walls and so we walk the final stretch, yellow dust settling on the cuffs of my jeans and over the toes of my running shoes.

We head down Xi Dajie, a semipaved street that runs through the heart of Pingyao. I read in my guidebook that centuries of poverty inadvertently preserved the town's Ming dynasty features; indeed, it seems almost forgotten by time, with red lanterns swinging from tiled roofs, the buildings low and capped with pointed eaves, the streets narrow. We weave our way among crowds of tourists, passing small shops selling cigarettes, postcards, and other tourist kitsch, before turning into a narrow alley. Tina stops at the crumbling gate of a courtyard home, identical to the others on the block, and the Shis tumble out to greet us, all four of them: grandmother, mother, father, and baby, whose split pants flash open to reveal that she's a girl. I sneak a glance at Tina and see she's arranged her features into an innocent expression. *"Ni hao!"* she calls out, her voice pitched silkily high, the way Chinese people think young ladies should sound.

Tina introduces me as "Li Jia, *nimen de waiguo pengyou.*" Your foreign friend. Mr. Shi rushes forward to shake my hand, a stream of *"Ni hao, ni hao, ni hao,"* flowing through the smile that broadens his weathered face. His wife, Wangmei, stands next to me, her strong hand patting my shoulder in a rhythmic beat. I turn to greet the grandmother, an older woman with cropped gray hair and proud posture, who holds a plump-cheeked baby in her arms. Her sharp eyes scan my face intently as she stretches out a leathered hand to touch my cheek. Forty years ago these people would have been proud to be called peasants. Now they are considered rough and rural, although unlike most country folk—who are suspicious of outsiders—their faces are open and friendly.

I call the younger woman *"ayi,"* or aunt, the grandmother *"nainai,"* the man *"shushu,"* or uncle, as if they are my own family. These are terms of respect in China and, after several months here, they roll off my tongue. It's difficult to determine their ages—their lined faces belie their youth, though not the bitterness of life. The baby is introduced as Baobei—I later find out that's not her real name, but a nickname meaning "precious treasure." She opens her mouth to emit a hungry wail and Nainai bounces her inside, the rest of us trailing behind her.

The rest of us, I should say, except for Tina, who seizes the opportunity to whisk herself away. "'Bye," she says, squeezing my arm so that the duffel bag slips off my shoulder and jars my elbow. "Meet the driver at the train station tomorrow at eight A.M. He'll bring you to the set." She gives a small wave and disappears around the corner, leaving me alone.

Nine-thirty P.M. Ohmigod, ohmigod, ohmigod. I'm wide-awake, my eyes round as gum balls. Next door, the Shis slumber. I can hear the measured rise and fall of their breathing through the house's thin walls. I already have to pee. How will I make it through the night?

Going to the bathroom is out of the question. Going to the bathroom would require putting on my shoes and finding a flashlight, making my way outside and down the dark street to the public toilet, where I would have to squat over a rotting plank, my stomach churning from the smell. No, I can't. I can face it during the day, but at night it's too terrifying. For the first time in my life I wish for a bedpan.

And something else is keeping me awake. Something that, with shortness of breath and an ache in the back of my throat, feels a lot like fear. I've never interviewed a Hollywood director before—hell, six months ago I had never interviewed *anyone*. My stomach heaves—and I'm pretty sure it's not from drinking unclean water. Even though I've watched all of Max Zhang's movies and read every scrap ever written about him (in English), a doubtful chill keeps creeping down my spine. I'm not sure my Chinese is good enough. I'm not sure if *I'm* good enough.

Turning on my side, I try to distract myself by mulling over my evening at the Shis' house. Ayi and I spent the evening in an elaborate dance of politeness: she kept trying to offer me things—food, fruit, tea, her bedroom—and I kept trying to refuse them. She won. She insisted that I sleep in her bed, her tone so vehement I feared she might burst a blood vessel. Now, she and Shushu lie tucked up on the concrete living room floor, their aged backs reclining against the unforgiving surface, while I lounge like a princess in their bed. Add guilt to the list of emotions that chase each other in my head.

At dinner, Ayi sat next to me, maintaining a towering heap of food on my plate. As the honored guest, I was treated to the fattiest morsels of cured sausage, while the dishes of vegetables—inexpensive, and thus ordinary—were kept far from my eager chopsticks. Bowls of *mao er dou*—cat's ear noodles shaped like pointed orrechiette—were mixed with scrambled egg and tomato, seasoned with sugar (because tomatoes are a fruit, after all), and doused with the region's famous black vinegar. Plates of sliced cucumber and tart, stir-fried shredded cabbage rounded out the simple meal.

I politely swallowed slice after slice of fatty meat and finished my bowl of noodles, until my stomach felt ready to explode. As soon as I had slurped up the last bite, Ayi snatched my bowl away and scooped in another helping, my exclamations of *"Chi baole!"* (I'm full!) falling on deaf ears. Afraid of offending her, I forced down the second bowl. When she refilled my bowl a third time, I thought I might burst from her kindness.

After dinner, Ayi and I watched Xiao Baobei toddle between the broken appliances and rusted bicycles that littered the small courtyard. The baby was actually her granddaughter, the child of her only son, Ayi revealed, holding his photo between tobacco-stained fingers. He's gone to Beijing to seek construction work, she explained. His wife lives with him and takes care of foreigners' kids. They send money home once a month. In the picture, a young man with rumpled hair stares out unsmiling, his jaw jutting forward in defiance.

Neighbors stopped to say hello, most eyeing me with undisguised curiosity. Though this courtyard home was built for a single family, the Shis share it with three other households, each living in one of the four buildings that border the square, central space. Running water spouts from a corroded tap, but bathing happens at the public shower down the street. To me, the lack of privacy is a gnawing discomfort—even the toilet stalls lack doors—but everyone else accepts it.

In Beijing, the explosion of new buildings and fleets of shiny Audis make it easy to forget about China's poverty. But in this rural village, *ayi, shushu, nainai,* and their neighbors still clearly struggle to find food and clean water. It occurs to me that they're among the lucky; thanks to a steady flow of tourist income, Pingyao is less impoverished than most. I shut my eyes and try to imagine my grandparents, my father's parents, Cantonese farmers who emigrated to California in 1925. They died before I was born, taking with them all traces of their former life. I'll never know if their Guangdong village was anything like this.

Sleep comes in the early hours of the morning and is brief. I am awakened by the sound of a rooster calling roo roo rooooooooo! I saw him clucking about the courtyard yesterday, his tail feathers bristling as he pecked circles around Baobei's fat toes. Outside, the sky looks milky gray, with clouds blanketing the surface. I climb out of bed and struggle into my jeans, which are fast becoming greasily soft with overwearing. With light filling the sky, I am finally brave (or desperate) enough to visit the bathroom.

Despite the early hour, the family is already awake. As I slip out of the house, I see Ayi hunched over the dining table, the day's chores already started. Her hands blur as she skillfully rolls and presses dough into oat's ear noodles. "Good morning!" she calls out to me, waving a hand covered in flour.

In the morning chill, the bathroom seems more manageable and, thus emboldened, I vow to visit the public shower. I *need* to take a shower; my hair clings to my head like an oil slick. I walk quickly back to the Shis to gather my things, breathing in the heavy, smoky scent of coal that fills the air. In, out, in, out, the deep, calming breaths fill my lungs and a light vibration makes my leg tremble. Who is calling me at 6:30 A.M.? The name lights up the screen: JEFF.

"Hey there, you're up early!" A smile creeps across my face.

"Early? You mean late. I haven't gone to bed yet, babe. Where are you? You didn't answer my e-mail." His voice is husky with cigarettes and something else—desire?

"I told you . . . I'm in Pingyao. With Tina." My trip to Pingyao means I had to cancel our date, something I'm sure Tina planned.

"Ohhh yeahhhh." Is that a touch of anxiety in his voice? "How's it going?"

I take a deep breath, ready to complain about the Shis' primitive home, the smelliness of the toilet, Tina's suspiciously solicitous manner, but instead I let it out. "Everything's fine," I say.

"I wanted to see you last night," he says sulkily.

"I'm really sorry. But I'll be back Friday." I find myself using a wheedling tone, as if I'm talking to a child.

"That's so far away! I need to see you, Li Jia."

"Friday."

On the other end of the phone I hear a rising squeal of voices and then a whoosh as if Jeff has covered the mouthpiece with his hand. "Hello?" I say. "Hello?"

"That sounds great, babe," he says, suddenly distracted. "Look, I really need to crash, so I'll call you later, okay?"

"Sure. I'll talk to you later—" I hear the series of beeps, which mean he's ended the call. "'Bye," I say, but no one hears me.

Back at the Shis', breakfast postpones my shower. We sit down at the wobbly dining table to another bowl of short noodles mixed with scrambled egg and tomato. The meal is almost identical to last night's, featuring the same drizzle of dark vinegar, the same liberal sprinkling of cilantro, the same hurried movements that carry our food from bowl to mouth. We shovel the food in swiftly, with only the slurp of noodles and clink of plastic chopsticks on chipped plates punctuating the silence. This, then, is eating for sustenance, with every mouthful chewed, swallowed, and untasted. As I dig into my second bowl (Ayi insisted), it occurs to me that they have probably been eating this same meal for months. I ask about the local produce and am not surprised to hear Ayi say, "Tomato season is almost over. Soon it'll be only cabbage."

Well, I tried. I really, really tried. Determined to vanquish any CAP (Chinese American Princess) behavior, I gathered my resolve and a towel, marched to the public shower, paid my two *kuai* and tried to ignore the wet smell of mildew within. Clutching my towel around my body, I started to undress, awkwardly wriggling out of my T-shirt and storing it on the hook. The shower, a communal space with one nozzle, featured billows of steam and a light carpet of green algae, and my toes curled as I considered my lack of shower-friendly footwear. I stood there in my lace-edged bra, willing myself to strip and jump in, and began to feel the stares.

In Beijing my Chinese appearance means that I can pass as a local, as long as I keep my mouth shut. Here in this tiny village that's as close knit as a cable sweater, I am a stranger, an oddity, a welcome diversion from the unyielding stretches of monotony. The gaggle of women in the shower stood scrubbing themselves with quick movements and staring at me, their curiosity as naked as their aged bodies.

"It's that foreigner who's staying with the Shi family," said one, not bothering to lower her voice. "I heard she doesn't speak a word of Chinese."

"Is she Japanese?" someone hissed.

"No, I think she's Korean."

"She's too fat to be Korean."

Their cackles bounced off the tiled walls as I shoved the T-shirt back over my head and ran from the building.

Now, my stomach churns as the driver zooms along the rough roads, one hand on his cell phone, one hand on the wheel. I've scraped my hair back into a slippery ponytail but it still feels ready to crawl off my head. I smooth the trousers of my pale gray suit and pull down the soft cuffs of my cashmere sweater. I'll soon be able to give Gab tips on growing dreadlocks, but at least my clothes are clean and well-tailored. The driver swerves, narrowing the gap between our car and the oncoming traffic, and

I dig my nails into my wrist to distract myself from the nausea. I get out my cell phone to call Geraldine, but here, deep in the Shanxi countryside, the signal has faded.

Tina greets me with a face full of solicitous concern. "How's it going with the Shi family? Did you sleep well? Are you hungry?" she coos.

I brush her off and sweep out of the car, my sharp heels immediately sinking into a patch of sticky mud. Tina looks at me in amusement. "Didn't my assistant call you?" she asks. "We've had terrible weather and the mud out here is awful!" She lifts a foot and displays a Burberry-plaid Wellington that's delicately spattered with mud.

"I'm fine." The words barely make it through my clenched jaw. I follow Tina toward the set, my legs as shaky as a newborn gazelle, my embroidered velvet mules—a prize from the Barney's sample sale—growing more soaked with every step.

I'm shivering by the time we reach the trailer that's used as an office. "Isn't it funny how much colder it is here than in town?" chirps Tina. "You're going to need an extra layer out on the field. But don't worry, I'll find you something warm to wear."

"I bet you will," I mutter under my breath.

Tina pulls a walkie-talkie out of the back pocket of her low-cut jeans and issues a few commands. Soon I am swathed in a padded, khaki-green jacket, a replica of the military-style coats worn by Chinese security guards. A brown leather belt bundles in the waist, the sleeves fall below my fingertips, and the hem almost hides my feet, which slide around inside a scuffed pair of army boots. I catch a glimpse of myself in the mirror and choke back my horror. I look dirty and bedraggled, like I've spent the night on the ground, using my only set of clothes as a blanket.

How on earth will a famous Hollywood director ever take me seriously?

"Tina, I can't meet Max Zhang like this." I grit my teeth to keep the tears at bay.

She looks at me. "Why?"

"I look like a street urchin! Don't you have anything else?"

"This isn't Bloomingdale's, Isabelle." She snaps up her puffy silver jacket. "Besides, we don't have time. Max wants to wrap up the shoot today. You'll be lucky if we can even squeeze in your interview."

We sludge through the mud to the edge of a grassy field, the flat plain stretching for miles before breaking into rolling hills. Shanxi province features coal mines and drab countryside, and gazing into the distance, I can see why Max Zhang chose to film here; if you stare long enough at the horizon, the monotony sprawls into beauty, evoking the contrast in the film's title, *Iron into Gold*. Tina deposits me amidst a crowd of extras, who are dressed in khaki-green coats similar to mine, though, I wryly note, their clothes seem to fit. "Wait here," she instructs me. "I'll come get you after this scene wraps."

Hours later I have watched so many takes I could perform the scene as a one-woman show. The problem is not with the leads—impossibly glamorous creatures who stand about between takes smoking slender European cigarettes—but with an extra, a sharp-faced girl who keeps stuttering her single line. Max Zhang comes closer to exploding with every take, pressing his lips together in the controlled manner of one used to suffocating his frustration.

"And . . . action!" he calls out in English. Film-making terms are universal, one of the extras whispers to me. Chinese directors use "action" and "cut" (or "*ka*") even if they don't know any other English words.

The scene begins again and I follow along, unconsciously echoing every gesture and mouthing each line. The extras start milling in the field, the lovers embrace passionately, the servant girl runs in—everyone tenses—but no, she flubs her line one more time.

"*Bu dui, bu dui, bu dui!* Cut! *Ka!*" screams Max Zhang, throwing up his hands in fury.

I glance at my watch and sigh. At this rate it'll be midnight before I can sit down with him for our interview. And if I go back to Beijing empty-handed . . . I picture Ed's irate face and shudder.

"Isabelle." Tina hovers at my elbow, her forehead creased with concern. "Look, I'm really sorry about this, but it looks like we're going to have to cancel your interview."

"What?" I gasp. "Are you kidding me?"

"We're way behind already and we need to pare back the schedule. Max wants to wrap today and it's just impossible to fit you in."

"What about tomorrow?" I demand. Rage starts building in the pit of my stomach.

"Max is leaving for Hong Kong tomorrow morning. I thought you knew that," she says with a smug smile.

"Oh *really.*"

"Really."

We regard each other for a moment, and I wonder what it would be like to reach out and slap her. I can almost feel the sting on my fingertips.

"Tina." I take a deep breath and shove my hands in my pockets. "I know you have some petty grudge against me and frankly I don't care. But you cannot drag me out to Shanxi province, change my accommodations at the last minute, arrange a room that doesn't even have a bathroom, and then not grant me this interview." My voice rises but I quickly remember that to show anger in China is to lose face. "I don't think you want any negative publicity in *Beijing NOW*," I finish quietly.

She shrugs. "It's not like you're the *New York Times*."

"Tina. I am tired. I am dirty. And I am *not* going back to Beijing without this interview."

"Yes. You. Are."

"Excuse me," breaks in a voice I don't recognize, the consonants sharp with a light English accent. "But when you ladies are finished bickering, we'd like to try another take."

I glance over to see Max Zhang, his arms crossed, one eyebrow raised.

"Oh, Mr. Zhang, I'm so sorry . . . " I stammer.

"Who are you?" he demands, looking at Tina for an answer. "Who is she?" he repeats in Chinese.

"I'm a journalist," I say.

"*You're* the journalist?" He looks at me in surprise. "I thought you were helping the wrangler muck out the pig pen," he says as I shoot Tina a dirty look.

Tina bleats, "Don't worry about her, she's nobody."

Max examines my face carefully. "Hm. I need a nobody. Can you speak Chinese?"

"A little," I say, as Tina pipes up: "No!"

"I love this waif look," he muses. "It's perfect for the servant girl . . . dirty hair . . . we can add some streaks of coal dust to your face . . . yes. Yes!" He turns to his crowd of minions. "Wardrobe!" he cries out. "*Fuzhuang zu!*"

Before I know it, I am clothed in the baggy cotton clothes of a servant girl from the 1930s, my hair braided into plaits, my face streaked with dirt. The oversized coat remains. Max (he asked me to call him that) thinks it adds a Dickensian air—though the army boots have been exchanged for a pair of thin cotton slippers.

"Kuai! Zhuren zai majuan li deng ni. Ta yao zhao ni!" Come quickly! The master is in the stables. He's looking for you! I mutter the line over and over, humming the tones like it's a song. My heart hammers in my chest so ferociously I'm afraid it might explode. But there's no one I can turn to for help. The rest of the cast and crew are strangers, and Tina has stalked off in disgust. I can see her near the food service table, shouting into her cell phone.

"And . . . action!" I watch the lovers embrace and kiss, as if for the first time. The lead actress runs her slender fingers down the side of her leading man's face and sighs. Oops, that's my cue. I run in, my legs shaking. *"Kuai! Zhuren zai majuan li deng ni. Ta yao zhao ni!"* The words tumble out in a shrill screech.

"Cut!" Max walks over and places a gentle hand on my shoulder. "You're nervous," he says, and his tone is sympathetic.

I swallow. "I've just . . . never done this before."

"May I offer a word of advice?" he says. "Just lose yourself in the moment. Don't worry too much about the tones. You're a servant girl. You probably have a thick accent anyway."

I laugh shakily.

"We're ready when you are," he says.

"Okay." I take a deep breath. "I'm ready."

"And . . . action!"

This time I allow myself to shiver in the cold, and if my knees knock when I run out to the field, well, my character is probably scared witless by the imminent arrival of the master, right? I deliver my line in a breathless panic, cringing inside and waiting to hear the fateful *"Ka!"*

But for the first time today, the scene continues. The lovers embrace once more in a heaving heap of emotion, the lead actress wipes away her tears, extends her hand to me, and together we go running through the field.

"Cut!" Max beams. "Great work, everybody," he shouts in Chinese. "That's a wrap!" As the cast and crew start moving en masse to the trailers, he turns to me. "Isabelle, I can't thank you enough. I was about to throttle that poor Shanxi girl. But, because of you, we're back on schedule."

"It was my pleasure," I assure him.

"If there's anything I can ever do for you, please let me know. Really."

·"Well . . . " I shoot him a sidelong glance. "Actually, there is one thing . . . "

The rest of the day is spent hurrying to film the last scene · before dusk descends, but Max invites me to ride back to Pingyao in his car. He is surprisingly candid during the interview, opening up about his impoverished childhood in Taipei, his university years in England, his early struggles in Hollywood, his feelings on filming in China, which his parents fled before World War II.

Plus, he promises me it will be an exclusive.

Imperial

" . . . Both complicated and elaborate, and very time-consuming. Artistically sculpted food, such as abalones stuffed with minced chicken, decorated with hair moss and peas to resemble the heads of toads, is an important element. The use of expensive or rare ingredients, such as bear's paws, camel paws, and monkey head mushrooms, not to mention shark's fin and bird's nest, is yet another. A third is the penchant for aphrodisiac dishes, such as the obvious stewed deer penis and the more subtle deep-fried beavers."

—YAN-KIT SO, *CLASSIC FOOD OF CHINA*

"In the Ming dynasty, banquets often started at 11 A.M. and would last for six hours or more."

—A. ZEE, *SWALLOWING CLOUDS: A PLAYFUL JOURNEY THROUGH CHINESE CULTURE, LANGUAGE AND CUISINE*

Sitting at my desk, I scroll through the names in my cell phone, considering each one. There's Claire, but she went with me last month. Lily? Picky eater. Ed . . . not picky enough. Geraldine is detoxing with a raw foods diet. Jeff left for Shanghai right after

I returned from Pingyao, but even if he were here, he's made it clear he wants nothing to do with *Beijing NOW,* which he considers amateurish ("small peanuts," was how he described it, but I think he meant potatoes).

Honestly, I never thought it would be this hard to find people to eat out with me. Before I had this job, I would have jumped at the chance to dine with a food critic.

"It's not that I don't like you," protested Gab last week as we ate lunch together in the conference room. "I like you. I like going out to eat with you. Just not on your review dinners." He ripped the paper cover off a cup of instant noodles, releasing a cloud of steam,

But why?" I demanded. "It's a free meal."

"Only when we don't exceed the three hundred *kuai* limit," he pointed out. And it's true. *Beijing NOW*'s tiny budget means we usually end up paying most of the bill out of our own pockets. "Besides," he continued. "Eating out with you is like a tour through *Roget's Thesaurus.*"

"I had the exact same problem when I was the restaurant critic," piped up Geraldine, pushing away her Tupperware of sun-warmed barley mixed with shredded seaweed.

"What did you do?" I asked eagerly.

"I switched jobs!" She laughed.

Still, I've got to find someone. As I scroll through the contacts in my cell phone one more time, I hear a little pop from my computer. Ooh, e-mail. I click on the tiny envelope in the corner of the screen.

To: Isabelle Lee
From: Dwayne Keeg
Subject: New friends

Dear Isabelle,

    I am Dwayne.

    Your mother is friends with my mother.

    I will be in Beijing this weekend. I would like to invite you out
for dinner. Please let me know when you are available.

    Sincerely,

    Dwayne

I read the message a few times, looking for clues. Strange
e-mails from young men who reference my mother can only
mean one thing: setup. And after my mom's last matchmaking attempt—a starched corporate attorney who kept translating words off the Italian menu ("Now this is al dente. Al dente
means 'to the tooth.' Now this is linguine. Linguine means 'little
tongues.'")—I vowed never to be fixed up by her again.

But . . . maybe this is just a friendly gesture, a family get-
together. Besides, I could take him to Empress Impressions and
kill two birds with one stone . . .

"Isabelle, when's the weekly restaurant review going to be in?"
bellows Ed from across the room.

"You'll have it by Monday," I promise as I type a quick reply
to Dwayne, assuring him that I'd love to meet him for dinner. I'll
just need to coax someone into coming with us.

Shit!" I stare at my e-mail in dismay. My date with Dwayne is
rapidly approaching and I still haven't found a third person to give
me cover. I thought Geraldine might acquiesce, but she just sent
me an e-mail saying she's off to some silent hot yoga retreat.

"What's wrong?" Claire wanders into the living room and
perches on the arm of the sofa.

I groan. "It's Mom. She wants to set me up with one of her

friend's sons. We're going to dinner tomorrow but I can't find anyone else to go with me."

"Why do you want someone else to go with you?"

"So that Dwayne doesn't think we're on a date, obviously."

"Ah, yes. Safety in numbers." She nods. "Who is it? One of Mom's typical setups?"

I click on Dwane's e-mail and show it to Claire. Her eyes scan the screen of my laptop. "You replied to him?" She laughs. "He got the one-click response from me. Delete!" She mimes clicking her computer mouse.

"Wait a second. He wrote to you too?"

"Yep, the exact same e-mail. I guess he didn't care which one of us he ended up with." She turns back to the computer. "I. Am. Dwayne," she intones. "He sounds like a caveman. You, Isabelle. Me, Dwayne. Go. Eat. Dinner." She raises her eyebrows and continues to read out loud: "'My mother is friends with your mother . . .' Well, Mom certainly didn't pick him for his literary style."

"He's single and she knows his family. According to Mom, that's all us young kids need to fall in love. You know what she's like." I stiffen my spine and lift my chin in an approximation of our mother's upright posture. "'You girls,'" I shake my finger. "'You need to think about settling down and having some kids before your father and I go senile. Aiya'!" I heave a heavy sigh.

Claire giggles, before straightening her face and adopting the same upright stance. "'I know a nice young man,'" she says in our mother's clipped tones. "'Why don't you go out with him? Just one date. It won't kill you! He's very nice. Chinese.'"

We both dissolve into laughter. "Ugh. She's so annoying," I grumble. "She'd marry us off to the first two Chinese guys who came along."

"Chinese? Any guy. As long as he has a good job. You know how she feels about Jewish men . . . "

"'They're so smart,'" we both chorus.

"Why don't I go with you?" Claire suggests.

My eyes widen in astonishment. "Really? You'd do that for me?" I say gratefully.

She shrugs. "Sure. You know my mission in life is to thwart Mom's matchmaking." She laughs, but I'm not sure if she's joking.

I slip my arm around her slender shoulders and give her a little squeeze. "Thank you, thank you, thank you!" I cry with relief.

College, career, marriage, grandchildren. Like most Chinese parents, my mother has always expected these things of her daughters. And, like most Chinese parents, her hopes have soared high—the college should be prestigious, the career well-paid, the husband Chinese, and the children fluent in Mandarin. Oh, and we would live next door to her and Dad, so they could see their grandchildren every day. Obviously things have not quite worked out this way.

Fiercely competitive, my mother and her friends engage in a continuous game of one-upmanship, pitting their progeny against each other like pawns. For years Mom was the queen in the corner of the chessboard, sweeping aside everyone else's accomplishments with Claire's academic achievements at Harvard and Yale Law. But then Auntie May (we call all of our mom's female friends "auntie") announced her daughter's engagement to one of the Google founders, and started knitting booties exactly three months after the wedding. And then Auntie Teresa, who had been in disgrace ever since her daughter, Connie, moved to San Francisco and came out of the closet, gained ground by revealing that Connie's girlfriend was pregnant via in vitro, and they'd bought the town house next door to her. Scarcely a year later Auntie Daisy moved to New Jersey to live with her son— perfectly sweet, though he'd only graduated from community college—because he and his wife wanted their children to grow up speaking Mandarin.

My mother now stands alone among her friends as the only one with (a) two unmarried daughters, and (b) zero grandchildren. She watches from the sidelines as her friends cluck about the size of their daughters' engagement rings and red egg parties. She remains silent as they swap notes about Chinese banquet halls or sigh with mock exasperation over their precocious grandchildren. And she conspires to somehow, by hook or by crook, find us husbands. She's asked all her friends, visited a fortuneteller, and created profiles for us on Match.com. Claire claims she's even consulted a famous Taipei matchmaker. I wouldn't put it past her.

Of course, I'm partially to blame for the pestering. I haven't introduced my parents to a boyfriend in eons, so long that they're convinced I don't date, that I'm not interested in men, or they're not interested in me. If I did produce someone nice (e.g., Chinese), perhaps Mom would stop with the blind dates, the makeovers, the unsolicited fashion advice. In fact, the last time she criticized my unruly mane of hair—"Men don't like messy!" she'd insisted. "Believe me! I'm a hair professional!"—I was tempted to whip out my cell phone, speed-dial Richard, and demand that he hop the next Metro North train to Westchester, to hell with his fear of suburbs. But then I remembered what happened the last, and only, time I introduced a boyfriend to my parents.

I was nineteen, which explains why I was dating a frat boy. Blaine and I met in "Geology of Earthquakes," a freshman lecture designed for jocks (him) and liberal arts majors afraid of science (me). He saw the Greek letters on my sorority sweatshirt, invited me to a date party, poured me whiskey sours and told me I was mysterious and beautiful; one thing led to another, and for the first time in my life I fell madly in love.

Blaine had all-American looks and an all-American story. He was the first person in his family to go to college—his father worked in a coal mine in western Pennsylvania—and he had a boisterous laugh and a slight, but jagged, chip on his shoulder about privileged, upper-middle-class sorority girls. I was intrigued by his broad-chested confidence and hardscrabble childhood— so different from my own—and when my parents made their monthly visit to Manhattan for dim sum, I brought him along.

It was Blaine's first trip to Chinatown, and as we strolled hand in hand down Mott Street, I watched his face carefully. He seemed fascinated by the cramped streets, the long-necked roasted ducks hanging in shop windows, the sidewalks lined with rows of fake Gucci purses. As we entered the crowded dim sum hall, I squeezed his hand and our fingers remained entwined until we located my parents, sitting at a crowded round table.

"Mom, Dad, Auntie, Uncle, everyone . . . this is Blaine," I said shyly. "Blaine, these are my parents, Grace and Tom Lee, my aunt Marcie, uncle Gray . . . " I went around the table, trying to ignore their expressions of surprise. I had mentioned a boy, but not a boyfriend, and I certainly hadn't told them he was white.

"Howdy!" Blaine exclaimed, sitting and draping an arm across the back of my chair. "Grace, Tom, I've heard a lot about you. It's great to meet you!"

I cringed. None of my friends ever called my parents by their first name. But my parents seemed to take it in stride.

"Would you like some tea?" asked my mother, pouring us each a cup from the china teapot.

"Nah, I'll just have a beer," he said, gesturing to the waiter. "Can I have a beer?" He pantomimed drinking from a bottle. *"You know, beer?"*

"Um, I think he speaks English," I muttered. "Are you sure you don't want to stick with tea?" No one else was drinking beer.

"Are you kidding, babe? Beer's awesome with Chinese food."

To his credit, Blaine ate. And ate, and ate, and ate. He devoured dumplings, upending the small steamer baskets onto his plate. He loaded piles of noodles onto his plate, demolished half a dish of spare ribs and a heap of fried rice. My mother and Aunt Marcie kept ordering more and more food, and it kept getting scooped up by Blaine's fork and disappearing down his gullet.

Finally, four beers, three pairs of dropped chopsticks, and twelve baskets of shrimp *xiumai* later, Blaine pushed his chair away from the table and exhaled deeply. "That. Was. Awesome!" he exclaimed, stretching his arms and depositing a hand on the side of my thigh, squeezing it suggestively. "Babe, we're going to have to work some of that off." He grinned.

Four pairs of eyes swiveled toward us and I saw shock in all of them. Had my family ever alluded to sex before? Maybe once, when I was going through puberty and my mother bought me a box of sanitary napkins and told me about my period. But that was it. I was still embarrassed to watch R-rated movies with them.

"Um . . . " I blushed and muttered something about having to meet my roommate at the library. Blaine and I left soon after.

I felt sure my mother would give me an earful, but she didn't mention Blaine until I came home for the weekend, a few weeks later. I was on my way to bed when she beckoned me into the tiny front room she used as her office.

"Isabelle, come here. I want to talk to you."

I winced. I thought I knew what was coming. She sat at her computer, balancing a heavy dictionary on her lap.

"There's a word I want to know," she said seriously, pointing to the open page. She squinted at the book. "I can't read it without my glasses. Can you have a look?"

I followed her finger. " 'Callow,' " I read aloud. " 'Immature or inexperienced. Untried, raw, green, naive, puerile. A callow youth.'" I fell silent.

"Callow," my mother repeated thoughtfully.

What was she trying to say about Blaine? Was she going to ask me about my sex life? I squirmed under her gaze and my heart started to beat too fast. I licked my lips and wondered how I could escape to my room. "Um, I'm feeling kind of sleepy . . . " I feigned a yawn.

But it seemed my mother had expressed everything she wanted to say, relying on subtext to convey the rest of her message. "Give me a kiss," she said, holding up her cheek. "G'night, sweetheart. Love you."

I went up to my room, my cheeks burning with a shame and anger that I swallowed rather than express.

Blaine and I broke up a few months later—he cheated on me with a Spanish student while studying abroad in Barcelona—but our relationship had changed the day he met my parents and it never recovered. My mother's disapproval of Blaine tarnished everything, making our dorm room romance seem tawdry and juvenile. I wanted to ignore her, but my parents' opinion mattered too much to me. Fearful and resentful of their censure, I didn't introduce them to my next boyfriend, a long-haired, chain-smoking anthropology major. Or the next one, a Wall Street junior analyst, who I practically lived with. Or the next one, a sharp-tongued financial journalist, but we barely lasted three months anyway. As the years passed, maintaining silence about my love life became a habit I didn't want to break.

As a result, my mother assumes I've been single for the past ten years. And now that I'm hurtling into my thirties, her anxiety grows with each passing month and wasted egg. Two wasted eggs, actually, considering that Claire is also single.

She began the parade of eligible bachelors a few years ago, a string of pleasant young men with good jobs, straight teeth, and not an ounce of sex appeal among them. In the beginning they were uniformly Chinese American, but as we became older—and our mother became more desperate for us to settle down and bear her grandchildren—other ethnicities were added to the mix: American-born Korean, Japanese, a few Jews. At first it was amusing, but as the dropped hints piled up to Mount Everest proportions, I began to chafe under my mother's disappointment and concern. A conversation about something as innocent as shoelaces could instantly turn into a thicket of oblique suggestions. "You broke a shoelace?" she'd said the other day on the phone. "You could get a new pair in a man's shop. They have shoe laces. And you never know who you might meet there!"

Back in New York, a younger, more yielding Claire used to go on dates with these guys, eating polite bites of chicken breast at echoing midtown restaurants before chastely kissing them goodnight on the cheek. But then one day something changed. In the months before she moved to Beijing, she started to thwart her dates, never saying no, but instead inviting other friends to go with her. "I'm getting together a group of people to go birdwatching," she'd say, effectively squelching any romance on offer at the crack of dawn in Park Slope.

Faced with the same parade of nice young men, I simply said no. As in: "No, I do not want to be set up for the prom." Or: "No, I will not play mahjong with Uncle Clifford's son." Or: "No, I will not take tango lessons with the I.T. guy from Dad's office."

"You can lead a horse to water," my mother would grumble, "but you can't make it drink. Aiya! I'm getting old!" At this, I would roll my eyes. My mother, prone to dramatic displays, was surely exaggerating. I'd meet someone, someday, and he'd be intelligent and witty and charming, and, most importantly, he wouldn't be introduced to me by my mother.

Except, I haven't met him yet. And, in recent years, afraid of turning into a lonely spinster with a penchant for traditional Chinese medicine, no has started turning into yes.

After thirty minutes of waiting, cradling our cell phones, peering out the front door, and craning our necks to stare at every other customer at Empress Impressions, Claire and I finally locate I-am-Dwayne (as she insists on calling him) sitting at a table in the corner. A table that, I might add, is occupied by two people, not one.

Dwayne's thin moustache almost hides his surprise when I introduce Claire, but neither my sister nor I can conceal our astonishment at meeting Dwayne's companion.

"You didn't tell me he was bringing his mother," Claire hisses at me as we move to a larger table.

"I had no idea!" I insist.

"Ladies, let me introduce you all properly." Dwayne's weedy voice rises above ours. "Mother, this is Isabelle and Claire Lee. Isabelle, Claire, my mom, Dorothy Keeg."

"Please, call me Mrs. Keeg," she says, patting her iron gray curls into place.

"It's so nice of you to join us," I say as we settle into our relentlessly upright carved Ming chairs.

"It's such an unusual dining room," says Mrs. Keeg. "So *Chinese*."

"Well, we are in China," says Claire. I shoot her a look, but she has an innocent expression on her face.

One of Beijing's ritziest eateries, Empress Impressions advertises itself as an authentic imperial dining experience, serving a menu of the venerable Empress Cixi's favorite dishes (camel's hoof, anyone?) with a royal price tag to match. Entering the

dining room is like being transported into a modern interpreta-
tion of an imperial palace. Carved beams soar overhead, and a
colorful school of koi dart around the pond that flows beneath
the Plexiglas floor. The waitresses are all dressed to resemble the
eunuch staff of the Qing court, ambiguously sexless, their hair
cropped short. Though it's eight o'clock on a Saturday evening,
the restaurant maintains a quiet hush, born not of decorum, but
emptiness. We're one of three tables, I note. Not a good sign.

"We're not going to eat those koi, are we?" demands Mrs.
Keeg as a bright fish streaks by her left foot.

"Don't offend them, Ma! They're probably an ancient Chinese delicacy! Cut off a man's balls and let them eat goldfish!"
Dwayne's laugh is like a donkey's bray. Eeeh-heee, eeeh-heee,
heee!

I offer a polite smile and turn my attention to the menu. "Is
there anything you don't eat?" I ask.

"Oh, we eat everything," says Mrs. Keeg breezily. "Except
shellfish. Dwayne's allergic. Or peanuts. I'm allergic. That goes
for peanut oil too. I just blow up like a balloon! And no MSG."

"Allergic?" asks Claire, and I'm afraid to catch her eye for fear
we'll both start giggling.

"Chinese food syndrome," explains Mrs. Keeg. "I get terrible
headaches just thinking about MSG."

"And no carbs," inserts Dwayne. "South Beach Diet. Trying
to lose a few pounds," he says, patting his bulging waist.

I leaf through the menu, a hefty tome filled with page after
page of the slimy triumvirate of fancy Chinese gastronomy: shark's
fin, abalone, and sea cucumber. Imperial cuisine is meant to im-
press with its array of dishes, all laden with rare and expensive
ingredients, each more complex than the last, but in reality it's
my least favorite genre of Chinese food. In my heart, I guess I'm
a peasant. Give me *mapo doufu* over shark's fin soup any day.

Our waitress glides to the table, pen poised. "We'd like to start with this," I say, pointing to the characters for cabbage in mustard sauce. "And this." I point at tofu skins filled with pine nuts and spinach.

"*Dui bu qi, jintian meiyou,*" says the waitress. Sorry, we don't have that today.

"Okay," I say cheerfully. "Cold chicken in sesame sauce."

"*Meiyou.*"

"Flat mung bean noodles tossed with cilantro and shredded pork?" I ask hopefully.

"*Meiyou.*"

"Pan-fried cod fillets with chili Mandarin sauce?"

"*Meiyou.*"

"Hold the *meiyou*, please," murmurs Claire.

I flip desperately through the menu, trying to locate other dishes among the thick pages. But the jumble of English words and Chinese characters make my eyes slow. Beside me, the waitress shifts edgily, and finally emits an impatient sigh.

"What do you recommend?" I ask.

"The abalone is delicious," she replies, pointing to the most expensive item on the menu.

I manage to order a few of Cixi's favorites that are peanut- and shellfish-free and, most importantly, available. The waitress leaves and I turn back to the table.

"Did you order any dumplings?" asks Dwayne, licking his thin lips.

"Oh no, I didn't. I thought you were avoiding carbs—"

"We're in China. Gotta have dumplings," declares Dwayne.

His mother nods vigorously. "Oh yes," she says. "We just love dumplings."

The waitress returns with our cold dishes and I add an order of pork and chive *jiaozi* before sampling the pickled cabbage in mustard sauce, sweet and sour and drizzled with a wimpy mustard that tastes like French's, completely lacking in nose-tingling buzz.

Lackluster, I scribble in my notebook.

"Ooh! Spicy!" gasps Mrs. Keeg, fanning her face with her hand. "Be careful, honey!" she says, moving the dish away from Dwayne. "He can't eat spicy," she says, leaning in close. "Ulcers," she whispers.

"Mo-ther!" Dwayne's Adam's apple bobs up and down like a fishing lure.

"Well, it's best to be up front about these things, Dwayne." She leans back in her chair and surveys us. "I think it's so exciting that you girls have come back to China!"

"Back to China?" I say faintly, but she ignores me.

"Such a wonderful thing, to return to your roots," she gushes. "Now, tell me, I'm so curious. How does it feel to be back in your homeland?"

My eyes widen. "Well, I wouldn't quite call it our homeland. We were born in the States, and so was our father," I remind her. "Chinese people often find it difficult to understand that we're American because of the way we look. But if anything, living in Beijing has made me feel more culturally American. I don't look different from the local population, but I feel different and my reactions to things are different. Though, of course, people constantly question our ethnic identity, and wonder if we feel more American or Chinese." I've explained this so many times, I can rattle off the words without thinking about them.

"So, do you feel more American or Chinese?" she asks.

"Um . . . " Didn't I just answer this question? "American," I finally reply. "When I close my eyes and think of home it's definitely not China!" I laugh apologetically.

"How interesting," she says in a tone that indicates she's disappointed that I haven't found ethnic salvation. "Which one of you girls is more like your mother?"

"Oh, neither of us," says Claire, her voice brittle. "We're both dilettantes, I'm afraid."

"Really?" Mrs. Keeg looks surprised. "Isn't one of you a lawyer?"

"Claire is a partner with White, Shaw and Knorr," I insert swiftly, before Claire can come up with another flip comment.

"Oh, I'd love to have a lawyer in the family!" Mrs. Keeg clasps her hands together and gazes at Claire intently. "Are you the Harvard daughter?"

Silence.

"She is indeed," I reply. "Yale for law school."

"Dwayne is an Ivy Leaguer himself," says Mrs. Keeg, nodding vigorously. "Cornell. He graduated summa cum laude." Her eyes dart between Dwayne and Claire and I can see her picturing them side by side at the dinner table, their brood of brilliant little Keegs crowding around. "Family values are so important to Dwayne," she says, her eyes still fixed upon Claire. "Do you want a big family?"

A strange expression comes over Claire's face. If I didn't know better, I'd say it looks almost like grief, but that doesn't make sense.

"No, not a big family," I answer for her finally. "Just a couple of kids." I have no idea if this is true.

"Oh, yes," exclaims Mrs. Keeg. "I don't understand this fad of having large families these days."

I can practically hear the wedding march trumpeting in Mrs. Keeg's head. Before I can disabuse her of the notion, a flock of waitresses arrives with the rest of our food, setting the dishes gently upon the table and removing the silver domes with a co-ordinated flourish.

"Um, would you like some tea-smoked duck, Mrs. Keeg?" I

pass the plates around in an effort to dispel the awkwardness that's flooded the table. Dwayne unloads half the dumplings on his plate and pours a river of soy sauce over them.

I carefully seize a wobbly cube of imperial-style tofu and lift it to my mouth. The clear sauce is bland to the point of tasteless, and the tofu is cold. I circle my plate, sampling a bite of everything: the sweet and sour ribs, anise beef stew, a dumpling that I've managed to wrest from Dwayne's acquisitive chopsticks. Everything is ice cold and dully flat.

We eat the food, the silence punctuated only by the clink of chopsticks on our plates. Suddenly, Mrs. Keeg leans forward in her chair. "Remind me again," she says. "Which one of you girls is . . . divorced?"

My heart starts thumping in my chest. Claire's divorce is a taboo subject, something that no one talks about. Ever. Ever. Ever.

I glance fearfully at my sister, but she's arranged her features into a smooth mask. "That's me!" she says before I have a chance to speak. "I took him for every penny he had. Bastard never knew what hit him." Her mouth stretches into a tight-lipped smile. "You're right, Mrs. Keeg," she says. "It is good to have a lawyer in the family."

Mrs. Keeg presses her lips together into a thin line. "There's no need to be nasty, dear. There's nothing wrong with a little matchmaking. You're not going to be young forever, you know." She takes a bite of anise beef and the corners of her mouth turn down as she chews.

"You're right." Claire puts her chopsticks down and pushes her chair back from the table. "But I'm old enough to know I don't want to waste my time here." She grabs her purse. "Sorry, Isabelle. I'll see you later."

"Wait!" I call as she stalks from the table. "We still have three more courses!" But she doesn't turn around as she leaves the restaurant.

"More food for us!" mumbles Dwayne, shoving an entire dumpling into his mouth.

I push the food around on my plate, unwilling to take another bite, even if it is my job.

Mrs. Keeg's voice pierces the silence. "So, tell me, Isabelle," she says, regarding me with new interest. "Where did *you* go to college?"

Nine forty-five P.M. Back home in our apartment, I pour myself a glass of wine and take a healthy sip. So this is what it's come to. Drinking alone. On a Saturday night. My stomach growls and I add a bag of potato chips to the bottle of wine that I'm carrying into my room, firing up my computer as I settle into my desk chair.

Actually, it's not really that depressing, working on a Saturday night. After all, I have deadlines to meet, articles to write, magazines to put to bed. I bet Charlie works on Saturday nights all the time. Granted, he's saving the world from some sort of North Korean nuclear attack and I'm just writing restaurant reviews. But, never mind, food is important too. Sometimes I really wonder if the whole Middle Eastern conflict could be resolved through distribution of free falafel.

I contemplate the empty screen as I take pensive sips of wine. Mmmm . . . delicious wine. Really smooth and luscious. I'll just pour myself another little bit.

A little booze would have improved tonight's dinner by one thousand percent. Aided by a few more sips, I start composing my review.

Ten-fifty P.M. Ooh, writing a bad review is kind of fun. "Better bundle up before dining at Empress Impressions, because the icy food and haughty service will definitely cause a shiver. If this is how the Empress Cixi dined, no wonder she was such a bitch."

Eleven-thirty P.M. Oops, just upended my glass of wine all over the desk. I watch the crimson pool spread across the blond wood and drip onto the pale carpeting. Ooh, pretty, so pretty! The movement and contrast is like performance art. I try to clean it up but my body feels heavy, like it's being pulled down by invisible weights. How much wine have I had? I slosh a bit more into my empty glass and sit down to finish off the last sentences of the review.

Eleven-fifty P.M. I cannot stop hiccupping! I've tried everything from drinking vinegar to holding my breath, but still hic! Hic! Hic! Maybe another bit of wine would help, just a smidge. Besides, I better finish the bottle, there's only a drop left after I spilled so much on the floor—and wine spoils so quickly in this arid Beijing climate.

Twelve-thirty A.M. The review is a masterpiece! I didn't know I could be so witty, so droll! Surely even Ed will be happy with this piece—it's definitely the best thing I've ever written! Quickly, I log into my e-mail and send it to him. I can't wait to hear his response!

One forty-five A.M. When I close my eyes, everything spins. My bed feels like a boat. Ah. The floor is very solid. Much better. Much, much better. I'll just rest here for a while.

Oh. My. God. With each rhythmic twinge of pain, I think my head is going to split open to reveal my brain, shriveled like a raisin. What on earth possessed me to drink an entire bottle of wine last night? The bright sunlight streaming into my bedroom highlights the mess of last night: the sticky spread of spilled wine on the desk, the pillow and blanket that form a makeshift bed on the floor, my laptop, still on, hurtling psychedelic shapes on its screen . . .

Oh, no. No, no, no! Memories are flooding back—writing the review, sending it to Ed . . . Quickly, I open up the document and read it one more time, my heart sinking with each sentence. "With food this terrible, who needs to diet? Empress Impressions is better than any fat farm." I bury my head in my hands. What on earth was I thinking? There is no way I can publish this bitter, mean-spirited rant. Well, no matter. I have the entire day to rewrite it. My head throbs and my tongue feels oddly prickly, like it's seeping pure alcohol, but I resolutely sit down at my desk.

Ack! My cell phone's ring makes my heart race like I've been shocked. I peer at the display and reluctantly answer the call. "Hi, Ed!" I say with false cheer.

"Isabelle!" he booms as I wince. "I just read your review of Empress Impressions—"

"Uh, yeah. I was going to call you about that . . . Don't worry. I'm definitely going to spend today revising it."

"I think it's bloody great! Fucking fantastic! I didn't know you had it in you!"

"Don't you think it's a little . . . um . . . " I search my desiccated brain for a suitable adjective. " . . . mean?" I finally say weakly.

"Are you kidding? It's fucking hilarious! I've already told production to lay it out."

"No!" I exclaim. "Don't do that! I might . . . take another stab at it. Maybe soften it a little bit."

"Don't be such a pussy, Isabelle. It's running. As is." And he hangs up before I can say another word.

In the bathroom, I shake out two Tylenol and gulp them down with a sip of water. There's no way I'll be able to change Ed's mind—he protects his decisions like a dog with a bone. Anyway, it doesn't really matter. Based on the previous response to my restaurant reviews—none—I'm pretty certain that no one reads my column anyway. I'll enjoy my Sunday, nurse my hangover with a greasy egg McMuffin, take a long nap, maybe phone Jeff in Shanghai to see how his junket is going . . .

Except, there's a nagging feeling in the pit of my stomach that just won't go away.

At work, but the idea of working, of actually concentrating enough to put words onto the screen, is about as appealing as the stewed camel's paw at Empress Impressions. The afternoon stretches in front of me, vast as the Gobi Desert. I desultorily click the Refresh button on my e-mail and watch it reload. Zero unread messages. Refresh. Zero unread messages. Refresh. One unread message. Ooh!

To: Editorial Department, *Beijing NOW*
From: Gourmet in China
Subject: Who is Isabelle Lee?

Dear Editor,

    I was shocked by Isabelle Lee's cruel review of Empress Impressions in this month's magazine. Who is Isabelle Lee? Does she have some sort of culinary degree? How is she different from a typical customer like me or say, my neighbor Mr. Wang?

    I think the food at Empress Impressions is a wonderful representation of Chinese gastronomy. Isabelle Lee clearly has no taste.

Sincerely,

Gourmet in China

A flash of happiness—someone reads my column!—is instantly replaced by panic. They're going to unmask me as a fraud. Everyone is going to know that I've never spent time in a professional kitchen, never trained under an established restaurant critic, never set foot in the Cordon Bleu. My credibility? Zero.

I crane my head and peer into Ed's office where he is typing away at his keyboard, his lips bared in a strange approximation of a smile. I start to relax. Maybe he hasn't seen it yet. Maybe he'll get so busy that he won't ever see it. Suddenly, he roars: *"Who is Isabelle Lee?"*

Oh, dear God.

"Did you see this fucking e-mail?" he demands, covering the short distance from his office in a bound.

I take a deep breath and measure my words. "Ed, I'm really sorry. I shouldn't have written such a harsh review and—"

"Sorry? It's bloody brilliant! Fantastic!" He sees my confused face and chortles with laughter. "Aren't you happy? Most writers *live* for controversy like this!"

"But he's asking for my culinary qualifications! I don't have any qualifications!"

"Do you like to eat?" Ed demands. "Do you have opinions?"

"Well . . . yeah."

"Food is our common ground, a universal experience. You know who said that? James Beard."

I gape at him.

Ed snorts. "You think I don't know James Beard? Please. A little credit. We'll run this letter at the top of the section," he says decisively. "Let me know if you want to write a rebuttal."

"I can't believe this is happening to me!" I moan.

"Toughen up, Isabelle," snaps Ed. "If you want to see your byline run, you have to deal with the nut jobs."

"But—"

"You know what I saw on my way to work this morning?" He thrusts his chin in my face. "A family of migrant workers asleep on the sidewalk. The kids were so thin a gust of wind could have blown them away. So let's keep this in perspective, shall we?"

I shut my mouth.

"Besides, this is fan-fucking-tastic publicity for us!" Ed rubs his hands together with glee and strides back into his office.

Except, it doesn't stop with one e-mail. A week later, the *Beijing NOW* online forum rages with the topic.

Subject: Who is Isabelle Lee?
Number of posts: 103

From: Pengyou

I'm curious about her background. Is she from Beijing? Is she Chinese, foreign or what?

From: Splitpea

> With a name like Lee she must be Chinese. No wonder she
> has no idea about Western standards of cuisine.

From: Joy

> Don't you have to train as a professional chef to be a restau-
> rant critic?

From: Manager, Empress Impressions

> I challenge Miss Lee to test her palate against mine. We will
> taste the same dishes together and offer our opinions. Only
> in this manner will she learn the difference between good and
> bad food.

From: Blanc de Chine

> I heard she's the granddaughter of Mao's English teacher.
> She must have major *guanxi*.

From: Huangdi

> A friend of mine knows her and says she's gained at least 10
> kilos since starting the job!

The list scrolls down, covering five pages. I try to ignore them, but reading the posts is like finally hearing what the mean girls were saying behind your back in seventh grade. By the time Friday evening rolls around, checking the forum has become such an obsession that I'm late to meet Jeff for our long-awaited date.

"Where are we going?" I ask him, trying to stifle thoughts of the last post I'd read, something from a poster called Empress Orchid, who claimed I'd spent the last year working as a sous chef at Per Se.

"It's a surprise," he says with a smile as his driver pulls up to the neon-bright banks of Lotus Lane.

"Houhai," I say when I climb out of the car.

He slips a possessive arm around my shoulders. "I thought strolling around the lakes would be romantic."

Jeff looks dapper in his dark jeans and white shirt, though I want to seize his shirtfront and fasten all but the top two buttons. A soft breeze blows across our faces as we walk through the narrow *hutongs* that surround the artificial lakes (man-made in the thirteenth century), our hands casually brushing until Jeff entwines his fingers with mine.

"Look at us, out for an evening stroll around the lakes. All we need is a little Pekinese to be really Chinese," I joke.

"What do you mean?" He looks at me quizzically. "We are real Chinese."

We turn a corner and a rough metal door appears, with a discreet sign that reads: BED.

"Um, is this some sort of message?" I ask with a nervous laugh.

"Don't be silly, baby." Jeff opens the door and urges me in with a gentle nudge. "It's just the name of the bar."

Bed is filled with beds. Not run-of-the-mill princess-in-the-pea mattresses, but traditional Chinese *kang*, or wide platforms, piled high with satin cushions and draped with sheer curtains. Dim lighting and the heady smell of incense create a sensuous atmosphere, like a 1930s Shanghai salon—or an opium den. Peeking through the open door, I see a series of rooms and courtyards unfurling like a fan. Jeff leads me to a dark corner that holds an ornate red lacquer *kang*, and we curl up on the platform, our backs reclining against the soft pillows, the billowing curtains creating our own private nest.

"Champagne?" Jeff murmurs, and before I can answer, a waitress appears before us cradling a bottle of Veuve Clicquot.

"Lovely," I nod, because who doesn't like champagne? Even though this date is starting to feel a bit studied, a little like Jeff has . . . done this before.

Two fizzy glasses later it doesn't seem to matter quite so much. Jeff sits next to me, close enough to stroke my hand or tuck loose strands of hair behind my ear, which he does often. His attention is so focused, however, that I find myself wondering if he's really interested in the hot pot that I ate for lunch or if he's just faking it.

"Have you heard about the ruckus I've raised at work?" I try to fill the silence. "Ruckus. You know, like a controversy. An uproar," I say, in answer to the glimmer of confusion that crosses his face.

"I know what it means." He glances at me with mild irritation. "What happened?" He leans forward and refills our glasses, emptying the last drops into his crystal flute.

I launch into the story, and it almost feels like a relief to tell him, like I'm confessing my professional sins. When I get to the part about the online forum, he throws back his head and roars with laughter, his face flushed with amusement.

"Don't laugh." I poke him in the side. "They're discussing where I went to college, if I can speak Chinese, whether I'm fat or thin, the Michelin-starred restaurants I've supposedly trained at, whether or not I can use chopsticks . . . "

"You want my advice? Ignore them. They'll find the next big thing and move on."

"That's what everyone says, but—"

"Shhh. Trust me." He lays a finger on my mouth. "From one celebrity to another."

"I'm not a celebrity!" A giggle escapes my lips, but looking into his face, I see he's serious.

"You're with me, aren't you?" Suddenly, he's so close I can feel his lips brush my forehead. What am I doing? Everything about Jeff screams playboy, down to his very fingernails, which are buffed to a professional gleam. But as I close my eyes, I feel the champagne weakening my defenses. Despite myself, my head tilts back. His mouth is as soft as I remember, and a shiver runs down my spine as he trails a slow finger down my neck, dipping it dangerously beneath my collar.

"Isabelle," he murmurs. "Let's get out of here."

I open my mouth to protest, and he kisses me again, so deeply that my knees tremble. Who cares if Jeff is unreliable and dangerous? Geraldine and Julia are right, I do need a little fling. Jeff leans in to kiss my neck until the last of my resistance melts. He pulls me to the door, and I follow.

On the street, he unsteadily jerks his hand up to hail a cab and loses his balance, falling off the curb. "Ow! My foot!" he cries.

"Are you okay? What happened?" I ask, glancing at his face, which seems unnaturally flushed.

"I'm fine! Fine!" he exclaims, a little too loudly.

Could he be tipsy after only two glasses of champagne? That seems impossible. Shrugging my shoulders, I climb into the backseat of the cab. Jeff tumbles in after me, rolling the window down and leaning his head against the backseat. "Li Jia." He turns bright eyes upon me. "Come sit a liddle closher . . . uh, closer."

Good God, he is smashed! He lurches toward me and throws an affectionate arm around my shoulders, his head lolling against me for the rest of the cab ride. My apartment is empty, thankfully, as I'm not sure how I could explain my late night visitor to Claire. In my bedroom, I close the door behind us. The journey across town seems to have revived Jeff, and he shimmies up to me with a lopsided smile. In a flash we are kissing again and I feel myself melting against him. Slowly, he unbuttons my shirt, pausing to stroke my skin.

"You're so beautiful, baby," he murmurs, simultaneously sliding the shirt off my shoulders and easing me onto the bed. His hands move up to my bra, but as he touches the clasp, my doubts rear up again. Does it matter that he's not boyfriend material? And, if I sleep with him, will Tina Chang kill me?

"Wait," I whisper, but he's kissing me and it comes out more like, "Eh." I pull away from him. "Wait." He gives me a questioning look. "Hi, I, um, I'm just going to the bathroom to freshen up for a minute."

"You seem fresh to me, baby," he murmurs. But he untangles his fingers from my hair and doesn't protest when I pull my shirt back on.

In the bathroom, I wipe away a mascara smudge and run cold water in the sink. The cold, fluorescent light turns my skin sallow, and suddenly my jitters seem neurotic. I'm a modern woman. I'm allowed to have confidence-boosting sex. No strings attached. Although, Jeff is awfully cute. And the weekends would be less lonely with a boyfriend. And I wonder what it would be like to date a pop star . . . No, no no! I wrestle with my expectations, finally pinning them down. Okay, just sex, that's it.

I slip my shirt halfway off my shoulders and glide back into my room. "Sorry about that—" I murmur, but the words freeze on my lips. Jeff is on his back, arms outstretched, mouth slightly open, deeply asleep. I gently nudge his shoulder, but he simply turns to his side and emits a soft snore.

Great. While I dithered in the bathroom, he passed out. I stare at the even rise and fall of his chest. What the hell do I do now?

Buttoning up my shirt, I lie down next to him, flipping from my back, to my side, to my back again. I try to sleep, but thoughts keep thundering through my mind, like eighteen-wheeler trucks on a highway. How could Jeff just pass out? Does he find me that boring? Or unattractive? Or could he really be *that* much of a lightweight?

I toss and turn, but my jeans are digging uncomfortably into my stomach and, anyway, it seems kind of weird to go to sleep fully clothed in my own bed.

Maybe I should change. But I don't want Jeff getting the wrong message from my sleepwear, an extra-large NYU T-shirt that's not quite long enough to cover my butt.

Except, I'm really uncomfortable.

Oh, for God's sake.

What I really need is a pair of cotton pajamas, crisp and modest, the sort of thing Doris Day would have worn. Except, I don't own any pajamas. But I know who does.

I slide off the bed and tiptoe out my door, down the hallway to Claire's room. A flick of the switch and the room is flooded with gentle light. I kneel at the drawers in her walk-in closet. Let's see, socks and tights in the first drawer, T-shirts in the second. Enough yoga pants to outfit an entire studio in the third. Finally, at the bottom, a whole drawer of cotton pajamas, organized by color. I dig to the bottom to unearth a pair in pale blue and quickly change into them, fastening the buttons up to the top.

Tiptoeing out of Claire's room, I can't help but linger in the cool, white space. Unlike the rest of our apartment, which is outfitted in bland, birch wood furniture that's included in the lease, Claire's bedroom bears her personal touch. Dove gray curtains shield the windows, tumbling to the floor in a pool of shimmering raw silk. The rest of the room is in shades of white, from the thick, textured carpet underfoot, to the cloudlike duvet on the bed, to the cream-colored chaise longue by the window. The room is a pale, calming retreat from the hustle of Beijing.

On the mirrored Art Deco dresser stands a small flock of photographs in silver frames, and I pause to examine them. There is Claire in a Chinese water village, standing near a canal lined with weeping willows and lines of fluttering laundry. Our father's black and white high school graduation photo, his mortarboard dipping down onto his pale forehead, the shape of his eyes startlingly similar to my own. There are others—Claire and her expat girlfriends clinking slender flutes of champagne, Claire on a white sand beach, Claire in a kelly green dress with a bevy of identically attired bridesmaids, surrounding the beaming bride, who I recognize as Claire's roommate from law school.

Standing at the back of the photo frames is a bright snapshot, a picture of our family taken at Epcot Center, outside the China pavilion. Mom and Dad have their arms around each other, clutched together like they are survivors at sea, which, considering they're at Disney World, makes sense. I'm eight years old, grinning broadly at the camera, my mouth and teeth stained red with cherry Popsicle. The picture neatly fills the frame, but as I peer closely at it, I realize that's because Claire has trimmed the photo, cropping herself out of it.

Why would she snip herself out of the photo? I think back to that vacation. If I was eight, then Claire was fourteen and in that awkward tween-teen period with braces, glasses . . . you name the nerd accessory and she had it. It was the summer between Claire's freshman and sophomore years of high school, and I remember my mother nagging her about signing up for Science Club instead of writing for the school literary magazine. I stare at the photo, which is perfectly surrounded by an elaborate silver latticework frame. Did she remove herself because of unhappy memories? Or only because the photo fits so flawlessly within the frame without her?

I hear a rustle from my bedroom and hurriedly replace the

photo, switching off the lights as I leave. But in my room I find only Jeff, curled on his side. Throwing a blanket over him, I examine his face, but nothing—not even an eyelash—twitches. I try not to sigh as I crawl under the duvet, listening to his snores, before finally falling asleep.

The next morning, I awake early and lie in bed watching a thin line of sunlight stream in through the gap in the curtains. Jeff sleeps beside me, the even rise and fall of his chest testimony to his calm. Unlike me. My thoughts feel scrambled, beaten like egg whites into an insubstantial fluff. Memories of last night creep back. Oh no, we didn't . . . I glance down. No, still fully clothed in my pajamas, thank God. Okay, we were kissing and then . . . oh yeah, he fell asleep!

I tiptoe into the kitchen and start spooning coffee grounds into the percolator. Claire must have spent the night at Wang Wei's penthouse, thank goodness. We've never discussed her overnight guest policy and I'd prefer not to start now, not with Jeff here. The coffee drains nosily into the pot and I pour two mugs and stare at them. How does Jeff drink his coffee? Does he even drink coffee? I reach for the sugar bowl but stop when I hear a musical blast coming from the living room. In the foyer, I find Jeff's cell phone, blaring Christina Aguilera. It must have fallen out of his coat pocket last night. I reach for the throbbing, flashing phone, and as I attempt to switch it to silent, the display catches my eye. The caller ID reads TINA, and the accompanying photo is of a leggy, Asian woman, stark nude. Jesus! Is that Tina Chang? The face is blurry, but those perky breasts seem familiar. I hear a sound from the bedroom, hastily tuck the phone into Jeff's coat and dart back to the kitchen.

In my bedroom, I place a mug on the bedside table and pat

Jeff on the shoulder. "Good morning!" I say cheerily. I'm suddenly anxious to get him dressed and out the door before Claire gets home.

"Coffee? No thanks . . . Sleep. More sleep." He rolls over and pulls the duvet over his head.

I whisk the curtains open and sit next to him. "Are you hungry? I could make us some breakfast."

"Owwww, too much light," he groans. "What time is it?"

"Almost ten," I say, pulling the covers off his head.

He opens one eye. "Nice pajamas." His hand darts out and fingers my lapel. "What do you have on underneath—"

Quick as a flash, I move off the bed. "Uh, do you want to take a shower? I put out some clean towels."

"Only if you're coming in with me." He grins at me.

"Er, maybe next time . . . I, um—I'm going to the gym soon. Do you have any plans this morning?" I ask pointedly, hoping he'll get the message.

"I'm meeting up with my manager . . . I should probably get going." He rolls over lazily. "Unless you want me to stick around . . ."

"No!" I exclaim. "I mean, no thanks. My sister's probably going to be home any minute . . ." I allow my voice to trail away.

"Ah. Gotcha." He starts pulling on his clothes, groping for his socks, yanking his half-buttoned shirt over his head. Suddenly, he stands and throws his arms around my waist. "I had a fantastic time last night," he murmurs huskily.

Pressed against his chest, I feel my knees start to weaken. "So fantastic that you fell asleep!" I tease, but my voice is unexpectedly shaky. "I can't believe you were that tipsy after only two glasses of champagne!"

He flushes. "I hadn't eaten all day. . . Must have been the empty stomach." He kisses my lips softly, oh-so-softly. "You know I think you're special, Li Jia. Most Chinese girls are so formal and stiff, it's boring. But you—you're different. You're so open and relaxed . . . "

"I'm not Chinese," I point out, but it's hard to keep up the witty banter with his grassy, clean scent filling my consciousness.

"That's what I'm trying to say, baby. You American girls are so liberal." He plants a kiss on my mouth, which is slightly open with astonishment. "Mmmm . . . It's . . . " Kiss. " . . . very . . . " Kiss. " . . . sexy." Kiss. He pulls me with him toward the front door. "Thanks for going to bed with me." He cocks an eyebrow.

"Well, considering how you fell asleep, I hardly think— Oh! You mean the bar."

He grins. "I gotta run, babe. I'll call you later, okay?" The door clicks sharply behind him, and I lean against the wall, torn between desire and something that feels a lot like relief.

PART II

The South

Taiwan

"A huge change occurred in 1949, when the Chinese government forces, defeated by communists on the mainland, retreated to Taiwan. This brought in hundreds of thousands of incomers, including at least some from all the various regions of mainland China, bringing with them their own cuisine . . . The various cuisines of China thus dominate the culinary scene."

—*THE OXFORD COMPANION TO FOOD*

The rest of the weekend drifts by in a confused blur. I can't stop thinking about Jeff, but my thoughts are edgy, not dreamy.

I keep replaying our date over and over in my mind. Curling up against Jeff's hard shoulder at Bed. Lovely. The sparkling glasses of champagne. Delicious. The tingle I felt when his lips brushed my neck. Yum. But then it all comes screeching to a cringeworthy halt. Why did he fall asleep? Why does he have a photo of Tina's *naked* body in his cell phone? Obviously, not sleeping with him was the correct decision, right? I mean, how could getting involved with Jeff lead anywhere but down a path of heartbreak, sorrow, and too much Cracker Barrel cheddar (which I can't even find in China, anyway)?

Now it's Sunday night. Jeff hasn't called. I know I shouldn't care. In fact, I don't care. But . . . those worries are starting to creep through my brain again—the fears that I'm going to spend my life alone, taking in stray cats and practicing traditional Chinese medicine. Jeff and I didn't make any plans to see each other again, but I thought he might fancy me. But then again, what was that he said about American girls being open and carefree and . . . liberal?

"What was he implying? That American girls are easy?" My voice rises above the tinkle of new age chimes. Geraldine and I are at the Taipan Spa getting foot massages, yet despite the dim lighting and lingering scent of lavender, I feel far from calm.

"A lot of Chinese people do seem to think Americans are sluts," Geraldine says thoughtfully.

"Great. Nothing even happened and now I'm a floozy," I huff. "Who is Isabelle Lee? Oh, she's American so she must be loose." I squirm as the masseuse presses down on a ticklish spot in my arch.

"It's not you." She pats my arm reassuringly. "It's the movies and TV. Somehow people have the idea that sex is our national pastime."

"No wonder he hasn't called," I groan. "He thought I was homesick."

"I thought you said nothing happened." She raises her eyebrows. "Is there something you're not telling me?"

"I told you! Nothing happened. It was all very junior high, right down to getting smashed off three sips of booze."

"If you say so, Iz." She smirks. "Who knew Jeff was such a lightweight?"

"I think he must have Asian alcohol syndrome. You know, how a lot of Asians get all red and tipsy when they drink because they can't digest the alcohol?"

"Sounds exactly like my ex-husband. His face would get bright red from just half a glass of beer."

Before I can respond, a smock-clad spa attendant approaches us, an enormous paper cone in each hand. Creeping behind me, she brushes back my hair and inserts the tip of the cone into my ear.

"What is that?" I shriek, and jump away.

"I ordered us an ear-candling." Geraldine calmly pulls her hair into a ponytail. "They light the top of the cone and the heat draws out all your ear wax." She catches my look of horror and smiles. "It's really good for you. Rebalances your yin and yang."

"Well, if you're doing it . . . " I say doubtfully. The attendant reinserts the cone into my ear, lighting it on fire. Soon a pleasant warmth fills my ear, accompanied by a faint crackle.

"So, have you talked to Jeff since Saturday? Has he called?" Geraldine's voice is muffled.

"No." I try to concentrate on the gentle warmth suffusing my head. "You don't think I should call him, do you?"

"No," she says, giving me a steely look. "I definitely, definitely, definitely do not." Despite the flaming paper cone stuffed in my ear canal, her message is loud and clear.

By Wednesday, Jeff still hasn't called and my fingers itch to dial his number. But every time Geraldine sees me reaching for my mobile, she murmurs, "Don't do it, Iz. Don't do it." I keep one eye on my phone, ready to pounce in case it rings.

"Isabelle, where is the Max Zhang piece? I need to see it." Ed's large figure casts a shadow over my desk.

"I'm, er, just putting the finishing touches on it." I glance down, hoping he won't see the panic in my eyes. The truth is, I haven't started writing the story yet. Every time I glance over my notes, I feel a wave of terror accompanied by a little voice. *How could* you *write an exclusive profile on a world-famous, Oscar-winning director?* it says mockingly. When I slam my notebook shut, it disappears.

"For fuck's sake, Izzy. You haven't started it yet, have you?" Ed crosses his arms and scowls. "It's been three weeks!"

"I just want it to be perfect," I say quietly.

"Don't be intimidated." His voice softens. "If it's not perfect, I'll make it perfect. That's what editors do."

"Thanks." I smile at him gratefully and then quickly try to rearrange my expression. Ed hates sappiness.

"I'll expect it on my desk first thing tomorrow morning."

"Tomorrow?" My voice rises into a screech.

"Yep, that's right. Deadlines—remember those, Izzy? We're running a magazine here, not a bloody country club."

He stomps away, oblivious to the alarm on my face. I open up a new document on my computer and stare at it, my mind as empty as the blank screen. My heart starts to pound as I turn to my notebook and scan through the hurried scrawl. *I cannot do this.* Why did I think I could do this? I glance over at Geraldine and Gab, but they are both sitting calmly at their desks, happily plugged into their iPods. I watch Gab type a sentence, a smooth stream of clickity-clack on his keyboard that makes me want to rip his fingers out of their sockets.

I take a calming breath and stare bleakly at the screen. And then slowly, very slowly, I begin to feel a certain resolve—not confidence, but something that feels like . . . impatience. *Stop whining and get to work!* I grit my teeth, review my notes again, type a sentence and erase it. Type another sentence and erase it. I limp along, erasing one word out of every three, leafing through my notes, carefully piecing my story together like a puzzle. Before I know it, the afternoon has faded to dusk and my cell phone is ringing.

"Hello?" I answer distractedly, my mind still on Max Zhang's parents, wealthy Shanghai landowners who lost everything when they were forced to move to Taiwan after the war.

"Hey, babe."

It's Jeff. A smile creeps across my face, followed by the merest wrinkle of irritation. I mean, where has he been?

"Hi." I try to keep my voice light.

"Sorry I haven't called. I've been in the studio recording. My manager thinks this new album could be a real crossover for me."

"Um, that's great!" I try to inject some enthusiasm into my voice. Crossover? What the hell is he talking about? In my mind, all I can hear are Max Zhang's clipped tones saying: *First the war, and then the communists. It ruined my mother, absolutely tore her apart. She was never the same after we moved to Taiwan.*

"So, are you busy tonight? Wanna go to bed?"

"Excuse me?" I say a bit frostily.

"Some friends and I are meeting at the Bed bar tonight. I thought you'd wanna join us."

Oh, he means the bar, of course. Duh. How many times am I going to fall for this joke? "I'd love to, but I really can't. I'm on deadline trying to finish a story."

"Finish it tomorrow. You write fast."

"Ed's breathing down my neck. He gets uptight about deadlines."

"I don't know why you work so hard on that magazine," he says sulkily. "It's not like anyone reads it."

I ignore this because we've had this discussion before and, really, he's right. None of Jeff's friends read *Beijing NOW*. They're Beijing locals—why would they be interested in an expat magazine? And just because most expats only read it in the bathroom . . . well, he doesn't have to know everything, does he?

"Maybe we could get together another time," I suggest delicately. "What are you up to this weekend?"

"I have a gig Saturday night," he sighs.

"Well, I'd love to come. I've never heard you play live." In fact, I'm a little curious to see how his boy-pop band will translate to a live performance.

"It's some American embassy event. Apparently, security is going to be really tight and it's impossible to get on the guest list."

"Oh."

"But Sunday might work. Maybe you can cook me dinner and I can finally try your famous pasta. I'll call you later, see how things are going, okay?"

It's a good thing this piece about Max Zhang is so absorbing. I linger at the office until hunger drives me home, and then sit at the desk in my bedroom until 2:00 A.M. When I finally fall into bed, I'm almost too exhausted to think about how Jeff seems to be calling all the shots.

The piece is with Ed by Thursday morning, and by the time I get back from lunch, it's on my desk, splashed with red ink. And yes, he's reworked the lead and sharpened the nutgraf, circled numerous sentences and left the ominous remark: *Passive voice! You should know better!* But at the bottom of the last page, in a scrawl so untidy it's almost illegible, are the words *Good job*. From Ed, this is the highest praise, and even though he is more mercurial than a Beijing Internet connection, I still respect him as an editor, and a faint flush of pride creeps across my cheeks.

Though my fingers itch to start revising, I only have time to glance quickly through the pages before racing out the door for my two o'clock appointment, an interview with a Spanish chef about his high-concept tapas/dim sum bar.

I could never have guessed what would happen while I was away.

"It was like an explosion," says Geraldine. I'd invited her and Gab over after work, and they're sitting at the kitchen table taking turns relating the afternoon's events between swigs of cold Tsingtao.

"Tang Laoshi must have been snooping through your desk," Gab says. "I didn't see him, but all of a sudden he was standing there screaming, *'Juh juh juh juh juh!'*"

Well, Ed always said there was a thin line between being the office censor and office spy. I imagine Tang Laoshi slipping up to my desk unnoticed by my busy colleagues, his liver-spot-speckled hands rifling through my papers.

"And then he ran into Ed's office and shoved a bunch of papers in his face. It was almost like he was in a state of shock. All he could say was, *'Juh juh juh juh!'* and *'Bu xing, bu xing, bu xing!'*" Not okay.

"At first Ed was really calm. He asked Tang Laoshi to sit down and offered him a cigarette. They both lit up and just sat silently smoking for a few minutes."

"But then," Geraldine says, "Ed asked him what was wrong . . . " She looks at Gab and they sigh. I edge toward the pantry and grab a can of refried beans. We're having Mexican food straight from an Old El Paso kit: hard-shell tacos, grated orange cheese, bottled salsa, ground beef seasoned with a spice packet—all the greasy, salty, prepackaged foods we miss.

"I'm a little afraid to ask what happened next," I admit.

"Tang Laoshi started waving the papers around again and stuttering 'Zhang Daoyan, Zhang Daoyan.'" Gab scans my blank face. "Director Zhang. Max Zhang."

"Oh, no . . . my story . . . " I whisper.

"He couldn't even string a sentence together," adds Geraldine.

"He was so irate he could only shout words like 'cultural revolu-tion,' and 'Taipei,' and 'capitalist roaders,' and . . . " She takes a deep breath. " . . . 'censored.'"

I gasp. "Censored? But what about—I mean—didn't Ed—do anything?"

"I heard him mutter, 'I'm sick to death of you commie bas-tards,'" says Gab.

"Really?" I laugh.

"Yeah, and then he challenged Tang Laoshi to an arm wres-tling match," Geraldine injects, her voice dripping with sarcasm. "No, not really. What could Ed do? The Three Represents Press owns us. They pay our salaries, publish the magazine, and, as a Chinese company, it's their responsibility to censor us." Her glance is sympathetic. "Don't be too upset, Iz. We've all had pieces censored before. It's kind of like a badge of honor."

"But how can you stand it? This isn't—" This isn't journalism, I want to say, but I bite the words back. To imply that we're too good for *Beijing NOW* would only raise some painful truths about all our situations. I wrench open a jar of salsa and start spooning it into a bowl. "What will happen to my story?" I ask instead.

Geraldine looks at me sympathetically. "It was a terrific piece, Iz. You could try selling it somewhere else."

"How?" The word feels bitter in my mouth. "I don't know any newspaper editors. I don't have any magazine contacts." Except at *Belle,* I think bitterly. And my name is like seven-month-old mascara there.

"Maybe you could look on the Internet and send some query letters," suggests Gab.

I shake my head sadly. "I worked in magazines for six years. I know what happens to random query letters." I lean my arms on the counter. Behind me, the refried beans bubble thickly on the stove, with an angry pop. "Well," I say, trying to inject a cheerful note into my voice, "at least it's an adventure. I guess this is all just part of the China experience."

"Like bossy *ayis* and surly waitresses!" exclaims Geraldine.

"Or old men who hawk loogies on the sidewalk and police raids at rock shows!" chimes in Gab.

I raise my beer. "Here's to squat toilets and tapped phones!" We laugh and touch our bottles together with a heavy thunk, but when our gazes meet, the concerned look in their eyes matches the one in my own. It says: When did all of this start feeling normal?

Iz?" Claire's honeyed tones float across the apartment, through the bathroom door. The closed bathroom door. "Iz? Where are you, darling?"

I sprinkle a few more lavender bath salts into the tub, twist the taps shut, wrap a towel around myself, and sigh. After our ill-fated dinner with the Keegs, I'd hoped Claire would start sounding more normal, but she's still using the same affected tone, clinging to it as if it's hiding something. "I'm in here!" I open the door, releasing a cloud of fragrant steam.

"Oh, there you are! Ooh! It's humid! Be careful, I just had my hair blown out." She fans the air around her head with both hands. "Are you busy?" she asks.

"Er, no. Not really." I cast a longing glance inside the bathroom, the steaming tub edged with softly lit candles.

"Oh, goodie. Because I wanted to ask you—" She hesitates and looks into the bathroom.

"It's okay. You're not interrupting me. I can just add a little more hot water to the tub."

"No, It's just—do you mind if we move? I'm really afraid the steam is going to frizz my hair."

In my bedroom, Claire curls up on the bed and I try to wrap the towel around myself a little more tightly. "What's up?"

"Are you busy tonight?" She smooths her hair and tucks a stray strand behind her ear.

"Why?" I ask slowly. Claire's invitations often involve a lot of money, and too much conversation about torts and testimony— or tan lines, depending on who we're with.

"Well, the Marine Ball is tonight, and Wang Wei and I were supposed to go together, but something come up the last minute and he can't make it. So, I was wondering—"

"A ball?" I cross my arms and grab at the towel as it slips. "Oh no, I mean, it's really kind of you to think of me but I don't think—"

"Oh, Iz!" she sighs with an impatience that surprises me. "I knew you were going to say no."

"I'm sorry. You know these society events really aren't my thing and—"

"It'll be fun." She looks down at the cream-colored invitation. "And it's in honor of Ambassador Charles Eliot. I'd have thought you'd want to show him your support."

"What on earth would give you that idea?" I shrug. "Look, it's really sweet of you to ask me, but—"

"Do you have plans tonight?" she demands.

I run over my plans for the evening: a long soak in the tub, then curling up on the couch with a glass of wine, cashmere blanket, and the pirated box set of *Ugly Betty* . . . "Yes."

"What?" Her eyes narrow.

"Oh, some people from the office are going to Alfa for eighties night. You know how I love Madonna!"

"So you're going out with some of the girls?"

"That's right. Geraldine and Lily and, er, Gab."

"Alfa's eighties night is on Fridays."

Damn.

"Honestly, Iz. You don't have to lie to me. If you don't want to go to the ball, it's no big deal, you can just say so."

"Claire, I really don't want to go to the ball." I try to soften my words with a smile.

She slides off the bed and walks over to the door, where she leans against the frame. "Remember our lovely night out with the Keegs?" she says musingly. "I defended you from that walnut-faced woman and her pudgy son . . . "

"You abandoned me in the middle of dinner!"

"You asked me to go with you and I did. And now all I'm asking for is one tiny little favor . . . " She locks her caramel-colored eyes upon mine.

"Okay, okay," I grumble. "Guilt-trip me into it, why don't you?"

"Oh, thank you darling! Here's the invitation." She thrusts a card into my hands. "It's black tie. Be ready by seven, okay?" She skips out of the room, leaving me to stare into my closet, where there are no ball gowns.

At 6:45 I am standing in the foyer, stomach sucked in with a girdle, hair pinned into a loose bun, my temper black. Why did I agree to go to the Marine Ball? I don't even like swimming in the ocean.

"Are you ready to go?" Claire clicks across the marble floor, looking stunning in a silvery gray cheongsam. She snaps her beaded evening bag shut and inspects me. "Is that what you're wearing?"

I glance down at my dress, a chartreuse off-the-shoulder number that I'd worn as a bridesmaid at my friend Erica's wedding and brought to Beijing in a sentimental moment. Richard and I went to Erica's wedding together, and it was the last time I remember us having fun together. We'd danced the "Hava

Nagila" and when my hair tumbled down around my shoulders, he wouldn't let me pin it back up again. "You look all rosy and windblown, like Botticelli's Venus," he said. "A little, Asian Venus."

I don't know how he saw that, because the dress was supremely unflattering, even when I had a summer tan to offset the acid color (and bottomless champagne to offset my vanity). Now, it looks ridiculous. But without any other long gowns in my closet, what choice do I have? "What's wrong with it?" I ask sulkily.

"You look like you're about to dance the funky chicken and elbow your cousin out of the bouquet toss. Whose wedding is this from?" She fingers the faux satin fabric, lifting the skirt to expose my feet. "You wore the dyed-to-match shoes?" Her eyes widen. "Why on earth did you bring this to China?"

"I don't think it's that bad. My friend Erica really wanted her bridesmaids to be able to wear the dress again. Besides, I don't have anything else." I scowl. "The shoes make the skirt the right length."

She takes my arm and pulls me down the hall into her room. "Come on."

"Claire, I can't borrow your clothes. You're about twice as tall as me and half as wide."

"We'll find something," she says firmly, switching on the lights to her walk-in closet. "I refuse to be seen with you in that dress," she mutters. "Here, try this." She hands me a black tulle skirt.

I take a deep breath and try to suppress my annoyance. "Claire, this is never going to fit. Maybe I should just stay home . . ."

"Oh, no. You can't get out of this by cooking up some sort of fashion emergency. Come on, put it on. *Hurry.* The car is waiting for us downstairs." She starts flipping through the hangers.

I wriggle out of the green dress, suck in my stomach, and zip up the skirt. It falls just above my ankles in a graceful ballerina pouf.

"Oh goodie, it fits. I bought it before I went macrobiotic so it's a little loose on me. Have you ever thought about giving up carbs?"

"Thanks a lot."

"It's just a suggestion," she says, shrugging her shoulders. "Try this." She tosses me a black shirt.

I hold it out in front me. "This is a T-shirt."

"It's couture. Put it on."

I pull it over my head. The scooped neck exposes my collar-bone, while the clever twists of sleeves make my arms look long and slender. I turn to Claire and find her examining me in the mirror.

"Much, much better," she exclaims. "But still a little too plain. Here, these should do the trick." Before I can stop her, she's slipped her diamond and platinum hoops out of her ears and handed them to me.

"Oh, I can't take your earrings—what about you?"

"I don't need them," she says airily. "But you do. Don't forget to change your shoes. And for God's sake put some lipstick on. You look pale." She sweeps out the room, leaving me standing in my borrowed finery.

One chauffeured car ride later we are standing in the crowded ballroom of the China World Hotel. The room glows with candles and tiny fairy lights, but despite the ice sculpture and open bar, it feels like an adult prom: the men look stiff in black tie, while the women eye each other, trying to discern who has the best dress. I want to hide in the ladies' room, but Claire hands me a glass of champagne and pulls me to the center of the room.

"Stand up straight," she hisses out of the corner of her mouth.

I take a sip of champagne as she drifts away, and I hear her say, "Hi, Krissie! How are you? Mwah, mwah." I lean against a table and study the flower arrangement, a tight bouquet of white carnations.

"I didn't expect to see you here," says a voice behind me.

I turn and nearly drop my champagne flute. There, dapper and crisp in bespoke black tie, is Charlie.

"Charlie! Hi!" I swallow my surprise. I haven't seen him since that morning when he gave me a ride to the bus station. My cheeks flame when I remember how I thought Charlie might like me. Thank goodness I realized his interest was only platonic, before I embarrassed myself. I pray he can't feel the heat in my face as he leans forward to kiss me quickly on both cheeks in a manner both Euro and brotherly.

"How are you? I've been enjoying your restaurant reviews in *Beijing NOW*," he says.

"Oh, you shouldn't waste your time reading those." I wave a hand nonchalantly as the blush spreads further across my cheeks.

"Are you kidding? They're terrific! Your descriptions of food are so enticing—they remind of MFK Fisher. Have you ever read her? Besides," his eyes crinkle into a conspiratorial smile, "I totally agreed with your review of Empress Impressions. Awful, awful restaurant. You're so right, their shark's fin soup *is* like glue."

I take another sip of champagne and laugh. "Actually, I try to avoid that stuff. Did you know they kill sharks for their fins? Well, of course you probably do since you're such a supporter of marine wildlife."

A confused look crosses his face. To my right I hear Claire say: "Oh, that's just my little sister." I turn my head as Claire edges to my side. Next to her is a tall blonde, dressed in a body-skimming gold sheath. Kristin, from the embassy.

"Charlie!" she says, playfully smacking him on the arm. "You didn't tell me you were living in the same building as the Lee sisters."

"I didn't know you'd be interested," he says mildly.

"Isabelle, do you know Kristin? She works with Charlie," says Claire.

"It's so nice to meet you," gushes Kristin. "I didn't even know Claire had a little sister!"

"Actually, we've met before. It's nice to see you again." I straighten my spine as recognition dawns in her eyes and her smile grows chilly.

"We were just talking about shark's fin soup," Charlie says, smoothly filling the silence. "Isabelle is a shark preservationist."

"Really? How fascinating." Kristin puts a hand on her hip and simpers at him.

"Oh, well, I'm sure you all know much more about the endangered shark population than I do!" I say, take a nervous sip from my glass and look at them expectantly. Silence.

"Why would we know about that, darling?" Claire asks finally.

"Well, considering how this evening is in support of marine wildlife—" I stop as Kristin and Claire dissolve into giggles. Even Charlie smiles for a brief second.

"Isabelle," says Kristin slowly and clearly, as if she were speaking to a child. "The Marine Ball is in honor of the Marines. You know, the branch of the U.S. military. Army, navy, air force . . . "

"Oh!" I try to force a laugh. "How silly of me!"

"It's all right. How could you have known?" Kristin shrugs her bronzed shoulders. "You're a total stranger to the embassy community."

I stare at her, trying to think up a witty retort. When nothing comes to mind, I hold up my empty glass. "I think I'm going to get another glass of champagne. It was lovely to see you all again!" I trill and slink away. But not before hearing Kristin exclaim, "Don't forget, Charlie! You promised me you'd sit next to me at dinner."

In line at the bar, I squint at my tiny bejeweled watch (Claire's) and sigh. I have hours left in my pointy-toed shoes and snug skirt. I stand shifting from foot to foot, trying to relieve some of the pressure, when someone taps me on the shoulder. I turn to find Charlie, with two sparkling, full glasses in his hands, a wry smile on his face.

"Did you cut in line? How very Chinese." I take a grateful sip from the glass that he hands me.

"Listen, Iz." He pulls me into a corner of the room. "I don't know how much time I'll have to chat later, but I wanted to ask you—how was Pingyao? Did you make it to the bus in time?" His eyes are friendly, but concerned.

I smile politely even as a bristle of indignation raises the hair on my neck. Evidently, he feels the need to check up on me. "Fine. It went fine," I say shortly. But he smiles so encouragingly that I find myself continuing. "Well, I practically missed the bus, and then I stayed with this peasant family and almost had to take a shower in the public bathroom but everyone was staring at me . . . And when I finally met Max, he was totally behind schedule, but our interview went really, really well—" I take a sip of champagne, and try to stop the stream of chatter. Why am I so nervous?

He looks at me with a bemused smile. "Actually, I've been meaning to call you . . . "

I take a step closer until I can smell his clean, fresh scent, like laundry that's been left to dry in the sun. He was going to call me? Something flutters deep inside me.

But then I hear him continue: "Have you looked at this weekend's crossword puzzle yet? I can't figure out the theme and it's driving me nuts."

"Oh." I take a sip from my glass and try to ignore the sound of blood that is suddenly rushing in my ears. "No, I haven't . . . "

"I've also been trying to find time for our trip to Houhai," he says gently, as if sensing my disappointment. "But work. Ugh." He rolls his eyes and laughs. "It's been truly crazy. Nonstop. Insane. I've barely had time to eat, let alone see you, which is what I really wanted to do."

I can't believe he's using the work excuse again! And if lying makes him so uncomfortable, he should really stop. His gaze is so intense, I'm afraid it might burn through my skin. "Maybe you should talk to the ambassador about your workload," I babble nervously. "I'm sure he isn't the young tyrant everyone says he is."

"Er—that's another thing I wanted to tell you . . . " He looks at me anxiously as people start moving toward their tables for dinner.

"Yes?"

"Excuse me, sir?" A young marine, his dress uniform stiff and shiny, taps Charlie on the shoulder. "We're just about ready for you."

Charlie sighs and throws me a rueful glance. "I have to go," he says, squeezing my hand. "But I'll try to find you later, okay?"

"Sure!" I say with false cheer. He moves toward a group of marines who are carrying the American flag.

"Where have you been?" whispers Claire as I slide into my seat. "The ceremony is about to start."

I shrug as the room darkens and we rise to our feet. What could Charlie have wanted to tell me? I wonder. The high-pitched notes of the "Star Spangled Banner" start to soar and a small group of marines marches in, bearing the American flag. *I wonder if it was something about his work . . . I wonder if he's a . . . spy!* I stand there stock-still, my hand frozen to my heart. Could that be the reason for all the late nights, the mysterious disappearances?

A voice booms over the loudspeaker, causing me to jump in fright. "Ladies and gentlemen, welcome to the U.S. Embassy Beijing Marine Ball." A muscled young man in military uniform, his face flushed above his stiff collar, stands at the podium. "As you know, we gather each year to celebrate the birthday of the United States Marine Corps. But tonight we are proud to also honor a special individual, our ambassador." My stomach growls and I clutch at it, wondering what we'll be served for dinner. Probably dry roast beef.

"Not only does he bring superb leadership skills to the job, we appreciate his unflagging spirits and excellent sense of humor. Even when our hours are long, he always has a smile for all of us . . . " The young sergeant drones on, and I look longingly at the glass of red wine in front of me. "Through Six Party Talks and Sec-State visits . . . " I crane my head, trying to find Charlie. Hm. I wonder why he's standing back there by the door. "Please welcome Beijing's most eligible bachelor . . . " Laughter. "The United States ambassador to China . . . Charles Eliot!"

I start to clap, but suddenly my hands freeze in midair. Striding up to the podium, shaking hands along the way, is Charlie. The applause roars around me, but I sink into my chair, shock draining the color from my face. Charlie is the American ambassador? To China? It seems impossible, but as I stare open-mouthed at the podium, everything starts to click into place. The late night calls from the Foreign Ministry. The unexpected trips to Washington. The unrelenting work schedule.

Oh God. My face flames as I recall the disparaging remarks I made about the ambassador, all secondhand gossip from Claire's friend, Eric. Which, I realize now, could very well have been the bitter ravings of a jealous colleague.

"Isn't it amazing that Charlie's already an ambassador?" Claire murmurs. "His rise to the top has been incredibly fast. They say he's a shoe-in for Secretary of State someday." I can scarcely respond, let alone concentrate on Charlie's speech, which stirs up more laughter and another enthusiastic round of applause.

Dinner passes in a blur of cold beef and leaden roast potatoes. I smile politely at the guy on my right, who is more interested in punching buttons on his BlackBerry than talking to me, but I can't stop the swirl of confused thoughts in my mind. Claire shoots me a look, but she is occupied by her neighbor, a taciturn bearded man whom I recognize as a senior partner at her law firm.

When the waitstaff distributes small plates of soggy apple pie and a stage crew starts setting up for the band, I lean over to my sister. "Claire, I'm not feeling too well. I think I need to go home."

She looks at me in astonishment. "But the band hasn't started yet! I thought you'd want to hear Xiao Zhu play live."

"Who?"

"Little Zhu. Zhu Bian. Jeff. Jeff Zhu. You know, your boyfriend?" She pokes at her piece of pie and pushes it away.

"My what!" My jaw drops. "Jeff's not my boyfriend. We've barely even kissed!" I insist a little too vehemently.

"If you say so, darling." She smiles knowingly and pushes back her chair. "I must say hello to the Swedish ambassador's wife. See you later!"

I drain my glass of wine and stare at the plates littering our deserted table. First Charlie, now Jeff. Haven't I had enough surprises for one night? And how on earth did Claire get the idea that Jeff is my boyfriend? I start calculating the cost of calling Julia on my cell phone when my thoughts are cut off by a drum roll and blast of disco fog.

"Good evening, ladies and gentlemen." Jeff emerges on stage, dressed in dark jeans and a tank top that bares his muscular arms. "We are DownLoad."

The stage lights flash and two other band members join him, launching into a bouncy Mando-pop song that I recognize as their popular single, "China Love," complete with carefully choreographed dance moves. They're actually not bad—their boyish faces and pop beat would send a flock of adolescent girls swooning—but here at the sedate embassy ball, the dance floor remains completely empty. From the stage, Jeff scans the thinning crowd and his face darkens. I should get up and dance, I think. But . . . alone? My inhibitions glue me firmly to my seat.

The beat changes into something more familiar and I recognize a remixed version of Madonna's "Holiday." With Chinese lyrics. I take a deep breath, stand up and edge toward the dance floor.

"*Hey!*" Charlie appears at my elbow, shouting over the music. "*You gonna dance?*"

"*Maybe,*" I shout back.

"*What?*" He raises an eyebrow and steps out onto the parquet. "*Come on! Holida-ay! Holida-ay!*" he sings and moves around to the beat. He's so unabashed and carefree that I can't help but giggle. "*Come on, Iz! Don't leave me hanging out here!*" he calls.

I creep out onto the floor and before I know it the familiar, infectious beat has me shaking my hips. We throw up our arms and dance around the empty floor. Jeff plays some more Madonna, and soon another couple joins us, and then another, and another, until the dance floor is packed. When the music slides into a slow song, I somehow find myself in Charlie's arms, moving in an unhurried circle, everything very proper, with inches between us, just like a junior high school slow dance.

"You could give Beyoncé a run for her money," says Charlie. "I didn't know you could dance like that!"

"Well, we all have our secrets." I raise my eyebrows. "Some of us, more than others." My voice emerges sharply.

He swallows. "About the ambassador thing . . . I'm really sorry, Iz. I didn't mean to embarrass you."

"I just have one question."

"Anything."

"Why do you live in our building? I thought there was some fancy ambassadorial residence on Guanghua Lu."

He smiles. "Can you keep a secret?"

I nod.

He leans in so close I can see the faint stubble on his chin. "It has rats!" he whispers. "Bionic rats! We've been trying to get rid of them for months."

I laugh, and he looks relieved.

"Listen, Iz. I really wanted to tell you. Really. But at first I didn't want to scare you off . . . and then I didn't know *how* to tell you. I've been struggling with what to say for a few weeks—I thought for sure you'd think I was lying, or delusional. And actually, I kind of liked being incognito. You weren't intimidated by me, which was . . . a relief."

Before I can respond, the song trickles to an end and Jeff whispers huskily into the microphone: "I'd like to dedicate that last song to a beautiful woman. Isabelle Lee. My girlfriend."

What? My head snaps to the stage, where Jeff stands staring at me and Charlie. Is Jeff insane? Why would he announce to the world that I'm his girlfriend when I'm clearly not? Or does "girlfriend" mean something else in Chinese? Maybe I should ask Geraldine. I shake my head sharply and frown at Jeff, but he simply lifts his chin before a cloud of disco steam descends and his face fades from view, the beat changing into something fast and insistent. My heart sinking, I turn to Charlie, who remains frozen, a surprised look on his face.

"Charlie, listen. Let me explain, Jeff and I aren't—I mean, he's not—" I put a hand on his arm, but he turns away and rearranges his features.

"It was great seeing you again, Isabelle." Suddenly, his voice is as polite as if I'm the Swedish ambassador's wife. "But I should probably mingle among the other guests. Good night." He leaves the dance floor and I find my way back the table, where I collapse into a chair.

I don't know how long I sit there before Claire appears. "Iz? A bunch of us are going to Bellagio to get something to eat. Do you want to come?" She scans my face. "Is everything okay?"

"Yes. No. I don't know." I bury my face in my hands. "Charlie and I . . . Jeff dedicated the song to me, and—" I stop. What does it matter? Dancing with Charlie hasn't changed anything. His interest in me is obviously platonic, otherwise he would have made more of an effort to see me. Why do I care what he thinks? I take a deep breath and smooth the tremor out of my voice.

"It's okay, honey. Jeff's going to finish his set and meet us at the restaurant!" she says cheerily.

Before I can tell her that Jeff is the last person I want to see, she adds, "Besides, you have to come." She lowers her voice. "Wang Wei is meeting us there, and I told him you were coming. He wants to meet you. Isn't that great?" She beams at me.

I still haven't met Wang Wei, and after all these months, I'm dying of curiosity. Claire snatches stolen moments to be with him; the minute her BlackBerry lights up with his name, she reaches for her laptop, so she can simultaneously talk to Wang Wei while canceling her preexisting other plans. She says his schedule is crazy—apparently developing new properties built on the land of poor, displaced, uncompensated Beijingers takes up a lot of time—but I suspect something else keeps him very busy: his wife. Knowing Claire's hair-trigger defensiveness, however, that's an opinion I keep to myself.

Instead, I paste a smile on my face and try to repress a feeling of impending doom. "Great!" I echo her. "Come on, let's get our coats."

Later, much later, our group is still sitting around an enormous square table at Bellagio. Claire sits next to Wang Wei, who rests one thin hand on her thigh, while the other clutches his shiny leather man-purse. We've only exchanged pleasantries, as he's spent most of the night leaning across Claire to chat quietly with his business partners, the cueball-headed Yang Biao and the flat-topped Peng Bo, who insists that I call him by his English name, Chaos. Their girlfriends, Chloe and Pearl, two Taipei girls who rival Claire in beauty and thinness, sit beside them, emitting occasional giggles. Their voices are unbearably *dia*—high-pitched and sugary sweet.

Wang Wei is handsome, I suppose, with his sharp features and rimless glasses, though I've noticed that his thin lips rarely lift into a smile. I try to listen in on his conversation, but all I can hear is the quiet but forceful cadence of his voice as he issues instructions to his colleagues. Their deferential nods indicate their respect (or is it fear?). When Wang Wei stops talking to eat a piece of chicken, I open my mouth to ask him a question. But what? Where are you from? What's your favorite color? I want to get to know him, but I don't know how to push past that cold aura of quiet power that makes me shiver.

Next to me, Jeff and his bandmates smoke a steady stream

of Marlboro Reds and dissect the show in rapid Chinese. Jeff showed up about an hour after we did, bouncing in with a grin and kissing me on the lips, though I tried to avoid it. I haven't had the chance to ask him what the hell he was thinking when he introduced me as his girlfriend. But it's hard to stay angry with him. He keeps turning from his conversation to interpret for me, or scoop morsels of food on my plate. Plus, he looks damn cute in that cutoff T-shirt, which shows off his muscled arms.

I sip from my cup of chrysanthemum tea and try to imagine myself with Jeff as my boyfriend. Dating a Chinese guy would certainly be a first in my relationship history. Hell, I've never even had an Asian boyfriend. It's not something I'm proud of.

"Why don't you go out with a nice Chinese boy?" my mother would urge, her voice cracking with frustration. "Why?"

Why? There were so many reasons. For one thing, there were only three Asian guys in my high school—we only make up 3.6 percent of the U.S. population, after all—and one of them was gay. Then in college, after Blaine and I broke up, I did have a brief fling with a Korean guy, Rodney Chung. Unlike the sons of my mom's friends, who were all prelaw/premed, he was majoring in sociology, and planning to work for Teach for America. Unfortunately, he also had a fiancée, which I discovered when she called late one night while we were, er, studying. After college, while working at *Belle*, I got set up with a couple of bankers, Chinese Americans who'd relocated from the West Coast. Alas, one of them was convinced the Met was a hot stock on the Nasdaq and Tolstoy some sort of Russian media mogul. I'm pretty sure the other one had a gambling addiction—unless you could consider the off-track betting parlor a romantic venue for a first date.

And then there were all those subconscious reasons, the messages I unconsciously absorbed from the media but couldn't articulate. The Brad Pitts, Matt Damons, and Tom Cruises who strutted across movie screens with their golden skin and hair, high-bridged noses, and wide blue/green/anything but brown eyes. The choppy voiced, slit-eyed caricatures on TV who emasculated Asian men, depicting them as sneaky, or inarticulate, or nerdy, or most of all, undesirable.

But Jeff is different. For the first time, I've met a Chinese guy who looks like he could be comfortable on a motorcycle—and not just one that's attached to a Wii. Maybe he's never read Shakespeare, but his muscled arms and dimpled smile definitely make up for any missing brain power. Shouldn't I finally date someone Chinese? After all, I am ethnically Chinese. I'm living in China now. And—not that this is a major concern, but still—my mother would be thrilled. At the thought of Jeff's boyish smile, my stomach flips. But it changes to an anxious churn when I remember his high-handed behavior at the ball. Why did he have to call me his girlfriend in front of everyone? For a second Charlie's puzzled, pained face flashes before me, and my stomach twists with a feeling that I can't identify.

My gaze crosses the round table and rests on Jeff's band members. There's the drummer, Li Xing, a round-faced, muscular guy with a shaved head and kind smile. Next to him sits the guitarist/manager, Hu Jia, an arrogant expression resting on his sharp features as he surveys the restaurant's other tables. And then there are the triplets, as I've come to think of them, the backup dancers: three petite Beijing girls, their hair frizzed into identical mullets. They scoop spoonfuls of shaved ice and mango into their pretty mouths and offer squeaky monosyllabic responses to all our questions.

It's well after 2:00 A.M., but Bellagio remains packed with an energetic crowd, most of whom have spilled over from Baby-face, the swish nightclub next door. We've eaten savory strips of tofu with fermented black bean, and nuggets of Sichuanese fried chicken hidden in a nest of bright chili peppers. Claire ordered dessert: a towering mound of shaved ice piled high with red beans, green beans, tapioca pearls, sago chunks, canned fruit cocktail, condensed milk, everything, really, as its name *zonghe baobing,* indicates. It's cold and sweet, like ice cream with a rubbery chew.

Our waitress approaches our table and sets down one more dish, a chunk of braised meat in a dark sauce.

"Did we order this?" Claire looks confused.

"*Wo dianle. Wo yao ni de meimei shi shi.*" Wang Wei's gaze finds mine and I repress a shiver. Something about his thin face intimidates me. Now he's ordered up a dish, especially for me to try.

"What is it? *Shi shenme cai?*" I swallow. Claire insists Wang Wei's English is word perfect, but I haven't had a chance to find out. So far, he's insisted on speaking to me only in Chinese, seeming to relish my bad accent and halting replies.

"*Kong rou.*" He pushes the dish toward me, leans over and scoops a chunk onto my plate, where it glistens slightly, the slivers of meat lost in the stripes of solid fat.

"Uh, *xie xie!*" I poke at it with my chopsticks. "What's *kong rou?*" I make a fruitless attempt to separate the meat from the fat.

"*Ni pa fei rou ma? Ni kan! Hao chi!*" Wang Wei stabs at the meat and eats a bite, chewing thoughtfully. "You Americans are too afraid of a little fat," he says. Scorn compels him to finally speak in English.

My cheeks flame as I reluctantly take a bite. The fat squishes in my mouth and I quickly swallow. "Tastes good! *Hao chi!*" I say politely. "What kind of meat is it? Pork?"

"*Gou rou.*" Wang Wei's chilly smile stretches his thin mouth.

I blanch. "Dog?" I push my plate away. "That was dog meat?"

The table erupts in laughter. *"Kai wan xiao!"* says Wang Wei. "Just kidding! It's pork." He wraps an arm around Claire. "I told you she wouldn't eat it," he snorts.

Claire shifts uncomfortably and takes a sip of tea. "What did you think of the Taiwanese food, Iz?" she says, clearly trying to change the subject. Her eyes, when they meet mine, are beseeching.

I gaze at my sister, her face aglow in Wang Wei's presence. This isn't some casual, expat fling, I realize. Claire is in love. I resist the urge to fling a protective arm around my sister. I can understand why she would be attracted to Wang Wei's keen good looks, his undeniable intelligence, his high-profile lifestyle. But part of his allure is a carelessness that makes me fear for her. Swallowing my irritation, I take a deep breath and try to inject some warmth into my voice. "It was Taiwanese? It was good—like fancy *jiachangcai*. I can't tell how it's different from regular Chinese food, actually."

"Why would it be?" Wang Wei says in Chinese, leaning forward and crossing his arms. "Taiwan *is* a part of China." His eyes flash.

"Bu shi. Not really." Chloe pushes her bowl of rice away impatiently. "In Taiwan, we have a democracy. And a free press. You don't have that on the mainland."

"Well, according to our government, there's only one China," Wang Wei says testily, echoing the official view.

In the months since I moved to Beijing, I've become increasingly aware of the tensions between mainland China and the tiny island on its southeastern coast, Taiwan. The two governments have harbored ill will since 1949, when the Kuomintang lost the civil war to the Chinese Communist party and fled to the island, founding the Republic of China. Since then the issue of whether Taiwan represents all of China (as claimed by the Republic of China), or is an inalienable part of the motherland (as claimed by the Communist party) is a topic so pitted with mines, just thinking about it could set off an explosion.

My mind drifts to Max Zhang and his bitter Taiwanese childhood, colored by the chaos of political instability and debilitating poverty; about his twin sister, left behind on the mainland in 1949, who was beaten to death in a struggle session during the Cultural Revolution. His feelings about China—whether one China, or more—are more complex than I could ever hope to understand.

"Come on, guys," Jeff says soothingly. "Let's not argue about politics. We're so lucky—China is booming, changing so fast. *Yi ri quan qiu*. One day is equal to a thousand autumns. Who cares about Taiwan?"

Wang Wei shrugs carelessly. "You're right. As long as I've got my iron rice bowl . . . Prada in the closet, the Benz in the garage, what else really matters?"

Jeff leans back in his chair and smiles. "More importantly, let's talk about where we're going next. Babyface?"

Everyone groans. "Only if we can get a VIP table," says Pearl.

"Yeah," says Jeff. "Last time we had to sit next to the dance floor and people kept bothering me all night."

"Oh, you loved it." Hu Jia throws a crumpled napkin at Jeff. "All those teenage girls asking for your autograph . . . "

I watch them banter and force a smile to my lips. I'll go to Babyface and drink Chivas and green tea and feel the loud techno beat vibrate against my sternum. It's better than sitting at home, contemplating Taiwan, wondering if I'm part of something or tied to nothing at all.

Sichuan

"People from Sichuan, known to the other Chinese as pepper maniacs, like to make a distinction: 'la' is the taste that burns, while 'ma' numbs."

—A. ZEE, *SWALLOWING CLOUDS: A PLAYFUL JOURNEY THROUGH CHINESE CULTURE, LANGUAGE AND CUISINE*

For as long as I can remember, everyone has gathered at my parents' house for Thanksgiving. Easter, Christmas, and Chinese New Year are spent at Aunt Marcie's (except for one terrible year, when we all went to Las Vegas and Aunt Marcie lost a thousand bucks shooting craps), but on the last Thursday in November, my parents' ranch-style house drifts with the cozy smell of roasting turkey and crackles with the voices of my mother and her sister. Only three years apart, they are alike in their slight figures, bouffant hairstyles, sharp tongues, and unrestrained curiosity—especially when they're together. For me, Thanksgiving is traditionally a long weekend filled with food, TV, and difficult conversations.

Take last year. When Aunt Marcie arrived, she made a beeline for me in the kitchen, where I wrestled with a can of Ocean Spray cranberry sauce. "Don't you have a boyfriend yet?" she asked, gazing at me unblinkingly before sighing. "Aiya . . . I should introduce you to my plastic surgeon. It's such an easy operation now . . . not like in my day! Just a quick procedure and you'll be home in a couple of hours."

She meant blepharoplasty, of course, the cosmetic surgery that widens the eyes from single-lidded to double. My mother and her sister worshipped the surgeon's knife, both boasting eyes more marble-shaped than almond. The summer before she started Harvard, even Claire endured the procedure. Only I refused, and my resistance quickly became a bone of contention between me and Aunt Marcie, who could never see me without placing a manicured index finger on my lid and raising the skin, "Just to see what you'd look like, sweetheart."

It's not that I was opposed to the surgery, which is common and quick, and done in an outpatient clinic in just a few hours. It was so accepted among Chinese American families that my mom and her sister spoke of it in a normal tone of voice, unlike so many other topics that shouldn't have been considered shameful but were, like sex, or breast cancer, or being gay. Plenty of Asian women did it—including some whom I admired, like Connie Chung, and some I didn't, like Tina Chang. I just couldn't imagine having *my* eyes snipped. I didn't believe in changing my features so I could assimilate to an American ideal of beauty, and—remarkably, considering how vulnerable I am to other people's opinions—I thought my eyes looked fine.

Yet the more I refused to consider the surgery, the more frustrated my mom and Aunt Marcie grew, until their suggestions had rocketed from coaxing to coercion. They began to equate my single status with my single eyelids. Aunt Marcie even tried to bribe me into seeing her plastic surgeon by offering to buy me a handbag she knew I coveted—Gucci with bamboo handles—if I would just agree to a consultation.

"It will make you more confident," she urged. "I know you want to look pretty. Just meet with him. *Please.*"

It pained me to turn her down, knowing I'd never be able to purchase the handbag myself (and it's so beautiful, not to mention iconic), but I summoned up some hidden strength and said no. Aunt Marcie didn't talk to me for month.

After the Gucci purse incident, Julia suggested that I sit down with my mother and Aunt Marcie and tell them that under no circumstances would I ever consider eye surgery, and could they please stop asking me, because their insistence was damaging our relationship. "Just be calm and firm," she said.

I choked on my martini. "Are you kidding?" I gasped, after I'd finished coughing. "They're Chinese. They don't talk about their emotions. They repress them and tell you some obscure Chinese story about peacocks and the emperor. And then, months later you realize that was a metaphor and they were actually furious with you."

And so, I didn't confront my mother and Aunt Marcie. Instead, I moved to China, where the distance and twelve-hour time difference makes it difficult for them to badger me. I may be a dating disappointment, a single-lidded romantic failure, but at least I'm no longer reminded of my shortcomings every other weekend and national holiday.

And this Thanksgiving I'll finally be free of Aunt Marcie's probing fingers. I'll invite my friends, and we'll eat at 7:00 P.M. instead of three in the afternoon, the turkey will be stuffed with bread instead of rice, and no one will care if I have a boyfriend.

I've ordered the turkey from Jenny Lou's and already made pie crust and frozen it. Geraldine is bringing green bean casserole, and Ed mentioned something about a pitcher of Bloody Marys. It's going to be an ideal Thanksgiving, just the way the pilgrims imagined it. Except in China, not America, obviously

In fact, I've been so busy dreaming about pumpkin pie and sweet potatoes that I hardly had time to think about all those pesky doubts crowding the back of my mind. Like the hollow feeling I get when Geraldine teases me about Jeff being my boyfriend, even though he clearly is not. Or the frostily polite tone in Charlie's voice at the Marine Ball—not to mention his conspicuous silence (I thought I saw him in the lobby the other day, but when I called his name, he didn't turn around). Or the dead-end path my career seems to be taking, ever since my piece on Max Zhang got censored (I love *Beijing NOW*, but it can make *People* look like Pulitzer material).

I know I should have pitched the Max Zhang story to a few American publications. But as the days slipped into weeks, my ambition felt more and more like a fantasy that had drifted too far from reality. So, I was more than a little surprised when Ed brought it up over lunch one day.

"Isabelle." He raised his voice over the roar that filled our neighborhood noodle joint, shifted his bulk on the tiny chair and clutched at the table, nearly sending a bottle of vinegar into my lap. The waitress set down large, steaming bowls of soupy noodles, and Ed immediately dove in, slurping up a mouthful before turning to me. "Wha da fuck ish goin' on wi' dat Mash Ang piece?"

I allowed a spoonful of salty broth to slide down my throat. "Sorry—I didn't catch that?"

He finished chewing, swallowed, and sighed. "The Max Zhang piece. What's happening with it? I thought you were going to pitch it."

"Oh, yeah, well I'm still thinking about where to send it." I avoided his eyes and tried to pile noodles into my porcelain spoon.

"Why?" He slapped his hand on the table and soup slopped over the edge of our bowls. "What the bloody hell are you waiting for?" He glared at me before twining another bunch of noodles around his chopsticks. *Ssslurrp, ssslurrp, ssslurrp.*

"I'm still doing some research on the Internet . . . trying to figure out the best way to pitch it . . . "

"The longer you sit on it, the harder it's going to be to sell." He reached for his tea and took a long sip. "Look, I'll give you the names and e-mails of some editors, but only if you promise to pitch it by the end of the week."

"Really?" I felt my face grow pink. "You'd do that for me?" It was such a kind, generous act . . . in fact, totally unlike Ed. I crossed my arms and fixed my eyes on him. "Why?" I asked.

"Come on, Iz. Don't look at me like that." He shrugged, his eyes wide. "I'm not a *monster.* I've been known to *help* people."

"Please, I know you better than that. Now, *why?*"

He toyed with his noodles and then rested his chopsticks on the edge of his bowl. "Honestly?" He continued in a rush. "Life is pretty good here for us . . . we eat at all the best restaurants, hang out at the hippest clubs, get pissed at the coolest bars, the magazine keeps us busy, we're surrounded by beautiful women . . . " He caught my baleful stare. "Okay, erase the beautiful women part. Anyway, my point is, it's easy to drift along in an expat haze, not thinking about where your life is going . . . And before you know it you're forty-three and the only clips you've produced in five years are from *Beijing NOW.* I don't want to see that happen to you. You're too good a journalist." He offered me a wry smile.

"Oh, Ed—you're a great journalist. I'm sure you could—"

He lowered his eyes, but not before I saw a glimpse of regret. "Besides," he cut me off. "Tara Joyce, the *New York Trib* features editor, is a babe. We cut our teeth together at the *Sydney Morning Herald.* Be sure to mention my name—I want her to know

I'm your boss. Mentoring the young'uns . . . surefire way to get her in the sack."

"You're doing this so you can sleep with her?" I gazed at him, my disgust tinged with amazement.

"Obviously!" He threw back his head and guffawed. "Who do think I am? The Dalai-bloody-Lama?"

A week later and I've sent a casual, yet professional-sounding e-mail off to Tara Joyce at the *New York Tribune* (it only took me six hours to compose), finished my grocery shopping for next Thursday, and started sorting pecans. Alone in the kitchen, I hum to myself as I mix Karo syrup and eggs together, roll out pie crust and crimp the sides into a pretty edge.

"Hi, Iz! Are you home?" I hear the front door open and close, and then Claire's socked feet come padding through the hall.

"I'm in the kitchen!" I call out. Claire has seemed more re-laxed since the Marine Ball. It might be because she thinks I ap-prove of Wang Wei—when she asked my opinion, I raved about his undeniable good looks and sharp intellect, even though I can tell he's about as reliable as a tabloid journalist—or maybe it's because she billed 103 hours last week at her law firm. She still disappears for days at a time (but at least I now know where she is: Wang Wei's CBD penthouse), and still seems to exist solely on sweetened green tea and slim cigarettes. But a few days ago she invited me to get a mani/pedi with her and even asked me for advice on what nail polish color she should use, Chanel Splen-deur or Vamp. When I directed her instead to Shanghai Red, she didn't get annoyed but agreed that it was a much better match for her skin tone.

"Hi, sweetie." Claire comes into the kitchen, heads straight for the refrigerator, and pulls out a bottle of green tea. "What are you doing?" She glances at the pecan bits that litter the counter.

"Making pecan pie for Thursday."

"Oh yeah . . . " Her brow furrows. "About Thanksgiving . . . I'm not sure I can make it."

"What? Why?" My voice rises in dismay. Granted, I had a feeling she'd wriggle out of it, but still, Thanksgiving feels like something we should celebrate together. We are sisters, after all.

"I'm sorry, Iz. I know you've been looking forward to it. But we're closing on a huge deal next week and I have loads to do."

"Well, at least come for dessert," I urge. "I'm making pie— apple and pecan."

"I'll bring the pumpkin," she says with a smile. "They sell them at Paul's Steak and Eggs. I can just pick one up on my way home."

"At least we won't have to watch Aunt Marcie scrape the whipped cream off her dessert."

Claire affects a nasal pitch and mimics Aunt Marcie's whiny voice. "'You didn't put *cream* in this, did you?'"

"'Are you trying to *kill* my husband?'" I add.

"Meanwhile, Uncle Gray would be hiding in the kitchen, eating pie as fast as he could." We both laugh.

"Just think," I say dreamily. "A Thanksgiving without Aunt Marcie. Can you imagine?"

"No, I really can't." She pops a bit of raw dough in her mouth and chews thoughtfully. "Who else have you invited?"

"The usual suspects—Geraldine, Gab, Jeff, Ed . . . "

"Oh, Ed's going to be there?" Claire leans on the counter casually, but her cheeks suddenly seem to be very red.

"Yeah." I examine her face. "Why? You couldn't possibly have a thing for—I mean . . . you and Ed aren't— What about Wang Wei?"

"Oh, don't be silly. Of course, Wang Wei and I are still together, it's just that Ed and I—" She breaks off as the phone starts to ring.

"What? You and Ed what?"

"I better get the phone," she says, ducking out of the room and out of my question.

"Hi, Mom!" I hear her exclaim from the living room before I plug my iPod into the kitchen speakers and turn up the Aimee Mann. Things between my mother and Claire might be uneasy, but you'd never know it from their phone conversations, which are still as cozy as a cashmere blanket. Even though I can't hear my mother's exclamations of maternal pride, listening to Claire boast about her billable hours brings back all my feelings of inadequacy.

I heave a sigh and turn back to my pie, patting the dough into the bottom of the pan and accidentally tearing a jagged hole in the bottom. "Dammit!" I mutter to myself, trying to ease the edges together.

"What's wrong?" Claire wanders back into the kitchen.

"Nothing, I just need to patch up the crust. How's Mom? Didn't she want to talk to me?" I try to keep the hurt out of my voice.

"The call waiting went off." Claire makes a little face. "She still doesn't know how to switch back and forth."

"Oh, yeah." I start arranging pecan halves in the bottom of the pie dish, lining them up in a checkerboard pattern.

"She did say . . . " Claire's voice trails off uncertainly and I look up sharply.

"What? What is it? Oh God, is something wrong? Is it Dad? Is he sick?"

"No, no, no, Dad's fine," she says reassuringly. "But he has to go Geneva for some last minute molecular biologists' conference next week, and Mom was thinking she could come here for Thanksgiving. Apparently she has to use up her frequent flier miles before they expire."

"Oh!" My eyebrows shoot up. Despite their weekly phone conversations, my mother and sister haven't seen each other in almost two years. They both claim it's because of the distance, but that sounds like an excuse to me. I know Claire has secrets—namely, her married boyfriend—but what has kept our mother away? Try as I might, I can't think of a reason. "Well," I say slowly, "that would be . . . nice."

Claire sips from her bottle of green tea and stares into space, her expression unreadable. "Mom also said Aunt Marcie and Uncle Gray are going through a rough patch," she adds.

"Mmm." I make a noncommittal Chinese sound that could mean anything from *Poor thing!* to *You think I care about Aunt Marcie? Thanks to her, I was in therapy for six years!*

"Apparently, Uncle Gray's been having an affair with their neighbor."

"What?" I gasp.

"Aunt Marcie claims it's a mid-life crisis, but according to Mom they've been having trouble for years."

"Wow. Well, I've always wondered how he put up with her constant nagging." I shake my head.

"I guess he worked out his frustration next door!" We both start to laugh.

"There's one other thing," she says, her tone suddenly serious. "Mom was thinking that a change of pace might be good for Aunt Marcie . . . "

Something in her voice makes me glance up. I have a feeling I know where this is headed. "Oh noooo," I protest. "Not Aunt Marcie. Not here for Thanksgiving. Please. I've been looking forward to this for weeks."

"I know, Iz." Claire sighs. "But she's getting divorced. Her husband of thirty years just *dumped* her, for crying out loud. I just . . . I don't know . . . I kind of feel sorry for her."

"I don't," I huff. "She's single-handedly responsible for my low self-esteem."

"So she has some transference issues. She doesn't mean it." Claire sighs. "I bet she's so upset she won't have the energy to criticize you."

I grab another handful of pecans from the bowl. "You already told them they could come, didn't you?"

"Well—" She hesitates and looks down. "Yes. But what else could I do? It's the holidays, Aunt Marcie's depressed, Uncle Gray's moving next door, Dad's going to be eating fondue in Switzerland . . . Come on, it's not like I'm dying to see Aunt Marcie either. I'm going to have to take a day off from work . . . my boss is going to kill me. Besides, you know what Auntie calls me? *Yaqian*. Toothpick."

"Okay, okay, okay." I throw a handful of nuts back into the bowl and wipe my hands on my jeans. "It's fine."

"I'm really sorry. Look, I can call Mom back if you want—"

"No, really." I force a smile to my lips. "It's fine."

"Well, okay . . . " She sidles to the kitchen door. "I should probably go over some papers before I meet Wang Wei for dinner . . . "

"No problem!" I wave her away cheerfully. But alone again in the kitchen, I stir my sticky pie filling and sigh. Claire and I may have moved halfway around the world, but our roles remain the same—she is still the good girl, the filial daughter. I am the bad seed, disobedient and selfish. *Plus ça change, plus c'est la même chose.* Or, perhaps the Chinese saying is more apt: *Bu bian ying wan bian.* The best way to face ten thousand changes is not to change at all.

Of course, my mother and her sister have been back to China since they fled in 1949. But they are southerners, preferring

Shanghai's sleek sophistication to Beijing's chaotic sprawl. Though they speak Mandarin, it's imbued with the soft, lisping sounds of the South, and though they miss China, their memories are of the graceful French concession mansions of treaty port-era Shanghai, not the blocky buildings, polluted air, and vast avenues of new Beijing.

"Northerners!" Aunt Marcie sniffs, spotting a migrant worker sprawled out on his three-wheeled cart, enjoying an early evening siesta. "They're so lazy!"

"And dirty!" my mother adds, flicking at the grimy seat of our cab as it creeps down Dongdaqiao Lu.

We are on our way to the Sichuan provincial government restaurant, one of my favorite eateries, which Ed once oh-so-charmingly described as "better than a trip to Chengdu, shits and all." Their food is blazingly hot and weirdly numbing—something to do with the Sichuan peppercorn powder sprinkled on everything. I'm not sure Mom and Aunt Marcie will like it, but chilies are supposed to raise endorphins, right? I'm sure we could all use a spice-induced good mood.

Mom and Aunt Marcie arrived this afternoon on the Air China flight direct from JFK. Despite fourteen hours of travel, they look pert and energetic, their tiny bodies folded into the backseat of our rattletrap Xiali cab.

"It's so nice to see you two!" Our mother leans forward to pat Claire on the cheek. Again. After exchanging greetings, making tea, showing them the apartment—Mom will sleep in my room, Aunt Marcie on the pull-out couch in Claire's office, while Claire and I will share the master bedroom—the four of us have settled into a forcedly pleasant atmosphere, like the calm before the storm. I can feel my mother and Aunt Marcie straining to unleash a barrage of questions as Claire and I both retreat further and further into silence.

It's only 6:00 P.M., but as our cab screeches to a halt outside the restaurant, I see a queue spilling out the doors.

"Did you make a reservation?" Claire murmurs to me. I shake my head and she presses her lips into a thin line. "Looks like we might have to wait a few minutes," she announces.

"Oh, I'm fine, don't worry about me," Aunt Marcie says faintly. "I don't need to eat much, anyway. Must stay thin, you know, if I'm ever going to attract another man."

I close my eyes in order to resist the temptation of rolling them heavenward. Aunt Marcie's favorite role is martyr, which is currently at odds with her new status as gay divorcée.

We fight our way into a corner of the crowded waiting room, where we stand in a little huddled group. *"Er shi yi!"* calls out the hostess. Twenty-one. I look at the number in my hand. Fifty-five.

"Maybe we should go somewhere else," I suggest.

"No, we're fine," says my mother. "I'm not really that hungry." She heaves a deep, guilt-inducing sigh. "Getting old . . . losing my appetite."

"Mom," I object, "you're not old." But she ignores me.

By the time we sit down, we are all starving, hunger sharpening our fretfulness into a dangerous point. The waiter brings us one menu, as is customary in China, and I grab it before anyone else has a chance to take a look.

"Can I do the ordering?" I plead, anxious to show off my new knowledge of Chinese cuisine. Three doubtful faces look back at me—none more hesitant than Aunt Marcie—but no one protests.

My spirits lift as I page through the menu, and I order enough dishes to crowd the table, all packed with plenty of endorphin-boosting chili peppers. They arrive one by one, slinky cubes of *mapo doufu* in a deep red chili sauce, thin strips of sweet and savory *yu xiang rousi* pork, nuggets of *lazi ji* fried chicken hidden within a bright nest of dried chilies, crescent dumplings doused with an aromatic roasted chili oil.

We pick up our chopsticks and silently start eating. The food is fresh from the wok, spilled carelessly onto the plates, yet each dish a complex blend of salty, sour, sweet, and spicy. The sharp tang of ginger hides in the slivers of pork, while the tofu burns my mouth with chilies, then thrillingly numbs it with Sichuan peppercorn, each bite more intense than the last.

"*La!*" exclaims my mother. Spicy. "*Ma!*" Numbing. She quickly scoops some rice into her mouth.

"Did you order anything else? Anything not spicy?" Aunt Marcie fishes a piece of chicken from the chilies and blots the oil off on a paper napkin.

Oops. I knew I forgot something. "Er, no," I admit.

Aunt Marcie turns to my mother with an exasperated look. "Your daughter. She's lived in Beijing all these months and she still can't order dinner properly! *Ta hai buzhidao zenme dian cai!*"

"I know how to order!" I protest, but my words are drowned in their laughter.

"Look at all that oil!" Aunt Marcie tips the plate of *mapo doufu* so the deep red chili oil runs to the side. "*Zhenme duo you.*" She motions for another cup of tea and starts dipping cubes of tofu in it, rinsing them free of sauce before placing them carefully on her plate. "You need a boyfriend," she says, popping one into her mouth. "Then, you'll know how to order."

"Yes, how's that going?" my mother asks brightly, pouncing on Aunt Marcie's opening. "Are you dating anyone?"

Impressively, she's managed to hold out a whole five hours before asking.

"Not really," I mumble. That sounds better than no, right?

"I know it's really hard, honey. I just want you to be happy."
She pats my arm and I gaze at her gratefully. She finally understands! But then she continues: "Why don't you let me make you
an appointment with Dr. Wu? He's one of Beijing's top plastic
surgeons. Don't be scared," she says, as I draw in a sharp breath.
"I've done some research and he's the best for eye surgeries. You
want to look your prettiest, don't you?"

"Mother—" I say warningly.

Aunt Marcie thrusts her sharp chin at me. "You pluck your
eyebrows, don't you? Wear makeup? What's the difference?
There's no difference!"

Am I surprised by their insistence? I am surprised by my
lack of surprise. They've been pestering me for so many years,
their bluntness no longer takes my breath away; nothing they say
could shock me. Their mantra is practically tattooed on their
foreheads: find a husband, come plastic surgery or high water.

"Why are you so stubborn, Isabelle?" Mom pats her mouth
with a napkin and lays it on the table. "You can lead a horse to
water . . . "

I pick out a cube of tofu, dark with ground Sichuan peppercorn, and pop it into my mouth, willing the numbness to spread
through my body.

"Ma—" Claire breaks in. "Don't push her, okay?"

"She's being selfish!" Aunt Marcie hisses. "As for you, young
lady, Claire. I still don't understand why you divorced that nice
husband of yours."

Claire's face grows pale. "Oh, let's not get into that ancient
history," she says, picking at her sleeve. I can tell she wants a
cigarette, but our mother doesn't know she smokes—and neither
of us has any desire for her to find out.

"He had a good job, he came from a good Chinese family—
his mother is *such* a nice lady, *really nice*—your children would

have spoken Chinese . . . " Aunt Marcie ticks off my former brother-in-law's attributes on her fingers.

"I *almost* had grandchildren," cries my mother. "I just want a baby to hold and love before I become senile and decrepit." She folds her arms together and moves them in a rocking motion. "Claire, I will *never* understand why you had to go and—" She swallows. "It was unthinkable."

"I'd prefer not to talk about Tom." Claire's tight voice cuts her off.

I look sharply at their flushed faces, both of them close to tears. What was unthinkable?

"I just don't understand why! Why!" Mom lifts her hands in exasperation.

"He . . . didn't make me . . . happy," Claire says faintly.

"Happy!" Aunt Marcie snorts. "You think your husband is supposed to make you happy?"

"We wanted different things out of life," Claire says a bit more decisively, as she signals for the check. I push my chair back from the table to hide my surprise. What does Claire want out of life? This flimsy expat lifestyle? A job that consumes most of her waking hours? A boyfriend who's already committed to another woman? I have no idea, but what's worse is I'm pretty sure Claire has no idea either.

The heaping plates of food sit congealing on the table, their once delicious fieriness subdued into an unappealing solid mass.

"Such a waste," clucks Aunt Marcie, poking at the dish of pork. "Should we take it home?"

"No," I answer. "It's never as good the second day."

I don't remember much about Claire's wedding. But if I close my eyes and picture that day ten years ago, I see red. Red envelopes, stuffed with cash, discreetly pressed into the groom's thick hand. Claire's traditional, high-necked red gown. The swaths of red fabric that decorated the banquet room of Triumphal Palace, our local Chinese restaurant. Every seat at every round table was filled with a face reddened from wine—some were double-filled with children sitting in their parents' laps—the room was packed with our relatives, Tom's relatives, their friends, business acquaintances, and strangely few guests of the bride and groom. Not that anyone would notice amidst the sumptuous eight-course banquet of shark's fin soup and abalone, or among the roar of noise, the DJ cranking out the chicken dance, and the persistent tinkle of chopsticks on teacups, rewarded by a peck between the young couple.

Claire was twenty-five, an innocent bride, shy and oblivious to the double entendre in the best man's toast. She and Tom met through their mothers—a match made at the mahjong table—and he popped the question after only six months of dating. It seemed sudden to me, but no one else was surprised—and, really, who knew Claire best? Not her little sister.

Claire changed multiple times throughout the day (Aunt Marcie's idea), from a frothy white wedding dress, to a skintight red cheongsam, to a skintight hot pink cheongsam, to a plain black cocktail dress. I wasn't part of the wedding party—Claire only had one attendant, her pale roommate from law school, Kate Addison, who took one look at the whole roast suckling pig and spent the rest of the day slugging Johnnie Walker Red in a deep state of culture shock—but I helped my sister change clothes, zipping her skinny body into the array of dresses. At one point— I think she was wriggling into the hot pink cheongsam—she lost her balance and grabbed my arm. When I reached down to help her, our eyes met, and the expression in hers startled me. They weren't filled with the joy of a bride. Instead, they were clouded over with something that looked like resignation.

After the wedding, Claire moved into Tom's one-bedroom on the Upper West Side and I saw them on my weekend visits home. I wanted to like Tom, but I was nineteen to his thirty, a sophomore at NYU to his investment banker. We were worlds apart and my fragile relationship with Claire couldn't bridge the gap. At family gatherings he would offer me nuggets of advice in a voice loud enough for everyone to hear. "I don't know why you want to be an English major," he declared one evening at the dinner table. "You already speak English. Economics. That's what you should study. Basically, by majoring in English, you're setting yourself up for failure."

"Is that right, Tom?" my mother said, concern wrinkling her brow. "Isabelle, you should listen to him. He's in business. He *knows*."

Claire seemed happy during her first few months of marriage. Or, if not happy, then content. At work, she was on the fast track to partner; at home, she had a drawer full of take-out menus and a husband who liked pizza. I didn't see a spark between her and Tom, but I simply assumed, like with many arranged marriages, it would come with time.

Except, less than a year after their wedding, it was over.

Thanksgiving. After shooing Aunt Marcie and Mom out to the Pearl Market in the morning, I spent all day peeling and roasting, chopping and stirring. I whipped sweet potatoes, trimmed broccoli, and cubed bread for stuffing. I set the table, polished the wineglasses, and proudly displayed my two pies on the dining room sideboard. I used three pounds of butter, and even managed to hide the wrappers in the trash before Mom and Aunt Marcie returned from their shopping excursion (they have a radarlike ability to detect saturated fat).

Now, alone in the kitchen, I peer anxiously into the oven where the turkey sits, fat and pale—Roast faster! I think—and listen to the murmur of voices in the living room. After dinner last night, the four of us came home and went to bed, choosing to smooth over our harsh words in the traditional Lee family way: by pretending they never happened. Claire left for the office early and returned this afternoon with a calm smile pasted on her face. Mom and Aunt Marcie came home from the Pearl Market playfully bickering about who could negotiate a better bargain. Everything seems back to normal. Except none of us can quite look each other in the eye.

In the living room, Geraldine chats with my mother about Beijing's modern art scene, while Ed regales Claire and Aunt Marcie with tales of his gap year, spent on an around-the-world trip. "And then in New Zealand," he says, "I got so drunk I missed my bus to Wellington and had to nurse my hangover in a library carrel!" I hear Claire's roar of laughter and Aunt Marcie's disapproving sniff.

"Everything smells great." Gab comes into the kitchen and refills his wineglass. "I love your Aunt Marcie!" he exclaims. "Her bouffant rocks. I'm thinking of hacking off the dreds and going for something pouffy like that." He tries to run a hand through his hair but it gets caught in the matted tangle. "Like a mod Kim Jung Il . . . " he says thoughtfully.

"Really?" I examine his face for sarcasm, but he seems serious.

He grabs a spoon and starts stirring the gravy. "I'm starving. Who else are we waiting for? Wang Wei?"

"*Shhhh!*" I hiss. "Don't mention He Who Must Not Be Named at Thanksgiving!"

He widens his eyes in mock horror. "Why? If he finds out we're talking about him, will he swoop down and evict you?"

I swat his arm. "He's married, you idiot! My mom and Aunt Marcie don't know about Wang —him."

Gab slowly shakes his head. "You and Claire have more secrets than the CIA. One of these days you might want to try another approach. Like honesty."

"Are you kidding? If we were honest, everyone would be all judgmental and angry with us."

Gab raises an eyebrow but doesn't pursue it. "Well, if we're not waiting for anyone, can we start gorging ourselves in the great American tradition?"

"We're almost ready. Just waiting for Jeff to get here."

Gab looks at me with surprise. "I thought you said you'd rather shower in a Shanxi village bathroom for the rest of your life than—"

"I know, I know. But I invited him before I knew my mom and Aunt Marcie were coming. I couldn't exactly uninvite him. He's never even tasted turkey."

"Does your mom know?"

"No, but she won't be surprised. After all, turkey is indigenous to the States and very few Chinese—"

"I meant," he says with exaggerated patience, "does she know that Jeff is your boyfriend?"

"For the millionth time," I shake my wooden spoon at him, *"Jeff is not my boyfriend."*

Gab choruses the words along with me and then laughs. "I know you keep saying that," he says, "but then why are you always hanging out together? Hmmmm?"

I heave an exasperated sigh, but before I can explain— *again*—that Jeff and I are definitely not an item, the doorbell rings.

"That's probably your man now," says Gab with a mischievous smile.

Jeff comes bounding through the foyer, all dimpled smiles and flashy good looks. "Ayi, it's so nice to meet you," he says, shaking my mother's hand. "And, here's the chef!" he exclaims as I enter the room. "Happy Thanksgiving!" His hug lifts me off my feet and twirls me around.

"Um, hi!" I say, a blush rising in my cheeks. I try to disentangle myself from his arms, but he pulls me close. My mother and Aunt Marcie stare at us, their sharp gaze taking in every detail of Jeff's tousled hair and well-tailored clothes. Why does he always have to embarrass me like this? "Well . . . " I take a deep breath and try to suppress my irritation. "Would everyone like to sit down for dinner, now that we're all here?"

"Finally! I thought I was going to faint!" Aunt Marcie says in a pretend whisper.

"Is everyone here, Iz?" asks Jeff with surprise as he slides into the seat at the head of the table.

"As far as I know. Why, were you expecting someone else?"

"I thought Claire just mentioned—" But his words get lost as I go into the kitchen to carry in the turkey.

We pass the platters of food around and Aunt Marcie pokes suspiciously at the stuffing, while my mother helps herself to doll-size helpings of everything—a thimbleful of mashed potatoes, a sliver of turkey, a cube of stuffing.

"Yum!" Geraldine mounding sweet potatoes on her plate. "Everything is delicious, Iz."

"Brilliant turkey!" Ed gnaws on a drumstick.

"And the mashed potatoes are so creamy!" says Gab, drowning his plate in gravy.

"Babe, the jam stuff is awesome!" Jeff points to the dish of cranberry sauce.

"I like the stuffing," concedes Aunt Marcie. "You didn't use butter, did you?"

"Did you make rice?" asks my mother in a quiet voice.

Damn. "I'm sorry, Mom. I forgot." Without a daily bowl of rice, my mother feels incomplete. It gives her strength and comfort, like Popeye's spinach or Proust's madeleine. I fiddle with my fork, feeling simultaneously frustrated—can't she let it go for one day?—and guilty. I didn't mean to forget, honest.

"It's okay," she says. "I'll just . . . eat . . . other stuff . . . It's quite rich, though, isn't it?"

"Well, it *is* a holiday!" I say cheerfully.

"Yes, but that's no reason to pile on the calories," she says pointedly. "Those mashed potatoes look just like an arterial plaque."

I suppress a sigh. My mother's need for Chinese food runs so deep that she eats it every day, only occasionally deviating into certain foreign cuisines, like those of Japan or Korea (but never France or Mexico). When we were kids, she managed to build her empire of Asian hair salons *and* have a four-dish Chinese meal on the table every night at seven. She loves Chinese food so much, she'd happily go to Flushing for dim sum after stepping off a plane from Hong Kong. To her palate, Western foods like butter and cream taste too *ni*—heavy, rich, oily.

An awkward silence falls over the table, until only the clinking sounds of our silverware fill the room. I try to think up an innocuous topic before someone else brings up something loaded with minefields. Like Aunt Marcie's husband. Or Claire's relationship with He Who Shall Not Be Named at Thanksgiving. Or whether or not Jeff is my boyfriend. Or Gab's hair. Or—well, the possibilities are endless.

"So, Jeff. What do you do?" Ah. Mom beat me to it.

He turns to her with a brilliant smile. "I'm a hip-hop, R&B

singer-songwriter-producer in China, Hong Kong, and Taiwan, performing in Mandarin," he says glibly.

"Really?" She raises her eyebrows. "Is that . . . stable?" Disapproval creeps across her face . . . or is it alarm? Our mother envisioned us marrying doctors, lawyers, investment bankers— definitely not pop music sensations, the Lee family equivalent of an axe murderer.

"We had Beijing's hit single last month. Maybe you've heard it? *'Wo ai ni, wo renshi ni . . .'*" He throws back his head and sings a few bars, strumming on an imaginary guitar.

Mom leans back and regards him with the same expression she gave me in junior high when I brought home a C+ on my report card. "And what are your long-term . . . goals?" she says finally.

Jeff shrugs. "I don't know . . . maybe branch out into acting, do a soap opera or a movie, something like that."

My mother smiles politely. I realize with a start that everyone has stopped eating and is staring at our end of the table.

"More turkey, anyone?" I ask hastily. "Come on, it's Thanksgiving! Don't be shy! Aunt Marcie, more stuffing? No? Sure? Okay, I'll clear the table for dessert."

"I'll help you," says Claire, stacking plates.

In the kitchen, I sag against the refrigerator while Claire deposits a pile of plates in the sink. "Tough going, darling," she says, patting my shoulder.

"It's a disaster!" I moan. "Mom hates him and he's not even my boyfriend."

"If he's not your boyfriend then why is he here?"

"How many times do I have to tell you? We're just friends!"

"Oh, sure friends! Is that what you kids call it these days?" She giggles. "Well, I guess you can always use a few more 'friends'!"

"What is that supposed to mean?" I ask.

But she only smiles mysteriously.

Jeff pokes his head into the kitchen and flashes a smile. "Whoa, babe, you didn't tell me it was going to be the Spanish investigation tonight!"

Claire extracts a carton of ice cream from the freezer and slams the door shut. "Inquisition," she says, and is there just the faintest trace of annoyance in her voice? "Spanish Inquisition." She finds a spoon and leaves the room.

"Babe," Jeff cocks his head, "I have to bounce."

"What?" I reach up for the coffee machine and give him a confused look. "You're not staying for dessert?"

"I got things to do . . . can't stick around . . . but I'll call you later, okay?"

"But—"

"Don't make a big deal out of it, okay?" he snaps. "I said I'll call you later." He stalks out of the room and a few seconds later I hear the front door slam. A sigh escapes my lips, but I'm not sure if it's from anger or relief.

In the dining room, not even pumpkin pie à la mode can dispel the tense atmosphere. When the doorbell rings, I hope it's Jeff; that he's changed his mind about dessert after all. But when I look up from slicing pie, I'm surprised to see Claire leading Charlie to the empty spot at the table. Charlie? Why is he here? We haven't seen each other since the Marine Ball, when . . . Oh God. I still can't think about it without feeling absolutely mortified.

Charlie leans down to kiss me on both cheeks and my stomach starts to spin. But when I look into his cool, blue eyes, his kind gaze gives no indication that he feels anything for me. My crush is as hopeless as a schoolgirl's.

"Um, Charlie! Hi!" I force a smile and start babbling to hide my embarrassment. "Do you know everyone? Let me introduce you. This is my mom and Aunt Marcie . . . Ed, Gab, and Geraldine . . . and you know Claire." I look around the table. "Everyone, this is—" I hesitate. What do I call him? Ambassador Charles Eliot sounds so formal, but how can I call him just Charlie? The embassy protocol team would probably burst through the door and arrest me.

"Charlie Eliot," he says, smoothly filling in the silence.

Ed chokes on a bite of pie. "It's such an honor to meet you!" He turns to Claire. "I can't believe the—"

"It's an honor to be here!" says Charlie, adding quickly, "Mmm . . . the pies look delicious. Did you make these, Iz?"

"The what?" says my mother sharply. Her expression looks wary, like Charlie might be a well-known American fugitive or something. After all, we've already introduced her to a man who slept off his hangover in a library carrel, a musician-singer-songwriter, and a guy who hasn't washed his hair in three months. I can see her bracing for the worst.

"He's the American ambassador," says Claire quietly.

"The *what*?" Mom leans over the table. She's always been a little deaf—war damage, she claims, though I maintain it's from overexposure to the high-powered hair dryers at her salons—but, really, couldn't she be a little discreet for once in her life?

But Charlie seems unperturbed as he walks around the table to my mother's chair. "I'm Charlie Eliot," he says with a friendly smile. "The U.S. ambassador to China. It's a pleasure to meet you, Mrs. Lee." He reaches out and shakes her hand.

"Please. Call me Grace," my mother whispers faintly.

Suddenly, everyone is sitting up a little straighter, eating a little more politely, the conversation resumes a little more quietly. Aunt Marcie takes a sip of water and extends her pinky.

"The pie looks delicious . . . " Charlie casts a meaningful glance at the golden wedges.

"Oh!" I remember my manners. "Would you like some? We have apple with a cheddar crust, bourbon pecan, and pumpkin." I pile a plate and hand it to him. "What are you doing here?" I ask, under the murmur of conversation. "Er, I mean, it's such a surprise to see you!"

"I ran into Claire in the lobby yesterday and she asked me to stop by. How are things going with your mom's visit?" He raises his eyebrow conspiratorially.

"Let's just say we could use a hefty dose of diplomacy around here," I blurt. Oops. Maybe I've had too much wine.

"Don't worry, Iz. You're in the hands of a professional." He winks at me, and I feel a tiny jolt in the bottom of my stomach. Which is ridiculous because there is no way Charlie could ever be interested in me. Obviously.

Later that night, as I pile leftover mashed potatoes into a Tupperware dish and stack our dirty plates in the dishwasher, I'm still not sure how Charlie did it. One minute we were all stiffly eating pie and talking awkwardly about the Korean peninsula nuclear crisis. The next minute saw us sprawled on the living room couches, opening another bottle of wine and laughing hysterically. But not because of Charlie. Because of my mother.

Had I forgotten her skill at storytelling, or had I never known? Whatever the case, we hung on her every word as she described her salon's oddest clients. Like the woman who insisted on dying her Pekinese lapdog's fur the same exact blond as her own. Or the balding man who surprised her one day with his new hair plugs. "I didn't know what to say!" she exclaimed as we roared with laughter. "Should I mention the lush hair springing across his head, or pretend that nothing had changed at all?"

I'm still not sure how the conversation turned more serious, how we started talking about my mom and Aunt Marcie's child-hood during Japanese-occupied Shanghai.

But as they shared their memories, I snuck a glance at my friends' faces, which were somber. And riveted.

"During the war, we barely had enough to eat," said my mother. "Our mother would give up her bowl of rice for us, so we could have a little more food."

"Sometimes she'd make soup out of a spoonful of lard, a drop of soy sauce, and hot water. That was it," added Aunt Marcie.

"We'd be lucky for the vegetables we could scrounge from the market. Cabbage, cabbage, and more cabbage." My mother shuddered. "To this day, I can't stand the sight of *da bai cai*."

"How did you leave Shanghai?" asked Charlie gently.

Mom and Aunt Marcie exchanged a glance. "Our father was a banker. Before the war we lived in a beautiful house, an Art Deco in the French Concession with a garden for us to play in," said my mother. "By the end of the war it was crumbling to bits. We had the money socked away, but no way to fix it."

"And when 1949 came," Aunt Marcie added, "our father knew all that talk of communist revolution did not bode well for him. He decided to move to Hong Kong."

"Hong Kong in the fifties was still developing," said my mother. "When we got there, I expected a beautiful city, a fragrant harbor. Instead, it was just a little better than Shanghai. And we were surrounded by people who spoke a strange and loud language."

"We only learned a little Cantonese," said Aunt Marcie. "We studied English instead. Every day. That was your mother's idea." She looked proudly at her sister. "She was so smart, she got a scholarship to study in the States, in North Carolina."

"At the time, I thought it was the only chance we had," said my mother.

"When she first got to America, to Chapel Hill, Grace would write me letters about the strange food and strange people," said Aunt Marcie. "She was so homesick I thought she'd give up and come back to Hong Kong. But then she met Bill and got married . . . that's when she sent for me and our parents."

"I always thought we'd go back to Shanghai," said my mother. "We left in such a hurry. I didn't know I was saying good-bye forever."

"You could always go back," said Geraldine encouragingly. "To visit."

"You can't go home again," said my mother, with more than a trace of sorrow in her face.

Huh. Who knew she knew any Thomas Wolfe?

Now, as I dry the last serving platters and I load soap into the dishwasher, I imagine my mother and Aunt Marcie as little girls waiting out the endless, hungry drudgery of the war, later helping each other study English, planning and working and hoping for a better life. They've always seemed so formidable, tireless, with infinite energy burning in their tiny bodies. It's strange to imagine them as vulnerable.

I put the last plates away and turn the lights out in the kitchen. Many floors above me, Charlie is probably climbing into bed. I wonder if he knows what he did for me tonight, how grateful I am that he defused the tense situation. In the hall, I pause outside my mother's room. A crack of light shines from under the door, so I knock softly and push my way inside. She's in bed with a book, her reading glasses perched on her nose.

"Mom?" I say. "I wanted to tell you something." But I hesitate. How can I tell her that I think I understand why she criticizes me? That I know she just wants a better life for me than her own?

Her face fills with hope as she says, "You've decided to see my plastic surgeon?"

"No!" I roll my eyes.

She sighs, but at the same time a teasing smile creeps across her face. "You're going to dump that loser Jeff?"

I swat her leg through the covers. "Ma! He's not a loser. He's a singer-songwriter . . . Besides, we're not dating." Even to my ears, my voice sounds uncertain.

She raises an eyebrow. "Could have fooled me." But she lets it go, choosing instead to continue in that same musing tone, "You . . . Hmmm . . . Oh, I know!" Her face lights up. "Charlie asked you out on a date! I saw that way he was looking at you!"

"What? No! Mo-om!" I feel suddenly bewildered. She thinks I should date Charlie? He's not Chinese. And could it be possible that she actually approves of someone I might like? Too bad it's Charlie, Beijing's most eligible bachelor, who considers me his substitute little sister.

"Well, I give up. What is it?" She turns her face up. Devoid of her customary dark makeup, her eyes look lined and vulnerable in the glow of the lamplight.

I take a deep breath. "I just wanted to say I'm glad you and Aunt Marcie were here for Thanksgiving. And that I love you."

"Oh, my daughter." She reaches her arms out and I perch on the side of her bed to hug her tiny frame. "I love you too, my *xiao baobei,* my precious treasure. I'm so proud of you." She rocks me back and forth, back and forth, and whispers in my ear, "Just remember, it's never too late to change your mind about seeing Dr. Wu."

Dim Sum

"The familiar *yumcha* scene at a Cantonese restaurant, which is often on several floors, is one of young girls pushing trolleys replete with goodies in bamboo baskets piled high or small dishes set next to each other. As they mill around the dining tables, they call out the names of their wares and place the baskets or dishes onto the tables when diners signal their wishes."

—YAN-KIT SO, *CLASSIC FOOD OF CHINA*

To: Isabelle Lee
From: Julia Steele
Subject: Lost in Honkers?

Dearest, dear Izzy Iz,

    I know this is short notice but Andrew just got invited to a tech-geek conference in . . . Hong Kong!! Any chance you can meet us there in two weeks? Write back and say YES! It'll be just like old times—especially as little Miss Em will stay with her ever-doting grandparents. I'll keep this short because I want to catch up IN PERSON! Can't wait to see you.

    Love,

    Julia

A smile spreads across my face as I read her e-mail over and over again. After my mother and Aunt Marcie's visit, the holiday season dragged on. I missed Julia and Andrew almost as much as the devilled eggs they serve at their annual yuletide party. December passed with lingering, arid cold and a blur of articles about overstuffed hampers and roast goose dinners. I thought Claire and I might spend the holiday together, but when I asked her about it, she seemed reluctant.

"Maybe we could invite some people over for Christmas," I suggested one Sunday afternoon in early December. I was curled up with my book on the sofa, and Claire was parading outfits before the mirror, trying to decide what to wear out to dinner with Wang Wei.

"That would be nice, sweetie . . . " She smoothed a black pencil skirt over her nonexistent hips and looked critically in the mirror. "But Christmas isn't really a big deal here. No one really celebrates it. Unless you want to go dancing."

"I just think it would be nice to spend the holiday together with our friends, don't you?"

"I don't know, Iz. Didn't we just get everyone together for Thanksgiving? I really don't think I can handle another family holiday."

"I don't think Mom and Aunt Marcie have any plans to come back to Beijing, if that's what you're worried about. Besides, I didn't think their visit was that bad," I added, thinking back to Thanksgiving night, when my mother looked so small and vulnerable in the sharp lamp light.

"Are you kidding? It was a freaking nightmare. I didn't see Wang Wei for a week. And could Mom and Aunt Marcie have been any more annoying about the marriage and having children thing? They're obsessed." She rolled her eyes.

"But their story. About the war. It was so—so heartbreaking. Didn't you think? I never knew any of that."

"Me neither." For a second her face softened, but then her mouth set again in that straight line. "But I'm sick and tired of feeling guilty about not having kids. So what if I'm single and childless? Haven't I done everything else they always wanted?" She threw out the words as if she were talking to herself.

"They just want us to be happy," I said weakly.

"They want themselves to be happy," she snapped. "Mom and Aunt Marcie have this childish idea that we should be a perfect American family. Two loving, successful daughters who live next door to their parents, raising happy broods of romping grandchildren. Guess what? Life isn't that easy. Families are fucked up. People fuck up. I—" She broke off. "Why the hell do you think I moved to China?" she said instead.

I stared at her. Why? Because she felt pressure to have a baby? That seemed a little extreme. And what did she mean about fucking up? I opened my mouth to ask her. But after so many months, the words stuck in my throat.

"You're right," I said eventually. "Their expectations can be a little unrealistic."

Claire held a crisp white blouse up to the black skirt. "What do you think? Does this look too waitressy?"

"Who cares? You're already Wang Wei's slave. Why not dress the part?" I muttered. Not quietly enough as it turned out.

"I really wish you wouldn't talk about him that way. He's my boyfriend. And I care about him. A lot."

I sighed. Ever since the night of the Marine Ball, Wang Wei had become a sore subject between us. In my opinion, he seemed to symbolize everything that was wrong with Claire's life: the hollow friendships, her obsession with status, the charade of happiness. "I'm just worried about you," I finally said.

"You sound like Mom." Her tone was not affectionate. "Don't you think I know how to make decisions for myself? Okay, maybe I wasn't prom queen"—this was a direct reference to me, though I wasn't prom queen, just a prom princess—"but I've dated enough guys to know what I want."

"Claire, he's about as affectionate as an iceberg. He's married, he's dabbling in some shady business deals . . . Is this really making you happy?"

"*Don't.* Second-guess my decisions."

"I'm not," I said, even though I was. "I just want you to be happy."

"I told you. *I'm happy.*" She turned from the mirror to face me. "And you know something else? I don't comment on your 'love life.'" She spat out the last two words as if they had quotes around them. "And I would appreciate it if you didn't comment on mine."

She left the room, and a few minutes later she went out for the night without saying good-bye. When I apologized the next day, she seemed tired and flat, as if someone had pulled a plug and deflated her.

As it turned out, Wang Wei surprised Claire on Christmas Eve, whisking her away to Phuket for two weeks. And so, Geraldine and I spent Christmas day at the St. Regis Hotel, stuffing ourselves at the free-flow champagne brunch, where we drank a bottle of bubbly. Each.

We had fun, but after I staggered home at five in the evening, my stomach felt hollow—and it wasn't just from my alcoholic breakfast. It was my first Christmas away from home, spent in a country that didn't even celebrate Christmas. I thought I'd find it liberating, simpler. The truth was, I missed my family, even Aunt Marcie.

And so, Julia's e-mail arrives at just the right moment, finding me with a bit of spare cash (my parents very generously deposited a Christmas gift in my bank account), homesick for friends, and considering an escape from Beijing's smoggy, chilly skies, if only for a weekend. In fact, Jeff asked me last week to accompany him to Hong Kong, but I've been hesitant about accepting his invitation.

Ever since that ill-fated evening when he passed out in my bedroom after only two glasses of champagne, I've been uncertain about my feelings for him. On the plus side, who doesn't love being showered with attention? Sometimes when he shoots me that lopsided grin, my knees turn as wobbly as a cube of fresh tofu. He's funny and generous, always heaping gifts upon me. (Admittedly, I was a little taken aback by his Christmas present, a giant Hello Kitty plush toy that takes up a full corner of my bedroom, but I chalked that up to the cultural gap. For all I know, he thinks we crazy Americans celebrate the birth of Jesus Christ by exchanging stuffed animals.) He's always willing to accompany me to work events—like the opening party for the new Philippe Starck–designed restaurant, where the paparazzi snapped a shot of Jeff with his arm slung around Zhang Ziyi that appeared in all the local press. Plus, spending time with him is like taking my very own Chinese language immersion course. We hardly speak English at all anymore.

And yet . . . Something keeps holding me back. It's not just Jeff's unreliability in making plans or returning phone calls, or the naked picture of Tina that's still in his phone (it comes up whenever she calls). It's not just his offhand comments about the loose sexual mores of my fellow female Americans, gleaned from film and TV. (If I have to listen to one more bawdy joke about Rachel on *Friends* or Samantha on *Sex and the City*, I might actually renounce my American passport.) No, I think it has something to do with the feeling of despair that washes over me whenever I see Claire sigh because Wang Wei hasn't called. It's the leaden realization that she's settled for something mediocre, when she deserves more.

I lean back in my chair and sigh. Yes, Hong Kong could be just what I need right now—tropical climate, postcolonial charm, great restaurants, swish hotels, not to mention a visit with my best friends, Andrew and Julia. Just the thought of seeing them makes me exhale.

I'm not sure if Jeff's noticed, but throughout our three-hour plane ride south, and on the high-speed train that whisks us from the airport to the city center, I can scarcely sit still. I'm bursting to tell him about Julia and Andrew, how we met, how they've never been separated from their daughter before this trip, how much I've missed drinking wine at their kitchen table. But I can scarcely insert a word into the conversation.

"Can you believe it?" he says, just as I'm about to tell him about the time Julia and I saved her cat from choking on sausage casing. "There's *another* profile of Cui Jian, and this time they're calling him the grandfather of Chinese rock!"

"Outrageous." I repress a yawn. He's spent the entire morning dissecting the past three months of *Chinese Rolling Stone*.

"I just don't understand why they don't want to feature my band." He tosses the magazine aside in disgust. "D'ya think *Beijing NOW* might do an article of something?"

"Hmm?" I look up from my cell phone, which doesn't seem to have service in Hong Kong. "Sure, I can ask Gab, if you want."

That's odd. Jeff has always scoffed at *Beijing NOW*. But before I can question him, he smiles at me indulgently.

"Babe, I've got a surprise for you."

"Oh, what is it?" I try to look enthusiastic. Jeff's last surprise was a set of Pokémon hair clips, each festooned with a fuzzy, bobble-bodied Pikachu.

"You'll see . . . " He smiles mysteriously.

Through the train window, I watch the scenery flash by and try to relax. Two weeks ago, when I mentioned to Jeff that I was going to Hong Kong to meet my friends, his face lit up. Before I knew it, he had booked himself an airline ticket, and reserved (separate) hotel rooms, negotiating a matchless price at the guest house where Andrew and Julia are staying. When I opened my mouth to clarify that this was a friendly, *platonic* weekend away, he reassured me that he would be busy with meetings and appearances for his Hong Kong record label.

Our taxi slows and I peer out the window, my nervousness giving way to excitement at seeing Julia and Andrew in our guest house lobby. I leap out of the car and bound toward the double doors. The entrance seems far grander than it did online, with a circular driveway and a fleet of mint green Rolls-Royce limousines. And . . . that's odd . . . are we on the Kowloon side of the city? I look up and gasp at the grand cream-colored building, twinkling with stately, serene elegance.

"Surprise!" says Jeff. "We're staying at the Peninsula! My record label booked me a suite here since I have all those promotional appearances to do."

"Wow!" For a moment I am speechless. But then I realize what he's said. "A suite?"

"Isn't it amazing? A suite at Hong Kong's most expensive hotel!" he marvels.

"Yeah, I've always wanted to stay here!" But my smile feels

stiff. What about staying in separate bedrooms? "Um . . . " I hesitate.

"*Bie danxing!*" he says, with a trace of impatience. "Don't worry. I'll sleep on the sitting room couch."

"Oh, okay." I'm surprised by the relief that floods through me.

The white-suited bellhop gathers our bags from the trunk of the cab and I stare out across the harbor. Even the Peninsula's driveway has a view of the water, capped by the glittering towers of Hong Kong island. I hope it won't be too inconvenient to meet up with my friends, who are staying over there on the other side of town. I swallow a sigh. I guess it really doesn't matter. After all, what kind of ingrate turns down a suite at the Peninsula?

My resistance dissolves the minute I step inside. The airy marble lobby drifts with the seductive, heavy fragrance of star lilies mixed with cigar smoke, the strains of a string quartet waft politely over a curved staircase, potted palms dot the polished floor. The bellhop whisks away the tattered backpack I'm using as an overnight bag, and from the moment we check in, everyone greets us by name.

Our suite overlooks the wide mouth of Hong Kong harbor, with a view of the city's famous skyline. The towering high-rises gleam bright with glass and steel, dark mountains rising above them. I stare at the boats and ferries scudding to and fro and think of Julia and Andrew, across the water on Hong Kong island.

"I should call my friends." I reach for the phone and start punching numbers on the complicated phone/fax/CD/DVD player hybrid. "How do you get an outside line?"

Jeff grabs the receiver and replaces it. "Don't call yet. Let's have a glass of champagne and enjoy the view up here."

"But they're waiting for me," I protest. "I don't want them to worry."

But he's already moving toward the minibar, where he extracts a demibottle of Veuve Clicquot from the refrigerator. Popping the cork, he swiftly pours two glasses and hands me one.

"Li Jia . . . " He motions for me to sit next to him on the couch and reaches for my hand.

"Er, yes?" I try to whisk my hand away, but he's got a grip on it like he's drowning and I'm his only connection to the lifeboat.

He leans his head to one side. "We've spent so much time together these past few months, I really feel like we've become close."

Oh, dear Lord. How am I going to get myself out of this one? I cross and uncross my legs, trying to avoid Jeff's confident gaze.

"But I was hoping we could get closer . . . " he says.

"Uh . . . " I stall for time by gulping some champagne. "That's really, um. Wow. But—"

Before I can finish my sentence, he's set down his champagne flute, slid closer, and wrapped me in a hug. "You're so diverting," he says. I think he means funny.

I try to pull away gently and finally break free, flinging my hair over one shoulder in the process. "Oh my God, I'm so sorry!" I apologize. My ponytail has accidentally whipped him in the eye.

"Jesus, Li Jia!" He blinks several times, blotting at his streaming eye with the back of his hand. "You knocked my contact lens out. We need to find it. I can't do my appearances in glasses!"

I lean over to switch on the table lamp and the bright light kills any final hope of romance. "Don't move," I instruct.

I spend the next twenty minutes on my hands and knees, scouring the area for the minute plastic lens. Jeff remains frozen on the couch. "What if you can't find it?" he cries. "My fans won't recognize me if they see me in glasses!"

"The horror!" I tease. But he's not amused.

I'm just about to give up when I see a tiny gleam of light on Jeff's pants. "Oh, hold on! I think I've . . . got it!" I snatch the contact off his trousers, my fingers accidentally brushing against his crotch. "Oops, sorry." I blush.

He ignores me. "Give it to me." He holds his hand out. I deposit the lens onto his palm and he stalks into the bathroom.

Apparently, his amorous mood is over. I exhale quietly.

"What time is it?" he calls over the sound of running water.

"Six!"

"What?" He appears in the doorway, the contact lens now presumably firmly fixed in his eye. "I'm late!"

"I know! Julia and Andrew probably think I've been abducted. Don't worry, I'll call them right now."

"No! I'm late to meet my producers for drinks!" He pads into the bathroom and turns on the shower full-blast. "Babe," he calls, "do me a favor and bring me my dark jeans and Zegna shirt, okay?"

"You're working tonight?" I try to inject some disappointment into my voice, just to be polite. Secretly, I'm thrilled to have Julia and Andrew to myself.

He sighs theatrically. "Don't give me a hard time about this, babe. You know these HK producers could make my career. If we finish up early, I'll meet you, Judy, and Alan out later, okay?" He nudges the bathroom door shut.

"It's Julia and Andrew!" I call. But he doesn't hear me beneath the beat of the Peninsula's matte-finish shower column with six adjustable body sprays.

My ears pop as the elevator heads up and up and up twenty eight floors to Felix, the restaurant at the top of the Peninsula Hotel. I step out into a gleaming white and pink space, walk past a battery of sleek tables and chairs and up a Plexiglas stair-case to the tiny bar. I'm looking for Jules and Andrew, but what I discover instead is the view from the wall of floor-to-ceiling windows. The glittering city lights spread out before me, gleam-ing in the busy harbor; set against the tropical night sky, the city dazzles.

Half a vodka martini later I see them walking up the stair-case, their familiar faces turned toward the windows, caught by the view. And then Julia spots me perched on my spindly bar stool and she rushes over to enfold me in a hug. For a moment the three of us stand there, our eyes alight in the soft Philippe Starck–designed glow, grinning like maniacs.

"Can you believe this?" squeals Julia. "We're in *Hong Kong!*"

"I know!" I grin. "We just hopped from one island to another."

More drinks arrive and more chips—not the ordinary potato variety, but exquisitely thin, crisp, light salty bites—and we sip and crunch and Julia tells me about Emily's first sentence ("Want Camembert!"—that's my girl!) and then she and I pretend to nod intelligently when Andrew launches into a description of his computer programming conference.

Is there any greater happiness than being reunited with your best friends? Possibly. But as we sit and talk and laugh, I start to feel more relaxed than I have in months. It's just the three of us, the way it's always been. And, in this moment, with the view sparkling outside, and an icy martini gleaming in front of me, surrounded on either side by the two people who know me best, it is enough.

So, what's going with you and Jeff?" Julia asks again. She chases a wonton with her chopsticks. "I thought you weren't interested in him."

"I told you, we're just friends." I shrug. "Here, have some more Chinese broccoli."

We've finally made our way into the steamy night, lurching through the narrow, neon-lit back streets of Kowloon to a cheap and cheerful noodle joint. But after three rounds of drinks, their curiosity has sharpened.

"I don't get it. You're just friends, but he showers you with stuffed animals and is springing for a suite at the Peninsula?" Julia wrinkles her brow.

"I downloaded some of his music from iTunes," interjects Andrew. "It's . . . catchy."

"You don't have to be polite." I slurp up a long noodle. "I don't think we're exactly his demographic."

"What's going on? We want to meet him!" Julia waves her porcelain spoon emphatically.

"I told you. There's nothing going on." I busy myself trying to dehead a steamed shrimp with my chopsticks, but when I look up they're still staring at me. "Except . . . well . . . he did try to pull some moves this afternoon . . . "

"What!" Julia gasps. "What happened?"

And so I tell them about the champagne, the iron grip handhold, my flailing ponytail, and Jeff's lost contact lens.

"But, Iz, if you're not interested"—Julia's laughing so hard she has to stop to catch her breath—"why don't you just tell him?"

"It's different in China. I don't want to hurt his feelings. Causing someone to lose face is unforgivable," I point out. "Besides, he likes me. And it's refreshing to be liked . . . for once."

They exchange a glance. "And what happened to the diplomat? Any news from the mysterious Charlie?" Julia leans her elbows on the table.

"I've run into him a few times since Thanksgiving, but he's always too busy to chat. I'm starting to wonder if he's avoiding me."

"Or maybe," Julia picks up her chopsticks, "he's afraid to ask you out because he thinks you're with Jeff."

"Ha!" I snort. "I don't think so."

"Why?" she demands. "After the Marine Ball, it would be an easy assumption to make."

"Let's face it," I sigh, "the best thing in my life is work. And even that's not great."

"I love your column on the different kinds of Chinese food," says Andrew. "I never knew General Tso's chicken didn't even exist in China!"

"Are you holding out on me?" Julia looks surprised. "I haven't seen those articles."

"I Googled her," explains Andrew. "It's terrific stuff, really funny and personal. You should check it out."

"So *that's* what you do at work all day," I tease.

Andrew laughs, but Julia's thoughts are far away. "You should write a food column, Iz. About discovering China through its regional cuisines."

"And how I gained twenty pounds in the process," I quip.

"I'm serious," she says. "One of my authors is an editor at *Cuisine* magazine. I can ask her to take a look if you want."

"Oh, come on, Jules." I balance my chopsticks on the edge of my bowl. "You and I both know how hard it is to get freelance work these days." I start listing the reasons on my fingers. "I don't have a platform. My only clips are about stuff like 'One hundred Best Beauty Buys at Your Local Drugstore!' I got *fired,* for crying out loud. I'm . . . nobody."

"Iz, one . . . mishap . . . does not make you a nobody."

"Okay, filled with ignominy, then."

She crosses her arms. "You know, Isabelle," she says, and there's more than a hint of exasperation in her voice, "it's not tempting fate to think big."

"I know, but—"

"Just send me the articles and let me take a look, okay?"

"Sure," I say, even though I know I won't. In fact, I've never heard of a more ridiculous—not to mention potentially humiliating—idea in my life.

Later, alone in the suite at the Peninsula (I love saying that), I change into a pair of cool, cotton pajamas and eye the sitting room sofa, which housekeeping has turned into a bed with crisp sheets and a thick wool blanket. Should I sleep there? But Jeff did say he'd take the couch. Besides, he did ditch me this evening, not even bothering to check in by cell phone. I hesitate for only a second before moving to the bedroom and crawling into the downy bed, pulling up the fluffy covers and turning on the TV. Two hundred channels flip by before I settle on CNN. Propped up by a half-dozen pillows, I listen to the soothing American accents.

"And today in Beijing," says the announcer. "The lead U.S. envoy to the Six Party Talks arrives for another session . . . " I move toward the screen to see a group of dark suited figures stride through a hotel lobby. Hey, that looks like the St. Regis! I peer more closely at the TV. And isn't that . . . ? Oh my God, it is! It's Charlie! He's walking with the delegation, his head bowed. He looks . . . well, he looks busy.

I stare at the screen. How could I have been so vain as to think Charlie might have been avoiding me? He's not just busy, he's actually saving the world *from nuclear disaster*. If the tense lines on his face are any indication, I'm pretty sure I'm the last person on his mind.

I switch off the TV and glance at my cell phone. It's well after 2:00 A.M. and I still haven't heard from Jeff. Should I call him? But he's probably well into a second or third bottle of Chivas by now. Instead, I turn off my phone and switch out the lights, before closing the bedroom door and turning the key in the lock. In the dark, the buildings sparkle in the distance and I watch them, trying to stay awake for as long as the night's three martinis will allow. I don't know when I drift off, but when I wake to go to the bathroom, the digital clock glows 3:00 A.M. and I am still alone.

The next morning, creamy light creeps into the room, edging me out of sleep. I stretch and shake my head against the merest suggestion of a hangover hiding behind my left eye.

After quickly showering, dressing, and using the Pen's turbo hair dryer, I open my door and creep into the sitting room, which is dark, the blackout curtains pulled tight against the morning light. Perching on the edge of Jeff's pull out sofa, I hesitantly pat his shoulder. He groans and rolls onto his stomach. "What time is it?" His voice is muffled.

"I just wanted to tell you, I'm meeting Jules and Andrew in half an hour," I whisper.

"Babe, I feel like shit." I strain to hear him through the pillows.

"You poor thing. Are you hung over? Was it a late night?"

He winces. "Oh my God, those producer guys are crazy . . . We went to a club and they just kept ordering these bottles of Chivas . . . " He closes his eyes as if the memory overwhelms him. Though, knowing Jeff's tolerance, it was probably just one glass of Chivas that did him in. "Babe, don't go. Stay here and we can get room service!" His eyes still closed, he gropes blindly for my hand.

Whoops, I'm not falling for the iron handhold again. Swiftly, I stand to avoid contact. "Oh, that sounds really fun . . . but I really should meet up with my friends. They flew all this way to see me. Jules even took time off from work, and it's her crazy season. She has five authors on the New York Times best-seller list right now!"

Jeff cracks open an eye. "What does she do again?"

"I told you, she's a literary agent. You know, she represents authors and sells their books to publishing houses."

"Hmm." He struggles to sit up. "You know . . . I think maybe I'll go with you." He creakingly swings his boxer-clad form out of bed.

"What about your hangover?" I take a step back in surprise. Active suffering is most unlike Jeff. He's been known to cancel a coffee date because of an overly strenuous gym workout.

"You don't want me to go?"

"No! I mean, of course you can come. But we'll be speaking English. They don't speak Chinese."

He hesitates, but then heads resolutely toward the bathroom. "I'll be ready in fifteen minutes!"

At eleven o'clock on a Sunday morning, Maxim City Hall clatters with bustle. Families gather to gossip in loud voices, to sip tea, and nibble their way through the variety of small bites, treats that touch the heart, which is what "dim sum" means. Waitresses push heavy, hot carts, piled high with steaming bamboo baskets, throughout the dining room, noisily calling out their wares. The enormous room feels alive with a raucous, tea-charged, dumpling-fueled energy.

Jeff winces at the cacophony of voices, the rattle of dishes, the bright light streaming in the picture windows. But he follows me farther and farther inside the crowded room, my eyes scanning the crammed tables for Julia and Andrew. As it turns out, they are easy to find—their Caucasian features shine out like beacons.

Introductions fly around the table and we all sit down, peering at the contents of each cart as it whisks by.

"Li Jia told me about your work. It's so fascinating." Jeff flashes Julia one of his dazzling smiles. "Tell me, is your job anything like Carrie Bradshaw's on *Sex and the City*?"

"Uh . . . not really." Julia shoots me a look. "It's a lot more boring than that, I'm afraid. I spend a lot of time reading bad book proposals."

"I've been thinking about writing a book . . . " Jeff raises his eyebrows.

"A book?" I exclaim. "You've never mentioned that before– "

"Ooh! *Shagao! Chasiu bao!*" says Julia, waving at a passing waitress and holding up two fingers. "Sorry," she says to him. "Didn't want to let her to go by. I'm starving!"

The conversation falters as we nibble dainty dumplings filled with shrimp peeping pale and pink through their translucent wrappers. We dive into plates of soy sauce-scented rice noodles, unwrap bamboo leaves to reveal triangles of sticky rice, sink our teeth into golden egg custard tarts and watch the pastry flake into our laps.

"The food here is amazing. So fresh!" says Julia, her voice soft with awe. "This is the best dim sum I've ever had. Ooh!" she exclaims, flagging down a passing cart. "Chicken feet!"

"What kind of gigs have you been playing in Beijing?" Andrew turns to Jeff, who's become strangely silent. "You must have some interesting stories to share about life as a pop star," he adds kindly.

"Exactly!" Jeff says eagerly. "That's why I want to write this book. To inspire other young kids not to give up on their dreams."

"How'd you get your first break? It must've been hard to get signed by a record label," says Andrew.

"Oh, there's not much of a story there." Jeff pokes at a piece of shrimp. "My uncle is a music producer in Taiwan. But, you know, it's so important to keep going, despite diversity."

Andrew nods. "You must have had some rough times before you made it big."

"Yeah. I remember this one time when all my friends were going to Macao for the weekend, and I couldn't afford to go. I felt really lonely."

A look of incredulity creeps across Julia's face. She opens her mouth as if to say something, but then closes it.

"So, whaddya think?" Jeff flashes another smile at Julia. "Would you be interested in representing me? What kind of money could I get?"

"I—I—" Julia picks up an empty bamboo steamer basket and looks inside as if hoping another dumpling will appear.

"I don't think you can expect much of an advance, considering how you only have about three American fans and they're all sitting at this table," I jumped in.

"But didn't Jeff's band play at the embassy Marine Ball?" Julia interjects. "He must have some fans there."

"Maybe Charlie's a fan." Andrew elbows me in the side and winks.

"You should invite Charlie to DownLoad's next gig!" Julia says excitedly. "That would be a fun date for you two."

Jeff's face turns blank and for a second I wonder if he understood them. "I'm going to the bathroom." He shoves his chair back and stomps off.

"Did I say something wrong?" Julia looks at me doubtfully. "Is he mad?"

"I don't know." I try to divide the last egg tart with my chopsticks.

"Iz—" Her clear eyes meet mine, and I press my lips together so she won't continue. But she does anyway. "I know you think I always butt into your love life, and Andrew made me swear I wouldn't do that anymore. But . . . " She swallows. " . . . are you sure you and Jeff are on the same page?"

"I told you, we're just friends!"

"*I* know that and *you* know that . . . but does Jeff know? Look, he may be a self-proclaimed expert on American soap operas, but I'm willing to bet that dating expectations in China are a lot different than in New York. It might be time to have a talk with him to clarify things."

"We're on the same page," I insist, even though I'm not sure that's really true.

Later, many shrimp dumplings later, after Jeff leaves to meet his producers, after Julia, Andrew, and I take the tram up to Victoria peak and walk the nature trail, admiring the sea and mountains and lush tropical vegetation, after I hug and kiss them good-bye at their guest house, I ride the Star Ferry back to Kowloon and allow the salty breeze to cool my hot cheeks.

Upstairs, I find Jeff in the sitting room, the curtains still drawn, the room flickering with the light of MTV. "Hey," I say, ignoring the chill that hangs over the room. "How was your meeting?"

His eyes remain fixed on the TV, and even as I perch next to him on the couch, I can tell by the set of his shoulders, his silence, that he is upset. I force a smile and pat his arm. "What should we do for dinner? Let's go somewhere adventurous. That place on a boat—what's it called . . . Jumbo Floating Restaurant? Or maybe one of those underground supper clubs?"

"Whatever." He pulls his legs up. "I'm still pretty full from lunch."

"Yeah, me too, I guess. But it was worth it. I haven't had dim sum in ages."

"*Dian xin,*" he automatically corrects me, using the Mandarin pronunciation.

"And Andrew and Julia enjoyed meeting you," I keep talking. "They thought you were really . . . interesting!"

"But not as interesting as 'Charlie,' apparently."

"Um . . ." This would be the perfect time to talk about the expectations that Julia mentioned. I open my mouth to bring up the topic, but nothing comes out. Do I really need to have this discussion? Suddenly I feel irrationally neurotic. "Hey," I say instead. "I didn't know you were thinking about writing a book."

He barks a laugh. "Me neither. I just thought up the idea today. But it's not bad, huh? You think she's interested? I figured I should milk the *guanxi* while I could, ya know?"

"Milk the *guanxi*? But Julia's my friend, not a business contact. We were having a casual brunch, not attending some sort of networking event!"

"Babe, every event is a networking event."

"Maybe for you, but I don't use my friends just for their connections."

"I'm not using her just for her connections. But if she's got 'em, why not?"

"Do you think that about everyone?"

"Of course," he says easily. "Like you and me. I think you're cool, we have fun together, and if there's an extra bonus of a *Beijing NOW* cover story, why not go for it? It's not like your mag's *Rolling Stone,* but I've got to start somewhere, you know?"

"So all this time, you've just been hanging out with me because I work for *Beijing NOW*?"

"No! Of course not. But you know that's how business gets done."

"Maybe in China."

"Well, we're in China, aren't we?"

"I guess I'm just used to a different approach, that's all. Things are a little more subtle in the States."

He pats my arm indulgently. "But you're really Chinese inside so I know you understand."

Something in his voice makes me sit up and scan his face. "Can I ask you a question?"

He nods distractedly, his eye caught by the new Britney Spears video that flashes on the screen.

"Do you think of me as Chinese or American?" I keep my voice casual, despite the sudden thumping of my heart.

"Chinese, of course!" he answers immediately, bobbing his head to the groove of Britney's hips.

For a second I think, Wow, my Chinese must have gotten really, really good! But then his answer hits me in the gut. After all this time, all these months, I thought he saw past my black hair, my almond-shaped eyes, the shell of me that looks Chinese, to the American heart beating inside. It turns out, he didn't see me at all.

Later, I lie in bed and watch the lights twinkle across the harbor. Jeff snores softly in the living room, but my mind is too troubled for sleep.

As a child, I played with Barbie dolls and idolized Smurfette. I grew up in a middle-class world, a white world of girls with long blond curls and long last names that made my own—Lee—look like a stump. There were moments when I felt embarrassingly, painfully different, like when kids on the playground would push their eyes into slits and chant: "Ching Chong Chinaman, sitting on the fence! Trying to make a dollar out of fifty cents!" Or when my high school English teacher, Mrs. O'Grady, would urge me to toss my bobbed hair: "Shake your head! Just like a China doll!" But as I grew up and into my skin, dated frat boys, introduced my friends to a world of Chinese food beyond fried rice, perfected my tuna casserole, I felt less and less exotic. By the time

I moved to Manhattan, ethnicity had become chic, and race had spun far from the core of my identity. Chinese American joined the other labels I used to describe myself—editor, foodie, New Yorker—a part of me, but not all of me.

But then I moved to China. And suddenly all those forgotten feelings of belonging and alienation elbowed their way to the front. They're in the voice of the cab driver who tells me that I'm not American because Americans have yellow hair. In the face of the waitress who profusely praises Geraldine's simple *ni hao,* brushing off my years of study, the hours I've spent memorizing characters. They're in the glance of *laowai* friends, whose eyes slide over me when they pass me on the sidewalk, unable to pick my face out of the crowd. They're in the surprise of the Americans I sometimes meet, who compliment my fluent English. They're in the throngs that pack a restaurant, my dark head slipping in among the rest, indistinguishable from any other.

Before I moved to China, I thought I knew myself. In New York, no one expected me to speak Chinese or know anything about my ethnic background. Now that I'm in Beijing, I've realized that other people's perceptions are as important as my own. I may think of myself as American, but that is an identity that a whole city, a country, my friends, cannot accept. I may think of myself as American, but it is my race, my Chineseness, that is the only part of me people understand.

The pain of alienation surprises me. I thought I'd left it behind with my adolescence, but it turns out it's still there, still powerful enough to send tears sliding down my face.

Yunnan

"Yunnan is a large province in which Chinese were a minority until recently . . . Its cuisine . . . comes closer than other Chinese provinces to the Alpine preserved-meat model. The finest hams in China are made here . . . Another oddity of Yunnan is the use of dairy products."

—E. N. ANDERSON, *THE FOOD OF CHINA*

You can't just keep avoiding Jeff's phone calls and not returning his text messages, Iz. You have to break up with him." Geraldine turns and scans a row of laundry detergent boxes.

"Break up with him?" I jump as a shopping cart whizzes by my left foot. Even at 8:00 A.M. on a Sunday morning, Carrefour, the French hypermarket import, throbs with people. "How can I break up with someone who's never even been my boyfriend?"

"Iz," she says warningly. "Maybe you never considered him your boyfriend, but he obviously thinks of you as more than a friend. Unless you're interested—and in light of your experiences in Hong Kong, I'm guessing you're not—you need to end it."

"But any moderately sensitive guy would have gotten a clue by now. And don't quote your *Men Are from Mars, Women are from Venus* crap," I say as she opens her mouth. "We're in China and those rules don't apply here."

"You need to talk to him. The sooner the better."

"Let's just focus on finding the dishwashing detergent and getting out of here." I approach a smock-clad employee. *"Duibuqi mafan ni. Ni men de hua fen zai na'r?"* The shop girl shakes her head and darts away from me like I'm covered in open boils.

"You just asked for flower pollen," Geraldine says when she's finished laughing. "The dishwasher powder is over there."

"Smarty pants," I mutter, grabbing a box. And I thought my Chinese had improved.

I haven't seen Jeff since we hugged good-bye in front of the taxi queue at the Beijing airport. "I'll call you," he said, before hopping in the first cab, and eight days later he did. I heard the phone bleat from the shower, but for the first time since meeting him, I didn't feel like picking up. Three weeks later we still haven't talked, and I keep hoping Jeff will interpret my silence as a brush-off. Unfortunately, he seems to think I'm engaged in some sort of mating ritual, a prolonged form of playing hard to get that has only inflamed his interest.

I wheel the shopping cart around and follow Geraldine to the produce section, where we examine twelve varieties of fresh tofu. "You'll feel better once you talk to him, Iz." She selects a creamy square and pokes at the smooth surface. "It'll be like . . . what's that word?"

"Hideously awkward?" I offer as we move toward a towering pyramid of leeks.

"Closure," she says, shoving a few stalks into a plastic bag. "You need closure."

"Maybe." I toss a bunch of cilantro in the basket. "Hey, let's go check out the cheese aisle. I've got a hankering for a wheel of long-life Camembert."

"Ooh, cheese!" Geraldine's face lights up. I knew that would distract her.

Of course I should talk to Jeff. Even though our relationship never developed beyond the platonic level, he deserves my sincerity. It's the right thing to do, we're both adults, I should be honest about my feelings—sheesh, I sound like I'm on *Oprah*. But what I haven't admitted to Geraldine—or anyone, for that matter—is that I've never broken up with anyone, least of all a guy I never even considered my boyfriend. I'm thirty years old and a break-up virgin.

Sure, I've shot down first dates who wanted to go to second base, tossed the phone numbers slipped to me at crowded bars, ignored e-mails. But throughout my entire life, from my high school boyfriend, Patrick Black, to my office romance with Rich, I have always been the dumped, not the dumper. I could think of this as pathetic, which, alone on a Saturday night with a wedge of Gruyère and box of Carr's water crackers, I often do, or I could consider myself a hopeful romantic, someone willing to fight for love.

The weird thing is, now that the roles have been reversed, now that I'm the one who has to end things, I suddenly understand my ex-boyfriends' hurtful behavior. I now know why Patrick still escorted me to our senior prom, even though he'd slept with Jennifer Santora two days before. I know why Brett Corcoran insisted that the only reason he split up with me was because I said I disliked Canadians. (I was kidding!) I know why Rich pretended his parents had died in a tragic plane crash, when in reality they were happily ensconced in an Orlando condominium.

And now, as I pace the kitchen putting away my groceries, I try to think of the kindest, most thoughtful way to have the Talk with Jeff without hurting his feelings. In a coffee shop? Too public—I don't want him to lose face. Over the phone? A possibility, but given the language barrier, he's more likely to think I'm asking him to move in with me. At my apartment? No, no, no. What if he refuses to leave? I shove a six-pack of yogurt into the refrigerator and sigh. The path of least resistance has never looked so appealing.

My cell phone beeps, interrupting my thoughts. It's a text.

U CAN'T DISTRACT ME W/CHEEZ. DO IT TODAY!! GER

I toss my mobile on the counter. Obviously I'm not going to talk to Jeff today, Sunday, the day of rest. I have pedicures to indulge in, DVDs to watch, spaghetti sauce to simmer. I open a can of Diet Coke and decide to ignore Geraldine. My phone beeps again.

DON'T IGNORE ME! G.

Arrggh! She can be such a pest. I sip my soda and scroll through the received messages in my phone's tiny in-box. Geraldine, Jeff, Jeff, Jeff, Ed, Jeff, Jeff. Hmm, he has been calling me a lot lately. I glance at the column of names, and a twinge of guilt nips at me. Geraldine is right. I should talk to him.

I take a deep breath and try to figure out what to say. "Jeff," I mutter, "we need to talk . . . I think you're really great. But . . . " My fingers hover over his number, but before I can dial, I snap the phone shut. This is ridiculous. Jeff and I aren't in a relationship, we never have been. So why is my heart pounding in time to the jackhammers twenty floors below?

I stand there for a while, staring at my phone, trying to work up my nerve. Open phone, close phone. Open, close, open, close. Dial, end call, dial, end call. Oh God, it's no good. I can't tell him. I'll just have to screen his calls for the rest of my life. The phone beeps again, and I jump, nearly dropping my Diet Coke on the floor. What does Geraldine want now? Oh God. It's from Jeff.

HEY BABE, U UP FOR SUSHI 2NITE?

Clearly, this is a sign. I start punching in a message, my fingers moving faster than my judgment.

SORRY CAN'T DO SUSHI. BUT I DO NEED TO TALK TO YOU ABOUT S.T. THINGS MOVING IN WRONG DIRECTION 4 ME. THINK WE NEED TO TAKE A BREAK.

Quickly, I hit Send and watch the screen as a little envelope folds itself up and floats away. There, it's done. It may have been unorthodox, but at least I was honest.

The swiftness of his answer startles me.

R U BREAKING UP W/ME OVER TEXT MSG?!

Breaking up?! We were never together! Quickly, I press the buttons to reply.

DIDN'T THINK U THOUGHT OF ME THAT WAY. I THINK YR GR8, BUT WE'RE 2 DIFFERENT. R U MAD?

His answer is only one word but it worries me.

WHATEVER

Hm. Maybe a text message wasn't the best way to handle the situation. Oh well, it's over now and no one ever has to know.

The shaky feeling of uncertainty plagues me for the rest of the weekend, but I manage to tamp it down with half a bottle of red wine and a pirated *Grey's Anatomy* DVD box set. Now, thank God it's Monday morning and I'm back at work, surrounded by friends and colleagues and not my own thoughts. I stare out at the oddly tinged winter sky and wait for our editorial meeting to begin.

"Okay comrades," says Ed, plopping into a chair with uncustomary good humor. "It's February, I'm thinking twittering love birds, hearts, romance in old Beijing . . . Isabelle, let's start with you."

I glance at my notebook. "I thought we could ask the St. Regis's chef to do a recipe column on chocolate fondue. The dining feature is on track for romantic hot pot for two. And we'll do a rundown of the top spots in town to take your sweetheart on Valentine's Day."

"Yes, good," Ed nods. "But watch the clichés, we're not fucking zombies. Let's add something for all the bitter single people out there. Maybe a feature on the best and worst breakup spots . . ." He muses. "Or breakup horror stories . . . like Dear John letters, voice-mail messages, getting dumped by SMS . . . " He fixes me with a wicked grin as the room erupts in laughter.

My face burns. Do they know? Surely they don't know.

"Good idea." I nod, hoping my bland tone will distract them from my flaming cheeks.

"Great!" booms Ed. "I'll expect copy by this afternoon. Shouldn't be too hard since you're such an expert." More laughter.

"I told you to break up with him, Iz, not permanently emasculate him," Geraldine teases. "I hear he's furious! He'll probably never date again."

"Don't feel too bad," Gab smirks. "Think of it as a favor. This'll be great material for his next album."

"But we were never even together!" I protest. "Does everyone know?"

"Not everyone." Ed pats my arm. "Just everyone who reads the *Beijing NOW* online forum."

In other words, everyone.

Oh God. People keep sneaking up behind my desk, shouting, "You're texted!" and then bursting into laughter. It's become the new office slogan. Ed told Lily he was going to text her if she didn't come up with an exclusive interview with the designers of Shanghai Tang.

I stare at my calendar while waiting for my computer to chug to life. The empty boxes wink at me mockingly. Monday, no plans; Tuesday, no plans; Wednesday, young professionals' meet-and-greet—or should I say *meat*-and-greet; Thursday, no plans; Friday, Saturday, Sunday . . . ugh. Here I am, alone. Okay, so maybe Jeff and I had some issues, but in the grand scheme of things, were they really so important? We had some fun times together, despite the fact that he thought we were in a relationship that would lead to a *Beijing NOW* cover story and I didn't. Now that I've texted him out of my life, I miss him.

My e-mail starts to load and I scan the names hoping to see Jeff's. But no, just spam, spam, freelancer queries and . . . something that makes my heart stop.

To: Isabelle Lee
From: Tara Joyce, NY Tribune
Subject: Max Zhang feature

Hi Isabelle,

   Thanks for your query and sorry for the slow response. We'd
like to include your piece on Max Zhang in a special issue on
Asian filmmakers, to run next week. Are you still interested in
writing this? Time is short and I'd need to have copy by Friday,
2000 words, okay with you?

   Cheers,

   Tara

   PS Tell Ed I say hello and that he owes me a beer, the old
reprobate.

Ohmigod, ohmigod. The *New York Tribune*. The *New York Tribune*! The city's biggest newspaper, with an arts section read by anyone who's at all interested in modern culture? My stomach clenches and I swipe my sweaty palms on my jeans. It's been so long since I wrote to Tara Joyce that I'd given up on ever hearing back from her. Now she wants two thousand words by Friday? Okay, calm calm calm. Youcandothis. Deep breath. You can do this.

   Oh fuck. It's no good. I can't do this. I'm going to have to turn them down. I stare at my computer screen, at the words *New York Tribune,* and curse the day I ever wrote to Tara Joyce. I hit Reply, but before I can start typing Ed's red face looms over my desk.

   "Have you moved on to breakups by e-mail now?" he asks, his mouth curving into a sardonic grin.

   Grrr. "Actually, I just got an assignment from the *New York Tribune*," I snap, crossing my arms. But then the panicky feeling takes over again. "And I'm really freaked out," I admit. "I really don't think I can—"

   "You need an extension on your dining section this month?"

he booms. "Well, I guess I can give you a few extra days. How about Monday?"

"No, you don't understand. I truly don't think I'm capable of—"

He holds up his hands. "Okay, okay, no need to text me, Isabelle. How about next Wednesday?"

I swallow. "Wednesday is fine. But I really wanted to ask you how I can get out of—"

"Jesus, you're tough. All right, you can freelance a couple of the pieces out, but just this once, okay?" He leans against my desk and regards me thoughtfully. "You know, when you first walked into this office I thought you were a real pushover. Claire told me about what happened in New York and you just seemed . . . defeated. Talented, sure, but without the balls to really go for it." He pauses to sip his coffee. "But first you dump Jeff Zhu—who most women in this town would kill to date—and now you're really nailing this *Tribune* story. I guess I underestimated you."

I bite my lip. "Er, thanks." Shit. There's no way I'm getting out of this now.

He turns to stride toward his office, and as I watch his retreating back it takes all my resolve not to throw myself at him and croak, "Help."

The next days pass in a tense blur of too much coffee, too much anxiety, too much time spent on my cell phone trying to set up interviews. Finding people is surprisingly easy, but convincing them to go on the record with me, a freelance journalist with bad Chinese, almost makes me regret not studying the language harder when I was a kid. (Almost.) In the end I talk to Max's friends from film school, his rival directors, his first wife, the slinky actress Chen Mei, who starred in all his early films, and who, it's rumored, dumped him on the set of their last collaboration.

I spend hours taking taxis across town and back again, and even more time cursing my inadequate Chinese, which seems to run dry every time the conversation turns juicy. Thank God for Lily, who patiently helps me translate the sections of recorded interviews that I can't understand.

For the first time in a long time, I don't care that I'm home alone on a Friday night. I sit glued to my laptop, typing and deleting with harried fingers, until finally, in the early hours, the article is done. I glance over the pages one last time. Is it good enough? Should I show it to someone else for a second opinion? Well, no time now. A few clicks of the mouse and it's gone.

Tara's response arrives almost immediately. *Thanks,* she writes. *A fact-checker will contact you ASAP. This will run next Thursday.*

I lean back in my chair, eyes drooping with exhaustion, heart thumping with excitement. It's late, I should sleep, a whole weekend's worth of tardy *Beijing NOW* articles await me. But . . . I'm going to be in the *New York Tribune!* Me, Isabelle Lee! I want to feel the fizz of champagne on my tongue, crank up my iPod and dance around the apartment, or at least talk to my best friend. I dial Julia in New York, but after several rings her line goes to voice mail. I imagine her at lunch with an editor, enduring three courses and a dry sprinkling of small talk.

I glance at the clock: 2:00 A.M. Too late to call anyone else. Only Jeff would be awake and . . . oh, Jeff. I've been so busy this week I haven't had time to think about him, much less apologize for my careless text dump. Geraldine said he was furious with me, and I can't blame him. Now, I stare at my empty bed, overcome with guilt. What if he's alone and depressed, still wounded by my careless text breakup? I pick up the phone only to put it down again. Calling him isn't the answer.

I loosen my hair from its ponytail, pull on a pair of pajamas, slip between the clean sheets, and close my eyes. Sleep comes eventually, filled with dreams of Max Zhang's crisp voice as he directs a new movie. Jeff stars as a German shepherd, watchful and possessive, with a pointy muzzle. When he tries to get too close to the camera, someone dressed as a St. Bernard leads him away. Upon closer inspection, it's Charlie, his eyes peering out large and mournful from behind a furry mask.

Thursday. Gray morning light shines weakly through my bedroom curtains. Gosh, it is early. Can't say I've been up this early since . . . well, since that morning I needed to sneak Jeff out of the apartment. I bet Claire's been up for hours, simultaneously checking her BlackBerry, calling New York, and practicing her downward dog. Anyway, there's no reason why I shouldn't be up this early. Catching the worm. I leap out of bed to log in to my computer, checking the Internet first thing, just as I always do. Today's no different. Okay, here we go, *New York Tribune* website . . . arts page . . . movie section . . . where is it, where is it . . .

It's not there.

At work, I sip from a mug of weirdly acidic coffee that only makes my stomach churn. Why, oh why, did I mention the article to Ed? He just bellowed across the newsroom, asking me if it's appeared, and I had to say no. Oh well, it's still Wednesday evening in New York, only 9:00 P.M. They probably haven't uploaded Thursday's stories.

Almost lunchtime, thank God. I check the *Trib*'s website one last time before Geraldine and I head out to the corner noodle

shop. Fresh burst of hope when a special section on Asian filmmakers appears on the *Trib*'s website. Followed by gasping punch
in the stomach when I can't find my story.

After lunch. My eyes are starting to droop, encouraged by the
huge bowl of starchy ramen in an ocean of salty broth I just
slurped up at Mian Ai Mian. I inhale deeply in an approximation
of yogic breathing while simultaneously checking the *Tribune*
website. It's still not there. It's never going to be there.

Outside, the hazy gray afternoon has darkened into pitch-black
night. My thoughts feel as bitter as the scent of coal that lingers in the cold air. The article is really never going to appear.
I'm going home where I can cry without Ed hovering over me. I
know he's worried about me, but his pity is almost harder to bear
than his usual gruffness. Besides, I'm going to develop lockjaw if
forced to maintain this calm expression any longer. And no, I do
not want another motherfucking cup of tea! Or any more shots
of vodka!

Shit. Halfway home, I'm indulging in a few tears in the taxi,
when I remember I'm supposed to meet Claire for dinner at S'
Silk Road. Ssss ssssilk road. Allegedly her favorite restaurant in
Beijing. "You'll like it, I promise," she said. The last time I heard
those words she'd dragged me to a ladies' tea, which actually
turned out to be an Amway recruiting session. "I thought we
were at least free from Amway in China," I whispered to her.

"I know," she whispered back, equally horrified. Then, as we
went around the circle introducing ourselves, she ducked out,

claiming a work emergency. For three hours I listened to Amway spiel, too mortified to leave.

Now, I brace myself for an evening Claire-style: tiny servings of carb-free food, lots of air-kissing, and not enough booze to wash it all down. Could this day get any worse?

I find Claire waiting outside the restaurant. "I've had the most wretched, wretched day," she says, kissing my cheeks before fastening her eyes back on her BlackBerry. "The closing date for Axon's takeover got moved up and I spent all morning scrambling to review the paperwork. Then my tailor Xiao Fang called to say she needed me for fittings *today* if I want my clothes to be done by the time I go to Gstaad, So I had to skip lunch, which doesn't really matter because I've had absolutely no appetite all day—I must have caught a touch of food poisoning last night . . . I just hope it's not salmonella. Jacqueline Yang got salmonella poisoning last year and they had to medevac her back to San Francisco. She was forced to move back in with her parents for six months! Can you imagine?"

"Mmm." I'm sticking to monosyllables until that lump in my throat dissolves.

Inside, we climb a spidery staircase to the sleek dining room, all poured concrete floors, clean-lined furniture, and jewel tones. A young hostess jingles up to us, the tiny bells on her embroidered robes tinkling with each step.

"Isn't her outfit wild?" says Claire as we follow her to a table. "It's from the Miao minority, or maybe Dai . . . You know, one of the fifty-five ethnic groups that aren't Han? They live in Yunnan . . . "

"Yunnan?" I croak. "I thought this was a Middle Eastern restaurant."

"No, it's Chinese."

"Chinese food? You hate Chinese food."

"Not all of it," she protests. "It would be difficult to hate a cuisine that spans five thousand years, 1.3 billion people, 3.7 million square miles . . . Why, hello." Claire stops suddenly in front of a table where a couple sits tucked into a narrow booth. When I see who it is, my skin prickles: Tina Chang. And Jeff.

Why here, why tonight? And . . . wait a second, why are they together? Oh shit, they've seen me. Too late to hide. I straighten my back and hope my eyes have lost their puffy redness. Claire nudges me.

"Hi there," I say, forcing a smile to my face.

Tina leans into the table and looks up at me with a twinkle. "Oh, hello Isabelle. What a treat to see the Lee sisters out together. It's like spotting a wild panda!"

"Well, seeing you and Jeff together is like catching two wild pandas mating," Claire shoots back, smiling sweetly.

"What's that supposed to mean?" Tina threads her arm through Jeff's, knocking the table and rattling the dishes. "We're back together," she says in a stage whisper.

"And the satellites aren't even cold yet from Iz's text messaging," murmurs Claire.

"What?" says Tina sharply. "We're both over the moon with happiness."

I sneak a glance at Jeff, who is staring determinedly into the distance, a sullen expression darkening his handsome features. A pang of guilt shoots through me at his hurt and anger. I open my mouth to apologize but snap it shut at Tina's possessive glare. Today is not the day to clear the air with Jeff. Not when I feel as if my heart might splinter, speared by disappointed ambition.

"Well, we shouldn't interrupt your special evening any longer." Claire turns away and I follow her.

"Iz!" Tina calls out before we can escape. "When's that Max

Zhang piece going to run? His manager's been bugging me about it."

I freeze. Does she know? I open my mouth but I'm horribly afraid that sobs, not words, will emerge.

"Any day now!" says Claire, firmly leading me to a table on the other side of the room. I struggle to regain my composure as she confers with the waitress over the menu. "What was all that about? Are you okay?" she asks finally.

"I'b find," I say through my stuffed nose.

"Really? Because you don't seem fine. You didn't even glance at the menu and you let me do all the ordering. You're not upset about Jeff, are you? He's definitely not worth it. Anyone who could be in a relationship with Tina Chang is one chopstick short of a pair, if you know what I mean." She flaps a hand at me. "Besides, darling, you certainly showed him! Texting . . . " Her gaze is admiring. "You're so innovative. I wish I could be that firm with Wang Wei."

I shake my head. "It's not Jeff."

"Then what? Is it work? Did Ed fire you? Don't worry, he's all bluster. He doesn't mean it."

"It's not Ed."

Claire looks at me expectantly.

"I was supposed to have an article in the *New York Tribune* today, but it didn't run," I say as quickly as I can.

"The *Tribune*?" Claire clasps her hands together. "Oh, Iz, that's so exciting!"

"It didn't run," I say dully. "I killed myself over it and it wasn't good enough. It wasn't any good." I cover my face with my hands.

"Iz!" She leans forward and grabs my arm. "Pull yourself together. Anyone could see you! Besides, you don't know why it didn't run. There could be a million reasons that have nothing to do with you."

I close my eyes. "It was dumb of me to even try. Now everyone's going to be disappointed. Not just me, but Max Zhang and—"

"Max Zhang? Wait a second, your thing on Max Zhang was for the *New York Tribune*?"

"Yes, but it doesn't really matter who it was for. It sucked."

"Actually, I thought it was a really nuanced, balanced profile. That story about his younger brother's death was so raw, so tragic . . . You really drew together the connection between his personal life and his *oeuvre*." She scrapes the French word over the back of her throat.

"Wait a second . . . You read it? How—"

"You left a copy on the kitchen counter. I like to read in the morning while I'm microwaving my oatmeal."

"Well, thanks," I shrug. "But it got spiked all the same." I slump back and stare out the window at the blinking red lights as a line of cars inches its way through traffic.

"You should send it to some other magazines. Don't just give up!" She leans forward with an enthusiastic gleam in her eye, and there is something about her perky confidence that sends me into a rage.

"That's easy for you to say," I say furiously. "You've always been perfect at everything—National Merit Scholar, law review, your firm's youngest partner ever. I'm not like you. I'm not talented and bright and charming. I can't just swan in to some magazine and expect great things to happen to me."

"Are you kidding me?" Her voice rises in disbelief. "My whole life, ever since you were born, Mom and Dad have lavished attention on you. They let you do whatever you want. Go to NYU? *I* wanted to go to NYU. Get a job in magazines? *I* wanted to get a job at a magazine. But no, I had to be the stable one. Go to law school. Set an example. I'm sick of setting a good example!"

Her words flash through me so hot and angry that I want to put up my hands to shield myself. "Mom and Dad didn't hold a gun to your head and force you to become an attorney," I snap.

"No," she retorts, "they just told me they'd cut me off financially if I didn't go to Yale."

"Well, if you were a writer, I'm sure you'd be on staff at the *New Yorker* by now. You'd find a way to be the best, just like you do with everything else."

"Do you think it's been easy for me? You think I just snapped my fingers and became editor of the law review, or partner, or—or whatever? You think that's all it took?" She crosses her arms. "Get real, Isabelle. I didn't have anything handed to me on a silver platter. I *worked*. Hard work. That's why I'm the best."

"I worked my ass off on this article."

"Yeah, well keep working. Writing is only part of it. Now you have to sell it."

"You don't know anything about journalism."

"I know enough to tell you're giving up. For God's sake, for once in your life just stop. Stop. Stop being afraid of failure. No one cares if one of us is the good daughter and one of us is bad. Only you care."

I open my mouth to say something, but nothing comes out. All my life I've heard my parents' friends whisper about us, differentiating us as the smart one and the funny one, the one who went to Yale and the one who didn't. Could Claire be right? Could those comparisons have only been in my head? Surely she can't be right.

Claire glances around the room and lowers her voice. "Look, the truth is, I don't totally mind being an attorney. I'm good at arguing. And it keeps me in Manolos." She laughs bitterly. "But you. You're not cut out for law school—"

"Thanks a lot."

"I'm not saying this to offend you. You'd make a terrible attorney. But you'd be a great writer. You *are* a great writer."

The waitress arrives to set down the plates of food, but I'm too stunned by Claire's words to lift my chopsticks. "I didn't know that Mom and Dad—"

"Please. Let's not get all messy and emotional." Claire turns back into her polite and proper self, whisking away her feelings with a snap of her starched napkin. "It happened. It's over. I moved on. It took years of therapy for me to even think about it. I don't need to rehash it now over dinner."

As much as I want to probe her further, I know it's no use. When Claire decides she's done with an argument, she is done; she will not revisit it, no matter how much she is pushed. It's probably why she's such a good lawyer.

Instead, I turn to the food. Paper thin slices of ham, salty and raw-cured like prosciutto. Small white squares that look like tofu but are pleasantly chewy, like mozzarella.

"It's cheese," says Claire.

"Cheese? Chinese cheese?"

She laughs at my surprise. "Try the mushrooms. They're called *yang duzi*, sheep's stomach. But we know them as morels."

"Morels?" I pop one in my mouth, savoring the rich earthiness. "Morels grow in China?"

We dig our chopsticks into the dishes: a salad of giant mint leaves drizzled with a tangy, spicy dressing. Black chicken, the dark flesh akin to pheasant or some other wild poultry, stewed with mouth puckering pickled papaya, short-grained fried rice served in a hollowed pineapple. In between bites we sip cups of earthy, dark tea, rich and mellow.

"*Pu'er* tea is supposed to have medicinal properties," explains Claire. "They grow it in Yunnan, and store it for years in compressed cakes. It ages over time, like wine."

"Like wine?" I take another amazed swallow.

We end the meal with bowls of rice noodles floating delicately in scalding hot broth. "They're called *guo qiao mixian*." Claire dips in her chopsticks and stirs. "Crossing the bridge noodles. Do you know the story?"

I shake my head.

"According to the legend, in ancient times, a scholar was so desperate to pass the imperial exams, he isolated himself on an island to study. Every day his wife would cross the bridge to bring him a bowl of noodles. But the journey from the kitchen to the island was too long and his lunch kept getting cold. The wife was so devoted to her husband, she finally devised a way to keep the noodles hot during her walk. She poured a thin layer of smoking oil on top to seal in the heat, and thus *guo qiao mixian* were born." Claire laughs. "Can you imagine being so dedicated to your husband you'd invent a new dish for him?"

"Not really."

"Yeah, me either." She cups her chin in her hands. "But I guess it's all about determination."

"And different perspectives."

"Can you believe this food? It's so wild and exotic . . . totally different from what we ate growing up."

"I guess there are still a few things we don't know about Chinese food."

"A few things?" She snorts. "Try everything."

Later, alone in my dark bedroom, I try to sleep. But the tears come instead, running down my cheeks and into my ears, soaking my pillow when I flip over onto my side. When I was three, I saw Claire reading the funny pages and I wanted to read them too. I wanted it so badly that I hit her over the head with my jump rope because she could read and I couldn't. I got in trouble, of course. But a few days later my father started to teach me, patiently sounding out each letter until I could string them together, and once I learned to read, I never stopped. How could I know then that this childhood incident would form the metaphor behind our entire relationship? Claire would always be five steps ahead of me. And I would always get what she wanted.

Well, not everything, of course. Not, for example, the one thing I've always yearned for: to be a writer. For a scant minute I thought I might have a chance. I allowed myself to hope. Working on my *New York Tribune* piece made everything else disappear, all those worries about sibling jealousy, or texting Jeff, or being single in Beijing without a steady source of soft cheese. Foolish, foolish me. I should have listened to my instincts and never accepted this assignment. I thought I'd found something I was good at, but it turns out I'm still a failure.

Morning, finally. Unable to sleep, I spent the night tossing and turning, worrying about what I should do with the rest of my life. Journalist, lawyer, editor—obviously those professions are out. Maybe I could be a pastry chef? I picture myself, hands shaking from too much delicate precision work, stomach bursting out of my chef's jacket (come on, I have zero willpower). Maybe accounting? Except I'm hopeless with math and money. . . and that rules out so many other things—nuclear physicist, doctor, small business owner. Oh God. Perhaps my destiny lies in my mother's chain of beauty salons. I could move back home and sweep up hair.

I climb out of bed and head into the bathroom, running the shower hot enough to sting my dry skin. Mascara? Blow-drying my hair? Clean clothes? Those things are for people with plans. I grab a pair of jeans frayed at the knees and a pilled cable-knit sweater. At the kitchen table, Claire eats a bowl of steel cut oats while surfing the web on her laptop.

"Good morning, darling," she says with a bright smile. "Goodness, you're up early this morning."

"Couldn't sleep," I mumble, turning on the kettle. "I thought I'd get to work early and get started on all the backlog."

"Is that what you're wearing?" She glances askance at my shabby outfit.

"What's wrong with it? Our office is so casual, no one cares what I look like."

"That's no reason to lower your standards."

"Claire, I don't have standards."

"Dress like the *New York Tribune*, be in the *New York Tribune*," she says briskly, fixing me with an expectant gaze.

I'm too exhausted to argue. I totter back to my bedroom and find a nicer pair of jeans—skinny, she'll like that—and a crisp white shirt. I dry my hair using the big round brush so it falls heavy and silky down my back. I pat concealer on the bags under my eyes, and darken my lashes with mascara. I even fasten a pair of pearl studs in my ears.

Back in the kitchen, I present myself to Claire. "Better," she says, draining her cup of green tea. "Now, I want to show you something."

"Can I at least make myself a cup of tea?"

"Just come over here."

Sighing, I lean over her shoulder. "The *New York Tribune*?" I say, glancing at her computer. "I really don't think I'm up for this—"

"Just look at this article," she insists. "Read it aloud."

I peer into her laptop's screen. "'When Max Zhang left China in 1949, he had no idea it would be almost sixty years before he returned—' Oh my God." My voice falters and my heart starts beating so hard and fast I'm afraid it might burst.

"'Max Zhang: A Chinese director returns to his roots. By Isabelle Lee,'" reads Claire with satisfaction. "It's on the front page of the arts section! We'll get Mom and Dad to send us a copy. They're going to be so proud!" She smiles smugly. "See? I knew it was excellent work."

"I—I—" I open and close my mouth but only a stutter comes out. "I really can't believe it," I finally manage.

"Believe it, Iz." She shuts down her computer and gathers her dishes into the sink. "You're a real journalist now."

Later, after she's gone to work, after I've gone online and e-mailed the story to everyone I know, I stand in the middle of our cavernous living room and gaze at the line of cars crawling below, the tall buildings that soar high into the sky. And then I turn on my iPod to blast the music, louder and louder, as I dance around the room. Just me and my relief, and hopes, and plans, whirling around with the music, with everything I've got.

Shanghai

" . . . Richer, heavier and sweeter . . . on account of the amount of oil and fat, sugar and wine used in the cooking. If the greasy and sweet characteristics are partially responsible for the unpopularity of Shanghai food abroad, its reliance on special local ingredients is probably more to blame."

—YAN-KIT SO, *CLASSIC FOOD OF CHINA*

A free trip to Shanghai sounded like a dream come true when Ed first suggested it. But as it looms closer, I'm beginning to feel a familiar flood of Ed-induced panic. Don't get me wrong, I'm thrilled to finally visit the city of my mother's birth, and even more thrilled to do it under the all-expenses-paid guise of an assignment. And when I get back, I'll be thrilled to write a two thousand word travel piece, detailing the city's finest hotels, dining options, and shopping finds. Thrilled, that is, unless my schedule kills me first.

I click on an e-mail from Ed, which lists the contact information for yet another nightclub he wants me to visit, and suppress a groan. The trip started as a casual three-day stroll through the Pearl of the Orient. Thanks to Ed, it's ballooned into a seventy-two-hour marathon, mapped out in ten-minute increments.

Geraldine glances up from her computer to see me furiously erasing scratched pencil marks from a threadbare piece of paper. "Is that your schedule for Shanghai?" she asks, lifting it from my desk. Her eyes widen. "Whoa."

"Do you think it's too crazy?" I clutch at my pencil.

"No, Iz, I think you can do all of this . . . " She pauses. "Just bring a good pair of walking shoes and, oh, I don't know, a couple hundred grams of crack."

"Crack?"

"Crystal meth, speed, whatever. You've got to be kidding me!" she exclaims. "This schedule is insane. Can't you cut back?"

"You know how Ed is." I cast a nervous look at his office.

"I know you have a problem saying no," she retorts. "From ten to ten-thirty you're visiting *eight* stores for write-ups? You've only got *fifteen minutes* to check out the Bund? You're staying at *five* different hotels?"

"If I'm really organized it'll be fine."

She ignores me. "Oh good, I see you've allotted a whole *twenty minutes* to tour the French Concession and find your mother's childhood home." She looks up from the paper. "You're eating five meals a day—breakfast, two lunches, and two dinners?"

"I have a very healthy appetite," I say defensively.

She raises an eyebrow. "Whatever you say, Iz."

Shanghai, Hongqiao airport, 9:00 A.M. My plane touched down late, delayed by wretched Beijing fog, and already I am behind schedule. I squirm in the backseat of my taxi, wanting to pound my fist against the window at the cars that inch along beside us. The driver looks at me and grins. *"Du che!"* he exclaims. Yes, I know we're stuck in traffic! I grind my teeth together but manage a tight-lipped smile.

Ten-eight A.M. Finally, finally, finally at my hotel, the über-swish Maison de Chine. I hurl my bag into my room and follow the public relations manager, Summer, down the hall for a tour. "All of the hotel's 259 rooms feature 800-plus thread count sheets, flat-screen televisions, and wireless Internet," she intones. We pause outside a guest room door as she fumbles with the card key. "This is our superior room. You'll notice it is vastly different from the deluxe room you're staying in." I glance around at the brocade curtains and dark furniture, everything identical, down to the forty-five-degree angle of the desk chair.

"Er, how exactly is it different?" I ask politely.

"The deluxe room is thirty square meters, while the superior is thirty-five square meters." She shoots an exasperated glance in my direction. "Let's move on to the premier room."

Ten fifty-three A.M. I keep glancing pointedly at my watch, hoping that Summer will get the message and hustle up. No dice. "In the deluxe oriental suite you'll see that the bath products are positioned in the sink and shower area, while in our regular rooms they're only at the sink." She glances at me, concern wrinkling her brow. "Aren't you taking notes on this?"

Eleven-ten A.M. By walking very briskly through the F&B outlets, I've managed to shave a good eight minutes off the tour. "The last stop," says Summer, pushing the elevator button for the basement. Thank God! "Our full-service spa offers treatments for the hurried business traveler. Thirty-minute aromatherapy massages, a forty-five minute pedicure, sixty-five minute facial."

She hands me a heavy spa menu. "Too bad you're in such a hurry, or I'd invite you for a massage. Looks like you could use it," she smirks.

Grrr. Cheeky PR flak. I peer into a treatment room, which is dim and fragrant with lilies, echoing with the soothing sounds of rain and wind chimes. I imagine sinking onto the table and allowing someone to work loose the knot twisting from my neck to my shoulders. . . . I glance at my watch. Shit!

Two-ten P.M. My original plan was to eat lightly at my first lunch, stroll the Bund, and then proceed, with renewed appetite, onto my second lunch. But thanks to sluggish Summer, minutes after gulping crème brûlée at Sens + Bund (they comped me a full platter of desserts for the "Beijing travel writer"—I should never have let Ed's assistant make my reservations), here I am at M on the Bund, forcing down a forkful of lamb roasted in a salt crust.

"Complimentary risotto with shaved white truffle, madam," the waiter says, setting down a steaming dish, aromatic with the earthy perfume of truffles. I gaze helplessly at the food and feel the waistband of my trousers suddenly give. The waiter and I watch as the button hits the hardwood floor with a rattle and bounces toward his left foot.

Two-fifteen P.M. I. Am. Never. Eating. Again.

Two forty-five P.M. I swear those bitchy waitresses were pointing at my gaping trousers and laughing at me as I staggered out of the restaurant. My stomach feels hard and massive, like it's squeezing all the other organs out of place. Yes, I considered going to the bathroom to, well, you know, but it seemed a little over-the-top Roman. Plus, I'm about four hours behind schedule. I don't have time to purge. Must keep plugging along. Let's see what's next . . .

Two forty-seven P.M. There is absolutely no way I am going to the Four Seasons to check out their afternoon tea service! A cadre of Red Guards couldn't drag me there. As I stare down at the schedule, I glimpse a flash of hot pink through my flapping waistband. Oh my God, can people see my underwear? A portly guy, flattop bristly as a hedgehog, strolls by and throws an appraising glance my way. I yank down my sweater. Great. I haven't even been in Shanghai for six hours and already: (1) have consumed a month's worth of calories, (2) burst open my only pair of trousers, (3) am about to get arrested for indecent exposure, or, worse, (4) solicitation.

Two-fifty P.M. Oh, hell. I don't care if Ed shouts at me for not sticking to the schedule. I'm going to do something I want to do. I'm going to the French Concession to find my mother's house.

A battery of cars chokes Huaihai Zhong Lu, sending clouds of exhaust into my face. Up and down, up and down, I march along the busy avenue, trying to imagine my mother as a little girl, enduring the long walk from school, dragging her heavy book bag behind her. Shiny new buildings have replaced much of the Art Deco architecture that once characterized the former French Concession. But here and there I spy evidence of the neighborhood's colonial past. Perhaps my mother stopped at that bakery on the corner to buy cakes and sweet buns. Perhaps she hurried by the ornate, blue-domed Russian Orthodox church, afraid of the round-eyed, bearded, robe-clad men who lingered outside. Perhaps she took a shortcut through this quiet, tree-lined lane, or *long tang*, chasing a neighborhood tabby past the small gardens and attached houses.

I stop to peer at a street sign, but it's not the one I need. The map says to go west, but which way is west? A fluttery feeling rises in my chest. It seemed like a good idea, this defiant break from Ed's manic schedule, but a glance at my watch tells me that my hour detour has turned into two. I'll have to give up soon if I'm going to complete at least one-third of the day's planned activities.

Sighing, I turn around and make one last pass along the street, looking closely at every sign, searching for Lane 6. But, no. It might be there, twisting behind another street, but it's not there for me, not today. Tears of disappointment prickle my eyes as I turn toward the rush of cars and look for a cab.

"Isabelle!"

Is someone calling my name? Impossible. I don't know anyone in Shanghai. I face the traffic and stick out my hand.

"Isabelle!" There it is again. I glance around me but don't see a familiar face in the rushing crowds. This is ridiculous. All that food must be making me slightly delusional.

"Isabelle Lee!" Running footsteps behind me and then a steady hand on my arm. I look up into Charlie's calm blue eyes. "I've been calling your name—didn't you hear me?" he asks, slightly out of breath.

"Oh! Hi!" I tug frantically at my sweater. "I thought I heard something, but I had this huge lunch, well, actually two huge lunches and then my pants—" I catch myself. "What are you doing here?"

"Just in town on some embassy business. I managed to escape my minder for a couple of hours to do some sightseeing." His eyes crinkle when he smiles. "The French Concession is beautiful, isn't it? I haven't walked around here since I was an exchange student at Fudan."

"You studied in Shanghai?" Surprise streaks my voice.

"Years ago, only for a summer. I helped a professor research old houses for a book on 1930s architecture. I used to know this neighborhood like the back of my hand, but it's changed so much." He shakes his head.

"Do you think . . . I mean, I know you're busy but—" I swallow the words. What am I doing? Charlie is the American ambassador to China, busy improving U.S.-China relations and, er, other diplomatic stuff. He rides around in chauffeured Lincoln Town Cars and people address him as "sir." He's much too important to wander the streets of Shanghai with someone whose pants are falling down. "Never mind," I mumble.

"What is it?" He reaches to touch my shoulder. "What do you need? Please, let me help you. I'd like to help."

I take a deep breath. "I'm trying to find the house where my mother was born," I tell him.

Back again on Huaihai Zhong Lu, or Avenue Joffre, as Charlie tells me it was called during its French treaty port heyday. But this time we veer off a meandering side street, Charlie tracing the way with sure footsteps. We walk under broad plane trees, passing restored French villas and Tudor-style houses. We peer into the windows of slick new boutiques and admire overgrown gardens.

"It's so charming back here!" I exclaim. "It feels completely different from Beijing." I gaze up at the spread of wide branches against blue sky. "There are trees, and birds, and—and side-walks!"

He laughs. "Beijing is a pedestrian death trap. They say the Shanghainese are more interested in making money than in breathing oxygen, but if you walk around the French Concession long enough you start to understand why people become obsessed with this city."

"Are you obsessed with Shanghai?"

"Not really." He turns to smile at me. "But I like its international flair, its complex, seedy history. Like that building." He points to a majestic villa that spills over an entire street corner. "It's a boutique hotel now, but look at that high stone wall . . . Can't you imagine it as a gangster's headquarters? Back in the 1930s every kid was terrified of being kidnapped and held for ransom. The alleys were lined with opium dens and brothels." He shrugs. "The most interesting people and places have something to hide, don't you think?"

"Maybe you were a Shanghainese mob boss in another life," I tease.

He smiles. "Maybe." We walk along in silence for a moment. "How about you?" he asks suddenly. "Do you think you lived here in another life?"

"If you'd asked me that about Beijing, I probably would have been offended. But Shanghai?" I glance around at the quiet lane in the heart of a modern city, at the red-tiled roofs, the old-fashioned rows of attached houses, their terraces billowing with clean laundry. "Oh, I'm pretty sure it's in my DNA."

By the time we turn down another winding alley, I've almost forgotten about my ruptured trousers, my abandoned schedule, my fear of Ed's wrath. Charlie pauses in front of a large villa, elegantly Art Deco with clean lines and a curved bay window in front. "Could this be it?" he asks.

Most of the house is hidden by a large wall, but through the front gate I spy tall windows, an expansive garden, the high branches of a gingko tree. "Should we ring?" I ask, suddenly shy.

"Why not?"

"I'm not sure my Chinese is good enough to explain why I'm here . . . they might think I'm a crazy person."

"Don't worry." He smiles encouragingly. "We can explain together."

I press the buzzer, once, twice, three times. No answer.

"Looks like no one's home," I say. For the second time today disappointment floods me. I gaze up at the house but it's almost entirely blocked by the stone wall. I can only glimpse the top of a window, the edge of a door. "Well," I try to keep my voice cheerful, "I guess I'll just have to come back another time." I take one last look, teetering on my tiptoes for a better view, but it's no use. Regretfully, I turn to go.

"Wait a second. I have an idea," says Charlie. Suddenly he kneels next to me. "Get on my shoulders."

"What are you doing?" I laugh. "Get up! Your suit's going to get filthy."

"You'll be high enough to see over the wall. It's not the same as going inside, but at least you can see the garden."

I look at him, horrified. "Oh, I really don't think that's a good . . . Charlie, I'm just bumbling around China and you're—"

"I'm a friend helping another friend," he says firmly. "Now, come on. I'm going to keep kneeling on this dirty sidewalk until you agree."

"Please, I really don't want—"

"This is my best suit!" he says warningly.

I take a deep breath and reluctantly settle my weight on his shoulders, steadying myself as he stands. Oh God, why did I have to eat two lunches *today* of all days? But as we stand there, teetering like acrobats, I forget everything in the warmth of his hands as they hold my legs. I'm close enough to see the golden streaks in his hair, to smell his clean, fresh scent. A blush rises in my cheeks that I'm thankful he can't see.

"You okay?" he calls, moving closer to the wall.

"I'm fine—oh!" I cling to the top of the wall and gaze out at a spacious garden planted with a wide lawn and shaded by a graceful gingko tree. There, near a nobbly root, must be the spot where my mother buried her pet rabbit, Little Blackie. There, in the back, is the gardener's shed where my grandfather hid bars of gold bullion from the Japanese. Through long windows that flank the front door, I spy a curved staircase with wide banisters, perfect for little girls to slide down. I can almost picture my mother as a child, coming home from school dressed in a starched uniform, reading in the bay window, dancing around the garden with her sister. Inside, there would have been a polished dining room table where they watched their lavish meals dwindle to wartime rations of plain rice. Upstairs was their bedroom, where they trembled under the covers, fearful of the marching Japanese soldiers.

When my mother left this house as a young girl, did she know she would never live here again? Could she have imagined Shanghai's changes, foreseen its countless guises of anguish from the Japanese occupation, to the Cultural Revolution's worst atrocities? And when she returns now—as she and Aunt Marcy sometimes do—does she feel a leap of pride at the city's frenzied expansion, in the Pudong's gleaming high-rise buildings, in the moneyed sheen that coats the Bund? Or is there an ache in her heart for the years lost to the Cultural Revolution, the friends left behind and broken?

I could linger here for hours, the questions running through my mind, but when Charlie shifts his weight, I suddenly remember where I am. "It's okay," I say. "I can get down now." He lowers me to the ground and I scramble off. "Thank you," I tell him, and the sudden sting of tears in my eyes surprises me. "I am really grateful." I blink quickly, but a few tears still fall down my cheek and I glance away, embarrassed by my emotions, by our sudden intimacy.

"It's truly my pleasure," he says gravely.

"Anyway," I babble to fill the silence. "You're so busy, I'm sure you have a million things to do right now, so don't worry about me, I'll just—" Suddenly he is close to me again, so close that I feel the rough brush of his wool suit against my wrist, see the stubble darkening his chin.

"Isabelle," he says, "there's no place I'd rather be than here with you." He leans forward slowly.

The shrill ring of a cell phone make us both jump.

"Jesus! Is that me?" I throw open my handbag and dig inside, wishing I could hide my flaming cheeks in its dark, leather interior. There's the phone, blinking and throbbing. I press End call and turn back to Charlie.

"Don't you want to answer it?" he asks.

"It's not important," I say as casually as I can. "Now—" I put my hand on his arm, just as the phone rings again. Arrggh! Who the hell is calling me? I yank out the phone and glare at the screen. Ed. "Actually," I admit, "I think I better take this call."

He nods and reaches into his suit jacket to pull out his own cell. "I should check in with the consulate too," he murmurs as Ed's booming voice fills my ear.

"*Isabelle!* What the *fuck* are you doing? I've been getting calls from PR people all *bloody* afternoon. *Nonstop.* You missed Crystal at the Shangri-la, April at the St. Regis, Kelly at the Four Seasons . . . *you better have a fan-fucking-tastic excuse!*"

"Oh, hi!" I throw a covert glance at Charlie, who has his cell clamped between shoulder and ear. "Yes, everything is going just fine. Thanks for checking in."

"Where the fuck have you been?"

"Oh, you know how it is." I laugh weakly. "I just got a little caught up, er, checking out shops in the French Concession."

"Caught up! I'll show you caught up! You better not be off gallivanting around with some slick Shanghai pretty boy, or I'll—"

"What? Don't be ridiculous. You know I don't know anyone in Shanghai. I'm totally alone." I glance around nervously and jump when I see Charlie is off the phone.

"Don't think I won't come down there to straighten things out," Ed says warningly. *"Now get the fuck back to work."* He ends the call.

My hands tremble slightly as I shove the phone into my pocket. "Everything okay?" asks Charlie.

"Um, yes. Fine." I force a smile to my face. "Anyway . . . I'm sure you need to get back to the consulate, and I—"

"Would you like to have dinner with me tonight?" Charlie asks abruptly. "There's this gorgeous restaurant, Yongfoo Elite. It's in an old villa that used to be the British Consulate. You'd love it—it's like stepping back in time to 1930s Shanghai."

I hesitate, but the image of Ed's face, wrathful and red, looms in my mind. "I'd really love to, but I can't," I say regretfully. "My schedule is absolutely insane. I've already missed three appointments and I have to visit at least four bars and three restaurants before midnight and then there are all the nightclubs—" I snap my mouth shut, aware that I sound like a raving, self-important lunatic.

Charlie shoots me a puzzled glance. "How about a drink?"

I want to rip up Ed's schedule and throw the pieces in the Huangpu River. I want to entwine my arm through Charlie's and spend the rest of the late afternoon strolling the Bund. I want to take a taxi to the Grand Hyatt hotel, ride the elevator up eighty-seven floors to Cloud 9, sip champagne, and watch the lights twinkle. Instead, I shake my head. "I really can't."

I'm not sure how to interpret his silence as we walk back toward Huaihai Lu. But as I hail a cab and crawl into the backseat, I can't help but feel as if I've lost something. Charlie pauses with his hand on the car door. "You know, Iz—" His brow furrows with concern. "I couldn't help but hear some of your phone conversation back there, and I just want you to know that if you ever need to talk to someone, I'm here."

"Oh! Don't worry about me." I laugh. "The boss is crazy, all right, but I can handle him."

His eyes widen slightly. "The *boss*? Is that what you call him?"

"Oh, I know it's kind of archaic, but he really likes it. Soothes his enormous ego, you know."

"But you shouldn't feel like you have to lie to him. And no one should scream at you like that. Especially not your boyfriend." A look of distress crosses his face. "You can tell me to mind my own business, Iz, but I really hope you know that people care about you. You're not alone." He reaches in to squeeze my shoulder before closing the taxi door with a quiet thump.

The words don't sink in until the driver's careened halfway down the block. Wait a second—boyfriend? He thinks that I was talking to . . . Oh no, he doesn't know that Jeff and I have . . . I roll down the window and stick my head out. "Charlie!" I shout. "Charlie!" Oh, thank God, he's turning around. "That wasn't Jeff on the phone! *It was Ed!*" I clear my throat. *"Jeff and I—we were never together!"* Can he hear me over the buzz of traffic? I strain my eyes to see his face, but he merely gives a jaunty wave before my view of him is cut off by a bus. He didn't hear me.

Great. It's not enough that the one person I might be attracted to is the American-*freaking*-ambassador to China. No,
now he thinks I'm unavailable, held hostage in some sort of psy-
chologically abusive, codependent relationship. I slump in the
backseat of the taxi as it carries me to the first of the evening's
three dinners.

My plane leaves at noon, but I have one last stop to make, one
final appointment on the Ed Itinerary. Outside and in, Jia Jia
Tang Bao resembles a McDonald's, with its fluorescent lights
and plastic tables and chairs. I squint at the characters on the
posted menu and haltingly place my order with the cashier, a
gray-haired woman with eyes that grow curious when she hears
my Chinese.

"*Yi long xiaolongbao!*" she repeats in a soft hissing lisp that I
strain to comprehend. She examines my face. "Where are you
from? Aren't you Chinese?"

I repress a sigh. "I'm Chinese with an American passport."
And then I add, "But my mother—she's from Shanghai."

"You were born in America, but you came back to Shanghai?"

I nod and watch her smile expand until it fills her whole face.

A sign above the register reads: FIRST ORDER, THEN WRAP,
THEN STEAM, THEN EAT. I peer through a smudged window into
the kitchen to watch a trio of women knead and roll dough, their
fingers a blur as each lump flattens into a paper-thin dumpling
wrapper. A fourth woman, clearly the dumpling-wrapping expert, stuffs each circle with a dab of raw pork filling and deftly
pleats it into a plump little cushion.

I take a seat, grab a pair of wooden chopsticks from the
bucket on my scuffed table, and wait. And wait. And wait. With
each bamboo basket wrapped and steamed to order, the crowd

of hungry diners grows. They sit around me sharing communal tables, slurping bowls of clear soup (should I get a bowl of soup?) floating with squares of congealed blood (er, maybe not). Their voices rise around me, not the rough growl of Beijing, but a soft, lyrical lilt that I find incomprehensible. It's Shanghainese, the city's own dialect. Sometimes my mother speaks it with Aunt Marcy, each slipping into the comfort of their mother tongue, but she never taught it to me, dismissing it as impractical. It must be nice for her to return, to embrace her first language as a living thing.

A waiter plops a damp basket of dumplings on my table and hurries away. Steam clouds my face as I reach for a dumpling, careful not to break the delicate wrapper. The first scorching slurp reveals a secret pocket of soup trapped inside. A second bite and I taste flecks of ginger in the ground pork filling, chew the tender wrapper.

After five meals a day in Shanghai, I can't believe I'm still hungry. And, oh God, how many zillions of calories are there in a basket of pork dumplings? But they are irresistible, exquisite and so cheap, only six *kuai,* less than one dollar for twelve. When I get back to Beijing I'll go on a crash diet. I'll eat only brown rice and seaweed for an entire month. I'll get up at five every morning and go running. I pop another dumpling into my mouth, relishing the burst of liquid. How do they get the soup inside? How?

The line forming outside the door indicates that this is not a place to linger, but I wait for a moment before eating the last dumpling. An older woman, her dark hair streaked with gray, sits down to share my table. We exchange a nod and a glance before she opens her newspaper and settles down to wait for her food. Her eyes slide over me so casually that I know she thinks I am a local, just another office girl out for an early lunch.

Which, in a way, I suppose I am.

Back in Beijing, the multipitted construction sites and blocky
buildings are like a slap in the face. Up in our apartment, I watch
a yellow crane swing across a sky that's gray with early evening
smog. The raw steel beams of the high-rise shell across the street
have sprouted, though I've only been gone four days. A crowd of
construction workers streams out into the street, their hard hats
a flash of yellow against the piles of rubble. They're on their way
to the cafeteria, ready to hungrily gulp down a simple dinner of
rice and unidentifiable meat and veg slopped from a gaping vat.
They'll go to sleep on thin mattresses in a dorm crowded with
other migrant workers, wake up, and do it all over again. And
again, and again, day after day until the building boom ceases
and the need for their labor ends. What then?

A sound as quiet as a mouse's snuffle breaks into my thoughts.
I whip away from the window in time to see my sister disappearing back into her room with a swish of her hair. "Hi there," I call
out. No answer. That's odd. And what's she doing home at five in
the evening? Little Miss Ambitious is usually glued to her office
chair at this hour.

I pad down the hall and knock softly on her door. "Claire?"

She's sitting at the desk in her room, long fingers tapping at
her laptop, a pair of rimless glasses perched low on her nose. "Oh,
hi, Iz." She glances up with a harried air that says, *I'm working.*

"I'm just back from Shanghai," I remind her.

She glances at a stack of papers on her desk and keeps typing.
"Did you have a nice time?"

"Great," I reply, and wait for her to ask me about it.

"Mm-hmm." She peers closely at her computer screen.

"How are you?" I say finally.

"Busy."

Well, someone is Crabby Crab von Crabmeister today. I start to tiptoe from the room, hesitate and say, "I'm going to order some food in a little bit. Do you want anything?"

She looks up, a gleam of interest in her eye. "Where are you ordering from? Do you have a menu? Can we order now? I'm starving." She fires questions at me like I'm a witness on the stand.

"Uh, Xiao Wang Fu. There's a menu in the kitchen drawer. And, sure, we can order now, I guess." And I swear to tell the truth, the whole truth, and nothing but the truth, I add to myself.

"That's okay, I'll take care of it." She throws me a suspicious glance, like she's afraid I'm going to forget to ask for no MSG, or that I'll mispronounce "easy on the grease" so that we get an oil slick in our broccoli and garlic sauce. Like I'd make that mistake again.

I've just finished checking my e-mail (Ed, Ed, Ed, and more Ed, and nothing from anyone else, not Geraldine, not Julia, and definitely not Charlie. Sigh) when our buzzer sounds. At the door I find a delivery boy staggering under the weight of half a dozen plastic bags. "Apartment 2012?"

"How much do I owe you?" I pull my wallet from my purse.

"*Yi gong shi . . .* " He consults a long receipt. " . . . 420 *kuai.*"

It's over fifty dollars. "Are you joking?" I start to laugh, but he shakes his head.

"Is the food here?" Claire steps into the front hall.

"I think there's been some sort of mistake," I tell her. "Unless we're having a party and you forgot to tell me."

"Let me see." She pokes around a few of the bags. "Nope, this looks right." She hands over a wad of cash and shuts the door. "I'll get some plates," she calls to me as I heft everything to the kitchen table and start unpacking the moist, steamy bags.

I pull out container after container of food that is either fried, drowning in sauce, or swimming in oil. Fried pork dumplings, pork fried rice, shredded pork with green peppers, braised pork ribs . . . Claire has gone whole hog, literally. "Didn't you order any steamed broccoli?" I ask. "What about plain rice?"

She shrugs. "Thought I'd branch out a little today." I stare at the kitchen table, its entire surface covered in food. "I'm ravenous. Let's eat," she says, picking up her chopsticks. Soon, piles of food tower on her plate, kung pao chicken spills off an overflowing mound of fried rice, a heap of *mapo doufu* seeps its chili-flecked sauce into a neighboring mass of fried noodles. She shoves half a spring roll in her mouth while pouring vinegar over a row of pork dumplings.

"Claire . . . " I venture. "Is everything . . . okay?" I've only seen her eat like this once before—when she and Tom divorced. She dragged me to her local diner and proceeded to eat her way through the entire menu, from milk shakes to meat loaf, all in one three-hour orgy.

She delicately picks up a green bean from the plate of *gan bian siji dou*. "Why do you ask?" she says blandly.

"No reason." I lower my eyes. "It's just when you were going through your divorce . . . "

She pauses from popping another green bean into her mouth, chopsticks in midair. Her cheeks have gone dead white and I notice with shock that her hand is shaking. Damn it. I should have known better than to bring up her divorce.

"I'm sorry . . . I didn't mean to upset you. But if something is wrong, if you need someone to talk to . . . " I hear the echo of Charlie in my words, and put my hand on her arm to steady myself. "After all, I'm your sister. Not to mention your roommate," I joke weakly.

In one swift movement she shakes my hand from her arm,

scrapes her chair back, and runs from the room. Seconds later I hear the bathroom door slam, and then the muffled sounds of Claire being spectacularly sick.

I follow her to the bathroom and knock gently on the door. "Claire?" I turn the knob, and when the door swings open I see my sister kneeling by the toilet. Our eyes meet in the mirror. "Are you okay?" I ask.

"No." Her voice is small.

"Do you want to go the emergency room?"

She takes a shaky breath. "I'm pregnant." Her eyes fill with tears and then she is sobbing, her thin shoulders heaving.

I kneel down and put my arm around her, feeling each shuddering breath. I try to pull her to her feet, to get her to sit down on the sofa, drink a cup of tea, or at least a swig of Pepto-Bismol. For the first time in my life I need to comfort my sister, and I have no idea what to say.

P A R T III

The West

Xinjiang

" . . . The vast deserts of Sinkiang, Chinese Central Asia . . .
[are] inhabited mostly by people of Turkic stock, primarily
the Uighurs . . . Food in these areas is not related to Chinese at all, except for recent superficial borrowings . . . The
staple is wheat bread . . . cooked in large, flat, boat-shaped
or oblong loaves that puff up on baking. Grilled meats, especially small shish kebabs, are traditional accompaniments.
Vegetables except for onions and garlic are few, but this is
made up for by the incomparable fruit; apricots, grapes, and
melons . . . "

—E. N. ANDERSON, *THE FOOD OF CHINA*

Claire is pregnant. About ten weeks, she says, which is still not
too late. Too late for what, I don't ask. After I've coaxed her into
bed and made her a cup of oolong tea, I try to get her to talk, not
an easy task considering the sobs that continue to spill from her
small frame. Plus, we're not exactly, well, close. Still, in between
the tears—the silent, unceasing, scary kind—I manage to extract a few details.

At first she blamed the nausea on a dodgy plate of salmon
tartare. But when it didn't go away after three weeks, she got
worried, stopping in at Beijing United on her lunch hour. When

the doctor broke the news, she fainted. The clinic wouldn't let her leave alone, and so she called Wang Wei.

"He accused me of getting pregnant on purpose." Her cheeks burn indignant despite her distress. "He said I was trying to entrap him into spending the rest of his life with me!"

Wang Wei wants nothing to do with the baby; he made his feelings clear as he dropped Claire back at work because it was more convenient than taking her back to our apartment.

"I'm sure he was just in shock," I say soothingly. "He'll call—" I stop. Picturing Wang Wei's cold eyes, his careless charm, the cruel twist of his smile, I am not sure he'll ever call Claire.

"I haven't talked to him for more than two weeks," Claire continues, as more tears slide down her cheeks. "He offered to give me money for an . . . Anyway, he offered me money, and when I refused, he stopped answering my calls."

Two weeks! "How long have you known about the . . . the, uh . . . the . . . " I gesture at her stomach, unable to say the word.

"Almost a month," she admits as her eyes well up again.

I hand her tissues for her nose, a cold washcloth for her eyes, a tumbler of whiskey for her nerves, and eventually she stops crying. But I'm unprepared for everything else Claire is about to say. Because of course there's more.

Chinese families are often secretive, and ours is no exception. As her little sister, I knew better than to ask questions about Claire's divorce, to poke, to pry. Instead, I was left to fit together the clues and guess their meaning. Like the night, home for our weekly Sunday dinner, when my mother asked me to set the table for four, not five. "Where's Tom?" I asked when Claire showed up alone.

"He's not coming," my mother answered for her. When we sat down to eat, I noticed Claire's ring finger was bare of her plain gold wedding band.

And there were other signs, like that day in the diner when Claire ate her way through the entire menu and then puked everything up in the bathroom. Or the three weeks in a row she missed Sunday dinner, claiming she had to prepare for a trial, except when I stopped by her office with leftovers, it was dark and empty. Or the way my mother started to speak about Tom, in the wistful tone she usually reserved for pre-Communist Shanghai, or Bruce Lee.

Indeed, the clues were there—not obvious, but not obtuse either—and at the time I congratulated myself for piecing together the truth. But I should have known that it wasn't the whole truth. In all stories, there are layers, and I had scarcely cracked the surface.

Now, as Claire lies beneath her Frette duvet, sobbing, I sit awkwardly on the edge of the bed and try to comfort her.

"What am I going to do?" she moans.

I hesitate. "Have you thought at all about, um, maybe keeping the, uh . . . " My voice trails off as I glance around her bedroom, its varying shades and textures of stark white a defiance against sticky fingers and spit-up.

Her eyes widen in horror. "Have a baby? I can't even take care of myself!"

"Of course you can take care of yourself," I say soothingly. "You have a successful career, a beautiful, clean apartment . . . "

"Our *ayi* keeps the apartment clean!" she wails. "I don't even know how to use the washing machine." Which, come to think of it, is probably true.

"Well . . . " I swallow. "You know you have other . . . options. You don't have to . . . um, you know, you could . . . "

"I know." She takes a shaky breath. "But let's be honest. I'm thirty-six years old. This might be my only chance to have a baby." More sobs. "Besides, I just don't know if I can go through that again."

My hand freezes as I hand her a tissue. "Again? You mean you've had an—uh, before you—"

Total silence fills the room. For a second she even stops crying. "I thought you knew," she says slowly.

"No." I glance at her face, which is pale, her eyes dark and wide.

"It was Tom's," she says as the tears spill down her cheeks again. "The day I discovered I was pregnant was the day I found a pair of panties in his suit jacket. Someone else's." Her mouth twists. "When I confronted him, he admitted he'd been having an affair with someone from his office. He said it was a mistake, that he'd never do it again. I gave him another chance, but I waited to tell him about the baby. And then three weeks later I found credit card receipts on our dresser. Hotel bills from the Plaza," she says flatly. "We went to the Plaza on our wedding night."

I don't know what to say. Her voice is matter-of-fact, like she's briefing me on a deposition, but the tears don't stop flowing down her cheeks.

"It was a late-term abortion. Fourteen weeks. They say sometimes you can hear the baby cry, but I didn't hear it cry. For a long time that's all I could be grateful for. That I didn't hear it cry." She closes her eyes for a long minute. "I took a cab to the clinic by myself, but afterward they wouldn't let me leave alone. I had to call someone and—" She draws a ragged breath. "—I was all drugged up, and scared, and I didn't know who to call. So I called Mom."

"Oh my God. Claire." I wrap my arms around myself trying to shut out the image of Claire, pale and shaking in a hospital waiting room.

"I told her I'd had a miscarriage, but she took one look at the waiting room and I think she knew. She took me home and made me stay in bed for a week and told everyone I had mono. And we've never talked about any of it."

"Any of it? Not even Tom's affair?"

She shakes her head slightly, as if it's too painful to move. "I couldn't. I was too embarrassed. I didn't want her to think it was my fault . . . that my husband didn't want me . . . " She starts to cry again. "I didn't love him, Iz. I didn't love him. But I could have loved our baby."

"It's okay, it's okay, it's okay," I whisper over and over again, rubbing circles on her back.

"And now, I'm here all over again. Knocked up, with a boyfriend who cheats on me. You'd think I'd have at least learned my lesson about birth control." She tries to smile but it turns into another flood of tears. "What am I going to do?"

I stall for time by handing her another tissue and waiting for her to blow her nose. "You're going to be fine, Claire. Whatever you decide to do."

"Are you sure?"

No. "Yes."

"What will Mom say if I have the baby?"

"She'll be thrilled," I say firmly. "Thrilled," I repeat, in an effort to convince us both.

"I doubt it." Claire barks a laugh. "Unwed mother? Deadbeat dad?"

"Look, if her first grandchild has even the remotest chance of being one hundred percent Han Chinese, I know she'll be over the moon with happiness."

"Maybe." Claire turns anxious eyes upon me. "But don't say anything yet, okay? I still don't know what I'm going to do."

Later, as I lie in bed, something prevents me from drifting to sleep, a sticky, unsettled feeling that's caused by something more than Claire's distress. I can't stop fitting together the puzzle pieces, the veiled comments that now make sense, Claire's swift flight from New York, her sudden detachment.

We are not like those sisters in books, Claire and I, not loving like *Little Women*'s Meg, Jo, Beth, and Amy, or even playfully competitive like the Bennetts from *Pride and Prejudice*. Our relationship is characterized by distance. At times I've even forgotten that I have a sister. "I've always wanted a sibling," Julia once sighed, over the dregs of an umpteenth round of saketinis. "Me too," I replied without thinking.

Yet now that I know Claire's secrets—or some of them, at least—I can't help but wish I didn't. Of course I want to know my sister, to understand her. But to imagine her sad and scared is almost too great a gap to cross. She is the accomplished one, strong and smart, worthy of admiration. For Claire to become suddenly vulnerable would mean that our roles have changed, that we've outgrown them. That we have grown up. And I'm not sure if I'm ready for that.

At seven-thirty Centro's faux suede sofas are scattered with a stylish crowd of local and expat yuppies liberally sipping two-for-one happy hour cocktails. Geraldine plucks the olive out of her martini glass and pops it into her mouth. "Should we get another round?"

"Definitely," I agree, and drain my glass.

Our waitress shimmies up to our table, tosses her shimmering mane of black hair and hovers over us, shifting her weight from one stiletto clad foot to the other. *"Women zai lai liang bei, yiyang de,"* says Geraldine in her perfect Mandarin tones.

Confusion floods our waitress's face before she turns to me. *"Ta shuo shenme?"* she asks urgently. What did she say?

"Ta bushi wo de fanyi," says Geraldine politely, though there's

an undercurrent of exasperation in her tone. She's not my translator.

"*Liang bei futajiajiu ma-ti-ni,*" I concede. Two vodka martinis. My tones are far from correct, but the waitress nods and totters away.

"Sorry about that," says Geraldine. "I just get so frustrated when people can't understand my Chinese."

"I don't think she's the sharpest knife in the kit, if you catch my drift." I jerk my head toward our retreating waitress. "I hear they hire their cocktail waitresses based on their height and head shots. The ACLU would have a field day with this place . . ."

"I've only been studying Mandarin for ten bloody years . . ." she continues to fume.

"Come on, Ger, you know how it is. If you have a foreign face, there's no way in hell you'd ever be able to speak such a complex, intricate language as Chinese. You simply don't have the mental capacity," I tease. "But if you have an Asian face . . ."

"Then of course you speak fluent Mandarin. Silly me." She laughs and reaches for a handful of peanuts.

The waitress carefully sets down our martinis. "*Feichang ganxie ni de bangzhu,*" Geraldine thanks her elaborately, receiving another baffled glance in return. We both take a sip, clear and cold with an icy burn. "So," Geraldine places her glass back on the table, "is Claire pregnant?"

I nearly choke on my drink. "What?"

She shrugs. "Tina Chang's been pushing it around on the rumor mill. But I just can't imagine Claire—"

"As a mother? Join the club."

"In that situation."

"Yes, well, it could happen to anyone, I suppose."

"So it's true? And . . . Wang Wei?" she asks delicately.

"Out of the picture."

"Of course. God forbid that anything distract him from his harem."

There it is again, that strange, sticky feeling in my chest. "What do you mean?"

"Oh, Iz, I thought you knew." Geraldine winces. "Wang Wei hasn't exactly been the most . . . faithful . . . "

Of course I knew, I just didn't want it to be true. I stare at the beads of moisture that have collected on my martini glass.

"How is Claire doing?" Geraldine's voice is gentle.

I shrug. "Fine. Terrible. I'm not sure. She was a wreck last night but this morning she was back to usual."

"Calm and composed?"

"More like chilly and aloof." I sigh. The nagging feeling just won't disappear, and as I watch the sleek people who surround us, laughing and smoking, I recognize it. Worry. I'm worried about Claire. I take another sip of my martini, hoping the vodka will ease my anxiety; instead, my stomach heaves in protest. I set my glass down with a thump and wipe my hand from the vodka that sloshes over the side. "I think I need to eat, before I get totally trashed and pass out."

"Good idea." Geraldine nods. "And I know just the place."

"Where?" Suddenly my face feels extremely flexible.

She smiles and throws down a sheaf of pink one hundred *kuai* bills. "Have you ever been to the wild west?"

Before I moved to China, I didn't know Xinjiang from Xi'an, or Uighur from Ulan Bataar. Now that I've lived here for almost a year, I know that Xi'an is home to the ancient terra-cotta warriors, while Xinjiang is the country's western province, a rough, wild terrain that had its heyday during the Silk Road. Ulan Bataar is the capital of Malaysia. Er, Mongolia. As for Uighurs, they're one of China's fifty-four minority groups, far from Han with their high noses, tawny skin, and deep-set eyes. They speak a Turkic dialect, and when they use Chinese it has a singsongy lilt.

Even Xinjiang's cities sound mysterious, with names like Kashgar, Urumqi, and Turpan. They conjure up images of bazaars filled with spices and silks, bright desert sunshine warming the region's famous grape and melon vines, long-toothed camels roaming dusty streets. For many Chinese, Xinjiang is still uncharted territory, largely Muslim, resentful of the Beijing government—and a land of opportunity, with millions of Han migrating to seek their fortunes in Urumqi's building boom and natural gas reserves, and to take advantage of generous government-funded relocation packages.

A cloud of cigarette smoke mixed with the unmistakable sweaty, boozy whiff of *baijiu* greets us at Tian Shan Pai. The two of us huddle at the edge of a vast round table meant for twelve, and sip cool glasses of Yanjing beer.

"So, I have some news." Geraldine reaches for the basket of flat *nang* bread. "I'm leaving the magazine."

A mutton skewer drops from my hand onto the floor. "Well, you certainly buried the lede." I kick the stick farther under the table. "What . . . where . . . when?" The vodka, beer, and cumin-scented meat combine to make my eyes swim.

"Well, you know how I spend a lot of time at the 798 galleries working on stuff for the arts section? A few weeks ago I was at this China Contemporary opening and this man came up to me, very thin, very bald, very Euro . . . "

She continues in a happy rush. He approached her as she was examining a plaster sculpture of a gigantic Mao suit, and asked her if she was "the acerbic Geraldine Elenski of *Beijing NOW*." At first she thought he was trying to pick her up, but as their conversation progressed it became clear that he wasn't interested in, well, women. They wandered over to the Star Gallery and then the Beijing-Tokyo Art Project, discussing recent Chinese avant-garde movements, "cynical realism," and the postseventies generation.

"It turns out he owns 508 West!" She beams and looks at me expectantly.

"Er . . . remind me again . . ."

"You know, the gallery in Chelsea. Gillen—that's his name—discovered all these young artists before they were famous . . . Jeff Koons, Chuck Close, Matthew Barney . . . And get this!" She takes a deep breath. "He wants me to open up a branch of 508 West in Beijing!"

"Oh my God!" I shriek, loud enough so that half the restaurant turns around to stare.

"He's been checking out my columns online and thinks I'm the right person for the job! Can you believe it?"

"Of course!" I squeeze her arm. "You have great taste."

"After all those years I struggled in the gallery world in New York . . . eating Top Ramen and walking home to save money on subway fare . . . I can't believe this is really happening." She slowly pulls the meat off a kebob. "Isn't it ironic? Fifty years ago our grandparents left their native countries to make a better life in the new world. And yet two generations later we're in China, finding better opportunities than in the States. Back home we'd just be cogs in the wheel. Here, we're inventing the wheel."

"Yes, but compared to most Chinese, we're extremely privileged. We have college degrees and earn middle-class salaries," I point out. "But . . . then again, when I lived in New York, I made grilled cheese sandwiches on my waffle iron."

"And I bet you never thought you'd have a front-page feature in the *New York Tribune*."

"Front page of the arts section," I correct her. "But . . . no, you're right. I would never have even tried."

"Have you started pitching your next story yet?"

"No . . . still trying to come up with a good idea."

"You could always do something on Jeff," Geraldine suggests.

"Like a piece on break-up texts? I don't know . . . Don't you think I've done enough damage?" I tear off a chunk of bread.

"Are you kidding? You inspired him! His new single just hit the Billboard Hot 100!"

"What?" I examine her face for sarcasm, but she appears to be serious. "Single? What single?"

"It's called . . . " She pauses for dramatic effect. " . . . 'I've Been Texted.' I can't believe you haven't heard it yet. They play it at Babyface like forty times a night!"

"Oh my God." I cover my face with my hands. "Please don't tell me it was inspired by . . . "

"Er, yeah. I think it was. Sorry." Geraldine pats my arm. "But don't worry. The lyrics use your Chinese name!"

"Great." I drain my beer.

"Besides, you're off the hook now. There's no way Jeff can be angry with you now that he's got a platinum album."

Our waiter sets down a heavy dish of stew. Chunks of chicken fall off the bone in a savory sauce laced with tomatoes, onions, and peppers. Underneath lurk cubes of potato and flat, doughy noodles, rough with a handmade edge. I scoop a spoonful into my bowl and breathe in the chickeny scent before dipping into the rich liquid. "Yum! What is this?" I dunk a piece of bread into the delicious sauce.

"*Dapanji*. Big plate chicken."

"That's it? No fancy name like 'Phoenix Entwined in Earth's

Stalwart Roots'? Just big plate chicken?" I peer at her. "Are you
sure this is Chinese food?"

She laughs. "The Uighur separatists would love you, Iz. Did
you know that even though Xinjiang is technically three time
zones away from Beijing, they still have to operate on official
government time? When I visited Kashgar, we ate dinner at ten
P.M., except it was actually seven."

I slurp up a fat noodle and try to imagine a place where the
sun rises at eight o'clock in the morning. "Instead of 'one country,
two systems,' they should call it 'one country, one time zone.' The
great unifier of China."

Our laughter drowns out the loud voices around us, making
us oblivious to the stares.

In the cab home, a tiny fender bender on the Third Ring Road ra-
diates traffic like an open wound seeping blood. I crank open the
window and lean back against the seat, contemplating tonight's
conversation. Geraldine is right, of course. She and I, Ed, Claire,
Gab, Charlie—all of us came to China for different reasons—
study, work, Sinophilia, the chance to start over—but it's the
opportunities that have kept us here. Beijing is our new frontier,
offering us freedom, privilege, and possibility—the chance to
leave our mark on uncharted territory.

Before I left New York, my old boss, Nina, sent me an e-mail.
"Good luck in your new adventure," she wrote. "How wonderful
that you will have the chance to discover your roots." It only took
a second to delete the message from my in-box. After all, my
roots were in Manhattan.

Living in Beijing hasn't changed that, of course. But I've still
spent the past months looking for perfect Chinese moments, experiences that prove I wasn't crazy to move here. Because I love

food, it's not surprising that I've found most of them at the dining table, in that first scalding bite of a *xiaolongbao*, or in the numbing, burning thrill of anything Sichuanese.

But there are other moments. Like the night I sang an entire Mando-pop song at karaoke, and didn't flub one word. Or the first time a thirty minute cab ride didn't involve the question, "Where are you from?" Or the day my article was published in the *New York Tribune*. Or every morning, actually, that I walk into the newsroom, ready to begin another day of writing about food, fashion, and culture—all the things that I love most.

Maybe I could have been a journalist in New York, but there were enough talented, witty, and accomplished writers to intimidate and stop me. Here in Beijing, however, I've flourished in the small pond, the growing international interest in stories about China, finally giving me the confidence to try.

In the end, perhaps this is the gift China has given me: not the chance to discover my roots, but the opportunity to realize a dream.

The white floors of the Green T. House Living are shiny enough to reflect the bright colors of the silk and satin cocktail dresses swirling above. Claire and I are at the gala celebration for the Year of Italy in China, and while the free-flowing Prosecco and wheels of Parmagiano-Reggiano cheese mean it's not quite like every other Beijing social event, it certainly has the major characteristics: lots of air kissing, flashy jewelry, and smiles as stiff as the hairstyles above them.

"I'm so glad we came, darling." Claire sips from a flute of Prosecco, carefully holding the stem between her long fingers. Almost two weeks have passed since she dropped her bombshell news, yet she still hasn't made a decision about whether she's going to keep the baby. Whenever I've tried to broach the topic, she sidesteps it, as if she'd rather pretend the situation doesn't exist. I think that's why she's drinking Prosecco tonight, though her sips are tiny enough to be inconsequential. Outwardly, she's the same Claire, a blur of busyness keeping her unapproachable, though I suspect she's been hiding out at her office in an attempt to dodge the Beijing social scene. And, late at night, I'm pretty sure I've heard muffled sobs from behind her closed door.

She surprised me this afternoon, asking if I would attend the party with her. Of course I was inclined to say no, but as I watched her fingering the gilt-edged invitation with a wistful expression, I found myself agreeing to go. An hour later she'd buried all traces of unhappiness beneath a silver sheath in wild silk, its severe cut revealing her still thin figure. In the car, I was so busy navigating the Airport Expressway and narrow back roads of Shunyi while she drove (her driver is away) that I didn't have a chance to ask her any questions.

A waiter brushes past and I snag a glass of Prosecco as well as a chunk of Parmagiano-Reggiano from the enormous, hollowed wheel of cheese. Claire holds out her glass for a refill. Should she really be drinking so much? I'm trying to think up a way to ask her diplomatically when I hear a voice trill behind me.

"Ooh! Do I see the Lee sisters?" My heart sinks when I see a tall blonde striding confidently toward us. Kristin from the American embassy.

"Hel-woah," I manage from beyond my mouthful of cheese. I hastily swallow and manage a tight-lipped smile.

"Great to see you, mwah, mwah." Her perfume, lingering and musky, washes over me. "Eileen, have you lost weight?" she exclaims, eyeing my dress, black brocade with a flattering fitted bodice.

"It's Isabelle," I say through clenched teeth.

"Oops, sorry sweetie. And Claire! Gorgeous dress, darling. How are you? You look tired."

Claire opens her eyes wide. "I'm fine!" she says with a breezy laugh. She fingers her double strand of dove gray Tahitian pearls.

"How are you holding up?" Kristin cocks her head to one side. "Enjoying life as a single gal again?"

"Absolutely," Claire says with a confident smile. "Never been better." She crosses her arms on her chest and looks Kristin in the eye with a cool gaze. Suddenly, I realize why Claire wanted to come tonight. She needed to make an appearance, to show people that she hasn't collapsed in a heartbroken heap of misery. She may be pregnant (though no one knows) and dumped by Wang Wei, but she's holding her head high.

Kristin turns away from Claire with a disappointed air and regards me. "Have you seen Charlie lately?"

"No, not lately. Not since Shanghai." I shrug like I don't care, though my skin prickles at the mention of his name.

"Isn't he here tonight?" Claire moves forward slightly. "I thought for sure he'd give his support to the Italian year." To my surprise, she seems disappointed. She clenches her jaw, a look I recognize from our childhood when she couldn't get her way.

"So you haven't heard the news?" Kristin babbles on, oblivious. "Charlie's moving to Paris! Isn't that amazing?"

My heart swoops into a nosedive. "Wow, he's going to be the, um, ambassador to France?"

"Of course not! No!" Kristin bats at my arm with white-tipped fingernails. "You really don't know anything about U.S. foreign affairs, do you? The ambassador to France is always a political appointee. No, Charlie's taking a sabbatical to teach at See Ahnse Po."

See Ahnse Po? I nod knowingly, though I haven't the foggiest idea what she's talking about.

"Is he teaching a course on contemporary American politics?" Claire breaks in. "What a great opportunity for him." She turns to me. "Didn't our cousin Michael spend a year there?"

Oh, she must mean that French political institute, Sciences Politiques, or something like that. Trust Kristin to be pretentious and use the French nickname. "Yes he did! " I shoot Claire a grateful look.

"Will Charlie be leaving Beijing soon?" asks Claire as a waiter refills her glass again. Suddenly, I find myself hanging on Kristin's every word.

"In time for the fall semester, I think," she says vaguely, her eyes scanning the room. "Ooh, is that Mimi Zhou over there? I must say hello. Wonderful to see you both. Let's catch up over dinner. Byeee!" With a click of her heels, she is gone.

"What a shame about Charlie, darling," Claire remarks casually, though her dark eyes scan my face a little too closely. "We should invite him over for dinner sometime before he goes."

I swallow hard against the lump that's suddenly appeared in my throat. "That would . . . be nice," I finally manage.

My sister reaches out to squeeze my arm with a hand that is surprisingly gentle.

I want to slump in the corner, but it's occupied by a troupe of white-faced mimes mutely acting out a scene from Dante's *Inferno*. Instead I take the last sip from my glass and go in search of the bar. But when I find it, the white-clad bartender informs me they're out of Prosecco and so I settle for San Pellegrino, gloomily slugging the sparkling water directly from the glass bottle. Charlie is leaving Beijing? A dull ache in my stomach reveals a disappointment I wish I could ignore. I'm always looking for him, in the lobby, in the elevator, always hoping to run into him. What will it be like after he leaves? I know it seemed far-fetched that something could happen between us. But some small part of me thought that maybe he perceived me, the real me, and liked what he saw. Now that he's leaving, I'll never have a chance to find out.

At dinner, I'm seated between two impeccably preserved women with deep tans who smile and nod politely and then proceed to lean over me to chatter in Italian. I concentrate on the food, plates of cured meats, followed by penne dressed in a drizzle of sharp green extra-extra-extra virgin olive oil. Over the main course (veal chop) I watch Claire across the table laughing with her handsome neighbor, a suave Italian whose picture could be in the dictionary next to the word "gigolo." He adjusts his shirtsleeves, crisp with European polish, and gazes at her, a small smile on his lips. Claire tosses her hair, cheeks flushed, eyes dark and flashing, and I realize with a start that she is drunk. Not mildly tipsy, but flat-out, sorority-style wasted. Why is she doing this? Doesn't she know she could hurt the baby? I catch her eye in a stern glare but she ignores me. It's as if she's trying to freeze all her problems through alcohol.

I push back my chair and stalk over to her side of the table. "Claire," I whisper urgently. "I'm going to powder my nose." I glance meaningfully toward the bathrooms.

"That's nice, Izzy." She turns to the man beside her. "Marco, this is my ba-by sistah, Isabelle. Isabelle has to pee and is going to the bathroom." She smiles at me and gives me a slight push.

"Come with me," I urge.

"I'm fine here, just enjoying my wine." She takes another slug from a glass of Chianti.

I grab her hand and pull her out of her chair. "What are you doing?" I demand in the fluorescent chill of the bathroom.

"Havin' a good time. Whaddha *you* doin'?" She staggers toward the sink, leaning into the mirror to examine her eye makeup.

"Watch out!" I exclaim as she loses her balance and clutches the counter to steady herself. "Claire, I think we should go home. You're . . . you've had too much to drink. And you have other people relying on you." I look pointedly at her belly.

"Oh, please. Don't get all saintly on me now." She rolls her eyes. "I'm enjoying myself. I haven't felt this normal in weeks. Marco is cute and I think he's about to ask me for my number."

"He's about to ask you for more than that," I snort.

"Just one more drink," she pleads. "I haven't been out in ages. And then we can go."

"Okay," I concede. "But make it coffee. You need to sober up or I don't know how we're going to get home."

But either she ignores me or doesn't hear. As we exit back into the dark swirl of the party, her eyes are frozen on someone in the distance. Standing by the stage, directing a flock of masked acrobats on stilts, is the one person guaranteed to send Claire home: Wang Wei.

She whirls around, snatching my arm. "We have to go now. I was positive he wouldn't be here tonight. I can't *believe* the *bastard* . . . How could he do this to me . . . " Muttering under her breath, she strides toward the door, glancing back only to make sure I'm following her. "Hurry up!" she snaps, tossing me her beaded evening bag. "You're going to have to drive."

Outside in the dry night air, I stop walking. "What did you just say?"

"Let's go. You're driving."

"What?"

"Obviously I can't, and you've been sipping sparkling water all night. Come on." Her fingers shaking, she opens the bag and extracts the keys.

"Are you kidding me? There's no way in hell I'm getting behind the wheel in Beijing. Have you seen the way people drive in this city? Let's just call a cab. We'll get the car tomorrow."

"We're in the fucking sticks. There aren't any cabs." Her voice grows anguished. "Please, Iz, you have to do this for me. I can't bear seeing him. Please, please, please."

Despite myself, her desperation makes me climb behind the wheel, thanking my lucky stars that Ed forced me to get a Beijing driver's license for a story. The steering wheel feels slippery beneath my sweaty palms, and I pull onto the dark narrow road slowly, flashing the high beams.

"Just relax," says Claire. "Driving here is easy."

"Okay," I say, my voice pitched high.

I follow signs back to the main highway, my hands gripping the steering wheel at ten and two o'clock, foot hovering over the brake. I've been driving since I turned sixteen, but nothing could prepare me for Beijing's pothole-riddled streets, the cars that zoom out of nowhere, wafting in and out of my lane, drivers who never contemplate a glance to their blind spot. By the time we reach the Third Ring Road, my limbs feel shaky. Almost there, I think. Almost home. I press my foot against the accelerator to overtake a giant dump truck as it lumbers along the center of the highway.

Later, what I will remember most is how quickly everything happened. The dump truck veering sharply into my lane, the crunch of metal on impact, the way the brakes feel like air as I ineffectively pump them, the reckless skid of the car as it spins across traffic. Our shouts, not screams, but bellows that come from somewhere deep inside.

It seems like the car won't stop, but when it finally does, the headlights of the dump truck shine through the gaping hole of the driver's side window. Broken glass covers my lap, gleaming sharply on my black skirt, the seat, the floor.

"Are you okay?" My voice quivers as I turn to look at my sister.

"Oh my God, Iz, you're bleeding!" She reaches out to touch

my collarbone, her hands shaking as she removes a tiny shard of glass.

"It's just a scratch. I'm fine," I tell her. "Are you?"

"I think so." We climb out of the car—my door is crunched shut, so I clamber out her side—and slowly make our way to the side of the road. The driver of the dump truck approaches us; he is plump, his shirt unbuttoned to reveal a solid belly. I can't even look him in the eye when he apologizes.

We stand there on the side of the road, staring at the wreck of crushed metal that is Claire's car, the cab of the orange truck hovering above as if victorious. Later, the dump truck driver will file a police report accepting all blame, Claire and I will tell the story to our friends and agree to hide it from our family, we will say how lucky we were to escape with just a scratch. But now, as we wait in the dry night air, I can only clutch at each breath of air, filling my lungs as I've done instinctively from the moment I emerged into the world.

A gust of wind blows the hair off my forehead, and Claire crosses her arms and shivers. "Do you want to go to the hospital," I ask, "just to make sure everything is okay?"

She moves her head almost imperceptibly, but when she finally speaks her voice is clear. "Yes," she says.

A smog-streaked sunset tints the kitchen pink as I pour myself a glass of wine and put a pot of water on the stove to boil. In the foyer, I hear the thump of the front door as it opens and closes, and a few seconds later Claire wanders in.

"Are you making dinner? I'm starving!" She looks hopefully at the counter, where I've assembled my ingredients: spaghettini, butter, parmesan cheese.

"Just a little pasta. Want me to throw some in for you?"

"Ooh, yes please. I'm famished!" She grabs a bottle of water from the fridge. In the two weeks since our accident, Claire has been to the doctor four times, but all seems to be well with the baby, despite her momentary lapse in judgment. She's less nauseous now and her cheeks have regained some color, though a permanent look of worry hovers in her eyes. I think it's the expression of motherhood.

A hiss from the stove indicates the water is boiling, and I stir in the noodles, Claire watching me from across the counter. "Oh, so you wait until the water boils *and then* you put the spaghetti in," she says.

"You're joking, right?"

"Hey, maybe you can teach me how to make food that the Little Pea will eat. Ooh, like those smoked salmon scrambled eggs . . . or maybe caviar and buckwheat blini . . . "

"I see the Little Pea will share its mother's expensive tastes."

"Mais oui," she giggles.

"Actually," I grab the hunk of cheese and start grating, "you know who you should ask for recipes? Mom."

There's a beat of silence that lasts so long it grows uncomfortable. "I've been thinking a lot about Mom and Dad," Claire says finally. "I didn't want to say anything until I'd made a decision, but I'm thinking about going home."

"Back to New York?" I look at her with surprise.

"Yeah." She twists a lock of hair between her fingers. "It's not going to be easy doing this on my own, and frankly, I could really use the support."

"I think that makes a lot of sense," I tell her.

"Really?" Relief floods her face. "You're not mad? You'll have to look for a place to live . , , "

"Or, maybe I'll go back too." I shrug. "I've gotten some good experience here, had some good bylines. Maybe I could get some sort of assistant job at a magazine, working for Condé Nast, or something. And I could babysit."

"That's really sweet of you, but do you really want to be an assistant again?" She pulls a face. "Making coffee and copies, fetching and carrying, answering phones . . ."

"It's really not that bad."

"Huh," she snorts. "I've seen *The Devil Wears Prada*."

"Have you talked to Mom?" I ask, to change the subject.

"I left her a message. She'll probably call tonight."

We eat our spaghetti while watching TV, twirling the buttery cheesy strands around our forks. Our plates stand empty on the coffee table and Claire is in the bathroom again when the phone rings.

"Can you get that?" she calls. "It's probably Mom."

I answer the phone expecting the booming cheer of my mother. Instead, I hear another voice, familiar and dear.

"Iz? It's Julia."

"Hi!" I squeal. "Oh my God, how are you?"

She pauses. "I have good news," she says.

"You're pregnant!" I exclaim. "Your baby and my niece will play together!"

"What? No!" she laughs.

"Well, what is it?"

I feel her settling against the phone, making herself comfortable for a long conversation. "So, remember that author I mentioned? The one who's an editor at *Cuisine* magazine? I was having lunch with her yesterday and she couldn't stop talking about China. Apparently it's become this super fad and everyone—"

"Where did you go for lunch?"

"Lupa."

"Did you get that pasta I like? The one with the black pepper and pecorino cheese?"

"Iz," she says warningly. "This call is like eighteen dollars a minute." She takes a deep breath and launches back into the story. "She kept asking me about my trip to Hong Kong and how I knew about so many great restaurants. So finally to get her off the topic I told her about you and your columns on Chinese regional cuisine."

"How—"

"Andrew forwarded them to me. Anyway, I thought she would drop it and we could talk about her next book idea. But she got really excited and made me promise to get in touch with you."

"Why?" I smile at the enthusiasm in Julia's voice, but I have no idea why she's so excited.

"So I told her you'd call her today. Well, tonight for you."

"Sure, but why?"

"For the *column*," she says in an exasperated tone. "The one I told you to write. About regional cuisines in China."

Suddenly I am clutching the phone so tight my ear burns.

"She wants to hear your ideas," Julia continues. "It's just for the website, and it doesn't pay much, but I figured it could be a good way to make some contacts, you know? Hello . . . ? Iz?"

I want to answer her but I can only stare at the variegated shades of pink in our marble floor, unable to utter a sound.

Fusion

"Fusion (*fuoo zhen*) noun. 1. The act or procedure of lique-
fying or melting by the application of heat. 2. The liquid or
melted state induced by heat. 3a. The merging of different
elements into a union. 3b. A union resulting from fusing. 4. A
nuclear reaction in which nuclei combine to form more massive nuclei with the simultaneous release of energy. 5. Music
that blends jazz elements and the heavy repetitive rhythms
of rock. 6. A style of cooking that combines ingredients and
techniques from very different cultures or countries."

—*AMERICAN HERITAGE DICTIONARY*

There are just a handful of perfect days in Beijing, days unsul-
lied by smog or dust, sultry temps or frigid winds. Days when
the skies look scrubbed clean, when the sun brightens painted
eaves and glints off glass and steel office towers. I've been eyeing
the weather reports on CNN anxiously all week, but as I wander
among the cool, fragrant aisles of the Laitai Flower Market, I
feel silly for having worried. Of course Claire's last Saturday in
Beijing would dawn shiny and golden, a perfect autumn day.

I shift the flowers in my arms and add a bunch of white roses
before carrying them to the shopgirl. *"Waaaah! Neme duo hua'r!"*

So many flowers! She divides them into two piles and starts wrapping them in newspaper.

"They're for a party," I tell her, glancing at my watch. Only two hours left and I have centerpieces to arrange, champagne to chill, food deliveries to accept.

At our apartment, the giant space looks even larger, stripped bare of Claire's rugs and artwork. I pad quickly through the rooms, breathing a sigh of relief when I see that Claire's not home. Ed promised to keep her occupied this morning with a whistle-stop tour of the Forbidden City, which Claire still hasn't seen despite her five plus years in Beijing.

"Don't wear her out," I commanded. "And don't let her drag you home too early, or you'll ruin the surprise."

"Don't worry." He turned away, but not before I thought I heard him say, "I've been hoping to spend some time alone with her."

Claire asked her law firm for a transfer three months ago, and since then things have been a flurry of shopping and packing, doctors' appointments, ultrasounds, and a whole new wardrobe for her growing bump. Together we sorted through our belongings, discarding old papers and clothes (Claire spent a happy and merciless hour in my closet) in preparation for our move. Our relationship has become a bit easier since the car accident, despite Claire's black moods, which still roll in like summer storms. We haven't started swapping clothes or secrets, and we probably never will, but we admire each other now from a respectful distance, our glances no longer wary.

I didn't think she'd want to know, but a few weeks ago she came home and told me that she's having a girl. "Can you believe it? I just hope she doesn't grow up to hate me. You know mothers and daughters . . . " she said with a grimace. Later, though, when she thought I wasn't listening, I caught her patting her belly and whispering about third-wave feminism.

The doorbell rings and I help the caterers carry in trays of food: enormous bowls of cold sesame noodles, platters of poached salmon, grilled beef studded with Sichuan peppercorns, a mound of leafy salad greens sprinkled with lacy Yunnan herbs, tiny *pao de quejo* cheese puffs, all from Claire's favorite restaurant, an eclectic Brazilian-Chinese-European fusion bistro.

Geraldine arrives on the dot of one, immediately throwing an apron over her lime green sundress. We stack plates and napkins on the dining room table and arrange the flowers in vases, large masses of creamy white blossoms scattered throughout the apartment.

"The place looks gorgeous, Iz." Geraldine pauses in the living room, admiring the sun as it streaks over the floors. "Do you think you'll miss it?"

"Of course." I glance out the window at the gleaming buildings that rise around us, the cars inching their way along the Third Ring Road. "But I'm looking forward to having my own space. And my new neighborhood."

"And your new neighbors, I hope." She arches her eyebrows and grins. "I can't wait to have you down the street!"

With Geraldine's help, I've found an apartment near Houhai, a bright space with white walls and avocado green tiles in the kitchen. It's about one-third the size of Claire's apartment, but still far roomier than my old place in New York.

"How about Claire?" Geraldine asks. "She's not moving back in with your parents, is she?"

"Oh my God, no!" I laugh. "She's renting something on the Upper East Side. It's only a one-bedroom but it'll be big enough until she can find something else."

"And close enough for your mom to visit," Geraldine reminds me. "Or is she still too upset about everything?"

"Yeah, that lasted for about a day. She's already knitted twelve pairs of booties and started driving Claire crazy with her advice. Her latest e-mail warned Claire against talking on her cell phone and making photocopies. Apparently the flash of the Xerox machine can release radioactive rays to the fetus." I roll my eyes.

The doorbell rings again and I go to answer it, smoothing down the folds of my floaty silk skirt. The polite smiles of Claire's coworkers greet me, that reticent senior partner with the pointy Shakespeare beard, and his wife, a pleasant, buxom woman with pillowy arms. "Hi!" I exclaim, trying to buy time with enthusiasm. What are their names? "It's so great to see you, Don and uh . . . Barbara."

"Steven," he booms. Damn. Well, at least I got her name right.

"Brandy," she offers.

"Can I get you a drink?"

By the time I've wrestled open a bottle of white wine and settled them on the sofa, the bell has rung again and again, and soon the living room is filled with Claire's friends. There are the Chinese glamour girls, huddled by the window as far away from the food as possible. A gaggle of expats stands by the bar, pouring healthy slugs of gin and helpfully opening bottles of wine. Claire's coworkers relax on the couch, blinking in the unfamiliar freedom of being away from the office on a Saturday afternoon. Gab and Geraldine munch on handfuls of cheese bread in the kitchen, while Tina Chang and Jeff snuggle in a corner, oblivious to the stares of the other guests.

By three-thirty I've drunk three caipirinhas, refilled the platters of food twice, and unplugged the toilet once. "Irene! Great party! Where's Claire?" Kristin from the American embassy brushes past me on her way to the bathroom. That's weird, I don't remember inviting her.

Geraldine refills my glass from a tall pitcher. "Should I be worried that Ed and Claire aren't here yet?" I ask.

"I think you should relax and enjoy the party."

"But what if they got into an accident? What if something's wrong with the baby?"

"What if they're locked in a passionate embrace in Ed's apartment?"

My mouth drops open. "Are you serious? Ed and Claire?"

"Stranger things have happened." She smiles.

Before I can press her for details, two short beeps from my cell phone announce a text from Ed. "Oh my God, they're in the elevator! Everyone, shhhhh! They're coming!"

The room quiets to an unnatural silence, until I'm sure everyone can hear the wild pounding of my heart. Will Claire be surprised? Happy? Suddenly I wonder if throwing her a surprise party was a good idea. I hear the scratchy rattle of the key in the lock and take a hasty swallow from my glass. Claire is laughing as the door opens but she's soon drowned out in the chorus of our greeting.

"*Surprise!*"

Claire's eyes open huge and dark, her face flushes rosy, as she places one hand over her mouth and one on her bump. Her friends engulf her, hugging her and patting her belly to feel the baby kick. She stretches a hand to her face, and if I didn't know better, if I wasn't completely sure of Claire's rigid stance against any form of sentimentality, I'd have sworn that she brushed a few tears away. Someone brings her half a glass of champagne, which she sips slowly. Chatter floods the apartment, people eat and drink, spill and laugh, and I stand back and watch the party, happy that it is finally complete.

In the kitchen, I arrange squares of chili-infused brownies on a silver tray and unearth pints of mango ice cream from the freezer.

"Hello," says a familiar voice behind me. I turn and find Charlie's steady blue gaze, two flutes of champagne in his hand. "I thought you could use a drink," he says.

"How . . . Who invited . . . I mean, how did you know . . . ?"

He smiles. "I ran into Claire in the lobby last week and she told me about the party."

"What! That little fink! I can't believe she knew all along and—"

Charlie hands me a glass and raises his in a toast, "I hear congratulations are in order."

"Claire told you—"

"About your new column? Yes. Well done, Iz, though I must say I'm not surprised. I always thought you had a writerly look about you."

"Pale with bloodshot eyes?" I joke.

"More like extremely observant with a razor sharp wit." Our glasses clink and we each take a sip. "If you need help doing any research, trying new restaurants, I'd love to go with you—" He breaks off and looks at me shyly.

"Aren't you leaving soon? Moving to Paris?" I narrow my eyes. "Just because I'm not a litigator or—or a diplomat doesn't mean that you can't take me seriously."

"Take you seriously? All I've ever wanted was to—"

"Haven't you been avoiding me?" I demand.

He looks slightly abashed. "No! I know it might seem that way. But first I got tied up by the North Koreans and their nuclear weapons, and then after I saw you in Shanghai . . . "

"Yes?" I raise my chin

"I just couldn't understand why you'd give that guy—what's his name?"

"Jeff?" I say unhappily.

"Yes, him. Why did you even give him the time of day?" Before I can answer, he continues. "Look, it's true. I'm moving to Paris. But I still have a year left in Beijing and a lot can happen in a year."

I look at him doubtfully. "I don't know . . . "

"Take the noodle shop across the street—opened and closed within a year. Or, Claire—she went from Sexpat in the City to mother-to-be in less than a year. And you, how long have you been in Beijing?"

"Ten months," I admit.

"Well, if you can build a new life in a new country in only ten months, surely that's enough time to . . . fall in love?"

I feel myself wavering. "And after a year, then what?"

He looks at me hopefully. "Do you like Paris?"

And then he takes a step toward me and I smell that fresh, clean scent again. Gently he puts his arms around me, and my knees tremble as his mouth touches mine.

I don't know how long we stand there in the kitchen, but I'm about to suggest we move into the bedroom when a step behind us makes us break apart. I feel heat in my cheeks as I straighten my skirt and sweater, looking up to meet Claire's amused gaze.

"Well, it's about time!" she says. "Honestly, I've never known two people more resistant to my matchmaking . . . completely obstinate . . . " She grabs the tray of brownies from the counter and turns to leave.

"Wait a second!" I say. "You—You planned this? You were trying to set us up?"

"Let's just say it was obvious to me from the minute I met Charlie that he'd be perfect for you." Her smile is satisfied. "Bring in the ice cream, okay? You can make out after our guests leave."

Charlie gathers up the cartons and leaves the kitchen, but I linger behind, filling the kettle, turning it on to make coffee. Even from our kitchen window the view of Beijing sprawls blocky, dotted with construction sites, teeming with cars, always in motion. I can sense the crackle of energy in the air, the shaky levitation of hope, the busy, big world, so full of possibilities.

There will be work ahead, research and writing, and many, many difficult conversations in Chinese. And good things too, the birth of my niece, spending time with Charlie, picnics on the Great Wall, boat rides on the Back Lakes, late night strolls through shadowy *hutongs* . . .

The kettle whistles and I turn away from the window wondering if perhaps Charlie would like Chinese food for dinner, and if so, what kind.

ACKNOWLEDGMENTS

Thanks to Deborah Schneider, who believed in this book from the moment she read it, and Wendy Lee, for her enthusiasm and sensitive edits, which helped create a better story. At HarperCollins, Betty Lew and Amanda Kain created a beautiful package. Thanks also to Cathy Gleason for her support, and Katie McGowan for helping Isabelle see the world.

In Beijing, thanks to Michael Wester and Jerry Chan at the *Beijinger* for taking a chance on an inexperienced writer. Lee Ambrozy, Jehanne de Biolley, Adam Pillsbury, and Judy Pillsbury shared their city with me and their enthusiasm was infectious. Joey Guo, Susu Luo, and Belle Zhao rescued me from countless linguistic mishaps. A chance remark from Evan Osnos inspired the title.

For their early advocacy and advice, thanks to Jonny Geller and Gerald Howard, as well as Andrew Dorward, Andrea Joyce, Susan Hans O'Connor, Amanda Patten, Sarah Schafer, and Lucia Watson, who provided invaluable editorial comments and friendship.

I am grateful to my parents Robert Mah and Adeline Yen Mah, who aren't anything like Isabelle's (okay, maybe just a little bit—but only the good parts).

Finally, thanks to my husband, Christopher Klein, for encouraging me throughout many discouraging moments, for accompanying me on all my eating adventures, for translating between Chinese and English despite the weird stares—and for bringing me to China.

A⁺
AUTHOR
INSIGHTS,
EXTRAS &
MORE...

FROM

**ANN
MAH**

AND

AVON A

READING GROUP GUIDE

1. Have you ever considered uprooting your life and moving to another country? If so, where would you go and why?

2. Early in the book, Isabelle defines the term "kitchen Chinese" an the pidgin Chinese that she speaks, and she struggles with her rudimentary language skills throughout the story. Why do you think the author chose this as the title? What role does language play in the book?

3. Why does Isabelle initially resist the idea of moving to China? Do you sympathize with her reluctance?

4. In what ways does the relationship between Isabelle and Claire evolve throughout the course of the story?

5. Isabelle is the younger of the two sisters. Do you think it is true that the younger has to the live up to the perfection of the elder, or that the younger gets to do what the elder wishes she could do?

6. How does Isabelle's discovery of Chinese cuisine affect her perceptions of China? In your opinion, what is the best way to learn about or understand a foreign place or culture?

7. Have you ever felt like a fish out of water, culturally, socially, or otherwise? How did you adapt?

8. Isabelle discovers that dating in Beijing is equally—if not more—challenging and confusing than dating in New York. In what ways do cultural differences and/or similarities affect her romantic life?

9. Claire and Isabelle both feel challenged by their mother to achieve professional and romantic success. How does each sister respond to her mother's pressure? Are their feelings of frustration justified? Or does their mother really just want the best for them?

10. As Isabelle learns, many Chinese believe that "all Americans have yellow hair and big noses." In your experience, is this a widespread stereotype? How do you think people in other countries form their opinions of Americans? How do you form your opinions of other countries?

FROM THE KITCHEN OF ANN MAH

SPICY "MAPO TOFU"

I feel a little guilty calling this mapo tofu, because it's so far removed from its classic Sichuan roots—the meat (when I use it) is ground chicken or turkey breast, not pork, and the chili paste is Sriracha, not dou ban jiang (the famous, salty fermented soy bean sauce). I eat this when I'm feeling blue—after all, chilies raise endorphin levels! It's good with a bowl of white rice, but I also like it ladled over a deep bowl of long noodles and hot broth.

SERVES TWO AS MAIN COURSE (WITH LEFTOVERS FOR LUNCH THE NEXT DAY)

1 lb. firm tofu, drained and cut into 1½ inch cubes
½ lb. ground chicken or turkey breast (optional)
2 teaspoons canola or olive oil
1½ inch piece of ginger root, peeled and finely minced
3 garlic cloves, peeled and finely minced

1½ cups water
1½ tablespoons light soy sauce
2 teaspoons Sriracha chili sauce

To thicken: 1 tablespoon cornstarch mixed with 2 table-spoons water

Meat marinade (if using meat):

1 tablespoon soy sauce
1 tablespoon rice wine (optional)
1 teaspoon sesame oil

If using the meat, put it in a bowl and add the marinade ingredients, mixing to stir.

Place a large skillet over medium heat and add 1 teaspoon of the oil when hot. If using the meat, add it to the pan, stirring and mashing it with a wooden spoon to break it up. When the meat is fully cooked, remove it to a clean bowl.

Add another teaspoon of oil to the hot pan, and then the garlic and ginger, stirring until fragrant, 20 to 30 seconds. Add the water, soy sauce, and chili paste; stir. Add the tofu and meat (if using). Bring the mixture to a boil, cover and lower heat until the mixture is at a very gentle simmer. Cook for 20 minutes.

Uncover, raise heat to medium, and add the cornstarch and water mixture. Stir until thickened. Taste and adjust seasonings, adding more soy sauce and chili paste, if necessary. Serve piping hot.

SPAGHETTI CARBONARA

With only six ingredients, I make this simple pasta when I don't feel like cooking or grocery shopping (which is often).
SERVES FOUR

1 onion
3 to 4 strips bacon
2 cups white wine
1 egg, beaten
1 lb. linguine or thin spaghetti
¼ cup grated Parmagiano-Reggiano cheese, plus more for sprinkling

Fill a large pot with water for the pasta, cover, and place over a high heat to achieve a rolling boil. Peel the onion and finely chop it. Cut the bacon into small squares. Heat a large saucepan over medium flame and add the bacon, stirring until it starts to crisp. Add the onion and stir until it's wilted, about 8 to 10 minutes. Add the wine to the onion-bacon mixture, bring to a boil, turn heat to medium-low and simmer about 5 to 7 minutes until all the alcohol has burned off and the liquid has reduced by half.

Meanwhile, start cooking the pasta, which should take about 8 minutes. When it's done, drain it, reserving 1 cup or so of the pasta cooking water. Return the pasta to its pot and pour in the onion-bacon-wine mixture, tossing to coat. Add the beaten egg and continue tossing, adding dashes of the pasta cooking water so the mixture is smooth and supple. Add the Parmagiano-Reggiano cheese and season with salt and pepper. Taste it now! Adjust seasonings if necessary.

Serve immediately and enjoy with the remainder of the bottle of white wine.

SPICY SUMMER PEANUT SAUCE

I love this versatile peanut sauce, which I make during the summer. Drizzle it over shredded, poached chicken and finely julienned cucumbers for a refreshing salad. Or add cold noodles to the mix for a satisfying chilled dinner. If your sauce is too thick when you're tossing it with the noodles, dashes of cold black tea will help loosen it up.

3 garlic cloves, peeled
1 cup cilantro, washed and dried (including stems)
2-inch piece fresh ginger, peeled and roughly chopped
½ cup smooth peanut butter
2 tablespoons soy sauce
2 tablespoons sesame oil
2 teaspoons Sriracha

Place all the ingredients in the bowl of a food processor or blender and process until the mixture is smooth. Taste and add more soy sauce or chili sauce if necessary.

SALT AND PEPPER SHRIMP SALAD

In the book, I imagine Isabelle's mother making this shrimp salad, but in reality this is my dad's dish. A creative cook, he's been using this salt-pepper-sugar mixture since I was a kid (and probably before then). Over the years, the dish has evolved into a fresh, fusion salad that's ideal as an easy and elegant first course.

1 lb. shrimp (about 12), peeled, cleaned, and patted dry
1 tablespoon minced garlic
¼ cup minced green onions
2 tablespoons pine nuts, lightly toasted

2 to 3 tablespoons dry cocktail sherry (pale)

2 tablespoons salt-sugar-pepper mixture (recipe follows)

2 tablespoons cornstarch

Olive oil for stir-frying

For the salad:

4 cups arugula or mixed salad greens, washed and spun dry

½ tablespoon balsamic vinegar

2 tablespoons extra virgin olive oil

1 teaspoon sesame oil

Salt-sugar-pepper mixture:

2 tablespoons sugar

4 tablespoons salt

6 tablespoons ground black pepper

This is a master batch for your spice cabinet. You can increase the quantities to make more and store it in a bottle.

Toss arugula or salad greens with the vinegar and oils and distribute evenly to four salad plates.

Heat 1 tablespoon olive oil in a wok or sauté pan until smoking. Toss the shrimp with the salt-sugar-pepper mixture (about 2 tablespoons) and add at once to the hot pan.

As the prawns cook, sprinkle them with 1 tablespoon cornstarch. Add more oil if needed. Turn the shrimp and repeat with another 1 tablespoon of cornstarch; the cooking process only takes a few minutes.

When the shrimp have just turned pink, add the minced garlic and toss. Add the green onions and toss. Add just enough sherry to create a sauce that barely coats the prawns. Remove from heat. Add the pine nuts.

Distribute 3 prawns per salad plate. Serve immediately.

AN INTERVIEW WITH THE AUTHOR

Kitchen Chinese is your first novel. What inspired you to write this book? How and when did you start writing it? How autobiographical is the story?

A month after I got married, my husband's work moved us to Beijing. I found myself in a new city, unemployed (I had left my job in New York book publishing to move to China), attempting to build a new life armed only with the rudimentary Chinese that I'd learned in college. My first year in Beijing was the hardest as I struggled daily with identity issues—I thought of myself as American, but almost everyone else viewed me as Chinese.

Like Isabelle, I found my feet once I started working as the dining editor at a local English-language expat magazine. There, I met people who had chosen to live in Beijing—as opposed to the majority of expatriates, who had been assigned to the city—and their passion, not to mention their excellent Mandarin, helped demystify the city and ignite my own enthusiasm. Through the magazine, I also made local friends who gave me a window into the lives of Chinese twenty-somethings. And of course our daily staff lunches at local dive restaurants were the best introduction to Chinese cuisine that I could have hoped for. As I ate my way through China's regional cuisines, and discovered a lot about the country along the way, the idea for this book began to germinate—though I know it would have to be fiction because I wanted a spicy story!

When I started the book, I was working full-time and I would snatch time to write during my lunch break, on weekends, and not-so-busy times at the magazine (I hope my former bosses aren't reading this, but if they are—I'm sorry!). Aside from finding the time to write, the hardest part was simply continuing to work on the book, to keep going even though it had an audience of one: my husband. For a long time he was the only other person who knew about the book, but luckily he is very discreet—and extremely encouraging.

Obviously, Isabelle's story was inspired by some of my experiences, but our stories are not identical. For one thing, we came to China under very different circumstances. For another, I was happily married while living in Beijing, while Isabelle must navigate the single scene—that was fun to write about, but I was quite content not to experience it firsthand! Isabelle's family is actually a composite of many different families—some Chinese, some not. As it turns out, Asian parents don't have the monopoly on guilt! Finally, Isabelle is much braver and less squeamish than I am—I would never even consider setting a toe into a Chinese public shower room, for example—and she navigates her adventures with a grace and openness that I admire. She is also much funnier than I am—and lucky enough to have a sister.

You lived in China for several years. Was living there what you expected? Were there things that surprised you about the country or the people?

Before I moved to Beijing, I had only been there once, for a weekend when I was eleven years old. I had a vague memory of vast avenues and fleets of bicycles, and I had read lots of articles about the pollution. In other words, I had absolutely no idea what to expect.

My first, most visceral, surprise was how easily I could blend into a crowd, and how alienated this made me feel. Living in New York, I was used to being considered a minority, and it was initially disconcerting to be surrounded by faces that so closely mirrored my own. But the longer I lived in Beijing, the more I began to realize that I wasn't blending in at all—in fact, it was much the opposite. Whereas in the States we joke that all Asians look alike, in China, they think all Caucasians look alike—they have trouble distinguishing white people, but they'll remember a Chinese face forever and I was recognized regularly!

I was also struck by how private Chinese people were, especially compared to Americans. Working as a journalist, I often encountered people who declined to be interviewed about topics as innocent as men's handbags, or the city's best Sichuan food. But the concept of privacy extended to friends as well—for example, I have gay friends who have never discussed their romantic lives with me. Also, I know at least three different people who got married in secret without telling anyone until weeks later.

Most of all, however, I was surprised and impressed by the country's indefatigable sense of optimism. Though nearly everyone I met had been touched by the horrifying events of the Cultural Revolution, each seemed to put the pain and sorrow behind them, to face the future with the confidence that their children's lives would be better than their own. It's a feeling that's both powerful and contagious!

In the book, Isabelle makes the observation that the gift China has given her is the opportunity to realize a dream. Do you think this is true for many foreigners who choose to live there?

I think it can be a little easier for foreigners to shine in Beijing, if only because of their overseas experience. Much of Chinese culture is still rooted in status, and having a degree from a foreign university (especially a prestigious one), overseas work experience, or speaking fluent English, are all greatly admired. It's especially true in the performing arts like acting, modeling, or music, where simply having a foreign face or accent can really set you apart. I have several American friends in Beijing who are pursuing their artistic dreams successfully, whether it be playing bass in a rock band, leading a modern dance troupe, or starring in English-language instructional videos. They are all very talented, but as one friend once said to me, "In the States, I'd be a cog in the wheel. In China, I'm inventing the wheel."

There's also the powerful sense in China of a world made new. Beijing vibrates with a tireless energy—restaurants open and close within months or sometimes even weeks, a block of buildings can be destroyed in a morning, skyscrapers seem to mushroom overnight—and the feeling of change is palpable. With all this change comes an incredible feeling of opportunity: with a little money (things are still relatively inexpensive in China), and some elbow grease, anything is possible, especially as the country develops its modern cultural identity.

So, yes, I do feel that China is a place where opportunities abound and dreams are realized—but I don't think it's unique in that sense. In fact, I was just reading an article the other day about second generation Indian-Americans moving to India to pursue work in creative fields. As people become more mobile—and cultural identity more flexible—I think we'll see many more young Americans—from all sorts of backgrounds—moving overseas to follow their dreams.

How did you become interested in cooking?

My parents like to tell the story of how, at three years old, I climbed up on the kitchen counter to watch my father chop vegetables, and shouted, "Bang the garlic, Daddy!"

So, I guess you could say my interest in food and cooking was cemented at a very early age. As a teen, I loved to bake and was also mad about England—I would prepare elaborate tea parties for my family, including fresh scones and finger sandwiches—

once, I even made crumpets from scratch! As I've grown older and traveled the world, I've come to realize what an important tool cooking is—for me, food is the most vital connection to learning about new cultures.

Cooking is something I enjoy, and I am extremely grateful for it. Unlike writing, which is a process that I find tortuous, it's an easier way to create. I find taking raw ingredients and turning them into something totally different—a cake, a pie, a bowl of soup—transporting, even miraculous. Of course there are times when I don't feel like cooking—especially if I'm on my own, when I'm more likely to eat a grilled cheese sandwich. I suppose, as with writing, I prefer to cook for an audience! Nevertheless, once I get started, I always find cooking contemplative yet absorbing, very sensory, and it can be either solitary or social. Plus, it gives great pleasure to others (except maybe the dishwasher!).

What are your favorite books about food, either novels, nonfiction, or cookbooks?

From the minute I found out about the concept of reading, I wanted to do it. And from the minute I started, I loved reading about food. When I was small, I loved all the Little House books, but especially *Farmer Boy*, the story of Laura Ingalls Wilder's husband, Almanzo. I was fascinated by the descriptions of food, particularly his breakfasts of ham and apple pie (pie for breakfast!), or freshly fried doughnuts and cider, or evening snacks of fire-popped popcorn, immersed in a glass of creamy milk. Laura's diet was grimmer, but I loved the story of the maple sugar boil, when she and her sisters make candy by pouring the newly boiled sap onto clean snow.

As a teenager I was a raging Anglophile, which started when my dad gave me some collected works of P. G. Wodehouse. I realize he's quite a controversial figure now, but I loved Wodehouse's silly, madcap tales of Jeeves and Bertie Wooster. Plus they were always eating things like kippers and bangers, or hot buttered toast with Gentlemen's Relish, all washed down with cups of scalding tea—oh, it sounded like heaven! Combined with a large dose of Agatha Christie (Miss Marple was always eating things like Victorian seed cake) . . . well, that probably explains my teenage mania for tea parties.

I've always admired Julia Child, even before I ever thought I'd move to Paris, so it was a delight to read her memoir, *My Life in France*. Of course, reading about her adventures at the Cordon Bleu cooking school was fascinating, but I loved this book most for its spirit. Julia was thirty-six when she moved to France; she had no expertise in the kitchen—and certainly no idea she would become one of America's foremost authorities on French cuisine. But she did—and her story reminds me that life-changing opportunities can arise at any age.

I have way too many cookbooks. One standby is *Italian Easy: Recipes from the London River Café* by Rose Gray and Ruth Rogers (published in the UK as *The River Café Cookbook Easy*). The recipes are very simple, but focus on delicious, different combinations of flavors and foods—and there are lots of creative ideas for pasta. My only quibble is that the recipes often call for unique and expensive ingredients, so I usually pull out this book when I want to make a special dinner for my husband. I've also developed a renewed appreciation for *Julia and Jacques: Cooking at Home,* by Julia Child and Jacques Pepin. I actually prefer this to Julia's *Mastering the Art of French Cooking*, which I find a little fussy. The recipes are simpler—classic and French, but homey—and I love how the two quibble over technique, each providing their own advice (which often disagrees). Plus, I recently made the book's boeuf Bourguignon for a French friend, who said it tasted just like a French person had made it. This was the highest praise, I assure you!

Finally, they don't discuss food much, but the following three books on China resonated with me for a long time, especially as each tells the story of a foreigner in Beijing. In *Hand Grenade Practice in Peking*, Frances Wood recounts her year spent as a British exchange student at Peking University, in 1975, during the Cultural Revolution. Her account of spartan dorm life and education through labor—the Communist party determined that she would learn more in the field planting rice than in the classroom studying Marxism, Leninism, and Mao Zedong—is witty, honest, and sensitive. In *Peking Story*, American David Kidd shares his story of marrying into a wealthy Chinese family and living in their vast ancestral Beijing courtyard home during the last days before the Communist party came to power in 1949. It's a fascinating glimpse into a rarified world that has totally disappeared—and the epilogue, in which Kidd visits the family again in the 1980s, is heartbreaking. Finally, as the wife of a diplomat in China, I was drawn to the novel *Peking Picnic,* by Ann Bridge, who shared my circumstances, albeit in the 1920s, during the tumultuous warlord era. It's an old-fashioned story—complete with a few off-color descriptions of locals—but Bridge weaves an atmosphere of old Beijing that is dreamy yet vibrant.

What types of food do you enjoy cooking, Chinese or otherwise?

Like Isabelle, I grew up eating Chinese food every single night, with very little variation. My dad, who is an excellent cook, made dinner each night, and though he has a wide-ranging palate, it was my mom's distinct preference for Chinese fare that dictated our meals.

As a result, I find that what I most enjoy cooking is a variety of different cuisines—I cannot eat Chinese food every day, but nor could I eat French cuisine, or spaghetti, or sushi every day.

(Except Indian food—I sometimes think I could exist on masala dosas.)

I usually make Chinese food during the week, when I crave something easy, fast, and healthy (you can sneak a lot of vegetables into a stir-fry). But unlike my dad, who really did make three or four different dishes every night, I tend to cook just one enormous pan of something, like a huge stir-fry.

I enjoy experimenting with North African food, discovering the play of spices, the contrast between sweet, sour, spicy, and salty. I studied Italian cuisine in Bologna, where I learned how to make decadent lasagna—and where, after watching Italian women labor for hours over sheets of dough, stretching, pulling, and rolling, I knew I would never make fresh pasta at home! Right now I live in Paris, where I am discovering the seasons by shopping in the open market—who knew sea scallops abounded in winter? I'm also enjoying the ritualized formality of French dinner parties, which involve four courses, eaten slowly and savored.

In fact, there's only one thing I don't like to cook: bread. I find the process of rising and kneading incredibly stressful. Plus, it always comes out heavy, lumpen, and dry, and I usually think, Why didn't I just buy a loaf at the store?

What advice would you give to a beginning writer and/or cook?

First, I would say: consume. If you want to be a writer, read, read, read. Read everything—fiction, nonfiction, the newspaper, magazines (both highbrow and pop culture), the classics, and pulp fiction. This will help give you a sense of different styles and voices, with the ultimate goal of developing your own. Likewise, if you want to be a cook, eat. Save your pennies and splurge on amazing meals. But also wander ethnic neighborhoods in search of crowded restaurants. Spy on your neighbors' table and order what they're eating. Also, experiment with new flavor combinations, or buy a new vegetable at the farmer's market because it looks cool and you want to try it. Explore and discover what you like and dislike.

Second, develop a thick skin. For cooking, you'll need it to survive nicks, scrapes, and burns, all of which will occur no matter how careful you are. Writers need a tough, protective layer, because they face a lot of discouragement. Unfortunately, they hear the word "no" often. You have to be brave enough to persevere in the face of despair.

Third, make sure you have excellent tools. This is more important for cooking, when sharp knives and heavy pots and pans make all the difference in slicing, dicing, and heat distribution—you don't need a lot of fancy gadgets, just good quality basics. Obviously, writers only really need a pen and notebook. But to this I would add a good dictionary or computer spell-check—no one wants to read a short story littered with typos (and editors notice these things)—as well as a thesaurus (I like Rodale's *Synonym Finder*).

Fourth, as the old joke goes: How do you get to Carnegie Hall? Practice! Practice! Practice!

Are there restaurants you would recommend in Beijing and Shanghai? What is the dining scene there like?

As China's capital, Beijing reflects the diversity of the country. In fact, each of China's twenty-two provinces has a government office in Beijing, and almost all of them have restaurants that serve the cuisine of their region. These are state-run eateries, with absolutely no ambiance, but the food is extremely authentic—some even fly in special vegetables or other hard-to-find ingredients! One of my favorites is the Sichuan Provincial Government Restaurant (5 Jianguomen Gongyuan Toutiao, Dongcheng district, tel: 86 10 6512 2277), where the chefs skillfully blend chilies and Sichuan peppercorns—I can still feel the tingle of their *mapo doufu* on my lips. I also love the refreshing salad of giant mint leaves and "crossing the bridge" noodles at the Yunnan Provincial Government Restaurant (in Chinese, Yunteng Shifu—7 Donghuashi Beili Dongqu, Chongwen district, tel: 86 10 6711 3322 X7105).

If you want to taste Beijing's northern cuisine—stodgy and wheat-based—*zhajiang mian* noodles are a must. I like the bustle of Beijing Style Noodle King (35 Di'anmen Xijie, Dongcheng district, tel: 86 10 6405 6666). As for Peking duck—everyone has an opinion, but my favorite is still the elegant, crisp-skinned bird at Made in China in the Grand Hyatt hotel (1 Dong Chang'an Jie, Dongcheng district, tel: 86 10 8518 1234).

Alas, I don't know Shanghai as well as I'd like. But I still dream about one restaurant there, a tiny dumpling shack called Jia Jia Tang Bao (90 Huanghe Lu at Fengyang Lu, Huangpu district, tel: 86 21 6327 6878). The décor is quite dismal—think McDonald's. But the soup dumplings (in Chinese, *xiaolongbao*), which are stuffed, folded, and steamed to order, make you forget your surroundings—they're delicate, with a rich meaty flavor and a luscious squirt of soup within. And, believe it or not, a basket of fifteen dumplings is only 7.50 RMB—that's less than one dollar!

You've lived in New York and currently live in Paris. How do these cities compare to Beijing? Do you miss China and would you ever live there again?

Of course, the differences between Paris and Beijing outweigh the similarities. But the two actually have more in common than one might think. They are both very old cities, very proud, very historical. Both bear battle scars—in Paris, it's not uncommon to see statues or monuments dedicated to the monarchy that were defaced during the French Revolution; the same is true in Beijing, where many old buildings were destroyed during the Cultural Revolution. As capital cities, both represent the diverse regions of their respective countries, and attract residents from all over. Also, both have thriving and enthusiastic food cultures—though they realize them in very different ways.

Of the three cities, I probably feel most comfortable in New York, with its manic energy and diversity and sense of possibility. In fact, Beijing and New York are pretty similar (aside from racial diversity): they both burn with a vivid intensity, plus you can get a good meal in either city at any hour of the day or night. But New York also has an openness, a permissiveness that I love: expressing yourself is good, creativity is rewarded, being different is desirable. Only thirty years after the end of the Cultural Revolution, Beijing hasn't reached this level of openness yet. But I hope it will soon.

I miss many things about living in China—above all, I miss friends and food—and I would love to live there again. But next time I'd like to live in Shanghai, where my mother was raised. As a former treaty port, it has a history of gangsters, spies, turncoats, and glamour—it would make a great setting for a book! Anyway, I don't know if I'll ever have the opportunity to live in Shanghai, but I can dream . . .

ANN MAH lived in Beijing for four years, where she was the dining editor for *That's Beijing*, a monthly English-language magazine. Her articles have also appeared in the *South China Morning Post*, *Conde Nast Traveler*, the *International Herald Tribune*, and other publications. In 2005, she was awarded a James Beard culinary scholarship to study in Bologna, Italy. Born in Orange County, California, she now lives in Paris.

www.annmah.net

Ann Mah